Wha

"This book was one of the best I've ever read. The stories are magical, captivating and I couldn't stop! From one sister to the other, the story weaves a fantastic web across a universe peopled with fascinating characters. Each story is unique, yet each is tied to the other. Read *The Way Of The Wolf*. You'll be transported to an incredible world you won't want to ever leave!" - *WordWeaving*

"Riveting and hard to put down." - *Timeless Tales*

Discover for yourself why readers can't get enough of the multiple award-winning publisher Ellora's Cave. Whether you prefer e-books or paperbacks, be sure to visit EC on the web at www.ellorascave.com for an erotic reading experience that will leave you breathless.

www.ellorascave.com

Ellora's Cave Publishing, Inc.
PO Box 787
Hudson, OH 44236-0787

ISBN # 1-84360-448-5

The Way of the Wolf: The Northlanders I, 2003.
ALL RIGHTS RESERVED
Ellora's Cave Publishing, Inc.
© Copyright Shelby Morgen, 2001/2002/2003
.

This book may not be reproduced in whole or in part without author and publisher permission.

Edited by Tina Engler and Martha Punches
Cover art by Christine Clavel

Warning: The following material contains strong sexual content meant for mature readers. *The Way of the Wolf: The Northlanders I* has been rated NC17 erotic, by a minimum of three independent reviewers. We strongly suggest storing this book in a place where young readers not meant to view it are unlikely to happen upon it. That said, enjoy…

THE WAY OF THE WOLF: THE NORTHLANDERS I

Written by

Shelby Morgen

Introduction

The fire crackled in the fireplace as the wind howled outside. The mother rocked quietly before the blaze, trying not to think. She should have been there to fight at his side. She should be there to protect him. She should…

"Tell me a story, Momma."

There was comfort to be had in familiar stories. "Come sit with me, daughter."

The child hesitated at her mother's side. "Will I hurt the baby?"

Ayailla laughed softly as she stroked her firstborn's hair. "No, Travanya. Thee canna' harm the baby."

The child crawled into her lap, snuggling her head against the mound of her unborn sister. "Tell me about the moons, Mother."

Ayailla smiled indulgently at her young daughter. "Ye know the story of the moons, Child."

Travanya stroked gently over the mound that was her sister to be. "Evalayna has no' heard, Mother. Tell us about before."

Before…

In the long ago before, the magic that had been in the world since the beginning of time fled, hiding from the great unbelief. People no longer acknowledged the gods. Humans ruled, and the races became as one. The gods lost touch with the world.

In this way the centuries passed, and the people began to build machines to take the place of the gods. They worshipped the machines and ignored Earth. The people warred among themselves. Earth suffered, and at last she began to die. Disease and pestilence ruled. Kine and other domestic animals died by the thousands. Famine ruled the lands. The air was no longer pure. The plants and the young trees suffered and died. The great waters rose to swallow the land.

The machines the Humans had built to protect themselves failed as the knowledge of their maintenance passed away. Eventually mankind was reduced to a shadowy existence, living in caves and under the earth.

Earth was no longer strong enough to defend herself, and at last the cosmos itself conspired against her. Asteroids bombarded her, pieces set adrift from another dying universe far from here. Among the debris was the moon of a long ago world, drifting homeless and bereft. That moon sought to join the dying Earth, that they might end their grief together.

Of the gods, only Wind and Rain still maintained hope. Those two roused the others to assist Earth, to revive her from her deadly lethargy. Despair was rampant, but their end was eminent. They had to act to survive. Together they bent their wills to revive Earth's spirit. The six pleaded with Earth to resist the new moon's pull. At last she roused herself, shaking off some of the layers of her despair. Still, she was not strong enough to fight the influence of the new moon completely.

Instead, as is her way, Earth compromised. She made a pact with the new moon to provide him a home, an end to his ceaseless journeying. In exchange, the moon would awaken the old magic.

The moon's compromise was not without price. The tides changed, and the cold returned to the planet. Some of the waters receded as the ice caps froze again, and Earth revealed herself once more to mankind. The tundra spread down from the north, and mankind fought to survive against the elements.

The changes the magic wrought were subtle at first. Earth found that there were those among us who could hear her voice once again. The old races, absent since before the magic fled, returned. The gods spoke, and we learned once again how to listen.

Seven gods we learned to name. Earth our Mother guides us all. Wind and Rain are ever her spokesmen. Wolf and Bear and Cat and Falcon are our totem spirits.

We of the Northlands are the first among the peoples. We are the chosen ones. Our Shamen are gifted with strong magic. We have the task of guiding our peoples. Our daughters are prized, and welcome in every household on Earth. We follow the Way of the Wolf.

To the East live our sisters, who sing the Song of The Bear. Their daughters and their sons like ours are great Warriors and Clerics. Where the earth is warmer the Cat people bask in the sun, in a place called Talismar, where the Elves walk in the trees.

The oldest magic belongs to those who have returned from before. The spirits of the Fey often lead them to serve as mages. As the Falcons they watch over us, their mission to serve and protect, their ways mysterious.

The Dwarves are the keepers of Earth, her core, and her center, and they burrow within her, being privy to her secrets. They are the smiths of fine weapons and sturdy armor for those with the strength to bear such encumbrance.

The Humans have scattered, like the Wind and the Rain, living at all points of the compass. Dark races there are, as well, lurking ever in the shadows, but theirs are tales for another day.

"Mother?"

"Daughter?"

"Do ye think Evalayna heard thy story?"

"Indeed I do, my daughter, and I think she knew ye were the one to have thought of her, and she knows as well that ye shall always hold her in thy heart."

"Will she love me, Mother?"

"There is no stronger bond than the love of a sister."

A Slave's Price

Chapter One

The noise of the marketplace rose like the shrill whine of wild fire. The press of bodies around her became oppressive, sucking the air out of her lungs. Cassadara shifted her armor, automatically standing taller, straighter, as if her imperious stance could remove her somehow from the filth and squalor. Her nose wrinkled in distaste, but she refused to acknowledge the underling who groveled before her. The Dwarf was not worthy of her attention.

The trader's voice droned on, extolling the virtues of yet another chunk of Human waste. The slaves all looked the same. The Dwarf dragged them out of their pen in a string, chained together like so many goats on a tether. Warriors, indeed. None of them would even raise their eyes to look at her. She terrified them. To a man they would rather die here than travel with her.

Something inside her turned cold as the arctic spring. These Humans were nothing. Spineless bundles of flesh huddled together, trying to hang on to their miserable existence. They meant nothing to her. Let them stay here and earn their freedom in the pit if they could.

Cassadara crushed the courier's message and tossed the paper into the fire. Unfortunately, she could not rest until she had fulfilled Lady Evalayna's directive. Irritated, perhaps unreasonably so, she thumped the small bag of gold coins against her leg. Even with the words burned to a crisp, Cassadara could hear Mother's voice as if the Lady had just spoken aloud.

"Although I am pleased to ken ye survived the Orcs' assault on thy escort, I fear for thy safety. I would na' have ye travel alone. Go ye to the Dwarf called Argolyn in the City of Stone. This vile creature claims to have one of our own amongst his slaves. Such a thing canna' be allowed. In freeing this Warrior ye shall also secure a second sword arm to stand at thy back. May the gods be with ye."

A second sword arm. A slave. Cassadara felt her frustration mount as she surveyed the expanse of Human degradation. She would find no Warriors here. She had sent to Mother asking for a company of Northland Soldiers—her own men, who would gladly follow her into battle if need be, rather than cower in fear of *her* while the enemy hacked them to pieces. Instead Mother sent the Mage Shammall and a small bag of gold. Cassadara would rather have traveled alone than take on the added burden of another responsibility. But there was no defying Mother.

At least the errand boy had spirited himself away after delivering Mother's instructions. She'd rather deal with the Dwarf than that damnable Mage.

"This one is a true Warrior, Lady. He is strong and well-endowed."

Cassadara looked down, trying to focus on the matter at hand. Argolyn was attempting to call her attention to yet another of the objects huddled in the mud. His sales pitch, delivered in Dwarven, sounded like he was trying to clear phlegm from his throat.

"Stand up!" the flesh-monger hissed. The slave made no move to obey. The trader kicked the battered body at his feet. The Dwarf received as his reward a glare of defiance from deep green eyes glinting like ivy-etched steel. Her attention secured, Cassadara watched the scene unfold like a play. The trader yanked ferociously on the chain by which his property was bound, cutting off the slave's air supply. Cassadara wondered why blood didn't spurt from the Human's neck.

The Dwarf kicked the slave yet again, ignoring the choking wheeze of the Human's strangled breath. The lack of oxygen had the desired effect. Almost insolently the man at Argolyn's feet rose. Grabbing hold of the chain threaded through the torc around his neck, he hauled himself up hand over hand, using the sturdy Dwarf as anchorage. Up and up and up the Human rose, until he towered over the Dwarf, who reached barely to his crotch.

Undaunted, the trader fisted his hand in the fabric of the man's tunic, yanking the thin covering from the battered body with one swift jerk. A grubby paw poked at the slave's testicles, as if to make sure Cassadara had an unobstructed view. "You see, Mistress, there is enough here to satisfy even a member of the Wolf Clan!"

To his credit, the Human barely flinched as the Dwarf displayed him.

Cassadara's focus lingered for a moment on a cock that hinted, even flaccid, at enough size and girth to be worth a second look, before she let her gaze wander back to the slave's face. His attention still centered on the Dwarf, his eyes blazed with cold, bare defiance. This one could not have been a slave for long. Although his body had been damaged, his spirit had yet to be broken. Still, he had obviously learned better than to actually attempt to attack the Dwarf. One move of the slave's hands, chained although they were, and the guards would beat the man to a bloody pulp.

What did his spirit matter? She was not here to secure a personal slave for the night's usage. She didn't want a man who would fight her, and the Human would never travel willingly at her side. Besides, without the guards around, the Human might be hard to control. He was not the clansman Mother had sent her to free. Cassadara didn't bother to look back at Argolyn. She answered in the common tongue of merchants, refusing to expend the energy necessary to spit out the words in the Dwarf's own language. "Thy merchandise is unacceptable." She turned away, as if to move on.

"You need not fear me, Mistress. You would be safe with me." The words were spoken in High Elven, a language that managed to capture the essence of poetry in its most common vocabulary. The voice caressed her, sliding over her skin like silk in the darkness, little more than a low rumble that might have come from Earth herself.

Who...

Cassadara raised an eyebrow in surprise as she turned back, surveying the man again. The Human had dared to address her—and in a language almost unknown in these parts. He had taken great risk to speak to her privately. Why? 'Twas a foolish risk that might well earn him yet another beating.

Cassadara's curiosity trapped her. Did he not know who she was? Did he not know *what* she was?

Deep green eyes clashed with hers, anything but subservient. Surprisingly, she saw no trace of fear. Instead she saw wariness mixed with desperation. The Human knew his fate. Unless she purchased his contract, the man would undoubtedly die here.

So. This slave was willing to cross the lines of race and class to save his own life. Yet somewhere within his battered body the man retained enough pride to keep him from begging.

Intriguing.

She stepped closer—close enough to smell the foul odor coming from the pen where the men were kept. By the gods, this one was tall. He was almost as tall as her brother Tyrell—the slave was certainly the tallest Human she had ever seen. Taller by far than her own six-foot-four. At this distance she would actually have to tilt her head to meet the man's eyes, so she didn't. Instead she looked down, surveying every inch of him, looking beneath the filth to see the long, lean, muscled body built on a powerful frame, capable of grueling days of marching and hard hours of fighting.

The Human was too large and well built to have escaped the arena. The spectators would love to see this one fight. She let her gaze wander over the length of him again, brushing over those other attributes the Dwarf had mentioned. This time his cock responded, jumping to life as if she had stroked him with her fingers instead of her gaze.

Intriguing.

He was indeed well endowed—far better equipped than she would have expected for a Human. As she watched, his cock grew harder, bobbing its deep crimson head as if straining to reach her.

She hadn't even touched him yet and he was already hard for her?

Despite the chill of the arctic spring, a fine sheen of sweat stood out on the Human's body now, trickling down his smooth, naked chest. She found herself imagining licking the sweat from his bronzed skin. Her nipples hardened at the thought of what he might be able to do with that equipment.

Did he want *her*? Or merely the freedom her money could purchase for him?

She had heard tales of Human lovers. The Humans might not be good for aught else, but they were said to make incredible mates. She followed the line of sweat back up, gradually returning her attention to the man's face. He let her look her fill without comment, though his cock jumped again as if she'd caressed him rather than merely admired from a few feet away. A single drop of moisture leaked from its tip. She wondered briefly what he might taste like. Just how different *were* Humans?

Cassadara hid her smile. She was fairly certain he was *not* what Mother had had in mind.

She answered in the common tongue, wanting to be sure the Dwarf understood every word she said. "Why should I trust ye, Human? I know what thy people think of my kind. Ye call *my* race *Barbarians*. Yet ye condone *this*."

The sweep of her hand indicated not just the squalid pens huddled at the base of the cliffs, but the amphitheatre-like arena at the far edge of the camp, and indeed the whole system by which men were bought and sold like sled dogs.

"Why would I pay this Dwarf for thy services? As soon as we are away from this place, ye shall try to kill me. Then ye shall die, and I shall be out a great deal of gold. I have no time to worry over the likes of ye."

"Then do not hold me as a slave," he answered, once again in Elven. "Let the price of my freedom be my indenture. I will pledge myself to your service. Allow me to earn my freedom and I will prove my loyalty beyond the boundaries of race and class."

The Dwarf looked perturbed by the banter, but if he did not understand, Cassadara surely would not translate. This time she answered the Human in Elven as well. "Ye would never live to see thy freedom, Human. Not where I go."

The man didn't deny the truth of her words. Instead he stared back at her, holding her attention with the intensity of his gaze, his eyes asking for her faith. "I know where you're bound, M'Lady. I will gladly die beside you if that is the will of the gods." He swayed unsteadily on his feet, righting himself before he toppled back into the mud. "Better to die in battle at your side than here in the pits for the entertainment of the Lords and Ladies. Death in the arena robs a warrior of his honor."

Cassadara examined the Human again, using her gift this time. A long half-healed gash ran the length of his shield arm from shoulder to elbow. Heat radiated from the wound, a sure sign the cut was infected. She looked deeper. Beneath the bruises his ribs were cracked, and his knuckles were swollen and bloody. He had undoubtedly survived several rounds in the arena already. His face, half-hidden under untrimmed fur, looked hollow and gaunt.

He'd take a great deal of healing to be of any use. If she bought this one she would be spending days in this hellhole of a town before the man was ready to travel. Worse yet, healing him would leave her exhausted and vulnerable—and at his mercy.

Cassadara let her gaze drift down to that thick, weeping cock again. "If I buy thy indenture, what will ye do for me?"

"Whatever you wish, M'Lady." Deep green eyes warmed slightly, lending character to the face where she'd seen only anger and despair. "In my homeland I am known as a man of my word. I pledge to serve you loyally."

Cassadara touched the tip of her tongue to suddenly dry lips. At her frank perusal, the Human's cock bobbed stiffly against his belly, looking painfully hard. Dampness stained the inside of her thighs. Yes. If he knew how to properly entertain a woman he might be worth the time and trouble he would undoubtedly cause.

When her gaze traveled back up the length of him, his eyes met hers with a trace of something that might have been a grin. "I can *cook*."

The man knew he had her attention. Cassadara fought to keep her expression distant as she turned back to the Dwarf, addressing him once more in the common tongue. "How much?"

Argolyn answered in his own tongue, disdaining the common vernacular. "For you, fifty gold pieces, Mistress."

"He paid but fifteen," the Human offered in that same guttural language.

The powerful Dwarf snapped the chain in a move that dumped the man back on his knees in the mud. "Silence! Your upkeep alone has near bankrupted me!"

"I have earned you ten times my purchase price," the Human argued. "If your word meant anything, I would own my freedom by now!"

If she left the man here, the Dwarf would surely beat him for such audacity. Cassadara stepped between them, distracting the Dwarf. She moved her shoulders in a studied show of disinterest. "This Human is indeed well-endowed, but he is insolent. He is not worth the fifteen ye paid for him. Where is the Northland Warrior ye promised?"

The Dwarf allowed himself to be distracted. "This is the Warrior we spoke of, M'Lady. Truly he has done well in the pit, though he has not yet won the Grande Mêlée. That event does not come here until after the thaw."

Cassadara tapped her foot impatiently. "Warrior or no', he is not one of my people. Ye have lied to Mother. Lady Lochinvar will be much angered with ye."

Argolyn spread his hands wide, his face a mask of innocence. "He is big. He is strong. He is well equipped. I sent word to Lady Lochinvar only that I had an acceptable candidate. Come back tomorrow. I will have broken him for you."

Broken. Aye. That he would be. Cassadara felt a surge of pity well up. She suppressed her weaker emotions with the harshness of reality. "I have no time to waste with ye. If he is the best ye have, he will have to suffice. I will give ye thirty and leave with him now."

"M'Lady, surely you jest. A big strong fighter like this will bring near to one hundred after the Mêlée."

"Then wait for the Mêlée. Away with ye." From down below in the mud, eyes flavored with desolation searched for hers. Did he understand nothing of trading? Cassadara intentionally looked away. She spun on her heel and headed toward the gates.

A filthy little hand tugged at her sleeve. "Please, Mistress, let us not haggle over money. I can see you desire this slave. Enjoy him. My gift to you at only forty gold pieces."

A slight metallic ping sounded as her short sword leaped into her hand. Her voice hissed out low and flat. "Remove thy hand from my person while ye still possess a hand to remove."

The Dwarf drew back stiffly, but swallowed his pride in the face of the threat in her eyes. "You drive a hard bargain, M'Lady. Thirty it is."

Her upper lip curled in a sneer. "Twenty-five."

Argolyn stared up at her for the space of two long, deeply drawn breaths. "Twenty-five."

The sword slipped soundlessly back into its sheath. Cassadara withdrew the coins from her leather pouch and dropped them. Argolyn picked the coins deftly out of the air as they fell. Short stubby fingers extended a large iron ring toward her. "Your keys, M'Lady."

She stepped back, refusing to touch the tainted metal. "Ye may keep thy chains."

"M'Lady! Think what you say! Surely you cannot mean to—"

Her hand still rested on the pommel of her sword. "The purchase is made. The Human belongs to me. I do not wish him to serve me in bondage. Remove thy chains."

The protest died on the Dwarf's lips. Wordlessly he unlocked the wrist cuffs, yanking the chain through the rings on the torc that shackled the man's neck. Ignoring both the Dwarf and the pain of the twisted torc, the Human kept his gaze fastened on Cassadara. He still clutched his tattered tunic. Cassadara watched in fascination as he tied the remains about his waist, concealing that rigid cock. Despite his privation, he retained some degree of modesty.

"You were not told to dress!" Argolyn barked, snaking out a grubby paw to yank the shredded tunic away from the man.

Cassadara caught the Dwarf's wrist in a grip as strong as his own. "Ye shall not touch what is mine. Not now. Not ever. Neither ye nor any of thy men."

Rage colored the trader's face. With his free hand he grasped a Talisman hung about his neck on an ancient leather cord. "Take him and be gone."

Something sharp brushed against her mind. Cassadara dropped the Slaver's arm, suddenly finding him far too filthy to touch.

"You shall regret your treatment of me," the Dwarf hissed as he turned and stalked away, rubbing his injured wrist.

"Harm what is mine, and ye shall not live to ponder my fate," Cassadara promised his retreating backside.

Truth be told, she already regretted having dealt with the little Slaver at all. She had no wish to *own* another, nor be responsible for anyone other than herself. Yet here she was.

She turned back to the Human. Eyes fixed on her feet in a traditional show of subservience, the man knelt before her in the mud, his ripped tunic clutched around him. Ice crystals were already forming in the man's beard. Pity swayed Cassadara yet again. She unbuckled her cloak and settled the heavy wool over his shoulders. Green eyes raised up to meet hers, still wary, but there was something in them she hadn't seen there before.

Hope.

The hope was tempered by uncertainty, but it was there.

The torc still marked the man as a slave. Cassadara saw no smith about whose forge she might use. She hated to touch iron. Still, she would have to touch the man if she was to heal him, probably more than once. Better to deal with the cursed iron now than endure its taint.

Sliding one hand under the twisted band to protect his neck, she closed her eyes and focused on the welded lock. She pictured the metal heating under her fingers until it was soft and malleable. Using all of the strength of her race and her magic, she twisted the welded hasp until the metal crumbled beneath her fingers. The lock sprung, allowing another few inches of space between the ends of the band. As gently as she could she spread the worn collar apart and removed the hideous thing from about his bloodied neck. Venting her anger on the metal, she flung the filthy piece of iron out across the tundra.

The Human said nothing, only continued to stare up at her as he rubbed dirt stained fingers against the raw wound at his throat.

She extended her hand to him, but he made no move to accept her help. Her temper leapt to the surface again as she let her hand drop back to her side. This was a poor start to things.

No. She would not judge him on the basis of race alone. Perhaps he had simply misread her intent. She tried again, choosing her words with care as she addressed him in his own language. "Are ye fit enough to travel?"

Understanding flickered across his face. Still watching her intently, he rose cautiously to his feet. "Aye, M'Lady." Even as he spoke he swayed like a drunkard.

She sighed, knowing he was not fit to go anywhere but to bed. "Have ye a name?"

He blinked in surprise. "To my friends I am known as Mâkakao."

Cassadara twisted her tongue around the foreign name. "Makâ..."

"Mâkakao," he repeated.

She laughed at her own clumsiness with the name. "Mâk?"

His lips turned up slightly at one corner. "Mâk."

"As much as I admire thy body, I would not have ye to travel with me naked, Mâk. Ye will attract the wrong sort of attention. Get ye to yon merchants and see to thy clothing. Something sturdy, but light enough to travel in. Get ye outfitted. A warm tunic and light armor and a traveling cape. Whatever else ye shall have need of. And get ye a good sword."

He stared at the bag of coins she pressed into his hand. His voice sounded odd when he finally spoke. "You would trust me in this, M'Lady?"

Cassadara looked up and down the one mud path that ran between the stone huts of the merchants. "Would ye rather remain here?"

A smile, a real one at last, stole through his reserve. The smile touched his face with the promise of beauty. "No. No, M'Lady, I would not."

"Mâk?" She spoke softly as he started to turn away.

"M'Lady?" On his lips the word sounded like a caress.

"Find ye a bath and a barber."

Green eyes turned stormy gray. A flush stole over his cheeks. "As you wish, M'Lady."

He thought she meant him to prepare himself for her bed? The idea was not unpleasant, but he was in no condition to enjoy such exercise at the moment, and she had no wish to kill him. Cassadara smothered her laughter. "Have the barber see to thy arm. I would not have thy wound heal badly."

He flinched as if she had hit him. "'Tis nothing, M'Lady. A scratch of no importance."

"Have the wound seen to," she insisted. "And get ye something to eat. A good dinner may cure what ails ye."

The Human inclined his head in a show of respect. "M'Lady."

She liked the way the title sounded when he spoke. Almost as if his words caressed her. Still…

"Cassadara. If we are to share this journey, ye might as well know my name."

One corner of his mouth lifted up. "I know your name, M'Lady. In the language of the Fey your name means Daughter of the Wind. I think all in these parts know your name by now."

"Then ye shall have no trouble finding me when ye are outfitted and ready to depart. I shall be at yon tavern at the edge of what passes here for a town. I have paid for a room there for the night, but I would rather leave this place behind us." She let her attention flick briefly toward the Slaver's hut. "Have caution. I do no' trust the Dwarf."

His eyes warmed slightly. "I will return to you, M'Lady."

If he did not, she would be out nothing but a small bag of Mother's coin. She watched the tall Human turn and walk away, admiring the hard angles of his shoulders beneath the cape. Somehow she trusted he would be good to his word. Cassadara thought briefly of the Human's other attributes and smiled to herself. Perhaps she would not regret this bargain, after all.

Even as the thought occurred to her, the Human stumbled up the steps to the nearest merchant's hut, clutching at the doorframe as he tried to right himself. Cassadara sighed. With a movement as swift as her name implied, she reached his side. Although she was shorter by a hand's breadth than any of her clansmen, she had at least inherited the strength of her race. She gathered the man into her arms as she would have an injured child. Even through the wool of the cape she could tell he was burning up with a fever that had not been there a few minutes ago.

Eyes the color of wintergreen sought hers as thick ebony lashes parted. "The Dwarf…"

She too remembered the Dwarf laying his hand on the Talisman.

His voice trailed off and his eyes slipped closed, only to jerk suddenly open again. "Please, do not let me die in this place, M'Lady," he implored. "Not here. The tundra…"

"Ye shall no' die. No' here. No' today. I give ye my word."

His eyes slid closed again. "Clan of the Wolf is known for keeping its word," he whispered. As if the effort of speaking had been too much, his head lolled loosely to one side.

The door before her gave way at a kick from her fine steel-clad boot. A tiny merchant woman looked up at them in terror, reaching for a pitiful excuse for a knife.

"I have need of thy assistance," Cassadara explained calmly. *"I shall pay thee well."*

Chapter Two

The Human drifted in and out of consciousness throughout the day. Despite the spells she used to heal his wounds, he seemed no better. Using her gift once again, Cassadara placed her hands on the man, chanting softly, but the healing prayer only served to keep him clinging to life. If anything, his fever had worsened. The man spoke in his sleep, sometimes giving orders to his troops, sometimes negotiating trades in exotic languages.

Her magic was not strong enough to war with the curse of the Dwarf. Dread began to take hold of her. Had she not feared to leave the man alone, she would have hunted down the Dwarf and his Talisman. If the Human died, Cassadara would have lost not only Mother's money, but her respect as well. Cassadara had chosen to accept the Human rather than wait to find the Clansman her mother had sent her for. The Dwarf's curse had been brought on by her temper. If this Human died, his death would be her failure.

If the man died, she would have failed him as well, for he had entrusted himself to her care. Admittedly, his other options had been none too good, but that was not the point. He had entrusted himself to her, and she had given him her word he would live.

Cassadara knelt beside the straw pallet, withdrawing the small leather-bound *Book of Ways* from her satchel once again, cursing her weakness. Mother could have healed the Human with a mere touch of her hand. Cassadara could not. Yet there were spells...

Now was not the time to decide to devote herself to learning new spells. She searched through the book again, trying to find an alternative, something within her reach, a spell she had already mastered. She kept coming back to the same page—Breath of Life, a full healing spell. She had never practiced this one. The spell was not to be used lightly, the book warned. The recipient must give his consent. He must surrender himself to her. Would—could—this Human give that much of himself?

There would be consequences. How much of herself would she lose to him? Only desperation led her to memorize such a difficult and dangerous spell now.

A groan from the pallet beside her alerted her to the man's return to consciousness. Cassadara put her book away.

There were always consequences…

* * * * *

"Mâk?"

He opened his eyes, and then closed them tight again. "No. No. You're not real. This is not happening to me." This was but a dream. The same one he'd had for years. The creature from his favorite dreams had come to haunt his nightmares now.

"Mâk…"

The Druid priests had warned him against his dream-lover. They called the Wolf-Woman an abomination, saying he was possessed. He shut his eyes tightly. "A fever. I'm down with a fever. You are not real."

The effort of speaking tortured his neck. Chains. The Dwarf had kept him in chains. His hands rose to claw at the iron collar that choked off his breathing. He fought back the panic. He would not let the Dwarf see his fear. That one would only use his fear against him.

Soft, cool hands closed gently over his, stilling his panic. She felt real. "Mâk."

The odd accent made his name sound like an endearment. His body responded inappropriately, as it had when the dream-woman had stared at him down by the Slaver's pit. He remembered the way she had looked at him, like a piece of merchandise she was inspecting. He closed his eyes, trying to escape the nightmare.

"Stay with me, Mâk. I need ye in this world before I can attempt this."

She could not be real. This could not be happening to him. Yet the voice persisted softly, patiently demanding. She spoke his own language, though strongly accented, as if she'd managed to weave sensuality into every word. He opened his eyes cautiously. The Wolf-Woman was still there. Whatever hell the gods had dropped him into this time, they'd chosen to mock him with the creature of his secret desires. A she-wolf in Human form stood beside the pallet, a small book in her hands, concern radiating from dark amber eyes.

She was naked. He was dying and a naked Wolf-Woman adorned with the runes of a Priestess stood over him, a mocking reminder that he'd taken a vow of abstinence five years ago to find favor with his gods. Perhaps the gods were rewarding his sacrifice now, for this woman appeared to be the answer to every devotion he'd ever made.

He *knew* this woman. He'd made a bargain with her—indentured himself for the price of his freedom. The Wolf-Woman *owned* him now. The chains she held him with were of his own making, and stronger than any bonds the Dwarf might have forged.

She'd made a poor bargain.

She was beautiful, in a wild, dangerous way. Her dark hair hung in a heavy braid the thickness of a ship's mooring rope over her shoulders. As she swayed closer, peering down at him, the ends of the braid brushed over his skin, branding him with a feather touch. Unbraided, her hair would reach well past her waist, a dark cloud that might swallow him up.

Nothing about her was small. Her shoulders were broad and powerful, no doubt from fighting with the massive staff leaning against the crudely plastered wall. He vaguely remembered her picking him up—no easy feat for a man of his own race, let alone a woman.

But she wasn't of his race. She wasn't Human. She was a Barbarian—a Wolf-Woman.

She was the youngest daughter of House Lochinvar.

Back at the Slaver's Pit she'd been in armor that showed both quality and service. She was no arrogant child of privilege, this daughter of Lady Evalayna. When she'd drawn her shortsword, he'd believed she would not hesitate to cleave off the Dwarf's hand.

The armor was gone now, all sign of her rank and station with it. Bared, her arms and shoulders were roped with muscle. She wasn't completely naked. A band of soft leather bound her breasts. Those weren't small, either. The binding, rather than making her look less feminine, pushed her breasts up into two large swelling mounds split by deeply shadowed cleavage. Swallowing hard, he let his focus drop lower.

She still wore her kilt. That left for a great deal of exposed skin. Human or not, what there was of her was all woman. Glorious, powerful, deadly Wolf-Woman. She was the dream he'd saved himself for. The answer to his prayers and devotions.

That she would appear as he lay dying was just too great an irony.

"Ye are awake. Good." Her voice mesmerized him, making him forget whatever question he'd been about to ask. She stepped across the pallet so that one long, slender foot rested on either side of his hips, slowly lowering herself to straddle his waist.

His breathing took on a ragged desperation, sending pain shooting through the broken ribs. He felt as if his cock might burst with the wanting of her. "I think I must be dreaming."

"Can ye find it within thyself to trust me, Mâk?"

"Trust you, M'Lady?"

"Aye. I have never done this before." She slid the book she'd been reading back into a small leather case. "I must have thy consent."

His consent? For what? Was she trying to tell him she was a virgin?

She settled herself astride his hips. The feel of her flesh against his told him she wore nothing under that kilt. Great. Just great. He'd eagerly listened to the legends of the Wolf-Women since he'd first left his childhood behind. The whispered tales of their sexual abilities were the stuff of a young man's wet dreams. Many a man of his township would kill for the chance to be where he was now. Yet he knew he was in no condition to take on a virgin Wolf-Woman, no matter how his cock responded to the feel of her heat pressed against his thighs.

"Can ye trust me?" she repeated.

His mind lost out in the argument with his burning erection. The gods had brought them together against all odds. He had asked for her trust. She had paid his price. He only prayed he might live long enough to give the woman her money's worth. "I am yours," he consented. "Do what you will with me." She might well be the death of him, but he could think of no better way to die.

She smiled, looking somehow younger and more vulnerable than she had in her armor. Further down she folded herself, until her bound breasts pressed painfully against his aching ribs. She took a deep breath and covered his mouth with hers.

Whatever he'd expected, if he'd actually been capable of thinking at all, he was totally unprepared for what happened next. She breathed out, gradually filling his lungs with her breath until he fought her, fought to break her hold, to shove her away, to do anything to remember where he ended and she began.

Trust her? What was she doing to him? Panic set in. He wanted to run, but he could not escape. He was too weak to fight her. Strong hands held his head clamped firmly in place. The kiss that was not a kiss deepened until he thought his lungs might burst. When at last she released him, his breath exploded, leaving the room awhirl in swirling colors. He coughed hard, desperately sucking in fresh air.

When his vision cleared, she was still there, looking more beautiful and exotic than ever as she sat straddling his waist, the heat of her bared pelt only inches from his burning cock.

The raw agony in his throat was gone. His shield arm itched savagely, but when he ran his fingers over the wound, the skin felt smooth and whole.

What had she done to him?

Strength flowed back into his body like a powerful aphrodisiac. Whatever she'd done, however she'd done it, he felt whole—renewed and hungry. By the gods, he'd never needed a woman so in his life! He tugged at her kilt. The soft, worn tartan came loose easily under his demanding hands. He had to see, to touch. He grasped her hips, dragging her closer, desperate to feel himself inside her. He wanted her. He needed her. Now. Now!

The Wolf-Woman snarled at him as he tried to pull her over his urgent cock, freezing him in place. She stared down at him, her teeth slightly bared, as if deciding his fate. One wrong move, and he was sure she'd rip his throat out.

Somewhere in the clouded recesses of his brain he knew this was wrong. A man did not force a woman. Did not demand more of her than she was willing to give. It had been a long time, five years, but he still remembered, women expected certain things. Some lingering trace of common sense told him not to push her any farther. You didn't just grab a woman—a Wolf-Woman at that—up and stab at her with a randy cock like—

Like mating wolves?

Her lips parted a little farther, the snarl becoming a grin as she rocked forward. She moved at her own speed, rising over him, torturing him, but still ending up exactly where he'd wanted her in the first place—her body sliding slowly down the length of his thick, throbbing cock.

Brother Wind, take my soul.

If a man could die of pleasure his time had come.

The muscles of her vagina rippled against his cock, allowing him access at a pace so excruciatingly slow he felt as if he would burst from the need for her. Too much. Too much. He couldn't stand the torture. He wanted to be in her. Now. With a strength he had not known he still possessed, he grappled with her, pulling her down on the pallet beside him. They rolled together, twisting and turning until he knelt between her thighs, their hands grasped tightly in two locked fists.

She was like nothing he'd ever felt before. Firm and muscular and tight, yet so wet and ready for him she whimpered when he pushed deeper into her hot sheath. Her low moan of pleasure rewarded him for his control. Slowly, as slowly as she had done, he pushed into her, pleased when her fingers tightened in his, trying to escape his hold. Her muscles pulsed around his cock, pulling, demanding, protesting his restrained pace. A grin settled over his face. Whatever she had done to him was nothing compared to what he would do to her.

"Mâk..." she gasped, writhing against him. "Now, Mâk. *Now.*"

No. Her urgency lent him strength. He'd waited five years for this. He would not rush. Not now. Withdrawing himself, he pushed her back, lowering his mouth to the soft patch of fur between her legs. "I have heard the women of the Wolf will sing for the right man. Sing for me, Wolf-Woman. I want to hear you howl."

Releasing her hands, he lifted her hips, tilting her pelvis as he slid his tongue over the silky-smooth folds of her flesh. She was different, but not so different. The source of her pleasure still formed a hard bud of desire. He circled the tiny head of her clitoris with the tip of his tongue, pleased when she bucked beneath his touch. He licked and kissed and sucked until her hands fisted in his hair, pulling, demanding.

Somewhere in the back of his mind he noticed his hair was trimmed shorter and neater, and his beard cropped. His arm, where the wound had been, supported his full weight as he hovered over her, driving his tongue into sensitive flesh that convulsed around him again and again. He felt no pain when he drew in his breath.

He would ponder these things later. For now, there was this compelling need, stronger than anything he'd ever felt before, and there was the Wolf-Woman, her body responding to his touch without reserve. The tension was more than he could stand. Lifting his head, he kissed his way up her body until he found that small strip of soft leather. The imprint of her nipples stood out against the hide. When he nipped at her through the restraint she moaned out a cry of desire.

Her hands released him long enough to fight with the knot in the lacings between her breasts. She growled and bit at him like the wolf he had named her, desperate in her need for his touch. Bare breasts spilled out before him, demanding his attention. The blue runes marking her face trailed down over her left breast, leading like a path to a deep coral nipple that waited before him, fully erect. Blackened steel rings adorned each nipple, piercing the flesh. He ran his tongue around the circumference of the closest one, tugging gently, pleased when she moaned again, pressing herself harder against him.

There was a power in this, in being able to answer her need. Yet her body was addictive, an intoxicant, eroding his restraint with each whimpered response. The tip of his throbbing cock brushed against her scorching heat, bringing another cry of tortured desire to her lips. He sat up again, pushing her slightly away from him. With one hand he spread her labial folds apart, the other hand moving the head of his cock against her clit — circling, teasing, maddening her with desire.

"I...want...ye!" she gasped. "Now!"

"Have you always had whatever you wanted, M'Lady?"

"Aye!"

"Very well." He dropped forward, supporting his weight on his hands, brushing against her welcoming body with the head of his cock. He allowed but an inch to slip inside her. No more. "Here I am," he murmured. "Come and get me."

She took him at his word. Strong legs wrapped around his waist, pulling her desperate body hard against him as she impaled herself on his waiting cock. He felt his control snapping as she arched up to meet him, each thrust a testimonial to her amazing physique. Breasts bobbed before him. He snagged one, sucking hard, scraping the sensitive nipple with the edges of his teeth.

"Is this what you want?"

"Aye..." she managed as she surged against him.

"Then give me what I want. Sing for me, Wolf-Woman. I want to hear you howl."

He slammed into her, sinking the length of his cock in until his balls smacked against her with the sound of wet flesh colliding. He pulled back out swiftly, then entered again, thrusting hard now, demanding his price.

"Sing for me!" he demanded.

She rocked her hips under him, tilting her pelvis, allowing him even deeper access to her tight-muscled channel. Her legs slid up from his waist toward his shoulders. The more he gave, the more she claimed. Taut muscles clamped down on his cock, shuddering in pleasure, yet demanding still more. All control gone, he slammed into her mercilessly, driving her body forward across the floor until the wall stopped their advance. He felt his own climax building, coming on him with a force like nothing he'd ever experienced before. She cried out again, a strangled noise somewhere between a moan and a whimper.

No! It was not enough! He wanted more. He wanted — with a final thrust he burst into her, spilling his seed in a hot, burning gush that seemed to go on forever.

Her body answered his, shuddering deeply, milking him of all he had to give. She arched hard under him, her breath a whine that rose to a long, high-pitched note, the call of the mating wolf.

As the light in the room faded into a blackness swirling within his head, he heard another voice answering hers. With the surprise of a spirit detached from his body he realized the voice was his own.

* * * * *

Cassadara sat up slowly, trying to clear her head.

How had she gotten here?

Where *was* here?

The night was far advanced. She must have fallen asleep, though she felt more like she had passed out. She groped blindly about her for something familiar.

What she found was a body. A still warm body.

What she didn't find was her weapon. She tried the process again, increasing the diameter of her groping, but still moving as soundlessly as possible. Nothing but the body within reach. Fine. She would have to search the body. She needed...

The body was naked. Naked and *alive* and very definitely male. Arms befuddled with sleep reached out to her, sliding around her as if their owner thought they had the right to do so. Her hands traced up those arms, searching for some remembrance of where she was and who she was with. Her fingertips read a scar, running from his left elbow to his shoulder.

Like a kaleidoscope, the pieces came slowly back into focus. Long, thick hair. A close-cropped beard. A broad expanse of hard, muscled chest.

Human. She had mated with the Human. Healed him with *Breath of Life* and mated with him. A Human male who was hers, bought and paid for. A male who had done incredible things to her body. A male who held her possessively even now. Even knowing the consequences, she had allowed this.

There would be a price to pay.

One large hand stroked her hair. The move was oddly comforting. She snuggled closer against his chest, thinking that whatever the cost, he had been well worth the price. Their limbs intertwined, and she drifted contentedly back to sleep.

* * * * *

"Woman, you have bewitched me."

His voice, low and deep, did not sound angry. Cassadara stretched languidly against him, enjoying the coolness of the early morning contrasted against the heat of his body. As she snuggled closer, his cock prodded her ass, hard and hot as a branding iron. "Good," she growled.

"Good? This is all you can say?"

Something about this conversation was slightly wrong, but she wasn't quite awake enough to figure out what was bothering her. Yet. Cassadara shifted her shoulders until she could see his beautiful green eyes smiling down at her. "Good. What is mine should be bewitched."

He propped himself up on one elbow to stare down at her, his hand brushing over his face. Curling his head down he pressed his lips over hers. She found the sensation oddly sensual. She would have protested when he nipped gently at her lower lip, but as she opened her mouth he slid his tongue in between her lips. His movements reminded her of what else he could do with that tongue. She nipped at its tip as he lifted his face away from her. "What have you done to me, woman?"

She ran her fingertips over the shortened beard, feeling a little guilty. "The Dwarven woman at the barbers helped me to bathe ye. She also trimmed thy beard. I did not know how ye were wont to wear it. If it is too short 'twill surely grow back." Her hand strayed to his distractingly naked chest. "The tailor and the cobbler both measured ye. Presumably ye will not leave here naked."

Warm green eyes searched hers. "That is not what I meant and you know it. The fever is gone. My arm is healed. My body...my body desires you more than I have ever known I could desire any woman."

She was already wet and hot with the need for him. The sensation was strange, but mysteriously pleasing. She twisted far enough to run the tip of her tongue over his nipple. "Thy body desires to mate with me? What about thy mind?"

His hand rested on her breast, rubbing the tip of her nipple between his thumb and forefinger until she thought she might go mad with desire. "My mind is filled with nothing but you."

Cassadara sighed. "Then perhaps like all men thy body rules thy mind."

"Perhaps you have bewitched me."

"Perhaps," Cassadara agreed as she snuggled back against him.

Damnation. She knew now what it was that had bothered her. "Mâk?"

"*Mel~amin?*"

"How came ye to speak my language?"

A chuckle sounded deep in his throat, like the growl of a wolf. "I speak ten languages, M'Lady." He answered in Ogre, a sound so guttural it might well have been the bark of an animal.

"What others?" she inquired in the language of the High Elves.

"Elven, Orcish, Gnomish, and Troll."

The feel of his cock pressing against her ass and his hands sliding over her skin made intelligent conversation nearly impossible. She already knew he spoke her language and his own as well as Dwarven and Common Tongue. She counted them twice to make sure. "That is only but nine."

"Both ancient and modern Elven, *Mel~amin*."

Ancient Elven? That meant…

No. Surely she was mistaken. Others besides the sons of elite houses were educated in languages. "Thou art the son of a merchant, perhaps?"

"My father has been known to trade a bit from time to time."

His teeth closed over her earlobe, nipping at the clan symbol dangling from her ear. She arched her back hard against him, moaning with need. He slid his hand along her legs from behind, down over the outside then up along the inner curve of her thigh. She raised her heel to trace her toes along his leg. His hand slid into the space she'd left open to him. One finger circled her clitoris, already engorged and sensitive to his touch. Another slipped inside her, then two.

She knew what he felt. Mating had never been like this before. Raw. Urgent. She was already so wet at the thought of him that her juices flooded his hand. The need was like a fire consuming her from within. His fingers thrust into her while his thumb continued to tease the head of her clit, circling without touching, driving her mad with the wanting of him so that she moaned and thrust against his hand like a wanton.

He curled over her, her breast in his mouth, tugging on the nipple ring, and she could feel his hot, thick cock smoldering against her hip, so close, so close to where she wanted him. She spread herself wider, beckoning him to enter. The tip of his cock grazed along her inner thigh and up, promising the contact she so desperately needed.

She sought to turn in his arms, to grant him access, but he held her where she was. His fingers, wet with her own moisture, moved to her ass, spreading her gently. He wanted to enter her there? Was that possible? She clenched hard against him for a moment before his touch coaxed her to relax, allowing him access. His finger pushed against her, gently teasing, wetting, stretching her. She held herself rigid at first, then pushed back against him experimentally. Lights danced in her head as exquisite sensations bombarded her senses. She moaned, snapping angrily when he withdrew his finger.

Still, she gasped in surprised when he slipped the tip of his cock into her anus. He paused there without moving, only the tip within her, stretching her, allowing her time to adapt to this new sensation. When she thought she would die if he didn't do something, his fingers began to stimulate her again, filling her sheath, teasing her clit until she wanted to scream. She rocked forward against his hand, accidentally pulling away from him as she strove to meet his probing fingers.

The arm supporting her found her nipple, tugging and twisting on her nipple ring until she drove against him of her own accord, pushing him back in, pushing him deeper and deeper until she felt his balls teasing her ass.

The dance took on a rhythm, filling her with an aching need as she shuddered against him. The first climax took her by surprise, ripping through her with a force she had never expected, while another crested right on its waning edge, and then another and another.

Still, he showed no signs of tiring. She clawed at him, desperate to reach any part she might touch or kiss or bite. Her cries of pleasure became animalistic, first little whimpers and then finally, as he moved faster within her, thrusting deeper, her voice broke to a crescendo, the mating call of the Wolf.

As his voice joined hers, his pace furious, she felt him break, shattering inside of her as his seed filled her ass. Her body shook in one last convulsive dance before the blackness overcame her.

* * * * *

"*Mel~amin?*"

Sleep still held her in its welcoming arms. "Mmm."

"The day is far advanced. Still the Dwarven woman has not knocked on your door."

Indeed, the sun was at a most annoying angle. She thought to ask which day it was, then decided she did not want to know. Still, she had no desire to rise. It had been so long since she'd actually slept. "Send the servants to fetch her."

Humor tinged his voice, his words stroking her like a soft hand. "I am your only servant at present, M'Lady, and I should prefer not to wander the town in your undergarments."

He had not the proper attitude for a servant, in any case. "Fear ye not my wrath for disobeying me?"

The humor in his voice turned to outright laughter. "No, M'Lady. I fear you not."

She turned her head away from the window with its annoying light. "Then come ye back to bed."

A warm, naked body slid onto the pallet beside her. "As you wish, M'Lady."

His arms encircled her as if to do so were his right. The burning heat of his cock teased her further awake as he snuggled against her. If his familiarity stole a piece of her soul she made no protest. She rolled in his arms to face him, her hands returning his caresses. "I meant to sleep, foolish one. Do ye never sleep?"

He inclined his head to nuzzle her ear. "I am bewitched, remember? I am destined to do nothing but lie abed with you."

She let her eyes drift closed, enjoying the feel of his lips on her skin. "Then we must away to somewhere with a more comfortable bed."

"My father's house has many comfortable beds. We could try them all until you pronounce a favorite."

"That sounds most enjoyable." Except…

Cassadara opened her eyes, searching the face before her. "Thy father be no simple merchant."

Deep green eyes settled their full attention on her, mesmerizing her. "No, Mistress. He is not."

A man who spoke ten languages and was raised in a house with many beds might well treat her as an equal. "Ye were raised in a house of privilege."

He smiled at her, humor still in the forefront, as if such information made no difference. "I was."

She sighed. "Thy father must mourn thy loss."

"As your mother would."

Uncomfortable feelings of responsibility settled firmly in place. Mother would see in this an opportunity to place one of the houses in her debt. Mother would see alliances and settlements. All Cassadara could see was the loss she would feel when he left her. "I must return ye to thy house. I would no' have thy father's grief on my hands."

He shrugged slightly, as if his birth made no difference. "Nor would I your Mother's. I pledged you my indenture. My word is my bond."

"Ye pledged me the bond of a slave. The son of a noble house has responsibilities outweighing any such bond."

He brushed his lips over the spot where her pulse beat in her throat. "I am still your slave."

The gentle caress of his lips stirred a heat in her that made thinking nearly impossible. Her lip trembled dangerously. "Thy bond to me is fulfilled."

His kisses made their way down over her chest, circling ever closer to her aching nipples. "What of you? Are you so anxious to be rid of me? Have you had your fill of me already, M'Lady?"

"What I want is of no consequence," she assured him, though her body betrayed her hunger. "We have responsibilities…"

"I am pledged to see this mission through with you," he insisted.

No matter the politics of the situation, she had no desire to dissuade him from remaining at her side. "What know ye of my mission?"

His kisses nuzzled her breastbone. "'Tis said you go to negotiate a truce with the House of Yarishet. A dangerous business at best."

"Aye. I canna' argue with thy logic."

"'Tis a fool's errand," he growled as he licked at the sensitive underside of her breasts. "What would possess House Lochinvar to send one of her prized possessions, a treasured daughter, across leagues of dangerous territory in the midst of a war to negotiate a treaty that will mean nothing four seasons from now?"

"Yarishet requested a daughter," she explained, attempting to keep her mind on the conversation. "House Lochinvar has daughters to spare. I am expendable. My mission is expendable. My death would gain a grievance against House Yarishet. I am but a pawn in a war fought by political advisors who know not the taste of the mud of a battlefield."

"You are more than a pawn to me, M'Lady." He licked the hollow spot above her breastbone, sending shivers through her nipples. "No. You do not taste of mud."

How could she talk politics while his lips did such incredible things to her breasts? She allowed herself the pleasure of one more night without politics, without allies or enemies, as she slid her hands along his body. She wanted to tell him how good she felt just lying there in his arms, letting go of all thought outside the room and their mating, but she kept such thoughts to herself. Instead she nipped his shoulder, teasing him with the caress of her tongue when he yelped a protest. She wriggled beneath him, nudging him towards the mating she desired.

Without further preliminaries he thrust his hard, hot penis into her.

She was ready for him. She knew she had always been ready for him. Her body leapt at his touch, slamming urgently against him. Her wet sheath tightened around him almost instantly, aching for climax. He thrust into her harder, deeper, filling her to capacity. She clenched around him, striving to hold him there, but he withdrew, only to slam into her again and again.

"By the gods," she breathed out.

She could feel the weight of his balls slapping against her, hot and heavy, ready to explode. She bit his shoulder, hard, leaving a trace of blood behind, which she licked away. Helpless to control herself, she contracted around him, feeling the waves of pleasure spread through her body again and again.

Her climaxes only spurred him to drive into her harder. Her hips bucked to meet him thrust for thrust, pushing their pace to the limit. She felt his breath against her like a blast of heat, scorching her breasts with an aching need to be touched.

"Sing for me," he gritted out as his teeth closed over her aching nipple. He took the black metal ring in his mouth, twisting it with his tongue.

She had no choice.

The cry spilled from her as his seed burst within her yet again, the final climax washing over her like the burst of a summer lightning storm. To her satisfaction, she felt him answer her call as he broke, a look almost like pain washing over his face.

The Dwarf had not lied, Cassadara reflected as she drifted off to sleep again, wrapped in Mâk's arms. She had gotten her money's worth.

Chapter Three

The sun was sneaking into the eastern sky like a thief trying not to be noticed. Cassadara opened her eyes slowly, cursing the curtainless window. She rolled until the sun could not find her, allowing her eyes to adjust. Pushing herself up on her knees, she surveyed the small room.

A table and bench lined the wall opposite the window. A door, closed and bolted, interrupted the wall in front of her. She knelt on a small straw-stuffed pallet providing no insulation from the cold floor. Her tartan had been draped across her like a blanket. Still, she was cold.

The space beside her where he had lain was cold.

She was alone.

She climbed to her feet. Perhaps his leaving was for the best. The aftereffects of her spell would have worn off by now. She need not see the remnants of lust in his eyes and wonder at the fire no longer burning for her there.

Her scattered weapons and armor had been gathered. Her clothing lay on the table, neatly folded, a mocking reminder of the wantonness with which she had discarded her garb. She laced herself into the brief leather bustier, noting the stain where his lips had darkened the leather. She brushed her fingers across her nipples, trying to recapture the magic, but all she felt was her own touch. Tears clumped her eyelashes into a wet, soggy mess.

Damn the man. She prayed a silent oath that his body might fail to respond to the next woman whose heart he wished to ravage. She had been a fool to have given so much of herself to the man. She had never let that happen before. She had broken every promise she had ever made to herself. She had allowed him to plunder her heart and her soul. She had *sung* for him.

Stirrings of life from beyond her small room called her to action. She had lost two days to this miserable excuse for a town. Two days while she'd done little but eat and sleep and mate. With a Human, no less.

She yanked at the buckles of her leather bracers, perhaps a bit more forcefully than was necessary. The mesh shirt snagged in her hair, testimony to the lack of care she'd paid it. She was hungry. Her rations were exhausted. She'd need to scout up food before she left—if the male hadn't taken all of her money.

The small bag of gold coin from her mother was gone, but her purse still resided in the outer compartment of her backpack. Its contents seemed undisturbed. There was one flask of water left. She rinsed her mouth and spat out the window.

Her breath caught as the door opened silently behind her. There was no noise, no sound of footsteps, but she could feel his presence as assuredly as if he had boomed out a welcome. She brushed the loose wisps of fuzz away from her face as she turned to face…a stranger.

A total stranger stood before her, dressed in worn leather and fine mesh armor molded perfectly to his hard muscled body. A pair of scimitars hug at his sides with the ease of familiarity. A backpack slung over one shoulder sagged with the strain of fresh provisions. His hair had been cut again and his beard trimmed very short. Only the eyes were the same. Deep green eyes smiled into hers with happiness that had nothing to do with his clothes.

"Mâk."

* * * * *

"Mâk."

Her voice made his name sound like a prayer. The backpack slipped from his fingers, unnoticed. In one stride he crossed the room to her, gathering her into his arms. A trace of salty tears clung to her eyes. He licked them away with the tip of his tongue. She responded shyly to his kiss, hesitant still, though her hands wrapped around his shoulders and into his hair, binding him to her as no chains ever could have.

"Why were you crying, *Mel~amin*?"

She swiped the back of her hand across her eyes. "I was no' crying. I never cry."

He smiled at that. "No. Of course not. Forgive me my foolishness, M'Lady." He kissed her again, caught up in the taste of her, already lost in her scent.

She buried her head in his shoulder, her voice barely a whisper. "I feared ye had tired of me and had returned to thy house of many beds."

The sob in her voice touched his heart. "What use is a house of many beds, when the only woman I could desire is not amongst them?"

"Ye are still besotted."

He sought to raise her head, but she would not meet his eyes. "Look at me," he whispered as he nibbled her earlobe. "Look at me, *Mel~amin*."

She drew a shaky breath and slowly raised her head. Deep amber peered out from under soggy lashes.

"I have faced your tribesman across the battlefield. I have seen one of your Shaman pluck a dying man from the ground and breathe life back into him. I have witnessed that same man, whom I would have sworn dead, unleash the fury of twenty men onto all those around him. My people fear these berserkers, these dead men, and call them abominations. Is that what I am to you? An abomination raised from the dead?"

She shook her head violently. "I have no' the power to raise the dead. Only to mend the living."

So there were limits. She was not all-powerful. Yet. He blinked once, filing that information away in his memory. "Do I look healed to you?"

She swallowed hard. "Ye look—ye look like everything the Dwarf said ye were."

"I was as dead, *Mel~amin*. I had lost the one thing that separates men from the beasts of burden. I had lost hope. When I looked up and saw you tromping through the mud, that imperious tone in your voice as you barked at Argolyn, I thought you were one of the goddesses, come to answer my prayers. That you are a flesh and blood woman as well does nothing to change my mind. You are the most beautiful goddess I could ever imagine, and you shall always be the answer to my prayers."

His words brought a tremulous smile to her lips. "Ye are still besotted. I am no' beautiful. My sister Tranorva is the beautiful one. When she does things, she does them right the first time."

The remembered image shook him. "General Tranorva is your sister?"

She nodded. "My elder sister. My mother's favored. I see ye have heard of her."

"Heard of her? I have faced her in battle. You think she is beautiful?"

"She is taller than I, and broader of shoulder, and stronger. She can hit a target with her throwing axe at one hundred and fifty feet. She is better at everything than I am. I do no' *think* she is beautiful. She *is* beautiful. Men fall at her feet. I am so unlike her I doubt I can be called her sister."

The humor of the situation hit him, bringing a chuckle to his lips. "Men fall *dead* at her feet from her war hammer, not from her beauty. She is the most frightening thing I have ever seen on a battlefield. I have seen her up close and I felt nothing but fear. Truly I thought her rather hideous. Thank the gods you are unlike her. Besides. She has not your talent. She is no Shaman."

Cassadara looked down at her feet. "I am no real Shaman. Not yet."

He kissed her again. "You are real enough for me. I am alive."

A commotion beyond the window distracted her attention. He sought to draw her back into his arms, but she was a single-minded woman.

"I think it is best you stay away from the window, M'Lady. Indeed, I think it might be best if we were about your business."

She turned back to him, suspicion mingled with humor overwriting her features. "Mâk, what have ye done?"

He did his best to look innocent. "I have but regained my armor, M'Lady, and purchased supplies. I think we might best be on our way."

"Where did ye find thy armor, Mâk?"

"Please, M'Lady. We must away."

"Mâk." She drew his name out, clearly desiring an answer.

He sighed, knowing he was defeated. "I but regained a few things from the pile the vile Dwarf had looted off of us." He displayed her bag of gold, still mostly full. "I purchased supplies for the journey."

He went to stand beside her at the window. The noises were getting louder as pandemonium broke loose on the city streets. Fires could be seen dotting the rooflines of thatched huts at the far end of town. "We really should go, M'Lady. I fear I have angered the Dwarf. He must have noticed his loss by now."

"How many men?" Her voice had lost its humor.

He swallowed hard. "M'Lady?"

"Ye have freed the slaves. How many of those men answer to ye?"

"Six, M'Lady. The rest were but a ruse to cover their escape."

"And still ye came back to me." There was a touch of wonder in her words.

He had tried not to. He had reached the edge of town before the scent of her on his skin hit him down low in his gut. "I gave you my word, M'Lady." He'd given her more than that, but he'd not tell her so.

She turned from the window and strapped on her sword. "Where did ye tell them to meet ye?"

He had not meant to draw her into this business. If only he'd managed to leave...But he had not bid her good-bye. "M'Lady, I—"

"Cease!" Her eyes blazed like yellow flames. "My name is Cassadara, and we have no time. The Dwarf will slaughter them all. Think ye not that the entire town has heard our mating calls? Think ye not that the Dwarf knows enough to know which men answer to ye? I humiliated yon Dwarf in front of his guards and his merchandise. Now ye have cost him his livelihood. Where?"

He knew when he was defeated. Inevitably, he thought with a trace of insight, he welcomed defeat. "The first knoll to the north beyond the river, M'...Cassadara."

She snatched up his pack and threw the strap over her shoulder, next to her own. He swallowed a protest, thinking the time might not be right to defend his injured manhood. Instead he bent his head to kiss her fiercely.

Her answer came as a growl. "Pray to the gods I am a better Shaman than I believe myself to be." With that she kissed him back and kicked open the door.

He was long of leg. He was strong. He was healthy. Perhaps the healthiest he had ever been in his life. He was unencumbered save for his scimitars. She was laden with both her pack and his own. Yet by the time she crested the hill near the river and stopped to orient herself, he feared his lungs would explode from lack of oxygen.

He bent nearly double, his hands on his knees, gasping for breath. She glanced at him, her look half-annoyed, half-amused. When her hand caressed his jaw he looked up at her, still gasping. Her kiss sealed off his air. She exhaled into his lungs again, though not so forcefully this time.

His body began to tingle, and his lungs quit aching from strain. He felt lighter, younger, stronger, and full of energy. He nipped playfully at her shoulder and she batted at him, her look pure amusement now. Then her eyes turned serious as they swept the surrounding hills.

"There."

He looked, but could not see where she pointed.

"Pray we are no' too late."

He did not bother to ask for more instructions. She could mean only one thing. The Dwarf had followed his men. "They are armed," he offered grimly. "They will not go down easily."

She glanced at him, saying nothing, but tossed him his pack. The bag felt incredibly light as he snatched it out of the air. She was off even as he slung their supplies over his shoulder, so that his first stride was almost a leap to catch up with her. They moved at least twice as fast as they had before. Yet this time he did not feel the strain.

He could see them now. His men had chosen a defensible position in the craggy stone hillside. Still, they were poorly armed, and but six against a party of eight well armed Mercenaries led by the Dwarf.

His men would be slaughtered. He cursed himself. He was their leader. He should have been with them. He should have died with his men the first time, never have lived to be taken captive. He stretched his long legs, asking his body for yet more speed, leaving Cassadara behind as he raced toward his fate.

A pack dropped at his feet and he slowed just enough to scoop the bag up as he ran. A white wolf streaked past him, huge and magnificent, its speed making his look like a mere attempt at running.

Her speed, he corrected himself—for the great white wolf that bore down on the Slavers could be none other than his own Wolf-Woman. The legends were true.

She might strike fear into the enemy and even harass a few, but what could she do without swords against eight armed men? Fear wrung his heart as she launched herself into the midst of the attackers. He landed into the fray as close to her side as he could, both scimitars dealing out death to the unwary. The cry she had taught him reverberated across the valley.

Chaos broke loose in the ranks of the Mercenaries the Dwarf had hired. At least one man went down with the giant wolf's teeth locked over his jugular. Before the other men recovered enough to counterattack, the giant ball of white fur and teeth had another man by the arm. Mâkakao's scimitar severed the arm well clear of her muzzle.

To their credit, his men did not cower at the sight of such an apparition. Rallied, they charged the Mercenaries with their spears and their pikes, as fearsome a sight as a maddened rabble. The Mercenaries broke and ran under the combined assault, his men hard on their heels.

Argolyn alone stood to battle the she-wolf. His hands fisted tightly in the fur of her throat, striving to shut off her air, while her teeth sought purchase in the armor-like skin of his neck.

"Kill me and you will earn the enmity of all of my race!" the Dwarf warned in a voice as harsh as the she-wolf's growl.

"You are an outcast and a traitor to your own people!" Mâkakao growled back in the Dwarf's own guttural language. "You trade with the spawn of hell. See what your greed has brought you!" His scimitars crossed neatly before him, like the blades of a pair of scissors. Argolyn's head dropped at the she-wolf's feet.

Lack of a head did not seem at first to diminish the Dwarf's power. The hands still held their purchase, clamped tightly about the she-wolf's neck. Mâkakao kicked at the thing with all of his rage, willing the demon to face its own death. The wolf faded before him, leaving Cassadara with her head thrown back, gasping for breath in a ragged wheeze. The scimitars leapt to life again, severing the headless body limb from limb. As they dropped back into their scabbards he wrestled the hands from her throat. At last torn free of the deadly grasp, Cassadara collapsed into his arms.

He carried her to a patch of grass where the wind had swept most of the snow away and laid her there, turning away only long enough to search for their packs. She was stirring by the time he returned with a flask of water. A snarl broke from her lips as her eyes trembled open. He slid a hand beneath her head, raising it enough to allow her to drink.

"Mâk," she whispered.

"Aye, M'Lady. I am here."

"Ye are unhurt?"

He took a moment to assess his bloodied armor. "Aye, I think so. None of this seems to be mine."

She smiled at that, scooping up a handful of snow and massaging her bruised throat as she sat up. "Ye were magnificent. Not even among my own warriors have I seen such skill."

"Never have I had so much at stake," he murmured.

If she pondered the meaning of his words, she did not say so aloud.

Chapter Four

The winds swept the hillside, drifting the last of the winter's snow into false hills that made the traveling slow and the camping tedious. From her post as night watch, Cassadara surveyed the small group of men huddled around the meager campfire, talking quietly amongst themselves.

She was ill at ease amongst them. She did not have to hear their words. Mistrust was written in their eyes, in the set of their shoulders, in the way they ceased their conversation whenever she came too near.

Not that she blamed them. Less than a week ago she'd seen them nearly starved and half-naked, huddled around a similar campfire, with chains about their necks. She would have walked out of their lives without a backward glance, except for Mâk. He had taught her to see beyond the bounds of race and class to the soul beneath.

These were his men. They were important to him, and as such they were important to her. Still, they were little better than they had been a week ago. True, the chains were gone, but they were cold, half-naked, and starving. They had little but the weapons and clothing they'd scavenged off the bodies of the Dwarf and his Mercenaries, and they were hungry.

Their hunger, at least, she could do something about.

She caught Mâk's eye as he glanced up. With a slight tilt of her head and a thrust of her chin she signaled to him. He said something else to the men and then casually strolled away from the fire. Within moments he was at her side.

He came up behind her, his light step so familiar she felt him as much as heard him. His hands circled her waist and slipped upwards, gently cupping her breasts as he lowered his mouth to nip at her earlobe. Her low moan of desire became a growl as his thumbs brushed over her nipples.

"How far is House Yarishet?"

"At the speed we have been maintaining, four days, M'Lady."

Too far. "And what of thy father's house with the many beds?"

There was a hint of laughter in his voice. "The same."

She snarled her frustration. "Four days is a very long time."

He seemed fascinated with her ear. Even through the leather tunic she could feel the heat of his erection as he brushed deliberately against her. "The men would not disturb us, M'Lady."

She placed her hands over his, caressing his fingers where they stroked her nipples into straining beads of desire. "They would resent me, even more than they do now."

His voice murmured against her ear, a caress in itself. "No, M'Lady. You saved their lives. They know this. They respect you for this."

"They know nothing but that a great wolf has bewitched their captain. They are cold and hungry and ye are not. They are sick. They are tired and sore and they long for their homes."

"Such is the lot of a soldier." Had she not known him as well as she did, she might have thought his words reflected a lack of concern.

"Ye were one of them when I first saw ye. Now ye are not."

His thumbs fell still. "Would you wish that I were?"

She turned to face him, displacing his hands. "Mâk, that is no' a fair question. Ye know I would no' have ye sick and starving. Nor would I have ye still bound by the Slaver's collar. I would have ye safely within the walls of thy father's keep, beyond the range of death and privation and the sheer weight of the elements. But since I canna' work that miracle at least I can see thy men fed!"

Amusement tinged his voice again. "You can conjure up food for seven men?"

She wanted to shake him in frustration almost as much as she wanted to mate with him. "I can hunt."

He shrugged, unimpressed. "Any of us can hunt. There's been nothing afoot. The Orc patrols have wiped the valley clean."

"I can hunt where ye and the men canna' go."

He drew back slightly in surprise. "You mean to travel as a wolf."

She wanted his approval for this plan. That alone surprised her. "The men already know I can take the lupine form. 'Twill come as no great shock to them."

"I do not wish you to hunt alone!" he protested.

She wanted to remind him that she'd been alone when he met her and none the worse for her adventures, but men's egos were such fragile things. Instead she nuzzled her cheek against his close-cropped beard. "I willna' be gone long. Perhaps an offering of a fresh kill shall improve their dispositions."

Worry clouded his handsome face. "Take me with you."

It was her turn to pull back in surprise. "Know ye what ye ask?"

His expression turned grim. "I ask only to stay at your side, *Mel~amin*. You know I will not get in your way."

She settled her gaze back on his men. "Know ye what they will think of ye?"

He grinned again. "They will be jealous because I travel at thrice their speed and in the company of my beautiful mate."

Mate. Shaken, Cassadara turned to scan the horizon, pretending to scout. Mâk spoke the word so easily. But he was a Human. Humans did not think the way her own people did. Still, she had to swallow hard. Mate. Was that what he was to her?

She wanted him. In the beds at his father's house or here in the snow. The where of it mattered not. She wanted him more than she'd thought it possible to want any man.

Mâk wanted to hunt. Could she run beside him and not desire to truly become his mate? Somehow she doubted that. Yet if she allowed this, she would lose another piece of herself. If he left her—when he left her—after this mating he would rip out a piece of her heart. She would lose a part of herself she might never again recover.

Her gaze ran over his men again. They would be more than jealous. They would be suspicious, thinking she had indeed bewitched their leader. If only she had the power to do so...

"I will not get in your way," he promised, his breath warm against her neck.

She turned in his arms, her teeth closing over his shoulder. "Tell them. Tell them we go to hunt."

He smiled the smile of a child, happy in the prejudices he knew not.

She watched him as he moved back down the hill, a strength and grace in his stride she'd never have suspected when she'd first seen him there in the mud. She could not hear his words as he spoke to the men, something low and reassuring, but she could see their eyes flick up to her and away again once they caught her watching.

He couldn't see the way this mating would further encumber his dealings with the men. All he could see was the chance to run at her side.

Perhaps that would be enough. She tried hard to hang on to that lie.

He stopped in front of her, his eyes smiling in genuine happiness. Too late to tell him she'd changed her mind.

Cassadara slipped her arms around his neck and exhaled gently, letting her tongue slip over his in that strange way he seemed fond of. His body lurched against her, his erection its own weapon in the battle against her defenses. She snarled as she felt their bodies falling away, thick, shaggy winter fur beginning to cover her, until they dropped to all fours and she raised her head to catch the message of the wind.

Instead all she smelled was him. Pure lupine now, he gave off the strong odor of pheromones and sex. She sniffed him behind the ear and nudged gently. By the gods he smelled good. She bit playfully, snapping at his shoulder, her teeth doing little more than yanking at his fur.

His first steps were tentative, but she turned and lifted her tail, teasing him with the scent of her need, daring him to follow her where he could. He was up to the challenge. She streaked away, across the snow-covered hills, staying just far enough ahead that he could not quite catch her until she was ready.

A copse of pine trees huddled along the river a few miles from their camp. She rushed into them, her nose already telling her they were empty. Laughing eyes met hers as she spun, sliding to a halt in the softly matted needles. His low growl told her he was here to hunt all right, and she was the prey. His nose against her cheek made promises she understood.

Ready, all too ready, she turned, lifting her tail. He growled again, deep in his throat, at the scent of her. She had never done this, but she knew what was coming. Fearful for just a moment, she tried to escape.

He lunged at her, his teeth grasping the fur at the back of her neck. She was not ready. She would lose too much of herself in the bargain. She whimpered in protest, but her attempt at self-preservation came too late.

Strong legs straddled her shoulders as the huge male rose over her, his entry quick and hard as he stabbed himself into her. She ran a few steps, trying to escape the intensity of his attack, but she fought against herself. She wanted him. By the gods, she wanted him.

The wolf had not forgotten the ways of the man. He entered her hard and hot and fast, withdrawing again and again, leaving her whimpering for more until she backed against him trying to move even closer as he thrust against her. His whole body strained with exertion. His front legs hooked around her chest, pulling her back as he pounded into her over and over again.

So hard. So hot. Like a burning fire within her. She wanted. She wanted more. The first orgasm hit like a pain that would slice her apart with its pleasure. Still he pumped into her, days of frustration behind his strength and endurance. His organ grew harder still, expanding until she felt she would burst. She clenched harder around him, feeling each thrust like a strike into her soul.

"Now!" she wanted to scream. "Now!"

But her voice was the voice of a wolf, and she lifted it in song as she shattered again and again.

* * * * *

He couldn't get enough of her. She smelled like sex, filling his senses. The world had focused down to the smell of her sex and the feel of her body beneath his. He felt bigger and harder than he ever had before. Her sheath burned like a fire, making him harder with every stroke. She held him all.

He bucked against her frantically, frenzied beyond his mental endurance, desperate to spill his seed as she convulsed around him time after time, but there was no relief. The harder he pumped into her, the more he wanted. She was hot and wet and slick, and he buried himself within her time after time, yet still it was not enough. Her moaning barks became howls, cries for release.

By the gods, she would be the death of him. Their wet flesh made a sucking sound as he drove into her, and he could feel his balls, which hung farther back now, contracting, ready to burst. Her muscles pulled around him again, tighter than ever, squeezing him painfully, demanding more. He had no more.

Yet from somewhere he found the strength. She whimpered as he pounded harder, his body responding to an ancient ritual his mind had not conceived of. At last. He could feel his release coming. At last, at last, he chanted. Her sheath became a vise, squeezing, milking, clamping him so tightly he could not withdraw.

Momentarily, he panicked, trying to break away, but it was no use. Trying to withdraw from her caused him unbearable pain. He surged into her again, hard, searching for release. He found it in overwhelming new sensations.

As her voice lifted to the stars, he bucked against her again, shattering like a broken vessel, her body milking him of his seed until his balls ached with the exertion. Still she did not release him. They collapsed together into the pine needles, her legs stretched backwards under his, their breathing ragged and their minds numb.

For nearly an hour they lay together, their bodies still joined, until they relaxed at last into a peaceful sleep.

* * * * *

It was her feral growl that awoke him. He awoke almost fearful, for he knew he had not the stamina for another such mating. But the bright shining eyes that looked down over him were not the eyes of a wolf. At least not all wolf. His body responded immediately—for he was indeed within his own body. He wanted to ask her by what magic his clothing had reappeared, but that would have to wait. He wasn't sure he would understand her answer in any case. Her hands moved quickly to help divest him of his armor and weapons.

It seemed impossible he'd managed without sex for five years, and now found such torture in just a few days abstinence. Yet it was obvious by the look on her face he was not the only one who'd been feeling this powerful need.

"No," she whispered, pinning his shoulders to the ground as he tried to move. "No' this time. My turn."

Again he felt that momentary flash of panic he'd felt when her wolf-body would not release him. He held himself rigid, but he didn't fight her. He could have, he told himself. He was bigger than she was. He wasn't afraid of her.

Right.

When the Dwarf's curse had struck him down, she'd picked him up and carried him away as if he were a small child. She was General Tranorva's sister. She could tear him limb from limb if she wanted to. He was playing a dangerous game. He'd known that from the start.

"Mâk?"

"*Mel~amin?*"

"Do ye no' trust me yet?"

He smiled up at her and lied. "I trust you with my life, *Mel~amin*." Which wasn't really a lie, after all. He had put his life in her hands. Things hadn't gone at all the way he'd expected them to. He'd certainly never thought to end up a slave on the auction block. He already owed her his life and more. If she was going to hurt him, she'd have done so by now.

He forced his body to relax. If she was going to hurt him, she would do so by breaking his heart.

"Remember that first night, when I healed ye?"

Remember. As if he could forget.

"I wanted to do this then, but I feared ye would go berserk after the healing."

The pieces came together. Her healing magic had left him with the energy he'd seen in men of her race on the battlefield. "I was berserk," he agreed. "But only for you."

She straddled his waist, her knees on either side of his pelvis, sitting up just a little too far for his aching penis to reach what he wanted. Her hands on his arms exerted no force to keep him pinned, but they could. He knew they could. The knowledge slid from alarming into exciting. "I am yours," he whispered. "Bought and paid for. Body and soul."

She lowered her head to kiss him. Her tongue darted between his teeth to stroke across his palate, sending waves of desire through his body. She'd taken his lessons well. She rocked back, settling on his hips so her soft mound just grazed the tip of his erection, then slowly rocked her body forward again.

He could feel the heat of her flesh dragging across him. He lunged desperately with his hips, trying to reach inside her, but she only smiled and pulled away slightly. As she moved back to glide over him again, her head dropped to lick his left nipple. The sensation was as much pain as pleasure. She bit gently, and he heard himself moan as he arched up into her, finding her sheath at last. She allowed him but one thrust before she lifted herself to the tip of his throbbing cock.

"You shall break my mind," he whispered.

She slid slowly back down his rigid member, rocking back slightly as she enveloped him all the way to his balls. "I would own more than thy body," she told him, reaching this time to flick her tongue over the tip of his right nipple. He thrust up into her harder. "I would have thy heart."

He laughed, though a little breathlessly. "You already have it, M'Lady. You have owned me body and soul since I first looked up at you from my place in the mud. Do you not understand what *Mel~amin* means?"

She raised herself up slowly to her knees again. "It is more than a pretty name?"

"My heart," he whispered. "It means my heart."

Her smile turned wondrous. "My heart. *Mel~amin*. Ye have my heart as well, *Mel~amin*."

The chains of a fear he had not known he harbored fell away as he surged up into her. This time she made no move to withdraw, but rocked hard against him again and again, driving him home to the place where he'd always wanted to be—the place where he had but dreamed of being. His restraint broken, release came quickly, but not before she convulsed around him with a strength that threatened to shatter his sanity. It was his turn to hold her tightly in his arms as hers lost their strength and she toppled to his chest.

"*Mel~amin?*" Her voice was but a whisper against the quiet of the night wind.

"My love?"

"If ye would stay with me then ye should know the truth."

His lips quirked up into a slight smile. "There is more?"

Her tone remained serious. "I have been sent to House Yarishet for more than just simple negotiations. The House of Yarishet holds a Talisman of import to House Lochinvar. This Talisman was stolen from our house long ago. Still, I canna' simply burst through the door and demand its return. To slaughter the entire house of Yarishet over a Talisman would be in bad form. We would lose many political allies."

Relief surged through him. If that was all…he dragged his tongue over the tip of her still darkened nipple. "Perhaps I can help you."

Her breath caught in her throat, making her response a strangled sound. "How?"

His body was recovering already, wanting her more than he had ever imagined he could want a woman. The legends were true. She was as an intoxicant to him. "I have been often within the walls of the keep at Yarishet. I know the castle layout well." As he indeed knew the layout of her body.

She smiled up at him. "Ye may well be useful in other places than beside me in bed."

"Useful?" he mocked, nipping at her bottom lip. "Is that what I am to you? Useful?" His rigid cock pressed against her thigh.

"And entertaining."

He pinned her hands to her side, his body over hers, brushing her mouth with his lips again. "Allow me to entertain you again."

"Ye shall entertain me to death," she whispered.

Somehow, the words did not sound like an objection.

Chapter Five

She sniffed the air cautiously. "Mâk."

He groaned in sleepy languor. "Rest, woman. There is no more. You shall be the death of me."

"Mâk, something is wrong."

He rolled to his haunches, his hands finding the hilts of his scattered scimitars in the dark. The stars reflected off their wicked blades, and the air made a tiny scream where they cut through the night.

She felt him change position silently until they were back to back, covering the night with their well-trained eyes. "Where?" he whispered.

"I know not. I simply awoke knowing something was wrong. I can smell it. I can taste it."

His tongue made a soft rasping noise as he moistened dried lips. "Orcs."

Orcs. Out here. Orcs were poor night hunters. What would they find on the open tundra to…

By the gods—*no.*

Mâk was already throwing on his armor. Cassadara slipped into her mail as quickly as she could. Orcs. Not again. His men would all be killed and their deaths would be her fault. She had enticed him away from the camp with the promise of hunting. They should have stayed together. She should have seen his men safely home, then bid Mâk farewell, allowing him to return to his safe, ordinary life. He had no part in her wars or her life. She had simply had the gold to free him from his chains. If his men died now because of her selfishness he would never forgive her. She would have lost his trust, as well as his friendship.

Whatever happened now, she would lose.

Orcs. The name tasted like fear on her lips. She had lost her escort to Orcs. It would not happen again.

She buckled the last buckle and strapped on her sword. She would not lose Mâk to Orcs, nor see him enslaved again. She reached for him in the dark, already finding his body rigid beneath her touch. She kissed him hard, blowing the gift of speed and strength into his lungs. For herself she chose lupine form, knowing that fast as he might be, she would be faster, and she would be deadly. This time she would be deadly.

"Cassadara!"

She crested the hill as he screamed her name. Already she was well outdistancing him.

"No! Cassadara! No!"

She had never yet taken orders from any man.

* * * * *

"Cassadara!" Terror struck through him as she crested the hill, the myths and legends stripped away to leave the naked soul of the woman exposed at his feet. He knew her fierce loyalty too well. She would sacrifice herself to save his men, and there was nothing he could do to stop her. He wailed in anger and grief even as he pushed his body to speed well beyond the limits of the spell she had cast upon him. The sound ripped from his lungs as the mournful cry of the lone wolf.

He crested the next ridge before he stopped to gasp for breath, searching the hills ahead of him as he did so. He was not lost. She was out of sight, but he was not lost. The river had been at their back as they raced toward privacy in the early evening. The moons had been before them. He could find his way alone.

A wolf's cry of warning split the night air. His senses responded as if he had learned this language as well. 'Twas the call of the she-wolf protecting her territory. Forgetting his aching lungs, he sprinted toward the sound.

The Orcs had tried to trap his men against the rocks. Now they were caught between an angry she-wolf and six men who would fight to the death before being captured again. Mâkakao altered his course to come in hard on the left, both scimitars singing their song of death.

Cassadara attacked their spell caster first. The she-wolf's hind claws raked the Orc Shaman's chest as she hung suspended in the air, her jaws still clamped around his bleeding arm, keeping the vile creature too distracted to heal his warriors.

Fear twisted Mâk's heart. He tried hard not to wonder if their Caster would be too much for a woman who swore she wasn't yet a true Shaman. The Orc Shaman *had* to be taken out of action. Cassadara couldn't hold out against him on her own for much longer. The Caster raised a yellow aura encompassing them both, and a wolf's whimper of pain echoed through the bedlam of battle.

Mâkakao fought his way toward Cassadara's side. Fear spurred on his battle lust. He was going to be too late. The Orc Scout had seen what was happening and he began to shove his way through his own troops to his Caster's side. Thank the gods the Orcs were too stupid to understand what their Scout was attempting to do. With a brain of any size behind that terrible physique, they'd be unstoppable.

Another cry of pain from the battling she-wolf ripped at Mâkakao's heart. The Orc he currently fought was giving him more trouble than the others had. This one was older, a veteran of many campaigns, and he knew how to use his body to his advantage. The Orc had a good foot of height advantage over Mâkakao. The scimitars slashed into the air while the Orc blade came down hard to nick into Mâk's rawhide bracer.

Cassadara was a better Shaman than she gave herself credit for. She could win this fight.

She had to win.

Mâk changed his tactics and dove to the ground, coming up hard into the Orcs groin, his blades flashing. A roar of pain and outrage shook the huge creature. His eyes turned blood red as he dove for Mâkakao, weapons forgotten in the lust for blood. Hands like vises clamped around Mâk's neck as he struggled to regain his feet.

A cry of rage and grief broke across the battlefield, the voice neither quite that of a wolf nor a woman, but of the both combined. Shards of ice hit the Orc who had hold of Mâk, slashing green skin and gouging gray leather armor. Before the Orc could get away, licks of blue flame singed the hair from his bark-like skin.

The thing howled in pain and terror, loosing his hold on Mâk's neck long enough for him to draw a full breath. A desperate slash left the beast looking down at the remnants of his armor under his own paw-like hands as he tried to keep his guts from spilling out onto the trampled snow.

Too late. He would be too late. The she-wolf battled both the Scout and the Orc Shaman now. The Caster raised his arms high above his head, chanting words that sounded as if they rose from the pits of hell, while the Scout lunged at the wolf with a ten foot long spear.

Mâk let loose a bellow of rage as the Scout continued to thrust and parry with the wolf's razor-sharp teeth. The Scout turned to face his newest opponent, rage glowing orange in his eyes.

As the Scout turned, Mâk saw how the she-wolf had kept him at bay. Vines had grown out of the frozen tundra to wrap themselves around the Orc's legs, keeping the giant rooted in place.

Her spells could not hold out forever. Holding the Orcs at bay this long must have required tremendous effort on Cassadara's part. Mâk drove in hard, attempting to shear the tip from the Scout's deadly spear. The scimitars met their match in the spear's shaft. The fine steel blades bounced back with a force strong enough to make the muscles of his shoulders burn.

Mâk could only see one way to get that spear out of the Orc's grip. He lunged in, exposing his side somewhat carelessly as he made a blundering attempt at shattering the spear once again. Taking the perceived opportunity, the Orc thrust the spear hard into Mâk's side. The tip grazed his flesh through the armor as he danced back, his sudden shift of weight offsetting the Orc's grip. Man and scimitars and spear all tumbled backwards into the bloody snow.

Unfortunately, Cassadara's spell chose that moment to loose its hold on the Scout's feet. The heavy Orc hurled himself after the blade, landing atop Mâk with the full force of his four hundred or so pounds. They grappled together, fighting hand to hand, rolling across the snow.

Digging desperately in the snow, Mâk closed his hand over not one of his scimitars, but instead the Scout's own spear. Mâk kicked out hard as he bashed his skull into the Orc's forehead, shoving the huge creature off him with all his enraged might. The Orc regained his footing just as Mâk rolled to his knees. As the Orc lunged to close the distance between them, Mâk raised the tip of the spear out of the snow. Understanding registered in the Orc's glowing eyes as he impaled himself on his own weapon. The fierce eyes went dead even as the Scout toppled back to the snow.

Mâk spun to find Cassadara. The she-wolf had faded. Now the fight was simply Shaman against Shaman. Cassadara raised her arms over her head, heavy shafts of lightning bombarding the Orc Caster. The Orc battled back with a ring of flames that scorched the earth beneath her feet.

With a speed more reckless than practical, Mâk pitched himself between the two opponents. The Orc Caster immediately changed the focus of his attacks as Mâk's scimitars sliced the air. With the customary self-preservation of his kind, the Orc Caster turned to flee.

Blue flames licked over the vile green body as the Orc Shaman spun away. The flames slowed the Caster's stride long enough for Mâk's scimitars to remove the arm holding the powerful war-scepter. Enraged, the Caster spun about to face Mâk once again. Shards of ice attacked the Orc. The Caster was already sinking to its knees when Mâk's blades closed over the space that had once been its neck.

Even as the head rolled away, Mâkakao sheathed his scimitars, turning back to find his Shaman.

One look told him she was drained. She sank to her knees in the mud, her body no longer able to support itself. He dropped to her side, his arms gathering her tightly against his chest. "Tell me you are not injured."

Cassadara fixed her eyes on his face. "I am no' injured, Mel~amin. Only weary." She raised a hand to touch his cheek. "Gather your men close. All of them."

He shifted his focus from her long enough to survey the battleground. Four men were standing, already looting the fallen Orcs for weapons and armor that might fit their needs. One man appeared to be down permanently. Another sat to the side, a hand pressed over a wound wrapped in rags. Mâk motioned for the men to come to him. The others helped the wounded one up the hillside.

Cassadara focused on them each in turn. "The sixth is dead?"

"Mortally wounded, M'Lady," Balthain, his captain, answered.

"Bring him to me."

Wordlessly two of the warriors turned away to fetch the dying man while the other two supported their less severely wounded companion. When all were gathered about she addressed them again, her voice weaker than he remembered. "Join hands." She closed her eyes. Just as the men began to get restless, her voice quieted them. She chanted softly, in words that they could understand.

"Bless these men, oh great goddess, with the spirit of thy health and the strength of thy might. Heal them with the purity of thy goodness. Fill them with the stamina of thy love. Guide them through the night with the light of thy way. Let thy will be done."

New strength flowed into Mâkakao's body. The snow around him lit up with the glow of a bright moonlit night. The pain in his side lessened, then faded. The men around him began to whisper softly to each other as they examined their wounds. Even the one he'd thought lost was able to stand on his own.

"M'Lord? Will the Lady recover?" Balthain's voice sounded truly concerned.

Mâk turned his attention to Cassadara, only to find her eyes closed once again. Fear overcame him. She had expended the last of her strength to heal his men, leaving nothing for herself. "Do not leave me," he begged, sinking to the bloodied ground with her head cradled in his arms. He stroked her hair away from her face. "Know you not how much I need you, Mia-Ell?"

"I must sleep for a time…"

* * * * *

Mâk awoke with a start. Fear washed over him. Everything looked unfamiliar. It took him a moment to orient himself. The tent was an Orc pavilion, but he had not been captured again. There were no Orcs here now. Mâk's small band of warriors had stumbled upon the deserted Orc camp only a few leagues from the site of the battle. Cassadara had needed to rest. The men had needed to rest. There were hides here to wrap themselves in against the cold and food of a sort to fill their bellies, and if everything smelled of Orc, they did not notice. They smelled of Orc as well.

Mâk shook the sleep from his body. He'd promised himself he would stay awake, guarding his Shaman. She had not opened her eyes since they had moved from the battlefield. Her dreams had been troubled. He had wanted to be near in case she awakened. Yet even he had succumbed to the terrible drain of battle.

Mâk rose quietly, thinking to check the perimeters of the camp. A low growl halted him in his tracks. He spun, searching the corners of the tent, looking for the intruder. There. The form was half hidden amongst the scattered hides. Mâk crouched down, a wrestlers stance, ready to meet the attack. Whatever it was, it moved silently in the dark, and its eyes glowed an eerie red.

A feral snarl warned him away as he moved closer. Cassadara. Where was Cassadara? He wanted to call her name, but if the creature hadn't spotted her he need not call attention to her presence.

The warning growl grew louder as he moved in. He heard the teeth snap together nervously as it shifted about, turning to stay face to face with him. An idea began to take hold in his mind, but the thought was so terrible he would not give it shape. Instead he pitched forward into a roll, coming up where his opponent should have been.

He grappled with air. His only warning was a deep-throated growl as she launched herself at him. As his arms sought to capture his attacker, his fear was confirmed.

"Cassadara!"

The legends were true. The creature was Cassadara. Or what she had become.

The Wolf-Woman was no longer quite Human.

"Cassadara!"

She was strong, true enough, but not trained in the ways of a wrestler. He lunged, catching her crouched form unprepared, pinning her arms behind her back. Her body, covered only by a thin leather tunic, felt like a woman's. But there was no humanity left in her eyes. It was the strain, he knew. The strain of the battle had drained her too low. "*Mel~amin*, do you not know me? I am Mâkakao, and I love you. Do not leave me, *Mel~amin*."

The sound of his voice seemed to give her pause. She stilled beneath his hands.

"You know me, *Mel~amin*. I am Mâkakao—Mâk. We have traveled together. We have fought together."

Her nostrils flared as she drew in his scent.

"That's right, my love. You know the smell of me. I am Mâk. I am bound to you, and by more then the gold you paid the Dwarf for my freedom. I am your mate. You know me. Tell me you know me."

She sniffed along his jaw line, pausing to nuzzle his ear. His hands on her arms relaxed just a little. She nuzzled more gently along his neck, licking him now.

Until her teeth locked over his jugular.

The move was so swift, so sudden, so paralyzing. Another small amount of pressure in the right place, and he was dead. He couldn't even yell for help.

Not that he would. He owed her his bond. He owed her his life.

Releasing her arms, he tried a move based in desperation. He brought his hands slowly up along her sides, worshipping every curve, until his hands captured her breasts. Using the skills he'd learned on the battlefield, he focused his attention on her body, ignoring the feel of her teeth on his throat.

Her nipples hardened to stiff little points under his thumbs. He could hear her breathing changing. Fear began to give way to desire. He could reach her this way. He could bring her back.

If she didn't kill him.

"I love you, Cass," he managed as her teeth loosed their hold.

She seemed to respond to the sound of his voice.

"I love the feel of your skin beneath my hands. Did I ever tell you how much I love your breasts? You have beautiful breasts." He kneaded them gently, brushing his thumbs back and forth across the sensitive tips.

Her growl sounded again, but this time it was a growl of desire. She shoved him to his back, rolling atop him. Their eyes locked as she straddled his waist. Her hands tore at him, but this time there was little malice in her movements. Or at least he hoped not. He helped her, raising his arms so she could yank the tunic over his head.

It was her turn now. She lowered her mouth to suckle his nipples, the first swipe of her tongue nearly unmanning him. He groaned in desire, more than willing to let her have her way with him. "I am yours, my love. Do with me what ye will."

She made it very clear what she would have, although she still spoke no Human words. That feral growl came again, as she licked and sucked her way down over his chest. Her hands — still the hands of a woman — unlaced his breeches, evidently finding the garments not to her liking. Her hands stopped to trace the length of his painful erection before she yanked the bindings loose to set him free.

He knew without the words this was what he had heard about in the stories and legends. The half-wild Wolf-Women would use a man for their pleasure, draining him of his seed, leaving his broken body behind. He was strong. He was healthy. He was up to the challenge. She was his mate. If he could but reach her, she would remember. Fear mixed with pleasure as she lowered her mouth to run the tip of her tongue over the length of his burning cock. He bucked under her, helpless to withstand her attack.

"I love you, *Mel~amin*."

Her hands fisted around his shaft, drawing him upwards until he was so hard he thought he might burst under her touch. He could feel the heat of her against his thigh. His body ached to fill her hot, wet sheath. He placed his hands over hers on his penis, drawing her up, urging her to mount him.

She moved, deliberately sliding her wet slit along his cock, responding at a pace so agonizing he cried out in frustration. She slid over him, pinning his engorged penis against his pelvis, massaging the length of her mound with its girth. "You're killing me," he managed. "Take me, *Mel~amin*. Ride me. Make love to me." His teeth ground together. "Now."

She rose up, coming down hard as she impaled herself on his waiting cock. Her muscles tightened around him, sucking him in, demanding his full length and more. She ground against him, wave after wave of rippling muscles pulling at him. Just when he thought he might burst from the pleasure that was so close to pain, she withdrew, leaving him hollow and aching with need.

He grasped for her hips, pulling her back, rougher than he'd intended to be. She responded in kind, coming down hard on him again and again, her sheath clamping down on his throbbing cock as she rode him, rocking to her knees and back time after time.

Each time she withdrew he felt as if he might die. When she consumed him again he thought she might destroy him. The dance took on a furious pace as she arched harder against him, crying out as her climaxes drove him to thrust up into her with all the strength he had left. The sound of their wet skin slapping together rose as loud as the hoarse rasp of their breathing. His balls burned with the need for release.

Her final climax twisted her so tightly around his burning cock that he could not withdraw. Her cry split the night air, the mournful cry of an arctic wolf. His own voice joined hers, singing the ancient song. As they'd bound themselves together as wolves, so it was now. He shattered within her, her body milking him of his seed, holding him captive as she slumped over his chest.

When he could move, when he was sure he was still breathing, he rolled with her, gently laying her beside him, his arm cradling her against his chest. Her eyes were shut. Her breathing was shallow now as her body relaxed against his. She lay so quiet he feared the mating might have been too much for her. He brushed his lips over hers in a gentle hint of a kiss. "Do not leave me, *Mel~amin*," he whispered again. "Now that I've found you, I don't think I could go on without you."

She snuggled closer into his arms. "I canna' leave ye," she whispered, her voice so low he bent closer to be sure he understood. "Know ye not wolves mate for life?"

Chapter Six

"Ye will take me to my daughter, and ye will take me now."

Cassadara knew that voice. She drew the blanket over her head and turned her face into the soft feather pillow. She was tired. So tired. Too tired to face her mother. Not now. Not yet. If only she had learned the spell to make herself invisible...

"M'Lady. Please forgive my servants. I have given orders Lady Cassadara was not to be disturbed. Such orders do not apply to you. Allow me to escort you to her."

"I accept thy apology, Lord Yarishet, but only because it is in my best interest to do so. Take me to my daughter."

Cassadara felt the shock of it reverberate through her system like the brute force of a well-placed blow. Yarishet. Lord Yarishet.

She knew that voice. Knew it as the call of her mate. Mâk. Mâk was Lord Yarishet. This castle she found herself in was his father's house of many beds. No wonder he had seemed amused when she asked the distance from her journey's end to his father's house.

She had told him everything. Far more than she should have. He had told her nothing, only enough to gain her trust without revealing anything of himself. Her mission, the deaths of the men, all was for nothing. Worse yet, she had mated with him. Now her mother was here to learn of her disgrace. Perhaps the day could get worse, but she had her doubts.

It would not do to have Mother find her abed. She threw off the covers, searching the room for any signs of her clothing. She swayed unsteadily on her feet. Damn the Orc and his magic. She was still so weak...

"Mel~amin!"

Before she could protest the faithless use of such an endearment, strong arms had swept her off of her feet and deposited her back into the pile of feather beds. One sword-callused hand swept her unbound hair away from her face. Warm, soft lips brushed across her features, as if taking inventory.

"You are not ready to leave your bed, *Mel~amin*." He spoke patiently, as if he might have said these words to her often. "I am sorry I was not here when you awoke. I went but to greet your Lady Mother."

She wanted to be angry with him. She wanted so badly to be angry with him. But his hands were so gentle with her and the concern in his voice felt so genuine. "Ye are Lord Yarishet," she chastised.

The smile lifted some of the lines of concern from his face. "Aye, M'Lady. I fear 'tis true. 'Tis a burden I was born with. I have discovered there is little I can do to change things."

She wanted to be angry with him and by the gods she would be. "Why did ye not tell me this?"

He bent down to kiss the tip of her nose. "You did not ask."

Her voice had turned sulky, but she did not care. "Ye could have told me. I did ask about thy father. I would have returned ye to him."

"My father has been dead these three years past, M'Lady. I apologize for my deception. I meant only to let you get to know the man before you had to deal with the title. Titles tend to get in the way. Truly, when one has been held in chains at the mercy of a vengeful Dwarf, titles seem to lose all meaning. I shall always be as a slave to the woman who freed me. For me, my title changes nothing." His voice held a trace of something alien. Could it be fear? "Please tell me it is the same for you."

She answered him the only way she knew how, pulling his head down to hers in the way he had taught her, sharing her feelings in that brushing of lips, assuring him he was still her mate.

Lady Lochinvar coughed softly into her hand, reminding the lovers of her presence. Cassadara giggled as Mâk turned a deep shade of crimson.

"So the Human speaks the truth, my daughter? Ye wish to be wed to this man?"

Cassadara glanced from her mother back to Mâk's brilliant green eyes. The look she saw there reminded her of the first time their eyes had met, when he had knelt before her in the mud. With a word she could shatter his universe. She smiled instead and touched the tips of her fingers to his cheek. "I desire this more than anything."

"When I sent ye to forge an alliance betwixt our houses this was not what I had in mind."

Cassadara swallowed hard. She met her mother's eyes when she answered. "It was ye who sent me to the Dwarf Argolyn, Mother. Knew ye not what I would find there?"

Mother's eyebrows rose slightly. "Ye think this meeting planned? I would no' have sacrificed thy escort so thoughtlessly. I had heard only that the Dwarf had a warrior of some promise in his arena. One of our own."

Mother's tone indicated she did not appreciate being questioned. Still, Cassadara pushed her point. "How does the Lord of a major house end up in a Slaver's camp and have such events go unnoticed?"

It was Mâk's turn to answer. "Orcs. Word reached me the Orcs were attempting to move into the tundra. I did not know of the Orc invasions when I asked your mother to send you as an Emissary. As soon as I realized I had put you in some danger, I set out to meet you myself, to provide an additional escort. Unfortunately I did not take the Orc threat seriously enough. We were overwhelmed by a large party only three days from here. The corrupt Dwarf had frequent dealings with the Orc raiders. He bought the lot of us within days of our capture. I thought at first he would ransom me back to my house. Instead he sent me to the arena. Had you not happened upon me..."

"Ye set out with six men as escort across Orc-infested territory?" The Lady Lochinvar made no attempt to keep the disapproval from her voice.

Mâkakao looked directly at her for the first time. "No, M'Lady. I set out with thirty men. But ten of us were captured by the Orcs. Six made it home. Without your daughter, none of us would be here now."

Lady Lochinvar said nothing for the space of two drawn breaths. "Thirty men. Ye know what this means."

Mâkakao nodded once.

Cassadara was the one to whisper the word aloud. "War."

Lady Lochinvar merely inclined her head.

"Mother, I should—"

"Ye have responsibilities, daughter. Ye must defend thy house."

Cassadara glanced at Mâk. She saw the turmoil in his eyes. That alone was enough to sway her decision. She would not leave him to wonder. "My place is here with my mate."

Lady Lochinvar merely inclined her head again. "This shall be thy house now, daughter."

"I have studied the *Book of Ways* much on my journey, Mother, yet I lack the skills of a true Shaman."

Mâk flinched. "I would not have you on the battlefield again! Know you not what seeing you brought down has done to me? I have been useless with worry for nigh onto a week now!"

Cassadara stroked his cheek again. "We won, Mâk. We won. And we will win again. It is no' the way of the wolf to fight alone. Wolves fight as a pack."

He closed his eyes, a look like pain crossing his face as his emotions warred with each other. When at last he spoke, his voice was as much a plea as a command. "If you will fight, you must learn to fight as a Shaman fights. You are not strong enough to take the frontal assault."

She adjusted her shoulders to the fit of it, slightly bemused by his concern. "Aye."

"You will take some small care to protect yourself, and quit using your body as a shield for mine."

"If ye will do the same."

He swallowed hard. "Aye."

"Ye shall devote thyself to thy studies and not plan ways to escape thy teacher." Mother's voice left no room for argument.

"Aye," Cassadara quietly agreed, trying not to cringe as she remembered the long hours spent in training with Shammall.

"Shammall shall arrive with the wedding party. He shall continue thy training. Heed him and honor his wisdom. He shall guide ye well." Lady Lochinvar turned to Lord Mâkakao. "What offer ye as a bride's price?"

Cassadara watched in surprise as Mâkakao rose from the bed to cross the room. From a drawer in an ancient chest he removed a small wooden box. Returning to her, he knelt beside the bed. "Cassadara, Lady of Lochinvar, it is my wish to make you my wife as well as my mate. I have asked your mother's permission. Now I ask you. I bring you this small token of my affection as my bride's price."

Cassadara took the small wooden box with trembling fingers. She knew what she would find inside. She had heard of the Talisman, of course, but it had been gone from her house for more than the length of her lifetime.

Her hands shook as she withdrew the ancient Talisman from the box. It was smaller than she expected. The ivory warmed almost immediately to her touch. She could feel the power within it.

Mâk took the worn platinum chain from her fingers and settled it over her head, fingering the carved wolf's head as it settled between her breasts. "I offer you this and my heart and my soul. Know you that I shall always be your slave, bought and paid for with far more than twenty-five pieces of gold."

"As I am thine, my mate."

"You will have me, then?"

"I will."

When his lips met hers, Cassadara lost track of the fact that her mother still stood in the room.

* * * * *

Lord Mâkakao did his best not to fidget, even though standing beside the altar waiting for his mate was driving him insane. He should have married her secretly, in private, so she wouldn't have to face such a huge crowd.

She was going to bolt when she saw the crowd. He just knew she was. He should have escorted her to the hall himself. Perhaps she was already gone. She was a private person. She didn't like crowds and ostentation.

Who had ever thought up these barbaric rituals, anyway?

He cursed himself mentally for even thinking the word barbaric. He was sure his soon-to-be mother-in-law could read his thoughts.

At last the door creaked open, and the most gorgeous creature he'd ever seen walked in, escorted by two young people who might possibly have been his niece and nephew, except they were too well behaved. If he'd thought about what he'd expected her to wear, it would have been armor, perhaps Mithral chainmail, something befitting her station.

Instead they'd dressed her in glimmering white robes, as befitted a Shaman. The outer robe floated open around her, while the inner one tied in the front just below her breasts. He tried not to stare at her breasts, though the gossamer robe left little to the imagination. Instead he moved his gaze back to her face.

She looked almost fragile. So beautiful. So terrified. At any moment, he worried, she'd change to lupine form and launch herself out a window.

The children scattered a trail of rose petals at the feet of the bride. He took her hand when she reached his side, as much to keep her from running away as to provide her support.

The priest had been speaking for several seconds before Mâk decided he'd better listen to see what the old man was saying. "We gather here today in the presence of the gods to celebrate the union of Cassadara, daughter of House Lochinvar, and Mâkakao, Lord of House Yarishet. Should anyone have cause why these two should not be united, let that person speak now."

Lady Lochinvar smiled munificently, but Tranorva's frowning face at her side concerned him the most. Mâk held his breath, waiting for the priest to continue.

"Marriage is a contract to be entered into only after a great deal of consideration. Houses make political alliances. People make marriages. Cassadara, come you here of your own free will, and without reservation?"

"I do so come." Her voice was strong. Determined. Mâk relaxed a little, but did not loose his hold on her.

"As a woman is not a slave to be traded at auction, I ask only who represents you, Cassadara, and if you come with the blessings of your house."

Lady Lochinvar stepped forward. "I, her Lady Mother, represent Cassadara and I bring the blessings of House Lochinvar."

The priest turned his attention back to Mâk. "Mâkakao, Lord Yarishet, come you here of your own volition, entering into this agreement freely?"

He swallowed hard. "I do so come."

The old priest smiled at him. "Mâkakao, neither I nor the gods have the right to bind you to Cassadara. Only you have this right."

"This is my wish."

"Cassadara, neither I nor the gods have the right to bind you to Mâkakao. Only you have this right."

Cassadara stared at the priest, refusing to meet Mâk's gaze. An eternity passed before she spoke. "This is my wish."

"Mâkakao, you may place the ring on her finger."

Darien stepped forward to hand him the ring. Mâk raised Cassadara's hand to his lips, kissing it once before he slipped the family crest onto her little finger. Their eyes met at last, and he saw hers were filled with tears, yet she was smiling.

Her fingers closed firmly over his. Something in his heart felt as if it would shatter at any moment.

"Mâkakao, have you words you would say at this time?"

He was supposed to say something, he knew. He had it written down, but then he'd left the parchment in his room, sure he had the words memorized. He'd worked on this speech until it was perfect, and now he couldn't remember a word of it. He stared into her eyes, hoping she couldn't see the panic in his face, and said the first thing that came to his mind.

"Cassadara, daughter of House Lochinvar, you are the answer to my every prayer. I once pledged to serve you loyally for the term of my indenture. I now pledge to love you faithfully until the hour of my death and beyond. You own my heart. I will stand beside you until the end of my days, through feast and famine, through adversity and in times of peace. I will respect your ways and beliefs and honor your house as my own. All that is mine I give to you freely. All that I am I pledge to you."

Well, he'd gotten most of it in there. Not as well as he'd written it, but it would have to do.

The priest spoke again. "Cassadara, have you words you wish to speak?"

Her smile reached her eyes, though the tears had clumped her lashes into thick dark smudges that made her look so vulnerable. "Mâkakao, I set off on my quest to unite our two great houses with little hope of a true alliance between our peoples. I stand beside ye today no' as an offering from my house, no' as a bridge to cement our alliance, but as a woman. Ye own my heart. I pledge to love ye faithfully until the end of my days and beyond. I shall stand beside ye through feast and famine, through adversity and in times of peace, until the hour of my death. I shall respect thy ways and beliefs. I shall honor thy house as my own. All that is mine I give to ye freely. All that I am I pledge to ye."

She had managed his name. Little else registered. She had practiced until she could twist her tongue around his full name. Tears misted his eyes, but he fought them down, concentrating on the priest's words once again.

The priest knotted a white ribbon across their joined hands. "You have pledged your love and devotion before the gods. We who stand with you today are witness to this pledge. You are now husband and wife. May your love endure as a guiding light to those around you. May your houses prosper even as your love. Mâkakao, you may kiss your bride."

A cheer rose from the crowd. Mâk felt a huge grin tug at his face.

She hadn't run. She'd wanted to, he was sure of it—if not from him, then from the crowd and the pageantry, but she'd stayed. His wife. His mate. The creature of his imaginings had been infinitely inferior to the reality before him. He drew her close with his free hand and nuzzled her gently as was her way before he placed his lips over hers—as was his way.

Cassadara's eyes widened in surprised. Her free hand found its way to the back of his neck, turning the kiss into something more passionate than the chaste public kiss he'd expected. Unadulterated joy filled his heart.

Her voice came as a soft caress against his cheek. "This mating of the lips is called a kiss."

He shifted back to her own language, lest their words become too public. "Mmm. I like your description better. 'Tis another kind of mating my body desires of you. I have hungered for you unimaginably during the days of your convalescence."

"Ye shall have to wait longer," she teased.

Desire warred with concern, dampening his spirits. "Are you not recovered yet, *Mel~amin*? We could have postponed this pageantry yet another week."

"I am well. I was recovered a week ago. Know ye not that I am a Shaman? I heal quickly. My mother's touch did much to fight off the Orc's fever spells as well. I meant only that ye would have to wait through a long afternoon of feasting and well wishing before ye can fulfill thy other desires."

He growled against her ear. "We shall see about that."

Grasping her bound hand in his, Mâkakao turned them both to face the crowd, raising their hands high together. "Friends, I present to you Lady Yarishet!"

Another cheer shook the grand hall. At his signal, the musicians began to play a traditional wedding ballad. The guests moved aside to clear the center of the marble floor.

Mâk swept Cassadara into his arms.

Epilogue

Cassadara felt the panic eddying closer again. "I canna' dance!" she whispered fiercely. Mâk merely grinned at her again, that foolish besotted look making him even more adorable.

"You can fence."

"Aye. But I canna' dance. My last master so despaired of me he quit our service."

"Watch my feet. Move with me as if we were fencing. Your robes hide your feet. If you are not perfect, no one will know."

Watch his feet. She could not even see his feet. He held her much too tightly. His people *would* notice. She tried desperately to remember the steps her dance-master had tried to teach her. She winced as she stomped on his instep. He only grinned at her.

"Relax, *Mel~amin*. 'Tis no contest. No one will grade you when we are done."

"I look the clumsy fool!"

He brushed his lips lightly over hers, pulling her even more tightly against his long, lean length. She could feel the scorching heat of his erection pressing against her. There was another dance she'd rather have been doing with him.

"Quit thinking." He lifted her till her toes cleared the floor. "Put your feet on mine. Move with me."

She had to. She could reach nothing else. His strength supported her with little obvious effort — no mean feat considering she weighed a bit over ten stone. Despite herself, she began to relax. Perhaps it was the aphrodisiac of his warm arms supporting her, or the feel of his erection pressed against her as they circled the dance floor, but her body began to move to the rhythm of the music. Almost hypnotically she felt herself flow to the music.

"How is it I want you more now than I did the first time, my love? You are my addiction. Truly I am bewitched."

"I feared that first time it was only the healing made ye want me and ye might see me as thy kinsmen did once the magic faded."

"The magic will never fade for me, my love. You are my fantasy lover, far more than anything I could ever have wished for."

She closed her eyes as she pressed her cheek against his neck, hardly noticing her feet had slipped to the floor and now seemed to move to the rhythm of their own volition. Neither did she notice the music had changed and their guests flowed onto the dance floor. "I thought never to find this, Mâk. Marriages for those of our state are so often for alliances rather than for love. I despaired of ever finding someone who would care for me for who I am, rather than for the power of my house."

He laughed, but the sound held no humor. "Since I was a barely more than a child, every eligible daughter from every house has been presented to me. They felt nothing for me, nor I for them, but still my father would have me marry. I wondered he did not auction me off to the highest bidder. I vowed with his death I would marry for love. You are indeed the fulfillment of my fondest fantasy."

A thought crossed her mind, and she spoke it aloud. "When ye asked for a daughter of my house as thine emissary was it thy plan to capture a Wolf-Woman for thine own?"

He laughed softly against her ear. "There was that in my fantasy, I suppose, though not to capture. I thought to court you, perhaps. I knew you were not betrothed. My emissary spoke of your beauty. I thought him besotted, but truly he understated the truth."

"Ye are besotted. I am not beautiful. I am short and plain and I have hair the color of Gnoll hide. And," she added, "I know none of the arts of being a Lady."

He stroked her hair. "I love your Gnoll pelt. I love everything about you. I want you more than I ever imagined I could want any woman. Let us leave the guests to amuse themselves while we steal away from here."

"Will not thy court be gossiping about us for weeks?"

"Do you care?"

His lips moved over her ear, tugging on the lobe, sending shivers down her spine. His hand caressed her hips, his erection swaying against her to the rhythm of the music.

She felt as if she might peak here on the dance floor from the sheer touch of his body against hers. "I care for nothing but ye. Take me. Take me here or take me away, but I must have ye."

He maneuvered them unobtrusively through the crowd and out onto one of the balconies that lined the great hall's corridors. Laughter danced in his eyes as he slipped out of the ribbon binding their hands and unwound his dress sash from about his waist.

Cassadara tried not to giggle as he looped it about the balcony post and slid to the ground. She could have made the jump safely enough in lupine form, but instead she followed him down the makeshift ladder. There were guards everywhere, but fortunately they were looking for intruders from the outside, not escapees from within.

"Where can we go?" she whispered.

Mâk held up his finger again for silence as he led her around the corner and through a gate at the rear of the courtyard. They stayed close to the battlement walls so the guards atop would not see them.

At the end of the first wall another gate opened into the orchard. The smells of spring were ripe here. The trees were in full bloom. Petals from the tiny flowers drifted through the air like snowflakes that would not melt. The grass was fresh and high and soft beneath their feet. Mâkakao turned her into his arms, caressing her as if she, too, were a fragile flower that might break in his hands.

Whatever their lovemaking had been, it had never been gentle. This new, slow pace might have been designed to drive her insane. She moaned out her desire as his fingers unthreaded the tie to her robe. Like the flower petals, the shimmering gauze floated to the ground, puddling around her feet. She stood before him naked, allowing him to look his fill.

"You are exquisite, *Mel~amin*. A sculptor could not ask for a more perfect model."

She giggled, embarrassed. "Ye are besotted."

"I am," he agreed. "But you are still beautiful."

He ran his hands up her sides, lifting her breasts with his thumbs, then cupping them to feel their weight. She could feel her nipples, already hard, elongate to sensitive spears of desire. He dropped his head to take first one then the other in his mouth, licking gently around the areolas, wringing another moan from her tightly clamped lips. There were people near. Too near. She had no experience in trying to be quiet.

"No fair," she managed. "Ye are still wearing clothes."

"What are you going to do about that, my bride?"

As an answer she reached for the buckle of his sword belt. The ceremonial blade tumbled with its scabbard into the grass. Next she lifted the surcoat over his head, followed by the shirt of fine light mesh mail. She would have wondered at its construction, but another time. For now all she wanted was to feel him naked beneath her touch.

The tunic joined the pile in the grass, allowing her to run her hands over bare flesh as she sought the laces for the leather breeches. She couldn't help noticing his breath came harder now, and his restraint showed signs of cracking. She smiled to herself, pleased with the power she had over him.

It was her turn now to make him wait as she raked her teeth deliberately across his nipple. With a groan of desire he fisted his hands into her hair, pulling her head tighter against his chest. She suckled there at his breast like a baby, enjoying the feel of his body responding to her touch. Her hands molded his well-formed loins, pulling him closer as she thrust her hips against him. She could feel the swell of his cock behind the thin leather.

The wanting of him was driving her crazy, but making him wait would be its own reward. She tilted her pelvis, rubbing her aching clit against his hard, pulsing cock. She was so wet she felt her juices beginning to moisten the soft leather.

"Dance with me," she whispered.

His hands slid low, pulling her back against his pelvis as he began to move to the distant strains of the musicians floating out on the warm spring air. He danced now as she'd wanted to before, his every move bringing him into contact with her aching breasts, his hands touching her everywhere.

Her fingers sought the lacings for his breeches, allowing them to drop around his feet. Without breaking his step he left them behind. Freed at last, his burning cock jutted against her, hard and hot and heavy. She moved against him in rhythm to the music, sighing when he lifted her high enough to grind against her clit.

She opened herself to him, but still he held her in the rhythm of the dance. Her legs locked around his waist, she leaned back, making room for his greedy tongue to find her breasts once again.

"Mâk," she whispered, still cognizant of the guards not so far away. "I need ye, Mâk." She strained to lift herself onto the tip of his melting heat. She felt as if a fire might consume her if he did not enter her soon. "I want to feel ye inside me."

"Do you always get what you want?" he asked hoarsely, using words he'd said so long ago.

"Always," she agreed. She bent her head to suckle his nipple, pleased when his self-control crumbled under her attack. He laid her gently into the grass, still taking his time as he poised over her. Her need was a pain that would not be satisfied. She growled deep in her throat, demanding more, raising her hips until she met him, swallowing his length with her frenzied thrust.

He slid into her in one hot thrust, searing her, driving her instantly toward the climax she longed for. Almost immediately he withdrew, leaving her hollow and aching for his touch.

He did not disappoint her. His lips followed where his cock had just been, his tongue thrusting within her as she convulsed around him, whimpering in both pleasure and distress at his absence. She looked for parts of him to torture, finding with a little work she could draw his hips toward her.

An idea took hold. She kissed the dark hair at his waist, following it down to the V where it pointed like an arrow to that waiting cock. The first touch of her tongue was tentative, experimental, but the results were all she could have hoped for. His groan of desire told her she had guessed well.

Mâk shuddered beneath her touch as she ran her tongue along the thick, hot length of his engorged cock. He rocked hard against her, his hands tightening over her breasts convulsively. She kissed the tip of his penis, then circled the head with her tongue, pleased when he strained against her in response. She slid her mouth over him experimentally, only to feel him go completely still.

"Cass, my love, if you continue on your present journey 'twill be a very short one."

She pulled back, disappointed. "Ye dinna like that? I thought ye would."

"Like it? *Mel~amin*, are you trying to drive me completely insane with lust for you? If so, I fear you have succeeded."

She laughed and slid her lips back over his engorged shaft. He sucked at her clit with a kind of desperation. She found the sound of his cock sliding in and out of her mouth mingled with the sound of his tongue sliding in and out of her hot, wet flesh made her ache for him even more.

"Enough!" he growled in a rasping breath. He rose up over her with one heave of those heavily muscled arms. His mouth closed over hers as he drove into her, sending her almost instantly into yet another hard, shuddering climax. Still he drove into her again and again, his balls slapping against her ass in rhythm to the dance, each thrust driving her toward the pinnacle of her desire. She met him thrust for thrust, arching up hard against him, taking the full length of his burning cock within her suctioning flesh time after time.

Wave after wave of pleasure broke over her, yet still it was not enough. She screamed his name, though his mouth on hers swallowed the sound. His hands worked her aching nipples, kneading the sensitive buds into one long wave of hot desire. He twisted the rings she wore in her nipples back and forth, tugging gently at first, then more roughly as she responded to his hands. "Now!" she screamed. "Now!"

His thrusts became the waves beating down on the rocks at the shore, breaking over her again and again, the sound of their wet flesh slapping together almost loud enough on its own to attract attention. He bucked against her hard and fast, pumping into her at a ferocious pace, demanding all she had to give, pushing her toward that edge with as much desperation as finesse.

She felt his climax building, smelled it with keen senses, his body shuddering as he spilled his seed into her. She convulsed around him, breaking at last, the pleasure coming in waves so strong they were nearly painful. His kiss smothered her mating cry, swallowing the sound even as she reached the height of her climax.

Exhausted, they fell back limply together onto the grass. When she could move, she raised a hand to trail it through his flower-strewn hair. Laughter spilled over her lips.

"What amuses you so, *Mel~amin*? Are you pleased you have managed to nearly kill me with the strength of our desire?"

She rolled to one elbow and studied the hard, powerful length of him. "I was just thinking."

"And what were you thinking, my love?"

"We have finally made it to thy father's house, and where are we? In a field of fruit trees. Ye promised me beds."

He grinned. "There are many beds within the castle, my love."

"Indeed. I believe we shall have to try them all before I can tell ye which is my favorite."

"You shall be the death of me, woman," he growled. "But I shall die with a smile on my face."

And for a while, as they lay in the grass that smelled of sweet springtime flowers, they shared no thoughts of the coming war.

A Rogue's Virtue

Chapter One

A soft murmur of whispers and hushes drifted around the crowded hall. Tranorva stood perfectly still, her position the formal parade stance the occasion demanded—feet spread slightly apart, hands clasped behind her back, eyes forward, every ring of her impeccably kept Mithral mail laying perfectly placed. She'd stood that way since she'd strode in to take her place at the head of the bride's honor guard.

Seanen studied her thoughtfully as he stood waiting. He hated waiting. Waste of time. Unless, of course there was a good reason. If, for instance, there was something large in the way that might kill you, then it was worth waiting…

Seemed like he'd been standing here for hours. He'd been one of the first ones in, naturally, making a thorough search of the room one last time. No hidden traps. No danger of any kind that he could find.

Except from boredom.

He didn't belong here. Not here with the wedding party, dressed up in his finest dress uniform, feeling like a stuffed bird on display. Most of these fine Ladies and Lords wouldn't have spoken to him on a normal day. They still wouldn't. Oh, they wouldn't complain that he had been invited—or rather commanded—to attend. No one would be so bold as to argue Lady Lochinvar's choice of a wedding party. No, the nobility wouldn't say anything. Nothing at all. They would just look right through him as if he didn't exist.

Not that that was anything new. It no longer even bothered him. In fact, their silence was something of a relief. Mostly such people had nothing to say that was of any interest to him in the first place. With a sigh he went back to studying Tranorva, hoping he could manage to stay awake through the long, boring afternoon to come.

*****

Yarwyn made herself small, sitting out of the big Northlander's line of sight, observing him silently before she made her move. Her breath caught in her throat. He was everything his Guild had promised, and so much more. She'd done her homework. So far, everything she'd learned about this man appeared to be accurate. But nothing in the Guild files had prepared her for the man who stood at the back of the bride's honor guard.

He was incredibly tall. Granted, he was a Barbarian — no, they called themselves Northlanders — so she'd expected tall, but not like this. She'd never actually seen one of them before, and this man stood half a head above his countrymen.

She'd expected something of a dandy. If anything, his dress was subdued for the occasion. He wore a plain black wool cut-away uniform jacket, remarkable only for the fine weave and tight finish of the fabric. Beneath it she could see an unruffled shirt of fine white linen. Even the kilt that covered most of his long, hard-muscled thighs was a subtle weave of brown on brown like the forest floor at dusk.

For a man who'd started out as a petty thief, her target had done well for himself.

The intensity of the man's emotions nearly overwhelmed her. She'd been prepared for reserve. She knew he wasn't really part of the gentry, and he didn't mingle with them. He was here to do a job — a job that by all accounts he was very good at. That didn't mean he had to like these people. Her carefully gathered intelligence reported no instances of his many affairs spilling over into his work. He was known as a ladies' man, always available for a good time, but not amongst women of this sort.

Nowhere in his files had anyone mentioned that the man was incredibly handsome. The broad shoulders and heavily muscled body were racial norms. The thick mane of long dark hair that cascaded over his shoulders and the strong, broad jaw with the tiniest little dimple in the chin were strictly his own. Even the scar that ran across his right eyebrow and down his cheek managed only to add character. He had the sort of looks that would only improve with age, too. His lips were broad and full, just made for kissing. If he smiled...

But he wouldn't. She could feel it in him. He rarely smiled.

Though the gentry didn't openly flirt with a member of the working class, the Ladies around him certainly enjoyed the scenery he provided. Seeing him in person, Yarwyn had to admire his professionalism. Women who looked at a man that way would go after him. Perhaps not publicly, but they would go after him, all the same. The fact that not a hint of scandal associated itself with his name did him worlds of credit in her eyes. She couldn't even feel him acknowledge the women around him as his eyes swept over them.

So far she'd seen him speak to no one, not even casually. Her trained eye told her he was surveying the crowd, watching, waiting, looking for signs of anything amiss. The strongest waves of emotion hit when his gaze strayed back to the bride's sister, the one with the unpronounceable name. *Travornia* or something like that. Cruel thing for a mother to give a woman such an unpronounceable name.

Yarwyn nearly reeled as the force of his desire washed over her. She knew without looking that Seanen was studying that woman again. When he did, when he actually let his eyes rest in one place, everything about him changed. The austerity slipped away. The lines about his mouth softened. The set of his shoulders became less severe. The carefully maintained distance he surrounded himself with fell away. The most incredible difference came in the fine lines about his eyes. If he ever looked at her like that she knew she'd be completely undone.

He was merely looking at some other woman and she was already undone. She felt her body respond to his fantasies. She wanted to strip out of her clothes in front of hundreds of people.

As if there was any chance he'd ever look at her that way. She had none of what a man like that looked for in a mate. He wanted what that one had. She was his own kind. A Barbarian woman. Tall with broad shoulders, hard muscles, and generous proportions.

Nothing about Yarwyn was generous. Besides, even if the big Northlander didn't despise her on sight for her racial heritage, he was much too young. He looked to be in his late twenties. Not even middle-aged for a man of his race. She was more than twice his age. Granted, she would outlive him by decades if she lived long enough to get old, but he wouldn't see it that way.

She was a fool to even think about the man as a lover. She was here to do a job. Nothing more. If that job put her in the way of one of the most attractive men she'd ever had to work with, she would manage to remain professional. She could handle spending days, maybe weeks, in close proximity to the first man she'd seen in ages who stirred her interest. As long as he kept his hands to himself she'd be fine.

It was a lie, and she knew it, but lies were the price a woman paid to keep her sanity.

* * * * *

Seanen let his eyes drift back to Tranorva. To the casual observer, she might appear detached or even bored. That wasn't the way Seanen saw the picture at all. Tranorva's eyes barely shifted, yet he knew she was surveying the room, even as he did, looking for the odd, the unusual, the dangerous. People who knew her, even those close to her, if anyone was truly close to her, described her as cold and efficient. Always efficient.

Seanen wondered again what she'd be like in bed. He'd have been willing to bet he could crack that cold reserve. Under it all, under the uniform and the military posturing and the years of training, was there still a flesh and blood woman in there? If he could get close enough to her, he could break through those defenses.

He was a thief, after all. Breaking into things was his specialty. Tranorva was a challenge he was up to, he was sure of that. If he could just find a way to get close to her...

"You're wasting your time, handsome. You're just setting yourself up for a heartache."

He jumped. By the gods, he never jumped.

The voice was breathy and feminine and incredibly sexy in a teasing, half-annoyed sort of way that said *Pay attention to me*, the way a woman did when she didn't like the direction a man's thoughts had taken. Made him feel like he should apologize. Not that he had a clue who he should apologize to or why. Yet the words were meant to be heard only by him, he was sure of it.

How in Hades had anyone known what he was thinking? He was good, damn it. Very good. No one ever knew what he was thinking.

Where had the voice come from, anyway, and who did it belong to? He was good with voices, but he didn't recognize this one. He wouldn't have forgotten a voice like that.

"You're not her type. She'll never even notice you exist," the mysterious voice assured him.

Even when she was mocking him, her voice fairly dripped with sex. Where was she? Who was she? Her voice came from his left elbow. He was sure of it. He searched the crowd, as discreetly as he could. He hated being caught off guard like this. Trouble was, there was nothing but a stone wall on his left. Yet his sense of direction and his hearing were both acute. A necessary trait for a thief.

Seanen surveyed those closest to him again, but he knew them all, knew their voices. Of course, those with magic could throw their voices, disorient the listener. If that voice was done with magic, she was going to break his heart. He'd already painted a picture of her in his mind, warm and pliant in his arms, contented that she was sharing his attention with no one...

"Some thief you are. Down here."

He blinked again, feeling like a fool as he looked down, and then further still. There, sitting atop the short cut stone footer that lined the huge hall, almost at his feet, was a tiny little woman.

"Hello, handsome."

Seanen snorted at her humor. Disappointment shot through him. He'd thought he'd been prepared for almost anything. Looks weren't all there was to a woman. With a voice like that…

But she wasn't a woman at all. Hardly more than a child, by the looks of her. She wouldn't be much more than chest high against him. How had one so young acquired such an incredible voice?

He rearranged his thinking. A child deserved some forbearance. Seanen buried his disappointment as he stared down at the little imp. "Who said I was a thief?"

"I'm a Ranger. I know things."

Sassy little bit of spunk she was. And that voice was going to drive him crazy. He gauged her to be no more than fourteen. Any moment now she'd be dancing off to join the children out playing in the grassy compound under the watchful eyes of the guards. In the meantime, she was more entertaining than waiting for the wedding to start. "You might be a Ranger. Someday."

She raised an eyebrow at him but said nothing else.

Child or not, he wanted to hear her speak. She was too young for him to even fantasize about without breaking every rule he'd ever set for himself, but he could still enjoy the sound of her voice. "Who said I was thinking about anyone?"

"Your face said so."

Nothing showed on his face. Ever. He snapped his mouth shut to avoid saying something he'd regret. Sexy voice or not, the child was beginning to bother him.

She giggled. Damn it, she was laughing at him! He hated to be laughed at. But if he said so, she'd know she'd gotten to him. Seanen had learned years ago that the best way to deal with those who ridiculed him was to ignore them. Give in, pay attention, and your tormentors never quit.

He'd learned the lesson on his own, just like everything else. He thought of the small stone hut where he'd spent the first seven years of his life and smoothed his face out into a flat plain of unreadable dirt, just like the dirt floor in that tiny hut. When you lived in a hut with a dirt floor, dirt got into your food. Dirt turned into grit between your teeth. The image steadied him, reminded him of who he was, where he'd come from. Reminded him too just how much his temper could cost him if he unleashed it here.

So much for listening to her voice. "Be quiet," Seanen warned. "The wedding's about to start."

The imp smirked up at him, but said nothing else.

It wasn't a lie, after all. The huge wooden doors at the end of the hall creaked open. Lady Cassadara glided in, looking as if she might actually have mastered the art of levitation at last, though he suspected she hadn't. Perhaps it was the fact that, for the first time in years, he was seeing her in something other than a full set of mail.

Tranorva would look like a goddess in that dress. He would spend at least ten minutes working his way down through the layers of fine, sheer lace. Maybe more. By the time he had her undressed—

"You're wasting your time, I tell you. She has no use for men."

It wasn't his imagination. The child sounded a little jealous. Damn it, this wasn't just his overactive libido responding to a sexy voice. She was flirting with him, and he old enough to be her father. His patience snapped. "Be quiet, little one!"

His irritation brought a note of humor to her voice. "Even if she had any interest in men, which I assure you she does not, she's the next Lady Lochinvar. If you get caught looking at her like that, you'll be out of the Royal Guard so fast you'll get a nosebleed."

Guilt washed over him. Damn it, his fantasies should have been his own private property. It wasn't as if he'd ever act on those fantasies. "I am looking at no one. What would a child like you know of such things anyway? 'Tis none of your business."

Yes, indeed. Her humor was back in full force now. "You know, lusting after things you can't have isn't good for you. Makes you forget how fortunate you are."

The child knew how to get past his defenses. She'd gone way past annoying. There was real anger here now, much too close to the surface—closer than it had been in a long time. He actually had to work to keep his tone light. "And just how fortunate am I, pray tell?"

She shrugged, her eyes glittering with laughter now. "You're a trusted member of Lady Lochinvar's household and a member of the Royal Guard, instead of being locked in a dungeon, where most thieves who get caught end up. Not bad for the bastard son of a bastard house. And you still have both of your hands. I'd call that fortunate."

Seanen told himself he wasn't going to argue with the child. He wasn't. After all, she was right. He laughed instead, until he found the humor in the situation himself. He tried his most charming smile. "How come you to know so much about me, little Ranger?"

She shrugged again. A slight movement of small, delicate little bones set so close to the surface that he could see them pull against her skin through the fine material of her tunic. Silk, he was sure. Fine silk of a costly sort. Though perhaps silk would not be so costly wherever she was from. Silk had to be imported back home. That added greatly to the price.

"Part of my job." She slipped to her feet so gracefully she hardly seemed to have moved.

His smile softened, becoming more natural. She really was a cute little kid. Soft and delicate with a small, narrow face that came to a point at her chin. "I know," he humored her. "You're a Ranger."

She shrugged again. He was almost disappointed. He'd lost her attention. Her eyes wandered the room, playing over faces and bodies, reading the crowd even as he did. She was much taller than he'd expected. She came even with his shoulder. It was the legs that had fooled him. All of her height was in long, long legs that had been folded up underneath of her while she sat. He had a weakness for legs, and hers were a thing of beauty. If she'd been a little older…not that she was that young. She was slight, but not quite the child she'd first appeared.

Still, he wasn't about to look at her that way. There was no one particular type of woman that caught his attention any more than another, but he did have his standards. He liked women, not girls. Once he was off duty, he enjoyed spending time with women from his own part of the city. He usually looked for older women.

Women with enough experience not to get attached. Women who expected nothing from him and wouldn't be disappointed when he moved on. It was one of his rules. Rules were important. If everyone knew the rules going into a relationship, no one got hurt. Entertain, enjoy, but don't get involved.

The priest was speaking. Seanen made an effort to pay attention. Ella and the girls at the tavern would expect a full report on the wedding later.

"Marriage is a contract to be entered into only after a great deal of consideration."

Right. From two people who'd known each other less than a fortnight. No one would catch Seanen entering into such a ridiculous contract. Why spend the rest of your life listening to one woman grow tired of you when there were so many others waiting to be entertained?

"What a fool. She just sold herself into slavery."

Seanen glanced down at the imp by his side. It annoyed him that she parroted his thoughts. Annoyed, and perhaps intrigued. "What makes you say that, little one? I thought women desired to have the lifetime devotion of a man."

She snorted. A most unladylike sound. "Trade my freedom for a lifetime of washing smelly socks and cooking meat and potato stew? I don't think so."

He found himself wanting to disagree with the little bit of a thing. "And freedom, that is more important to you than a home and a family?"

"What would I know about families? About as much as you do. I don't intend to find out, either. That's not part of my plan."

He detected a trace of bitterness in her words. She sounded so much like he had in his younger days. For a moment the years washed over him and he felt so old…

It was the child. Compared to her he was old. What did children know? When you were a child, thirty was old. "You have a plan, little one?"

One eyebrow raised in that peculiar way again. "I'm a Ranger. I always have a plan."

Seanen tried to concentrate on the priest, but it wasn't doing much good. The tiny woman-child at his elbow was too fascinating.

Lord Yarishet raised Cassadara's hand to his lips, kissing it once before he slipped the family crest onto her little finger. The priest knotted a white ribbon around their joined hands. "You have pledged your love and devotion before the gods. We who stand with you today are witness to this pledge. You are now husband and wife. May your love endure as a guiding light to those around you. May your houses prosper even as your love. Mâkakao, you may kiss your bride."

A cheer rose from the crowd. Lord Yarishet turned them both to face the crowd, raising their hands high together. "Friends, I present to you Lady Yarishet!"

Another cheer shook the grand hall. The musicians began to play a traditional wedding ballad. The guests moved aside to clear the center of the marble floor.

Lord Mâkakao swept Cassadara into his arms. Now they were supposed to dance. Seanen winced. It was hopeless. Cassadara had been his worst student ever. He couldn't watch this.

"Can you dance passably?"

Seanen blinked down at the tiny woman-child. She sounded worried. "I thought you knew all there was to know about me."

It was her turn to look annoyed. "I know you're big enough to break every bone in my foot if you tromp on me."

He should have been personally affronted, but she was an amusing little thing. "I shall endeavor to keep your toes safe should you decide to do me the honor of dancing with me, M'Lady."

"Was that an invitation?"

"'Tis not, M'Lady. For that I would need to know your name, and we have not been introduced."

"My name is Yarwyn. That's all the introduction you're going to get."

"Well, then, Lady Yarwyn, would you grant me this dance?"

"I'm no Lady, I can assure you of that. Just plain Yarwyn."

"My pardon, Mistress Yarwyn. Shall we dance?"

She bowed slightly from the waist as she offered Seanen her hand. A very small, delicate hand it was at that. Seanen thought briefly to ask if she had been schooled in the art of dancing yet, but decided against it. No matter. He could make the worst dancer look reasonably good. Except Cassadara. He sighed at the thought.

"What?"

Seanen blinked, turning his attention back to the tiny thing before him. He smiled again. "I thought you could read my mind. Did that thought escape you?"

She grimaced. "I never said I could read your mind. May the gods protect me from being able to read your or anyone else's mind. There's enough noise in the world already."

Seanen didn't say so aloud, but he couldn't help but agree.

Across the wide expanse of marble, Lord Yarishet seemed to have the situation in hand. Cassadara hadn't tripped and fallen headfirst through the large stained glass windows, at any rate. In fact, she managed to look almost graceful.

The steward gave his signal, and the guests surged forward onto the dance floor. Seanen turned his attention once more to Yarwyn. She moved into his arms. With the first turn his spirits lifted. She had the liquid grace of a natural dancer. As he pulled her against his chest for a turn, he discovered she had something else, too. She had breasts. The soft silk tunic hid them well within its flowing folds, but she definitely had breasts. When she moved against him he could feel them, high and soft and womanly, teasing his chest with thoughts that a man should never have for one of her age.

The music swept them along, creating a magical universe where beauty and grace blended, where the dancers all moved in harmony, and nothing of the world he had known could intrude. In this world, and in this world alone, he forgot who he was and where he had come from.

"Isn't this the part of the evening where you attempt to seduce me?"

Her attempt at humor broke his reverie, dragging him back to the ancient stone hall and the scattered rushes and torch light. He found himself scowling down at the tiny imp in his arms. She was laughing at him again. And looking older as the sinking sun gave way to the soft light of torches burning in the wall scones. "I beg your pardon?"

"Well, you do have quite a reputation, you know."

Surely it was humor he heard in her voice and nothing more. Seanen let his face relax again. "I admit, I do often enjoy the company of ladies. But there is the—ah—difference in our ages."

Violet eyes laughed up at him, sparkling like precious gems, tempting him to forget the rules. "I am a great deal older than you, but it's a liability I forgive you for."

Chapter Two

Yarwyn let her head fall back as she turned in his arms, and Seanen caught what he should have realized so much sooner. Her ears had been hidden by her silver, short cropped hair. Small, delicately sculptured ears rose to long, tapering points. The magic hadn't come from the music, after all. Not this time. The woman in his arms was the magic.

Yarwyn. Even her name was magic. She was supple and lithe and so in tune to the rhythm that her body seemed to pulse with the beat as the orchestra sent the couples whirling off into a waltz. His heart beat a faster cadence, until his racing blood blended with the music, much as she did, becoming part of the spinning magic.

An Elf. He held an Elf in his arms. How could he have missed that? What had happened to his famous sense of observation? Not a High Elf. She hadn't the alabaster skin they were known for. A Wood Elf, then? But no. That didn't seem quite right, either.

Though Yarwyn appeared tiny next to him, she reached nearly to his shoulder, which would make her close to six foot tall. No Wood Elf he'd ever heard of made it to that height. A Half-Elf perhaps. He'd never seen one before, but that was the only explanation that worked. He'd taken her for a Human. Perhaps he wasn't so far off, after all.

At any rate, she was a grown woman. Certainly old enough for him to think anything he wanted to about her. Her claim to be a Ranger even seemed plausible now. And just what was an Elven Ranger doing at a wedding on the edge of the tundra? And why had she bothered to learn so much about him? Maybe it was time he got to know this little Elf a whole lot better. She was up to something, and he wanted to find out what.

Her very presence here was unsettling. He needed to find out why she was here. It was his duty, after all. He maintained his position as head of security in Lady Lochinvar's household because things like this didn't happen. No matter that they were not currently at House Lochinvar. He hadn't been doing his job, or Yarwyn wouldn't have gotten so close to the wedding party without his knowing who she was and why she was here.

Seanen favored the little Elf with his most charming professional smile. "You are a rare pleasure, little Ranger. I am honored that you chose to dance with me."

One eyebrow cocked slightly up at him again. "Does that bother you, Seanen? That I asked you, rather than waiting for you to ask me?"

His most professional smile split into a much more honest grin. "I'm the bastard son of a bastard house, remember? I'm pleased when I get asked instead of ordered. And how could I object to dancing with such a truly gifted partner?"

A tension he hadn't realized she'd been holding went out of her.

"Good. I hate functions like these. I tend to—that is, people often..." She sighed. "My mouth gets me in trouble. I say the wrong thing to the wrong person and next thing you know I'm carrying messages between Guild halls like a first year Ranger."

She was such an odd mixture of sex-appeal and self-doubt. Somewhere in his years of studying women Seanen had learned that it was advisable to neither agree nor argue with a woman at such a point. Rather than answering her with words, he did what he'd wanted to do from the moment he'd first heard the sound of her voice. He bent his head to cover her lips with his own. A strange custom he'd picked up from the Human women...oddly satisfying, with many variations.

Yarwyn's eyes opened wider in surprise for just a moment before they fluttered closed. Her lips parted beneath his, perhaps because of her sharply indrawn breath. The tip of his tongue danced across her palate.

How could he have ever taken her for a child? Seanen let his hand slip down her back a little farther, resting the tips of his fingers on the curve of one soft, rounded hip, moving her breasts a little tighter against his chest as he pulled her closer. If he had any doubts about her willingness, they were dispelled when her free hand found its way to tangle in his hair, pulling his head down for another, deeper kiss.

He could feel the outline of her nipples, hard and ready, pressing against his thin linen shirt. A surge of pure lust fired his blood, hitting him hard, the way it had when he was a boy. He wanted to slide his hand under her silk tunic, to caress and stroke, until he could get her somewhere more private, where he could provide them both the ease their bodies coveted. He pushed his hips against her, knowing she could feel the heat of his engorged cock. She caught his bottom lip in her teeth, biting none too gently, demanding more when he tried to pull away.

Seanen shook his head. It was her Elven magic, working like an intoxicant, washing all the years of ingrained caution from his mind until he would have taken her here, on the dance floor, while hundreds of people looked on.

The logical side of his brain screamed in outrage, reminding him that he was too close, that he was losing his objectivity, that he was on the job, and he had responsibilities. Reluctantly he broke the kiss, holding her at arm's length while he tried to regain his focus. She faltered, nearly missing a step as he spun her in his arms. A foolish grin settled on his face. She looked a bit dazed, her violet eyes wide as she stared up at him.

Seanen risked a quick touch of his lips to her pretty little nose. "I should like to get to know you much better, little Ranger, but right now I am on duty, and I fear another such kiss would have me forgetting who I am and why I am here."

A light tap on his shoulder interrupted whatever reply she might have made. Seanen turned, a scowl darkening his countenance, ready to dismiss the interloper who was fool enough to try to cut in on him. But he recognized that suspicious little pointed face that looked up at him, knew those shrewd midnight-blue eyes, and knew immediately how close he'd come to being caught with something much less than duty on his mind. Still, he tucked Yarwyn's hard through his arm as he moved them all as unobtrusively as possible off the dance floor.

"What do you want, Ferret?"

The pinch-faced Human ignored Seanen as he bowed slightly before Yarwyn. "Antonius Faroott at your service, Ambassador. Forgive my interruption, but the Lady Lochinvar wishes me to invite you to take council in her apartments immediately after the bride and groom dismiss."

Ambassador.

Seanen glanced at Yarwyn out of the corner of his eye. Gone was the child-like waif façade. Instead a polished woman who might indeed have been his senior, and certainly his better in rank, stood with one arm looped loosely over his, as if he might have been her escort for the night. Her paid escort.

Seanen drew himself in sharply, isolating himself within his reserve. He wanted to click his heels together and mockingly salute, but he would give neither of them the satisfaction. Bad enough to have been played for a fool. Worse to let them know how badly it settled in his stomach.

He turned, instead, and raised Yarwyn's hand to his lips. "Then you must be going, Ambassador, for Lady Cassadara and her new husband have just slipped out. I shall see to their safety. May you have a pleasant evening."

She smiled and nodded, but if she attempted to say something, he didn't hear her. In truth, the bride and groom might well have slipped out some time ago. For the first time since he was a raw recruit, he hadn't been doing his job, and he'd been caught blindsided from all directions at once.

* * * * *

Lady Lochinvar paced the length of the spacious chamber that had been given her as an anti-room. Her stride belied both her advanced years and the necessity of her heavily ornamented black walking stick. Sense of purpose surrounded the Lochinvar matriarch. She truly believed that she alone was responsible for the fate of her people. Yarwyn wondered how much of herself she'd given up through the years in her search to fulfill her responsibility.

The oldest daughter, Tranorva, sat quietly in the chair beside her mother's writing table, her eyes focused somewhere out the window into the black depths of the night. Yarwyn could pick up nothing off that one. Her attention shifted back to Lady Lochinvar as the older woman began to speak.

"Lord Mâkakao set off to cover twenty-five leagues of relatively uncivilized territory with a patrol of thirty men. These men were no' raw recruits. These thirty men were his handpicked Home Guard. Lord Mâkakao led those troops personally. But only seven of those men are alive today.

"The Orcs that attacked Lord Mâkakao's party had both a Shaman and a Scout in their patrol. They were heavily armed. 'Tis no' the sort of Orc patrol we are used to seeing out on the tundra!"

Tranorva frowned down at her fingernails. "Thirty Humans, Mother. Do not forget that the Orcs attacked Humans. A patrol of Northlanders would no' have taken such heavy casualties. Give me an army of our own and I shall wipe these Orcs off the face of the tundra."

Lady Lochinvar raised one eyebrow at her daughter. "Never underestimate thine enemy, Daughter. The Orcs were better organized than we have ever seen them before and better equipped. They also traded their captives to Argolyn the Dwarf in the City of Stone near the tundra's edge. Since when has any Dwarf traded with an Orc? Granted this was an outcast Dwarf acting on his own, but this is no' an isolated incident. Orc Traders are beginning to make their way into many border cities. They trade captives and slaves for goods and services of all kinds."

Yarwyn shuddered at the thought of what services an Orc Warrior might trade for in a small border city. "Orcs don't trade. Orcs don't even take captives. Or at least they didn't. Though I loathe the vile Orcs, it is not they who are our enemy. Someone is behind this. Someone is inciting the Orcs against the peoples of the tundra. It is that someone who is our most pressing enemy."

Here was an emotion Yarwyn could read well enough. Anger. Tranorva stood, using her height to glare down at Yarwyn from over a foot above her. "The Orcs are our enemy. We wipe them out, and whoever is behind this has no tools left to attack us with!"

Lady Lochinvar held up her hand. "Both of ye are correct. We must wipe out the Orcs, or at least contain them again, so that our people can travel freely across the tundra once again. But ye, too, are correct, Yarwyn. We must find out who is behind these raids, who is arming and training the Orcs, and stop their interference. Tranorva, ye shall have thy army. Every Northlander and Human available shall travel with ye to clean this pollution off the tundra.

"Yarwyn, ye know why ye have been sent here. Thy mission is dangerous. We canna' take the castle of the Orc King by force. The place is a fortress, designed by Dwarven Architects to withstand any siege. Even Tranorva and her combined armies canna' take the castle itself. Still, the situation must be contained. I need to know who is behind this as well. I will give ye a small party of thy own choosing. Are there members of thy Guild whom ye would call upon? I shall personally guarantee their fees."

Yarwyn glanced around the small gathering, keeping her face suitably grave as she inclined her head toward Lady Lochinvar. These people didn't trust her. Why should they? They didn't even know her, and they never would. She would not choose from amongst this carefully selected lot. "The larger the party, the harder it will be for us to escape detection. I would ask for only one man, M'Lady. I would ask that your man Seanen accompany me."

Hushed voices whispered sharp little hisses of dissention around the room. Yarwyn kept her features bland, but all the while she was laughing inside.

"Seanen? Seanen of the House of Lindall, the dance instructor?" The horror in Tranorva's voice was enough to cheer Yarwyn considerably.

Lady Lochinvar held up her hand for silence. "If this is thy choice, I will respect thy decision. I am sure that both House Security and the dance instructions can manage to function without Seanen for as much time as this will require."

So even Lady Lochinvar knew not what she had here. Or, if she knew, she would not give him away. The man was good, she'd give him that. He'd played his hand just right with these people. Yarwyn inclined her head once more. "I shall inform Master Seanen myself, Lady, if you will but grant me your seal."

Lady Lochinvar wrote briefly on a small parchment, signed it with a flourish, and quickly affixed her seal. Yarwyn smiled to herself. Things were going better than she'd expected. Now she had but to find the gentleman in question and inform him that Lady Lochinvar had just signed his life over to her, to do with as she saw fit.

She just hoped her plan wouldn't end up getting both of them killed.

* * * * *

Seanen knocked back a pint of mead in the hopes that it would help. It didn't. He waved off yet another of the tavern's patrons who tried to get just a little too close. He wasn't interested. Not tonight. The scene he'd stumbled upon while trying to locate the missing Lord Mâkakao and his new bride had left him feeling hard and frustrated.

Granted, they were newlyweds, but they could have waited long enough to get back to their chambers. He'd known Cassadara almost her entire life. She was as close to family as he would ever have. He hadn't ever wanted to see her naked, let alone wrapped in the arms of her Warrior lover.

And he'd had to watch. Or at least keep the scene under observation. It was his job. How in the name of the seven gods was he supposed to maintain security when the couple he was guarding insisted on slipping out the back door to rut like animals in the orchard?

He'd done his best to ignore what was going on in that orchard while he kept his eyes on the perimeter, but he couldn't kill the lust that burned in his blood. He should find a woman. Any woman. There were several here who'd invite him to their room and relieve him of his frustrations. Unfortunately there was only one woman he was interested in tonight. He wouldn't hold one woman while he pretended to make love to another. He had his standards. They weren't very altruistic, but they were standards.

He shoved the second pint of mead back across the bar half finished. The woman he wanted in that picture was an Ambassador. An Ambassador of what and from whom he'd yet to discover, but it didn't matter. Whatever her game was, he'd been played for a fool. He'd...

Seanen drew in his breath sharply as two small hands settled on his shoulders from behind. No other woman would have been so bold. A man he'd have killed, and asked questions afterward. But he'd have recognized this touch anywhere. It was as if his body had tuned in to her. He forgot to breathe as the hands moved down over his shoulders and finally slid around his waist, making their way up again on the front until she'd explored every inch of his chest.

He was angry with her. He had to remember she had lied to him and he was angry with her. Yet as he turned on the wooden stool to face her, all he could think of was that she'd come back.

"Seanen, I must speak to you."

If possible, her voice had become even sexier. The words meant little as her hands continued to explore his chest, her touch as hot as if there were nothing separating their skin from one another. His hands framed her face perfectly, making her look small and fragile once again. He tried to be gentle, to make the kiss soft and welcoming, but her hands pulled at him, demanding more. She took what she wanted, grabbing anything she could reach with her teeth, demanding that he hold nothing back.

"Talk," he managed. "I don't think so. Talk is not at all what we need."

The sharp little Elven face seemed to have lost its focus. "Talk," she repeated, though with a degree of uncertainty. "I—yes. We must talk."

Seanen slid to his feet. He dropped his hands slowly down her back, until they rested on the curve of her delicious little rump, pulling her tightly against his aching erection, letting her feel his heat, warning her also of how seriously he took her little game. For he knew it was a game. No woman of her class went after a man like him for any more than one reason, and this was the reason. Her hips moved against his, teasing him with her own heat. Yes. There could be no doubt as to what she wanted.

He didn't usually encourage women of her class. Didn't follow through when they made their play. He knew the ways of the gentry all too well. This would mean nothing to her, and everything to him, because he wanted her as he hadn't wanted a woman in some time, maybe ever. She would break his heart when she left, and she would leave. As soon as her assignment was up, he'd be forgotten, just another amusement that had helped her pass the time. And he would be here, in this or some other back town bar that suddenly seemed even more squalid and hopeless.

"Let us get out of here," he muttered, almost angry at the place for being what it was. "We can 'talk' somewhere else. Your apartments, perhaps."

"Your apartments," Yarwyn argued. Her fingers stroked the length of him through his kilt, making him feel once again like a young boy, ready to spill his seed at her touch. He captured her hand and brought it to his lips, then tucked it through his elbow as he led her from the seedy little tavern. It was only a few blocks away. A stone's throw from the back gate where House Yarishet's walls kept the squalor of O'Shay's tavern at bay.

Right now he needed badly to return to his room in Lord Mâkakao's magnificent home, to reassure himself of just how far he had come. That desperate boy who'd gotten caught trying to steal a day's bread from Lady Lochinvar was years and worlds away. The man he had become was worthy of the woman on his arm, even if the lurking shadow of the boy cried out in fear.

They slipped in past his guards as easily as he'd gotten out. Remarkably easy if you knew how. In the shadow of the orchard where he'd found Lord Mâkakao and his new bride a few hours before, Seanen stopped to pull Yarwyn back into his arms, a little more roughly than he should have, but she didn't seem to mind. Her hands slid under his kilt in the dark, her breath drawing in sharply as she captured his cock in her hands. He jumped at her touch, breathing her name as his heart sought to escape his chest.

Through the thin silk of her tunic he cupped her breasts, caressing until her nipples budded like the points of ripe lemons beneath his touch. His lips grazed her face, sampling the moist, soft skin of her eyelids, stroking her delicately pointed ear with warm breath before he captured the tip.

Her hands convulsed on his shaft as her whole body stiffened. He could have sworn she'd forgotten to breath. Slowly, gently, he caressed the tip of her ear with his tongue, gauging from her response what she liked best. His hand found the other ear and stroked lightly with his fingertips. She moaned with a sound that could have been pain or pleasure when he nipped light on the sharp little edge.

"I haven't felt like this in years," she whispered. "Take me. I want you. Here. Now."

He could have. He was more than ready. But she was something different. Something special. This wasn't how he wanted it to be with them. If there was only to be this one time, this one evening, he wanted more to remember her by than a romp in the orchard. He reached down to grasp her hands firmly away from the work they'd become so occupied with and lead her on to his room. "Close now," he promised.

It wasn't. The room wasn't close. Not with an incredibly lithe nymph of an Elf who still had one hand free to explore whatever she could reach. He pulled her into an alcove off the main hall to let a party of house guests make their leisurely way back to their rooms. When her quick little fingers plucked at his nipples he had to press his lips over hers to contain the surprised gasp of something that was as much pain as pleasure. In retaliation his fingers slid under her tunic and between the tops of her leggings, exploring where they would, finding more similarities than differences.

The soft triangle of curls that awaited his touch was already moist and hot, bucking against his exploring fingers with as much wantonness as one of the girls from O'Shay's might have shown. He thrust one finger deep inside her, finding her tight and ready as he teased her with a promise of what was to come. She moaned again, and he kissed the sound away, lest the guests take notice of what was none of their business.

She was so tight he could almost have taken her for a virgin. He wondered, panicky for a moment, how he'd ever fit inside her. He didn't want to hurt her, but he didn't want to give her up. Not now. Not after all of this.

The visitors moved along, and, more impatient than he'd been in a good long time, Seanen swept the little Elf into his arms, slipping up the servant's stairs with a grace that denied his bulky size. The door to his room had barely shut behind them before she was on her feet, skimming out of her tunic, anything but shy as she stood before him naked, helping him unwind the pleated yardage of the great kilt, urging the linen shirt over his head.

* * * * *

Yarwyn caught her breath when he stood before her naked. Waves of lust mixed with an unexpected tenderness rolled over her. His emotions would be her undoing. Everything about this man was big. There was no middle ground. She felt as tiny and vulnerable as a child. As if he sensed that she wanted to look, he stood quietly, waiting for her. She placed her hands on his shoulders, letting them trail slowly down to his fingertips. "You're gorgeous," she whispered. "You take my breath away."

Large hands fisted over hers, pulling her against the whole long, hard, hot length of him. "You're daft, woman. But don't change. Not right now. Make love to me."

He wanted more than sex. She could feel it. She just didn't know what the more was. The need in him was so raw, so basic, so overwhelming. He held her hands captive, but he had not pinned her in place. Yarwyn brushed her breasts across his chest, trying to find ease for the burning ache that filled her. She wasn't sure if the need that possessed her was his or her own, but it no longer mattered.

She kissed the pulse at the base of his throat, then down, down, along the line of dark hair that pointed like an arrow to that hard, hot shaft awaiting her. By the gods he was big. She kissed her way down the length of him, still not struggling to free her hands, holding him captive far more intimately as she circled the tip of his engorged penis with her tongue, teasing, stroking, making him moan with desire.

Their hands still locked together, she straightened, pushing him backwards toward the raised dais that overflowed with pillows in exotic fabrics from around the world. He managed to drop back into the pillows gracefully, without yanking her off her feet or breaking the hold of their hands.

"Perfect," she assured him. "That's just where I want you."

Standing over him, more of her soul showing than she'd shown any man in years, Yarwyn found she felt at ease, trusting that he would not hurt her, though she knew he could have. He let her set the pace, making no objection when she knelt over him, testing their fit together as she sank slowly down onto his rigid shaft. He stretched her, filling her as no man had before, but somehow he fit.

He would have waited then, though she could feel the effort it was costing him, could see the fine sheen of sweat on the broad, muscular chest, but she was tired of waiting. She ached for more. She wanted all of him. Slowly she relaxed over him, sucking the last few inches of him into her greedy sheath. She rocked forward, driving him even deeper inside her, then back, their wet flesh making a sucking sound as she rode the length of him, rising up on the back stroke only to drive him down deep inside her again and again.

He could have taken control at any time, she knew, knew it from the strength of his grip on her hands, from the sheer size of the man, from the overwhelming intensity of his desire. He didn't. He let her set the pace, let her define their movements. Knowing that made the ache inside of her deeper, made her want him more. She rode him faster, grinding her hips against his, seeking a release that promised to shatter her. She sank her head down to his, capturing his lip in her teeth, claiming his mouth with the force of her desire until their tongues imitated the mating of their bodies.

It wasn't enough. She wanted more. She didn't know what. Had no words to explain it. Unfamiliar emotions washed over her. Lust, that she knew the feel of, but there was more. The need to possess, the need to become one. She wanted. She needed. "Please," she murmured against his lips.

All semblance of civility slipped away. His hands released hers, dropping to her hips, pulling her closer as he rose up, driving hard and hot into her, shaking with need. Their speed became a frantic dance, her whimpers cries of desire. His teeth caught at her nipples, sucking, nipping, as the hot, burning length of his shaft scorched her raw. The first climax shattered her like a pane of fragile glass, only to rebuild her again and again until she felt she could stand no more.

Pleasure and pain blended until there was no line between the two as the final climax ripped through her. Massive hands gripped her hips, slamming her down on him so hard that she knew she'd find bruises in the morning, but at that moment she just didn't care.

His seed spilled into her in a hot gush that threatened to ruin pillows that would cost a working man half a month's wages. She would ask the gods forgiveness later, but right now she truly didn't care. Her breath caught in an exhausted sob as she collapsed at his side.

* * * * *

Seanen spent the last of his energy rolling to one elbow to look down at her, cuddled against him, half buried in the pillows. "Say my name."

She didn't open her eyes. "Seanen." That sexy, sleep-drugged voice made it sound like an endearment.

"I just wanted to be able to remind myself when you break my heart tomorrow that you were really here. That this wasn't a mistake, that you know who I am."

She smiled, still without opening her eyes. "You are Seanen of the House of Lindall, a trusted member of House Lochinvar. You're also the best operative the Rogues' Guild has to offer. You come highly recommended. And it is you who will break my heart. But not tonight."

No one knew he belonged to the Rogues' Guild. No one. Even other members of the Guild rarely knew one another. She knew too much. How had she—unless…

"Do you have a token for me?"

She raised up enough to scan the room for her scattered clothing. "In my bag. Told you we needed to talk. Wanted to explain…"

Seanen let himself relax as he kissed the spot where the pulse beat in her neck, pushing her back down into the pillows. "Perhaps we shall leave tomorrow to its own fate then, Ambassador Yarwyn."

She groaned. "Ambassador. Ha. I told you I'd been reduced to carrying messages like a first year Guild member."

A Guild Ambassador who held his token. Seanen chuckled softly in the darkness. "So you did, M'Lady. So you did."

Chapter Three

He'd been three days without a bath, marching for hours in the hot sun with an army at his back, sleeping alone in his bedroll with the woman he wanted close enough to touch and so far out of reach that she might as well have been a continent away. Now she had him sprawled on a cliff, two hundred meters above the good, solid earth, and she wanted him to look over the edge.

Seanen fingered the small hand-struck bronze coin, flipping it from knuckle to knuckle like a trainer toy. She'd bought his soul with that tiny little coin. Absently he ran his fingertip over the coin's inscription. Tokens from the Rogues' Guild were not easily obtained. She had to know someone, have some pull somewhere.

The woman knew too much of him and he too little of her. Just the thought of her slim naked body disrupted his reasoning. He'd known her in the most intimate way a man could ever know a woman, yet he still knew nothing of who she was, what she stood for, what made her tick. He was being led about like a fool pup. A blind fool pup.

Yarwyn turned slightly on the narrow ledge, studying him with a shrewd, assessing gaze. "You still don't trust me."

He was cranky and irritable, and he knew precisely why. The closeness of her body to his on the ledge wasn't helping things at all. "You could have killed me in my sleep any of the four nights. You didn't. I'd say I trust you about as much as any man ever could."

Yarwyn pulled his head toward her, kissing him in a way that was sure to distract his attention from the mission at hand.

"I don't recall getting much sleep the last three nights. I can't seem to sleep without your arms around me."

Seanen grazed the back of his knuckles over the light chainmail shirt she wore, gauging from her face more than from what he could feel when her breast responded to his touch. If it hadn't been for this cliff she had him sprawled on, he'd have taken her then and there, and damn the army below. "I trust you in my bedroom. That doesn't mean I have a great deal of faith in this plan of yours. I've never fought beside you. Just because you haven't killed me outright doesn't mean you're not going to get yourself and me killed."

Yarwyn looked annoyingly pleased at his response. "You're worried about me."

He shrugged noncommittally. "You get yourself killed, I'm next."

She inched forward, until she was almost hanging out over the cliff. Seanen took a deep breath, steadying himself as he grabbed at the back of her belt. He hadn't bothered to tell her how little he cared for heights. Not a trait one really expected in a thief.

"See there? That is the main entrance."

Yarwyn pointed to a set of wide iron-bound doors that appeared to be the only entrance into the forbidding stone wall. Those doors were, unfortunately, straight down over the side of the sheer two-hundred meter high cliff. Seanen was suddenly very thankful they had marched the morning through without stopping to break their fast with a midday meal. He pulled back from the cliff's edge, drawing in his breath sharply before he dared to speak. "You mean to walk in the main doors in broad daylight?"

"That might work, but that's not the plan. My sources tell me there is another way in. A tunnel that leads from the moat into the dungeon, directly below the main halls. My plan is to assume our disguises then enter through the tunnel. Then I lead you about until we find what we're looking for."

Seanen risked another quick glance over the ledge. "What makes you think that water is empty?"

She stared at him blankly. "The water? In the moat?"

"Orcs are said to fill their moats with all sorts of foul things to keep trespassers out."

Yarwyn shrugged. "We are seasoned warriors. I doubt we will meet anything we cannot handle."

Seanen pulled back again, further this time, and regained his feet.

"Where are you going?"

He shrugged. "If I'm going to die it won't be on top of this gods-forsaken cliff. Let us get to work."

* * * * *

Yarwyn folded her mail shirt and undertunic into a leather satchel, hiding it carefully in a recess of the small cave's stone wall. She picked up the corked vial and held it for a moment, steadying herself.

Waves of concern rolled off of him, but not for himself. Concern for her. He truly cared about her. That frightened her more than any Orc ever could. "Are you sure?" he asked for the tenth time.

She shook her head. "It's not dangerous."

"It is if it doesn't work. Or if our own men see you. Or if you're wrong."

She shook the vial gently. "Do you have a better plan?"

He shrugged. "I'm a thief, remember? You stay here and I break into the castle, find what we need, and escape."

Yarwyn wished his plan weren't so temptingly simple. She glanced at him again. He stood waiting, all but naked, ready to trust his life into her hands, and all he worried about was her. He held his arms crossed over his naked chest defiantly, his oiled skin reflecting the light of the small campfire and outlining the tight, bunched muscles where his jaw knotted with tension. He'd wrapped a piece of worn, frayed tartan around his waist, concealing his other distractions. "You're too clean," she objected.

"Give it a few minutes. I won't stay this way."

That was hard to argue with. Yarwyn uncorked the bottle and drank, holding her nose as the vile concoction threatened to gag her. When it was down, she threw the bottle into the fire, crouching close to its meager light to watch for the changes.

Nothing.

Five, and then ten minutes passed. Still nothing. Her stomach churned with revulsion as the potion refused to settle. She edged away from the fire, fearing the worst, using all her willpower to prevent the inevitable. There was no privacy to be had in the small cave, but she stumbled toward the darkness of the far back corner. It was no use. He was there beside her, his huge hands stroking over her back, supporting her, offering comfort as her body rejected the enchanter's brew. When she would have collapsed into the dirt, sobbing in defeat, he scooped her up and carried her, careful to press her head against his shoulder.

"I'm sorry," she whispered.

"It's not your fault, little Ranger. We will find another way."

"No. There is no other way. I was too weak. I have ruined everything."

"Do you not know the Rogue's Guild motto? There is always another way. Trust me, little one. Even a castle such as this one has a back door. I will find it. Our mission will not fail."

The mission had already failed. Perhaps it had failed before it ever began. Tears slipped silently down her cheeks and onto his chest.

"Yarwyn."

He had stopped beside the fire, still holding her as if she weighed nothing at all. Yarwyn raised her eyes to his face, sensing a tightness in his voice. "What's wrong?"

"Nothing. Nothing's wrong. Look. Look at your hand."

She splayed her fingers over his heart, her hand a tiny presence in the deep hollow of his breastbone. A dark presence. Her skin had turned a deep shade of dusky ebony. Mingled joy and fear warred for dominance. "Everywhere? Did it really work?"

Seanen set her down, walking slowly around her as she stood naked beside the fire. "Everywhere." She feared his next question for she wasn't altogether certain of the answer, but he had to ask. "How long will it last?"

"Supposedly up to a month, unless I take the antidote. I never tried it. I couldn't afford to be found out back in the Human city. Even if I hadn't been recognized, I'd have been killed on sight. And now, since it didn't stay down, I know not whether I will have the full effect…"

Seanen gathered her waterproof pack and slung it over his shoulder. "Then we better work quickly."

* * * * *

The water was cold and murky, as dark as the sky above, and things floated past. Seanen didn't want to know what sort of things, as long as none attacked him. He suspected many of those things were long dead anyway. None of them seemed to have been reanimated.

He was a good swimmer, having grown up fishing naked in the ice locked northern ocean. He could stay underwater for many minutes at a time, having learned the art of controlling his breathing, but he was, as were all of his race, totally night blind. The pendant around his neck gave off a weak glow, lighting up a path that reached as far as Yarwyn's aimlessly kicking feet.

She was not a strong swimmer. In another place and time, her technique might have amused him. He could have done this more easily without her, simply by following the curve of the stone wall. At least they weren't anywhere where he had to look down…

He wished fervently he hadn't indulged that thought. The thing that swam under him moved fast, undulating through the water with a speed that belied its bulk. Seanen wished again that he'd kept at least his dagger, but a prisoner would carry no weapons. Maybe it was just passing by. Maybe—

Maybe Yarwyn's feet looked like dinner, kicking ineffectively as they were.

The worm-like monster changed from placid to ominous as it opened its massive jaws, revealing multiple rows of gleaming white teeth that lit up eerily in the glow of the tiny crystal pendant. Yarwyn chose that exact moment to head for the surface, twisting herself just out of the monster's range as Seanen dove headfirst towards its snout. Using the only weapon he had handy, he punched it soundly between the eyes, or at least where its eyes should have been. Changing targets, the thing writhed itself around, its long serpentine body attempting to trap this new attacker within its coils.

His hammering fists had no apparent effect except to enrage the monster. Wicked teeth snapped shut on the place where he'd been as he dove under it, hiding under its jaw, looking for something softer, more vulnerable. He found a target in the fleshy underside of the throat, where the hinged jaw made the skin more elastic of necessity. The sluggish beat of its pulse throbbed against his hand as he buried his fist up to the wrist in the fleshy throat. He could reach it here, but he couldn't kill it. Not with his fists. And eventually he would run out of air.

Air. Even if it had gills, which he'd yet to encounter, the thing had to breath. Seanen stretched his arms around its thick body, burying the top of his head into the soft fleshy underside of its jaw. He felt it make a soft strangled wheeze as he tightened his arms with all the strength he possessed, thrusting his head against its soft inner organs. It thrashed wildly, trying to get its massive body coiled around its smaller attacker, but it could not reach him without strangling itself.

Desperate, the thing rose up out of the water, standing almost on end, trying to smash him against the forbidding stone walls, bringing sound back into Seanen's world with an eerie rush that seemed almost deafening. He gulped in air while throwing his body weight away from the wall, shifting the creature's balance so that they toppled back down, falling far below the surface, down to the murky depths where the thing must spend its days.

The maddened creature began to spin like a gyro, its every twist threatening to break Seanen's hold. Still he maintained his grip, butting the top of his head up even harder as he felt soft structures give beneath his relentless pressure. He felt its gasping gurgle as the fragile windpipe collapsed, felt it gasp what surely would have been a cry of pain had there been any sound at all. It was dying. They both knew its remaining minutes were numbered. If only Seanen could manage to hang on, he had won.

The twisting stopped as quickly as it had begun. The creature launched itself straight down, surging forward toward the depths of the moat, as if seeking out its lair. Seanen felt his ears pop with the depths, felt breath giving way as he struggled not to panic. Surely there was only one of them. The moat was not big enough to support more than one such creature. If it had had a mate, the other would have come by now to help her dying partner. Surely...

One last flick of its mighty body drove the thing into a vast underwater cavern, totally devoid of any light. It ceased its movement, going flaccid in his arms. Seanen relaxed his grip, swimming back along the length of the creature's body. He'd won, all right. Now there was just one problem. Several tons of dead worm blocked the only way out, and he was out of air.

Chapter Four

Yarwyn searched frantically for the opening of the moat in the stone wall. It had to be here. She knew it was here. The drawings had shown it right here.

Terror pushed her beyond her limits as she searched again, determined to find her way to safety. Seanen was gone. She knew he was gone, had felt him disappear from her under that water, leaving her mind free of his emotions for the first time in over a week. He'd bought her safety with his life, and by the gods she would not waste his sacrifice. Her hands traced over every stone, pushing, pulling, looking for a trigger that might spring a trap door, swing open a porticos, anything.

A few feet further. She would search just a few feet further. Perhaps she'd lost track of the distance in the dark. Perhaps — nothing. Her hands encountered nothing. One moment there was a wall, the next moment there was nothing. She kicked forward, turning awkwardly in the water as she tried to explore the opening.

"What are you doing, fool?" The words were spoken in the musical lilt of Dark Elven. Dark arms reached to pull her out of the water. "Do you not know this water is not for swimming? Foul things live in there! You could have been eaten alive!"

She wanted to cry, to kiss the ground, to fall on her knees and thank the gods for their mercy in sparing her, to scream her rage at Seanen's loss. Instead she had to begin her deceit. She was a Dark Elf female, a Priestess. She wrapped her shredded dignity around herself, becoming austere and remote — and in control. If this was ever going to work, she had to maintain control.

"Fool? You dare call me fool?"

The smaller male pulled back in fear, recognizing her for who and what she was. "I beg your pardon, Mistress. I—I thought you but an acolyte, fallen into the moat."

And well he might fear her. She had the right to kill him for such impertinence. "I did not fall in. I jumped in. I had a prisoner—a large man-thing. He got away. I tried to catch him, but the foul worm attacked him and dragged him under the water."

The young male searched the black waters with his eyes. She knew his night vision was excellent—much better than hers. He shook his head. "I see no remains, but he must be dead, Mistress. Nothing survives the worm."

She swallowed hard. "What is your name?"

"Élandine, Mistress. Of the House of Tamall."

"Well, Élandine, since you are but a male, I will explain this slowly, so that you might come to understand. I captured my prisoner here within these walls. The man-things are attempting to invade the castle."

"Pardon, Mistress, but man-things are always attempting to invade the castle."

"This one was inside, I tell you, within the walls. If there was one there will be more. We must search the keep!"

The young male glanced up at her as if she'd quite lost her mind. "As you wish, Mistress, but will this not alert the hierarchy that you have lost your prisoner?"

Yarwyn bit the inside of her lip, thinking rapidly. This was the one part of her deception she had not had the opportunity to study thoroughly. The politics of the Dark Elves were so alien to her thinking. She could not accept the young male's advice without admitting that he was right, which no Dark Elf Priestess would ever do. And yet he was right. And she should have known that, considered the politics before she spoke. Well, Rangers had their own politics, and she knew a few things. "I said search. I have no intention of *alerting* anyone."

She caught her breath as the Dark Elf suddenly pulled a torch from its bracket on the wall and moved it toward her face. His fingers reached out, darting quickly to her hair. She was sure she'd been discovered, failing to fool even one of his race.

What she saw when he drew back his hand made her almost wish her fears had been confirmed. The young male held a leach in his hand. Humor tinged his voice. "Mistress, before we bring you before the King and raise the alarm that the castle has been invaded by crazed man-things, please allow me to order you a bath and dry clothes."

* * * * *

Seanen shoved as hard as he could, but the creature would not budge. It appeared to have wedged itself in the opening at an angle, so that it completely filled the opening. He changed tactics, pushing upward, praying that a pocket had formed at the roof where he might at least find enough air to keep himself alive long enough to search for another way out. If he had air, he could perhaps find a sharp rock, and hack his way through the thing. If he had air...

He pushed up hard, extending his hand, searching for the roof. Nothing but water.

Undulating his body like a fish he swam up through the murky depths. Up and up he went, still finding no roof or ceiling. At last he broke free of the surface, gulping in lungfuls of stale, dank air that had not seen the light of day in any lifetime remembered by man. There was another smell here he almost recognized. He treaded water, searching for the source of the memory.

Lye. Crude, coarse lye soap.

Many years ago his mother had used it for boiling the laundry. He almost laughed. The creature had brought him deep into the heart of the castle, to the place where the keep emptied its wastes. He was directly below the kitchens. Somewhere there would be a drain in the floor, a hatch, something. If the laundry water could get out, he could get in. There was always a back door.

For a thief.

* * * * *

Yarwyn soaked in the big copper boiler while the kitchen slave picked at her hair with a spatula-like comb. The Dwarven girl couldn't have been more than twelve, yet she bore her lot with the typical Dwarven stoicism. She pushed gently on Yarwyn's head, indicating that she should rinse the strong lye soap out of her hair. Apparently the leaches didn't like lye. Not that Yarwyn blamed them. Her hair would undoubtedly have the consistency of old straw by the time the girl was done. She slid under the water long enough to scrub her fingernails through her short cropped mane once again, assuring herself that the last of the loathsome creatures were indeed gone.

The Dwarven slave-girl's shriek brought Yarwyn straight up out of that water and reaching for her blade. She lunged toward the intruder, only at the last moment capping her desire to slide her arms around the ghost before her and instead follow duty, laying the fine sharp blade against his throat. He knelt before her, his posture the correct combination of subservience and fear. "Don't move," she ordered in Dark Elven.

Whether he spoke the language or not, he could surely understand the message in the dirk's finely honed blade.

Ignoring her nakedness and the water dripping from her hair, she addressed the man huddled before her. "Never have I seen such a pitiful pile of filth. Who and what are you, man-thing, and what are you doing in this place?"

"I do not understand," he responded in the Northlander's tongue.

"Perhaps another language," Élandine suggested. He kept his drawn rapier resting comfortably in his hand.

Yarwyn was careful not to acknowledge the male's comment, though she took his advice. "Who are you?" she asked again, this time in the ancient language of the High Elves.

"Know you the speech of the Humans?" Seanen countered.

Yarwyn turned to Élandine, her face a mask of frustration. "This is the one. The man-thing who escaped into the moat. I must interrogate him."

Élandine looked the huge invader over carefully, fear still his paramount emotion. "I should hope so. Can't have bunches of them this size running about. Perhaps he is so big that his body has no room for a brain. He may speak only gibberish."

Yarwyn prodded the slave girl. "See if you can communicate with it."

"Yes, Mistress." The girl eyed the huge Northlander warily. She spoke something unintelligible, and Seanen glanced up quickly, then looked down again. He shook his head, once, but his fingers moved in a quick gesture that Yarwyn was sure had some meaning.

"Know you my tongue?" the girl queried in Dwarven.

Seanen glanced up at the girl again, then focused his attention back on the stone floor. "Aye. A little."

"The Priestess would know who you are and how you come to be here."

"I am a slave," he replied in careful, halting Dwarven. "I was captured by patrols near the City of Stone on the frozen ground. I was—lifting—carrying barrels of—drink—mead—to the storeroom when the Priestess grabbed me. She frightened me. I was—I tried to get away through the water, but a giant worm creature attacked me and carried me under the water. I killed it. I came up through the kitchen drain."

"You killed it," Yarwyn repeated in the same guttural tongue. "You killed the giant worm creature with your bare hands underwater. Yet you profess to have been afraid of me."

Seanen still fixed his gaze on the floor. "Aye, M'Lady. Mistress."

Yarwyn glanced at Élandine. The Dark Elf didn't seem to find the slave's statement incongruous.

"Why don't you keep him, Mistress," Élandine suggested. "He may amuse you. But I would keep him chained. Even if there's only one like this, no one has ever escaped the worm before."

Yarwyn glanced down at the slave, disgust evident in her voice. "He's filthy. Clean him up. Bring him to me when he is presentable."

* * * * *

Seanen swallowed his outrage, painting himself the picture of a docile slave as he allowed himself to be shackled. Inside, every fiber of his being was screaming at him to throttle the small Dark Elf male in front of him and make his escape. He couldn't. He was an actor, playing his role, just like the cast of the traveling theatre troupes who'd visited the Northlands when he was a child. He'd dreamed of joining their troupe, of leaving that squalid hovel behind even then.

At least he was clean. Even his ragged kilt had been washed and wrapped back around him, though the technique could use work. He followed his captor down a long hall with a series of broad, stout doors lining its sides. The Dark Elf knocked softly on one near the end, waiting for a call from within before he lifted the latch to enter.

Seanen caught his breath, staring at the sight before him. The small chamber was simplistic in design, functional and sparsely furnished, hardly befitting a Dark Elf Priestess. The slaves had worked quickly, transforming the room with pots of scented oils and drapes of silk and pillows of deep, rich velvet until the room took on an air of exotic fantasy.

Yarwyn herself was the center of the tableau. The Dwarven slave girl had attended to the Priestess, anointing her hair with oils that made it reflect a violet sheen much like her eyes. They had dressed her in a fine, colorful silk robe and leggings that shimmered in the light of late afternoon. She might as well have been naked. The translucent silks did nothing to disguise the curve of her breasts or the outline of her nipples. Seanen felt his body respond both to the woman who was his lover and to the exotic ebony beauty before him.

Seanen found one set of chains exchanged for another as the male shoved him back hard against the wall. The Dark Elf yanked the tartan off him, dropping the plaid in a casual heap at his feet. Whatever he said made Yarwyn laugh, though her laughter stilled when she ran her eyes over his body, admiring him as an intimate stranger. The Dark Elf spoke again, his tone both familiar and suggestive.

Yarwyn shook her head, dismissing the Dark Elf with a casual wave of her hand. She slid off the bed, her attention fixed blatantly upon Seanen's naked body as she crossed the room to the open door. She waited, her hand pointedly resting on the latch, as the Dark Elf took his cue, bowing as he backed out the door. Seanen found that one's eyes on him most unpleasant. It was a great relief when Yarwyn snapped the latch shut behind him.

The relief ended when she turned back to face Seanen, crossing the room like a large, predatory cat stalking its prey. A shudder of something between fear and excitement passed over him. "Get me out of these chains," he demanded, though his voice felt less than forceful.

She traced a gold-plated nail over the manacle on his wrist, then trailed her fingertip along his arm. "I cannot. I don't have the key."

Yarwyn didn't look as if the thought of leaving him in chains disturbed her overly much. Seanen's heart thrashed against his ribs. Her sharp features reminded him more and more of a feral cat. She stopped before him close enough to touch him, but just out of his reach, dropping the bright flowing robe from her shoulders so that it puddled slowly on the floor like a misplaced scattering of flowers.

She moved in closer, brushing against him, then backing away. "Do you know what it did to me, thinking you were dead?" she whispered, her voice deep and husky with sex.

He would not respond to her. Not like this. He would not surrender himself to be used like a tool. He willed his body not to respond. Still, he had to swallow hard before he could find his voice. "Shall I apologize for having survived?" The words didn't come out nearly as angry or as defiant as he would have liked them to. Perhaps because as she brushed against him he had forgotten to breathe.

"Don't fight your feelings," she whispered. "I know what you want."

Seanen tried to focus on the anger, but it was slipping away as her body enticed him. "No," he managed. "You don't know what I want. Not if you think I would condone this."

Yarwyn ran a piece of red silk over his arm, trailing it down to his fingers, then slipping away so that he was left with nothing but the silk to hold. "Isn't this every man's fantasy, to be held captive by a woman who desires his body for sex?"

"No," Seanen argued. "I will not. Not like this."

Yarwyn moved in again, teasing, touching, deliberately grazed the edge of her teeth over the tight, hard nub of his nipple. "You cannot lie to me," she scolded. "I will always know."

To hell with not responding. He would have her, and have her now. He lunged against the restraints, determined to tear them from the wall until he could get at her.

"Cease!" Yarwyn ordered, concern in her voice. "You will hurt yourself!"

When he ignored her, she simply stretched her hands over the length of his arms until she stood pressed flat against him, so that he could not shift a muscle without feeling her skin against his. His cock twitched convulsively in response to her nearness, just grazing the mound of soft curls at the top of those long, long, silk covered legs.

Frustration warred with desire. It didn't help any that he was sure the little Dark Elf male stood listening at the door. "Have I no rights over my own body?" he demanded, not even trying to shield her from his anger.

Yarwyn drew her hands back up his arms to capture his head, holding him with a strength he had not suspected her small body capable of, stretching up on her toes to plunder his mouth with a deep, seeking kiss that stilled his hands and nearly stopped his heart. Her hands slipped slowly down to trace the full, hard length of him, while her mouth tasted everywhere, outlining his jaw, working down and across his shoulder, outlining his nipples until he didn't know which was worse, to have her lick and suck and send him shuddering towards what he could not reach, or have her not touch him at all.

"Now what do you want?" she teased.

He tried and failed to remember what he was angry about. "I want you," he admitted.

She nipped his lower lip hard enough to hurt. "But what you want doesn't matter at all, does it, slave?"

He wasn't sure if she was serious, or simply toying with him. She picked up her discarded silk robe and draped it across his chest, teasing him with the feel of the soft fabric as it dripped down his body to hang across his distended shaft. She moved her hands over him again, stroking him slowly with the silk. "Say it."

"No." His tone was more whimper than defiant. He tried again. "No. I will not."

She was so familiar, yet so different, her dark ebony skin a dusky contrast to his expanse of bronze chest. She brushed her nipples across his chest, circling until they rubbed over his, leaving him shuddering with desire. "Say it." Her voice was softer this time, almost an invitation.

He almost moaned the words. "It doesn't matter what I want."

She cupped his straining balls in the silk, lifting, kneading, testing the weight of him, until he meant the words he'd spoken. "Then what does matter?"

"You," he rasped out. "Pleasing you."

She moved closer, rubbing the tip of his penis over her mound, stroking herself with him until he thought he might spurt with the need of her. "Good. You may yet make an excellent slave."

Her breasts brushed over his chest again, the nipples tight and hard, but he couldn't quite reach them to take them in his mouth. "Let me taste you," he almost begged.

She raised one small breast with her hand. "This is what you want?"

His heart thudded against his chest like it might explode. "Please."

Her thumb slowly encircled her nipple as she considered his request, until the delicate plum colored tip hardened under her touch.

He strained towards her, his body ready to burst with this new frustration. "Please," he managed, his voice thick with need. "I promise, you will enjoy this as much as I will."

Stepping closer again, she raised one breast just far enough for him to suck the nipple into his greedy mouth while she continued to stroke herself. Her moan as he circled the hard bud with his tongue told him that he had not lied to her.

Sure, strong hands stripped away the silken barrier of her leggings. She was through teasing him. In a show of athletic prowess she raised herself over him, her long dancer's legs wrapping around his waist to support her as she impaled herself on him, shoving his hips back against the wall.

She set the pace, fast and furious, demanding satisfaction and taking all he had to give. Her hands roamed everywhere, stroking his outstretched arms, caressing his chest, urging his hips on as he pumped into her time and again. Her fingernails clenched into his thighs as the first orgasm shattered her, then stroked up his back as she crested again and yet again.

"Seanen!"

Fear washed over him. It didn't really matter what they did, not here where there was no right and wrong, only master and slave. But out there, on the other side of the door, she wasn't supposed to know his name. He released her breast in favor of her lips, smothering her cries as she gasped his name again. Pulling her closer with the tip of his tongue leveraged against the back of her teeth, he sucked the cries from her with the force of his will.

Despite his fears, or perhaps because of them, he found the experience heightened his sexual appetite until she was an all-consuming need, until touching her with as much of his body as he could became paramount. He felt as if his balls might burst from the need to fill her, yet he managed to hold back, giving her pleasure as long as he could, knowing that his release would end this, would move her out of his reach, would leave him alone here and desolate.

Need overpowered the fear as he thrust into her again and again, straining against his bonds to fill her tight, wet sheath with all of his length. Desperation drove him into her with all his strength.

The male Dark Elf might reappear at any moment. Seanen pushed himself toward climax with a final frantic fury. She was slipping from him as her sated body began to wilt against him. "Now!" she demanded, her nails clawing his back. "Now!"

The release was shattering, as if his balls had opened up to spill a lifetime's treasury into her. His heart felt as if it had exploded in his chest, and the room went black for a moment before he tumbled slowly back to the world where he hung naked, chained to a cold stone wall, while the woman he'd come to need more than life itself slid slowly down his drained body.

A soft rap sounded at the door. Yarwyn roused herself enough to recover her robe and her silken leggings, wiping herself down with a piece of toweling as she did her best to restore her careless Dark Elven Priestess image. Just as he'd suspected, the Dark Elf male leaned lazily against the doorframe when she opened the latch. Seanen had no doubt but that he'd never moved farther than the corridor when she'd dismissed him.

The ebony face took on a trace of cynical humor as he surveyed the scene. "I see that you have finished with the slave, Mistress. I return to offer my services."

Anger flushed Seanen's face. He would not stand by while some other man used his woman. But as the Dark Elf moved across the room, understanding dawned. The Dark Elf wasn't interested in Yarwyn's person. He had his eyes fixed on Seanen's naked, exposed body.

Chapter Five

Yarwyn glanced casually over her shoulder as Élandine followed her into the room. "I have no need of your services at the moment."

Élandine had his eyes fastened on Seanen's naked body. The young male would enjoy this, she was sure. The lust that trailed off that one was dark and evil. "I know your tastes, Mistress. I shall endeavor to provide you with ample entertainment."

Entertainment? A Dark Elf Priestess would find *that* entertaining to watch? Yarwyn searched frantically for some way to divert Élandine's attentions without alerting his suspicions. She tried to sound bored. "The slave will not be of any use for a while."

Élandine turned back to her, amusement blending into his lust. "That will not matter, Mistress. He will only be more compliant."

Compliant? She didn't think so. Not Seanen. Not for anyone but her.

Anger stirred within her, and perhaps a bit of jealousy at the way Élandine eyed Seanen's exposed body, but she kept those emotions out of her face. Instead she ran the tip of her fingernail down Élandine's bare chest. His skin was as smooth and soft as a young girl's. "Perhaps you shall entertain me after all." Her low laugh was calculated to stir Élandine's blood. "Do you think it is safe to unchain this one?"

Élandine let his eyes drift over her. "I trust the prisoner will not escape you again."

Yarwyn smiled her agreement as she turned back to latch the door, waiting until the Dark Elf's attention was focused once again on Seanen to reclaim her small leather pack. She could feel the anger and defiance radiating from Seanen from across the room. Though he wasn't attempting to tear the manacles out of the wall this time, he drew his breath in deeply, prepared, she was sure, to fight Élandine with every ounce of strength he possessed. Seanen might have played along with her game, but he'd never allow this. If she didn't act quickly, she knew he'd hurt himself.

She wasn't sure Seanen saw her slide the little dirk into her hands, but she didn't dare leave it exposed long enough to make sure she had his attention. Élandine stood before Seanen, just out of reach, slowly disrobing. "It won't do you any good to fight me, big man-thing, but go ahead and try. I shall enjoy your efforts."

"He doesn't understand you," Yarwyn commented blandly. "He doesn't speak our language."

Élandine turned to face her, his naked body revealing the strength of his desire. "Too bad. Perhaps if he understood me he might fight me even harder."

Seanen's eyes fixed on her over Élandine's shoulder, calm and steady. She relaxed just a little. Seanen had seen her draw the little dirk and he was ready. She moved in on Élandine, running her hands over his chest. "I won't fight you at all." She lowered her lips to his chest, circling the areola with the tip of her tongue before she bit down hard.

Surprised by the sudden pain, the Dark Elf took a step backward, away from her, and much too close to Seanen. Strong muscled legs clamped around the small, dark head like a vise while those mighty forearms supported Seanen's weight against the wall. Yarwyn plunged her knife between the ribs and pushed and twisted toward his heart, hoping she'd hit hard enough to finish things off quickly. Fury blazed from the pale silver eyes, then hatred as they gradually grew dim. Yarwyn pulled her little dirk free and wiped it clean on his shimmering silk robe as Seanen let the body slide to the floor.

In the robe's pocket she found what she was looking for. She dangled the iron ring from her finger as she turned back toward Seanen. "Now I have the keys."

He said nothing, his eyes fixed on her as she unlocked first his left wrist, and then his right. His wrists were raw and bloodied, and she would have healed him, but when she tried to capture those wrists again he captured her instead, wrapping his arms around her possessively.

She was as unfamiliar with the emotions pouring off of him as she was with the way his arms wrapped around her. There had been few hugs in Yarwyn's life. She stood absolutely still for a moment, unsure how to respond, but the simple affection was her undoing. Her arms rose, almost of their own volition, to tighten fiercely around him, holding, possessing, sheltering, protecting, even as he protected her. All the emotions she'd kept carefully in check since she'd seen the worm drag him under came crashing through, until her fear burned itself out against his chest in hot, angry tears.

* * * * *

Seanen held her, satisfied for now to know that they were both safe. The feel of her body against his, small and soft and whole, reassured him that they were both alive and relatively unscathed. He didn't expect the sudden strength with which she returned his embrace, couldn't have predicted the way it would overwhelm him with a jumble of unfamiliar emotions, all soft and tender and protective. Her tears against his chest sealed his fate. He slid one arm down, behind her knees, scooping her up to carry her gently toward the bed.

She curled herself around him under the covers, her head against his chest, her arms and legs entwining with his, as if she needed to touch him as badly as he needed to feel her skin pressed against his. He whispered her name softly, then again.

"Yarwyn."

"Seanen." She smiled up at him, her eyes wet with tears. "You see, I still remember your name."

He kissed each eye, admiring the soft, beautiful skin of her eyelids. "I know the timing isn't good, but I need to tell you something."

She pulled back a little, sudden fear in her eyes as she looked up at him. "What?"

He was a fool. He was going to frighten her, chase her away, destroy the closeness that had built up between them. What had he been thinking? He was but a child to her, a toy she'd soon tire of.

"What?"

Fear tinged her voice. He recognized the sound of it. Not the fear of death in battle. A far stronger fear. The kind of fear that could only happen when you trusted someone with your heart. Seanen caressed her head with one hand, trying to reassure her even as he found the courage to speak the words. "I'm falling in love with you."

"No." She shook her head, like a dog trying to clear its ears. "No. You love making love to me. You love the way my body feels in your hands. You might even like being chained up occasionally as long as I have the keys. But you don't love me."

He wasn't sure what response he'd expected, maybe none at all, but whatever it was, he'd never expected the fierce, almost angry denial she threw back at him. He kept his tone low and even, trying not to frighten her any more than he already had. "I admire your body, and your spirit, but you don't need chains to hold me, little Elf. You have my heart."

"No—"

"I love you, Yarwyn."

She drew up into a tight little ball, hugging her knees to her chest as she rolled away from him. Hard, angry sobs shook her slender frame. "You don't even know me. I am a lie, built upon lies. I am nothing anyone could ever love."

Seanen jackknifed his knees under hers, his arms encircling her as she cried out her grief. "I love you, Yarwyn. No matter who or what you really are. It doesn't matter, Yarwyn. I love *you*." He kissed her ear, where he knew she was the most sensitive. "Unless…"

She turned toward him, her sobs quieting, her eyes desperate. "Unless what?"

"You're not really an Orc, are you? That would take very strong magic."

She blinked once, twice, a hint of a smile appearing. "I'm not an Orc," she murmured.

"Or a troll?"

Despite herself she was beginning to giggle. "Or a troll."

"Good, because I really don't go for green skin." He kissed her lips, tasting them thoughtfully. "I suppose an Ogre might be feasible, though we'd have to be careful, or you'd crush me."

Her voice came through low and frightened and even sexier for its breathiness. "How about the bastard daughter of a tavern whore who sold her child to the temple Priestesses for the price of another bottle of mead?"

This—this was the secret she'd tried to keep hidden from him? He did his best not to laugh. Instead he kissed her gently on the forehead. "How about you give me a lifetime to think it over?"

"A lifetime?" Her voice caught, then steadied. "What shall we do while you're thinking?"

Seanen glanced at the traces of light beginning to filter in through the slits of the castle walls. "Well, we could kill the King and another Dark Elf or two and get the hell out of here. Then if there's anything left of our armies we could help clean up the mess and get an escort back to House Yarishet or House Lochinvar or just about anywhere in the known world you'd like to go next."

"Anywhere?"

"Anywhere."

"I'm not fond of cold."

"Mmm." He kissed the top of her head. "What about the desert cities, then? Too hot?"

"You would leave Lady Lochinvar's household for me?"

"Lady Lochinvar has been more than an employer to me. Almost a mother at times. Her faith in me kept me from losing my hand, and gave me the means to become whatever I have made of myself. I would not like to part company with her, though I would, if it were necessary to keep us together. But I was thinking of a post she asked me to take some time ago. Ambassador to Port City, on the ocean at the edge of the desert. She felt my talents might prove useful there."

Yarwyn pressed her face against his chest. "Seanen?"

"Mmm?"

"If I tell you something, will you try not to laugh at me?"

He held her slender form tightly, lest she feel him tremble. "I will not laugh at you."

Her breath came out in a hot rush against his chest. "I think I fell in love with you the first time I saw you. My knees went so weak I had to sit down. I thought my heart might fall right out of my chest at your feet."

"Ha." For some reason the image pleased him enormously. "I thought you were still a child. But your voice...your voice had me wanting things a man has no right to want from a child."

Worry crept back into her voice. "Seanen, I've never...that is, I don't know if I'm any good at—I've never felt more for a man that just the need of the moment. The idea of a relationship...I'm frightened."

He blinked hard at the picture. "A relationship. I guess that's what this is. The thought has never occurred to me. I never expected to find a woman who'd consider me as more than a temporary diversion. Perhaps we shall have to learn how this works. Together."

"It will mean a change in our lifestyles."

Seanen glanced around the small stone-walled room, taking in the manacles hanging from the wall, the blood pooling around the corpse on the floor. "Maybe our lifestyles could use a change."

He felt more than heard the laughter that shook her. "You think?"

"Yea." Seanen ran his hand over the long, dark length of her thigh and up the curve of her hip until it rested on her waist. "You know, I never properly thanked you for preserving my virtue."

She snorted. "Your virtue had nothing to do with it. I was jealous. I don't share what's mine with anyone."

"Good." He kissed her tenderly, a sweet, soft, bonding of lips that brought his blood to a slow, languorous boil. "I think I'm going to like being yours." He kissed her eyelids, working his way slowly across to her ear, feeling her shiver in anticipation as he touched his tongue to the lower lobe, lifting it into his mouth to suckle gently before he moved on to the sensitive upper tip. He rolled over her, supporting his weight on his elbows as he looked down on her small, fragile body. "And who do you belong to?"

Tremors shook her body as he drew the point of her long, delicate ear into his mouth. "Seanen," she breathed. "Only you."

She was ready when he entered her, already tight and wet and hot as the fires of all the hells. He moved slowly, sinking into her welcoming flesh, then pulling back, savoring, tasting, enjoying the feeling that was so much more than anything he'd felt with any other woman. "You make me feel like a virgin again," he whispered.

"You make me feel like I'll die if I can't have all of you now."

He pushed in again, plundering her depths, finding a better fit than he had with any other woman. "I've had sex before. You know that. But I've never made love to any woman but you."

Her hands moved to frame his face as she kissed him, her eyes soft and damp around the lashes. "I've never loved anyone before. I love you, Seanen. Only you."

He stilled within her, feeling her pulse beating frantically against him in long, shimmering waves. She'd said she'd fallen in love with him, but this, this was different. Nothing in his life had prepared him for the depth of this emotion. "No one's ever loved me before," he whispered.

"Well, I do. Maybe we have a lot to learn together."

He laughed at that, happier than he could ever remember feeling. She moved against him, trying to pull him further into her hot, wet depths. Instead he withdrew, just a little, giving her more room to move. "Yes? Is there something you want?"

"You. I want you."

He grinned at her, sliding out, then slowly back in, feeling every ridge of her as she pulsed against him. He ran his tongue over her eyebrow, watching her shuddered response as he moved closer to the ear he'd neglected so far. She cried out as he pushed farther into her, then withdrew again, picking up the pace just slightly. She was almost there. He could feel his slow, careful movements pushing her over the edge. She tightened around him like a fist, building the answering need within him until the pace he'd set for himself seemed unbearably difficult to maintain.

"Seanen." She thrust her hips against him, urging him to increase his pace.

"Not yet, my love." He withdrew completely, sliding slowly down her body until he held her hips in his hands. He spread her lower lips, caressing her thighs as he sucked her juices into his mouth. His tongue circled her clitoris, tracing its outline while her hands fisted in his hair.

"Seanen!"

He blew soft, warm breath onto her sensitive flesh, holding her when she would have twisted away, then licking gently, loving the torture he'd created for her. Another hot flood of juices poured from her, and he licked them up, exploring her flesh with his tongue. She thrust against him, her hands grasping at him, her voice a whimpering moan as she burst under his gentle, slow ministrations. He ran his tongue around her clitoris, wetting her with her own juices.

"I want you," she whimpered as she broke under him again.

"And I want you."

She cried out as he thrust into her again, no longer gentle, and she clenched around him as he felt his own need build to the point of no return. He set a furious pace, giving her everything she asked for, suckling her ears in turn as they moved toward the final precipice.

She came beneath him with a final spasm, clenching so tightly around him that he felt as if she'd pulled the final response from him. His orgasm shook him so that he felt the room go dim for a moment, felt himself collapsing over her, without the strength to support his own body weight.

When he finally remembered to breath again, she still held him fiercely, as if determined not to let him get away, apparently not at all concerned that he might crush her. Which was just as well, for he still hadn't the strength to move.

"You shall be the death of me," he managed. "But what a way to die."

Chapter Six

"The sun's up."

"I know."

Yarwyn propped herself up on one elbow so that she could study his face. "Have I ever told you how much I enjoy looking at you?"

He snorted softly. "You're daft, woman."

She cupped his chin to plant a gentle kiss on his lips. "That's one of the things I like about you. You really have no idea how incredibly attractive you are."

His eyes closed when she kissed him, and a look almost like pain stole across his face. The emotions she felt from him now were alien to her experience, but so comforting. Possessiveness, mixed with something akin to lust, but softer and yet more powerful. If this was love, it would surely be her undoing. She snuggled down in his arms for a few stolen minutes, not wanting to be the one to move first.

* * * * *

She fit into his arms so perfectly. Who'd have ever thought that such a fragile creature could take such a powerful hold on him. Seanen sighed. "This is like a dream world, and as soon as we move, it's over." And if anything happened to her, more than these few stolen minutes of peaceful intimacy would be lost. If he'd had it in his power, he'd have done the job alone, kept her somewhere safe and protected.

"I wish I could do this alone, without putting you in so much danger," she whispered against his chest.

Seanen snorted softly. "Aye, girl, I feel the same. I guess we shall have to learn to trust one another to do our jobs. If you're busy worrying about me you won't have your mind on your work, now will you?"

Yarwyn curled a little tighter against him, her ear pressed against his chest. "I love listening to your heartbeat. It sounds so strong. So alive."

"Yarwyn."

She sighed, the sound an admission of defeat. "I trust you. You're the best. I came for you because you are the best. But if anything happens to you, how will I live with myself?"

He ran his fingers through her short silver hair. "I checked on you, you know. You're very good at what you do. Remember that. Do your job, and trust me to do my job. Once we leave this room, we're two professionals. That means the mission comes first. If you want to keep me alive, focus on the job at hand."

Yarwyn kept her ear pressed to his heart. "You have my word. Now you promise me. No unnecessary risks. No more unarmed water-worm hunting."

He stroked her head again. "You have my word. No unnecessary risks."

But then, part of his job was to keep her alive. Toward that end, there were no unnecessary risks…

* * * * *

The door clicked softly shut as the Dark Priestess led her slave from the room. Behind them, the form on the floor that had been Élandine slowly shifted. He was tired. So tired. But, as he had heard the others remind themselves, there was a mission at hand. He drew in the blood that had pooled around this body, consuming it as fuel for his magic.

The current illusion took too much energy. He let it go, shifting forms once again. His bones ached from the torture of being pent up so long. He laid one long, bronzed finger over the wound in his chest, his eyes pressed tightly closed.

Slowly, so slowly, the wound drew together, from the inside out, until at last the skin sealed itself shut. When he could draw his breath again without the burning pain, he crawled to the bed, throwing aside the soiled sheets as he wrapped himself in the bedcovers.

Even if a servant entered the room, they would not know. He was just another dark creature, sleeping off a night of too much wine. He'd recover. He just needed some sleep. He'd be better in a short time. Time enough to finish his mission.

* * * * *

Even in full daylight the corridors were dark and dank. Yarwyn followed in Seanen's footsteps, moving as he moved, marveling at his stealth. She knew how to glide quietly through the forest, making herself almost invisible as she traded shadow for shadow. Seanen could do the same thing here, blending into the stone walls until he was part of the floor, so that at times even she couldn't find him with her eyes.

Her skill at hiding was not nearly so adept. Instead, she used her own small magic to wrap herself in a mist the color of the stone, dissipating the shadow of her body. She kept her breathing slow and even, even as the stone itself breathed in the early morning breeze, and they moved at the speed of a cat stalking its prey.

The corridors were a maze that made little sense to her, though she had the feeling that Seanen led her up and towards the west with each progressive twist and turn. They had studied the same drawings together, and she understood in theory where she needed to go, but she didn't feel it the way Seanen did. The forests were her place. She felt no affinity for the cold stone walls.

The castle was nearly deserted. They occasionally glided by a household servant, but she could sense the body of the Orcish troops had swarmed from these corridors not long ago, in the early hours of the morning, massing, she knew, to face the army of Northlanders and Humans who now stood across the moat before the front gates.

She sensed their emotions now, from where they stood ready to do battle. There was no fear. The army puzzled these brutish creatures more than it frightened them. The thick stone walls were nearly impenetrable, as they well knew. The army could lay siege, but such a siege would be difficult if not impossible to maintain so far from their own supply lines.

Yet the Orcs would open their doors and charge straight into the waiting army simply because it was there. She wondered belatedly if Orcs could even feel fear. They ruled their land because they were physically powerful and well disciplined and they cared not for their own individual lives. Their loyalty was unquestioning. They lived to fulfill the will of their King.

Much like a colony of ants.

Seanen had disappeared again, so well camouflaged that she could only feel his presence as he stopped before a massive bound door sealed with an elaborate looking lock. She heard the slight metallic ping of picks on tumblers as he went to work.

Yarwyn blended into the stone wall, her own magic shimmering around her like a blanket of darkness, as three huge Orc Palace Guards came marching down the hall.

A sharp click sounded. The guards paused by the door where Seanen had stood only moments before. She looked, and looked again, but she could not see so much as a shadow of the man. She couldn't even feel him in her mind now. He'd shut down all of his emotions, becoming truly invisible to her.

The Orc Guards' faces blanked in amazement as the Treasury doors drifted open. The Orcs sprinted into the room, turning left and right as they searched amidst the chaos for intruders. Yarwyn slipped her arm around the last one's neck, slicing him from ear to ear to drop him where he stood.

Ahead of her and to the right another one of the ugly gray creatures spun to face his invisible opponent as she moved toward the third. Attacking had broken her magic, but that didn't necessarily hurt her any. The leader of the Orc guards had heard her victim fall and he turned now to jabber loudly at her, pointing in obvious agitation at the bloodied corpse in the doorway.

Yarwyn shrugged as she stepped over the body to cross the room. The Orc's level of agitation rose as she failed to answer his protests, but she still felt nothing from him but surprise as she plunged her dirk into his heart.

"I think you will find this weapon more to your liking."

The Orc fell dead at her feet, and still she felt nothing. Not even a vacancy where it had been. She stared at the twisted thing as the blood dripped from her dirk. How could they hope to win a war against things that felt no fear?

Seanen's voice pulled her back. She wiped her blade on the dead Orc's tunic before sheathing it, only then turning to see what Seanen held in his hands.

She nearly forgot to breathe. Her mouth watered with an ache to possess at the sight of the ancient bow Seanen held in his hands. She'd heard of the bow, of course. Nemesis. Every Ranger had heard the legend of Nemesis. The bow was smaller than she would have expected, her experienced eye telling her the silver-inlaid rosewood measured but sixty inches from tip to tip. The bow glowed dully in Seanen's hands, a dim light seeming to emanate from the deep blue crystals set into the risers. No one had laid hands on the bow for generations. Not since Talandar had fallen in the battle of the Lost Races.

Seanen seemed to sense her reverence, placing it gently in her nerveless fingers. She lifted her eyes to thank him, but he was gone again, searching amid the reckless piles of debris for some new treasure. Practicality took over. A bow that had lain tossed in the corner of a massive storeroom such as this for over a century might not take well to being forced into service.

There were no polishing clothes to be had in a place like this. Yarwyn wiped the bow down with a rag hacked from the dead Orc's tunic. The silverwork was badly tarnished, looking more black than silver. Numerous dings and scratches marred the ancient surface. One of the Iolite stones was missing. She searched the area where the third Orc had dropped, his neck snapped easily in Seanen's strong grip. On a haphazardly stacked wooden shelf she found a cracked leather bow case containing the missing blue-violet stone and a neatly rolled package of bowstrings. Several quivers of age-hardened arrows lay scattered about as well.

The strings felt like a fine silk-spun wire. She checked each string carefully for wear and rot, but they appeared ageless. Yarwyn fitted the first string to one ivory tip and drew the other down carefully, listening for any sign of weakness. Better to hang it on the wall in the Rangers Hall as a reminder than to break it now after all these years. The wood curved easily under her hands, amazingly light and springy for its age.

She had no tools to reset the missing stone. Still, she cleaned the small bit of blue fire and placed it into its hole, taking the assembled piece to the small slit of a window to see it more clearly in the sunlight. A small gasp of astonishment escaped her lips, and she almost dropped the bow as the Iolite gems caught fire, blazing forth an eerie blue light that burned the tarnish away from the silver, heating the wood so that it came alive in her hands.

"You will need this," Seanen offered.

Yarwyn looked up to find him holding a set of finely crafted Elven mail of emerald green. She had no soft leather tunic to wear beneath the mail. The colorful silks would have to do for padding. She smiled at the picture she would present. Her smile faded as she looked beyond the mail to the man who held it easily in his hands.

Gone was the cowed slave in remnants of a tattered kilt. Before her stood the most impressive Warrior she'd ever laid eyes on. Seven foot tall and broader of shoulder than the average doorway, he was one of the few men she'd ever seen capable of wielding the mighty battleaxe he now held. The blackened chainmail he wore might have been made for him. The belt at his waist held both an ebony hilted dirk and a short parrying sword. Even the crest on his helm—a green drake etched into the metal and swooping down with wings widespread so that its head rested between Seanen's eyes—looked right.

The kilt sash that crossed his chest was different, a blend of muted blues and greens of a fine woven wool that had survived the years with little signs of age. A bronze-gold broach the size of a man's fist clasped the tartan plaid at his shoulder. Seanen of the House Lindall looked, indeed, the Lord he should have been.

More than the kilt about him was different. He felt different to her. Almost a stranger. "The mail was your father's," she speculated.

"My father drank himself to death when I was four. This was my grandfather's."

Something akin to anger began to form at the back of her brain. She shook her head, trying to make the pieces go another way, but they fell together too neatly. She recognized that thing that burned within him now. Pride held its own lust, as strong as the one he'd felt for her only this morning.

He wanted retribution. He would restore his family's honor. "This is why you entered the Rogues' Guild. To learn the skills that would bring you here one day. To take back what has been stolen from your family."

His voice remained quiet, calm in the face of her accusation. "I am the bastard son of a bastard house, remember? I joined the Rogues' Guild because I was hungry, and a boy on the streets had few choices. I stayed in the Guild after I came under Lady Lochinvar's protection because I wanted to. And because she asked me to. I stand here beside you today because you went to that Guild and asked for a token. Think you now that my Guild picked the wrong man for the job?"

Yarwyn opened her mouth, then shut it again, trying to find the words to answer truthfully. "I think I am afraid. Afraid of who you will become once this is over."

His face softened. "I am who I am, Yarwyn. I am a Rogue. That means I can be a Warrior or a thief as the need arises. The thief got us in here. The Warrior will get us out. Would you have me lie to you, and tell you the chance to reclaim my grandfather's legacy meant nothing to me? I will not. But these things, they are just trappings to me. The chance to avenge my grandfather's death, however, means everything."

It would be easier, so much easier, if things were as they had always been. If she hadn't learned to care. Yarwyn did her best to swallow her fear. She felt drained and as cold as the stone beneath her feet. "Then we will deal with what comes after when the time comes. Let us get the deed done and over with. I am ready." She held out her arms and Seanen slipped the mail shirt over her head.

Seanen tried, she conceded that point to him. She could feel him try to contain the laughter that bubbled up. It was no use. She looked down at herself and shook her head. The mail fit well enough, but bits of colorful silk stuck out at all the edges. She pulled the mesh cap over her head, knowing it would pull at her hair when she tried to take it off. Attired much like the court jester on a very bad day, she slung the ancient bow over her shoulder, gathering up as many quivers as she could carry.

Seanen's hand on her shoulder stopped her. She turned to look up at him, expecting to see the laughter in his eyes. Instead there was something else, something that moved her in a way no words of apology ever could have. He leaned down to kiss her, to stamp her with his own possessive seal, to tell her the only way he could that nothing between them had changed. She moved into his arms, holding him fiercely until she had absorbed as much of his warmth as she could.

"It is time," he whispered.

Chapter Seven

Siege cannons had moved into place. Gallons of hot oil rained down upon the Orcs, setting the closest ones on fire, and blinding those around them. Showers of boulders crashed amongst the lines. The archers loosed thousands of arrows on every target within range. Still, the Orc line held, as indeed the attackers had known it would.

Seanen watched, sickened by the carnage, by the useless waste of it all. So many would die today, and for no purpose. There was no reason for this war. No reason for the Orcs to have strayed beyond their mountains. In all their search of the castle, they had found nothing beyond the occasional slaves and a few Dark Elf males whose bodies they had left to molder in the small stone rooms below. Something, someone, had stirred the Orcs to threaten the Human and Northland populations, and still they did not know what. Nor were they likely to find out, as all who knew the answer would soon be dead...

Tranorva's battle cry split the air. Hundreds of Humans and Northlanders took up her cry. Tranorva's troops held the left-hand side of the field. The combined forces of the Human Houses, under Lord Mâkakao, held the right. Swords and battleaxes rang out. Casters traded spells till the air lit up like fireworks at a festival. Rank upon rank of Orcs went down, their blood making the stone-paved courtyard slick. When one Orc fell, another one would shove the body out of the way and take its place.

From the parapet above the courtyard, separated from the mêlée by a hundred meters and a wide moat whose depths Seanen could attest to, the Orc King watched the battle. Twenty members of the Royal Guard surrounded the King, waiting to do his bidding as he growled and pointed toward the battle. More troops were massed at the gates, waiting for the King's signal. As the numbers on the field began to thin, the King would wave his hand and order the replacements up.

It was a slaughter, really, more than a battle. The Orcs had neither the numbers nor the discipline to counter the highly trained warriors under Tranorva and Mâkakao. They fought with a persistent brutality, swinging their war hammers and hatchets with strength enough to tear a man in two, and many a man went down, but not enough to turn the tide.

Angered by his losses, the Orc King threw up both hands, ordering his reserves into battle en mass, no longer holding back. It was the signal Yarwyn had waited for.

From high above on the watchtower parapet he caught a glimpse of brightly colored silk. The Orc Guard to the right of the King went down, a single arrow protruding from his left eye. Almost before the first Orc had hit the ground, the Orc to the left of the King had joined his fellow, a small shaft vibrating from his chest as he toppled back on his heels. Chaos ensued as the Guards tried to move the King to safety, only to find bodies piling up in their way.

Seanen stepped from the shadows and raised his battleaxe high above his head. "Lindall!" he cried as he brought the axe down, cleaving the first Orc in his path from crown to stern. "Lindall!"

The Orc King was shouting now, ordering the reserves he'd already sent into battle to come to his defense. Yarwyn had thinned his party until there was but a handful of Guards left clustered about him, and those were crowded close as much for protection as his own personal defense. The Orc King turned to face Seanen, his heavy silver battleaxe ready in his hands. The axe might have been largely ceremonial, but the Dwarf who crafted it had given it a finely honed blade as well.

Arrows rained down on the King, but refused to penetrate his enchanted mail. The Orc King stopped where he stood, staring at Seanen with eyes that held more intelligence than

Seanen had expected. The Orc King spoke, his voice harsh and guttural, his thick tongue managing to make himself understood in Seanen's own language.

"So. You have come again, Man-thing, as your words once promised. I had feared you would not come in time. I have grown old waiting for you. Your death amused me last time. I will make the torture longer this time, until you beg me to end your life again. I have sent out Raiders searching for you, so that I can go to my grave in peace. This time I will defile your body, placing your head on a pole, so that your ancestors will not welcome you home. You shall not return to trouble me for a third time."

Rage clouded Seanen's vision as he raised the dripping axe high over his head. "It is you who will die, King, this very day. I will defile your body when you are dead, and I will throw your head to the men below! You will not return to trouble my people again! Your nation shall lay in ruins, and your ancestors shall not write your name in their family books for the shame you have cost them. You will regret the day you decided to war with House Lindall!"

The Orc King charged, feigned, then backed away, circling to Seanen's left, then swung again, bringing the mighty battleaxe up with a back swing that almost caught Seanen off guard. The old Orc was quick on his feet for one of his age, and powerful enough to chip the stone when his swing came down short of its mark.

Seanen waited, darting in, then pulling away, trying to test the old one's strength. They both feigned, looking for any sign of weakness in the other's defense, then swung, their blades locking in midair with a jolt that numbed Seanen's shoulders. The axes tangled on the rebound, and the old Orc attempted to use his weight advantage to knock Seanen off his feet.

Prepared, Seanen stretched to his full height, attempting to twist the weapon from his smaller opponent's grasp. Neither tactic worked. The two battled in a test of strength and agility for the space of several minutes, until Seanen changed his tactic, lunging suddenly forward, letting the Orc King's own weighted resistance pull him off balance.

The battleaxes slid apart with a loud metallic ping and the Orc King staggered backwards, regaining his footing all too quickly for Seanen's peace of mind. The rain of arrows had stopped, as the King's Guard had fled or died beside him, and any attempt Yarwyn made now to hit the King himself would be just as likely to find Seanen as its mark.

The Orc King was old and shorter than Seanen, though not by much. But he was still an excellently engineered piece of fighting equipment, and age did not seem to have slowed his reflexes or dampened his strength. Their blades clashed again with a sound like a storm moving in. Seanen had counted on his relative youth to turn the tide of battle, but the Orc King showed no signs of tiring. He circled warily, an evil grin splitting his ancient gray skinned face.

"I am glad you have returned, Lindall, for I had grown weary of waiting. I have lived long, and killed often, but I would not have missed this opportunity to kill you again. I shall go to the halls of my ancestors as the only king ever to have defeated the same enemy twice. This battle shall be legendary. When we share our ale around that table in the great hall of beyond, I shall tell the story of your deaths with great enjoyment. You were worth waiting for."

Seanen felt the anger boiling in his blood threatening his reason. He swung again, intent on cleaving the old Orc asunder. Instead his axe met air as the King danced out of his way. He felt a searing pain split his right thigh as the King's parry grazed him, the blade deflected by the ancient mail, but not the force of the impact. Seanen reeled backwards from the blow, nearly losing his footing.

The air around the Orc King shimmered with angry blue heat. A wave of fear hit Seanen, like a fist to the gut. He would die here, and there would be no one to protect Yarwyn. He had to get away. He had to run, had to find her...

The Orc King simmered in bright red flames before him, breaking the chain of the magic. Vines rose up from the stone floor, twining about the King's feet. Lightning crackled through the air, spitting at the defiantly raised battleaxe. Recovering quickly, Seanen surged back into the circle of magic, battling against the Orc King with all his strength. It mattered not that he no longer fought alone. The victory would be no less poignant for having shared it with his mate. For no other could have come to his rescue.

His feet rooted in place, the Orc King still managed to swing his mighty battleaxe with a force that threatened to splinter the handle on Seanen's axe as he parried the blow. The air around them had turned purple now, and Seanen felt a renewed strength flow into his arms. He swung again, pulling back at the last second as the King reached to parry the blow that never landed, trusting the magic to support his weight. The vines chose that moment to dissipate.

With the strength of three generations of rage, Seanen reversed his battleaxe's swing, bringing the sharp honed blade up to split the creature from groin to gullet. The Orc King looked only mildly surprised as his entrails spilled out over his sundered mail. With a strength that defied all logic, he raised his axe again, catching Seanen with a swing that split the black leather greave from his forearm and stained his grandfather's mail with a hot smear of dark red blood.

"Die, you bastard!" Seanen bellowed, swinging the axe once again with all the power of his rage and pain. The Orc King merely offered up an evil grin, making no attempt to block the blow that severed his head from his shoulders. A hiss of swirling blue-green smoke rose from the corpse as the body sank slowly to the stone floor.

Seanen ignored the blood that ran down his arm as he grabbed the sundered head from the cold stone paving. Raising the head high in one arm and the battleaxe of his grandfather's house in the other, he moved to the edge of the parapet. "Lindall!" he screamed. The battling troops paused to raise their eyes to the madman on the wall. "Lindall!" Seanen swung the gory trophy by its meager hair, sending it sailing down into the midst of the Orc soldiers. "Lindall!"

The Humans and Northlanders surged forward, overrunning the outnumbered remains of the Orcish army. The Orcs broke, turning to run, but there was no place for them to go but into the moat or across the bridge toward the castle.

Blood stained the paved courtyard below until the stone turned a dark crimson. Seanen turned from the carnage, the battle rage fading, to leave him feeling older and tired beyond belief. The axe dangled from his arm, almost too heavy to hold. He needed to do something about the blood running from his arm, but first he needed to find Yarwyn. He needed to hold her, needed to feel once again that sense of peace and rightness with the world.

"Seanen."

He raised his eyes to her face, too tired to ask how she had come to him or when, too tired to care. She had taken the antidote. Her skin had faded back to its natural ivory, looking pale against the colorful silks. Magic flowed from her, healing his wounds even as his arms closed around her, his lips finding hers as she returned his embrace.

"Seanen."

The voice jolted, shocking him down to his toes. It was Yarwyn's voice, the same as it had been only moments before, but filled with deep foreboding now. He raised his eyes to the place where the voice had come from. The axe dropped from his nerveless fingers. Yarwyn stood, at the far side of the parapet, next to the door, her colorful silks streaming from beneath the Elven mail, the ancient bow slug over her shoulder, her dirk ready in her right hand.

The woman in his arms turned to face the one across the courtyard. Seanen pulled back, comparing the two. They were the two sides of the same woman, one dark, one pale, one dressed in silks, one in mail.

"What are you?" they demanded, both speaking at once. They circled each other, moving slowly, like dancers in the mirror. Anger stabbed between them, raking the air with uneasy blue magic.

Changeling. The word came to his mind unbidden. Seanen studied them both, looking for differences, finding more that was the same. The lips that had touched his had felt so right, the magic that healed him so familiar. Yet the other Yarwyn looked so much like his own. He'd heard of changelings, of course, knew they existed, a magic as old as the stones. He'd never seen one before, or if he had, had never been aware of its existence.

"Seanen," the darker one warned, "There can be only one reason for this deception. The Changeling will hurt you. You must destroy it."

"True," the paler one agreed. "And you have no way to know which one of us has been sent here to kill you. There can be but one solution. Destroy us both."

The darker Yarwyn drew in her breath sharply. "I hate to agree with this one, but I see no other solution."

Seanen moved slowly toward them, running through the possibilities in his mind. If he chose wrongly, the damage the Changeling might do him would be of no consequence, for he would have lost the woman he loved. He had to choose, and choose correctly, for he could not accept their solution. The Changeling would be counting on that. He held out his arms to the pale one. She sobbed against him, turning to look over her shoulder at the other one. "You should have known he would recognize me," she hissed.

The darker one paled visibly, fear filling her eyes. "Seanen," she breathed.

He met her eyes, hoping she really could read his thoughts. "I'm sorry," he offered. With a swift move of his hand he brought the other one's arm up behind her back, laying the edge of his dirk against her neck. "What are you, Élandine, or whatever your name is?"

The thing in his arms shrieked and twisted, changing forms even as it attempted to escape. He held it tight, refusing to let it escape, though even the bones beneath its skin seemed to be viscous.

It was an Orc, then a troll, his strength almost overwhelming Seanen before the blade against its skin pressed deep enough to draw blood. It went limp in his hands, but even that did not persuade Seanen to loose his hold. It shifted again, this time reverting to its Dark Elven form. "How did you know?" he asked calmly.

Seanen shrugged. "When you looked at me, all I could see was the lust. There was no love in your eyes."

Élandine shrugged.

"I killed you," Yarwyn sputtered, staring at the Dark Elf in horror. "You died in my hands."

"Simple magic. Feign death. Had you truly been a Dark Elf, you would have known that our hearts are on the opposite side from yours. But I must say, you're stronger than you look. You nearly managed to finish the deed from the blood loss alone." He looked up at Seanen over his shoulder. "What shall you do with me now, Northlander? If you're going to kill me please get it over with. It's been a very long day."

Seanen used the silk scarf wrapped around Élandine's waist to bind his wrists. "Your day will be longer, Dark One. I shall leave your fate to other hands." He pushed Élandine ahead of him as he slipped his arm around Yarwyn's waist. She had retrieved his battleaxe, though she held it with both hands, supporting its weight with her arm. He wrapped his hand around the shaft, lifting it easily from her fingers. "The battle is won, but it is far from over. Let us give aid where we can."

* * * * *

The bonfires blazed at the center of camp, an act of defiance against the few Orcs that had survived the day's massacre. The Humans and Northlanders mingled freely now, sharing the treasures in the Orc King's wine cellar. Many of the Northlanders had stripped to their kilts to dance in a circle around the fire.

Yarwyn knew the revelry would last far into the morning. She almost wished she could join in the celebrations. She didn't know how to explain to Seanen that she could not, or why. Not without revealing her deception. He'd insisted she stay by his side, and she had, but the swirling emotions of the revelers were slowly tearing her apart. Emotions bombarded her from all sides. The chaos of the battle lust mixed with the drunken frenzy about her until she could no longer discern which emotions came from where.

The strongest emotions she had to battle were from within. She was jealous. There was no way around it. She was angry and jealous and bitter. Not of Seanen. No. True enough, he was the one at the center of everyone's attention. When ballads were sung of this war it would be Seanen's name that people remembered, not hers. But that was the way of things. House Lindall had had its long overdue moment of triumph. Seanen deserved his recognition.

No, it was not Seanen who sparked Yarwyn's ire. It was Tranorva. Tranorva was at her best tonight. Filthy and bloodstained and covered with the gore of her enemies, she sat amongst her soldiers as their equal, her mail tossed aside, her long black hair lifting lightly with the breeze, her magnificent figure clad only in a sleeveless leather undertunic, and her mind was focused where it had no business being.

She had finally noticed Seanen.

Any woman would notice Seanen. Tonight he looked the part of the Warrior. He stood half a head taller than those around him. His grandfather's helm made him look even fiercer. The dragon swooping down between his eyes reflected the firelight until it looked ready to attack. He moved easily amongst the soldiers, for position and status held no rank here. He smiled and laughed and retold the story of the Orc King's death, as he might have back in the taverns of Yarishet.

And Tranorva watched. She talked to those closest to her, and she shared their ale all too freely, but her thoughts were focused on Seanen. Yarwyn could feel the lust rising in her, bringing her blood to almost as hard a boil as the battle rage had.

How could she ever have thought that one cold? Tranorva might have no lust for the court or the dance floor, but here she was in her element, and here she was the soul of passion. The woman was predatory. She would not sleep alone tonight, and she had set Seanen as her target.

Seanen's attention focused on the storytelling. Yarwyn slipped slowly back away from the crowd, trying to regain control. She paced the line of the shadows, blending into the darkness, trying to do battle with her unreasonable anger. She wanted to strike out, to unsheathe her dirk and slip up behind Tranorva before she had a chance to touch what Yarwyn had no intention of sharing.

Yarwyn knew she could get in close enough to do real harm without ever being detected. As the woman's eyes raked over Seanen's body as if he stood before them naked again, Yarwyn decided it was time to test her theory. She moved with the stealth of a cat stalking its prey. Closer. Closer. She was within a meter of her victim before strong hands lifted her off the ground, turning her in the air so that she came down plastered against a massive chest that could only belong to Seanen.

His breath came in a hiss against her ear. "What do you think you're doing?" He bent his head over hers so that the drunken revelers around them cheered, thinking their newfound hero embraced his lady-love.

"I'm going to kill her."

"I could see that. Why?"

Anger flared up hot and red before her eyes, venting itself on Seanen. "Do not play the innocent with me! If you want her enough to defend her take what you want! I am done with you both!"

Seanen merely scooped her up into his arms, despite her attempt to free herself, and carried her away from the bonfire and the heat of the lusts that lingered there. He pried the dirk from her fingers as he carried her, tucking it safely out of her reach. When he stopped they were alone at the perimeter of the camp, in front of a large pavilion tent. Seanen thrust the door aside with his shoulder to gain them entrance.

"Put me down," Yarwyn ordered, calmer now, but still angry.

Seanen did as she requested, depositing her none too gently into a pile of pillows that shifted atop a thick feather bed. He ran a hand through his thick mane of hair, his mind a jumbled mix of emotions. "You know Tranorva would have killed you."

"She would never have known I was there."

"Think you this a logical plan? To kill the daughter of the House I am sworn to protect? Would you ask me to choose between my duty and my heart? Would you leave me bereft of all honor?"

"Honor?" Yarwyn's voice rose to a screech. "What honor is there in this? You profess to love me, yet you would defend that—that—monolith when she would steal what is mine!"

Seanen stared at her, his expression unreadable, her mind too overloaded to sort out his emotions from all the others. With slow, deliberate movements he stripped off his armor, setting his weapons in the rafters, well out of her reach. His eyes alone held her captive, for she was too confused and overwhelmed to know whether to run or attack. When he had done away with his own armor, he began on hers.

He had stripped her naked before his intent registered on her beleaguered mind. Her rage rose to the heat of the bonfire the men had built. "Do you think that sex can cure everything?"

He captured her fists in his hands before they could attempt to do him damage. "I think," he answered carefully, "that you have lied to me. You told me once that reading people's minds would overwhelm you with noise. I think also that you are very angry. If you wish to vent that anger, vent it on me. Whatever is wrong here, it stays here, between us. You will not leave here until I can trust you again."

"I cannot read minds," she insisted once again. "But perhaps you can read mine." She brought a knee up hard into his groin, but he was not there. A leg wrapped around hers, sending them both tumbling into the pillows, their hands still locked. He landed on top of her, his mouth coming down to cover hers, his lips hard and demanding. His hands released hers to stroke over her body, lighting the flames until she could not tell anger from desire. She shoved hard at him, and he let her roll him to his side, though his leg stayed hooked over hers. She attacked again, but this time with her mouth, licking and nipping her way down his neck until she reached his chest.

That broad expanse of chest would always be her undoing. She traced the lines of the blue runes with her lips, following the longest one down, until it blended with the dark hair that led up from below. She would make him pay.

She felt the sharp intake of his breath, pleased with herself, knowing she had already won. He breathed her name when she took his rigid shaft into her mouth, pushing the foreskin back, circling the tip with her tongue.

It was hard to remember that she was angry with him when these other emotions threatened to overwhelm her, but she tried. She would punish him. She would…

Strong hands moved to stroke her head, stopping to fist for a moment in her hair, then moving on to trace the outline of her ears. His fingers slid down, lifting her until she found herself face to face with him again.

There was no limit to how low he would sink. He took her ear in his mouth, sucking gently on the tip until the room faded to a swirling mass of colors. A long shuddering moan broke from her lips. Her eyes slid closed, and she knew she had lost.

"Emotions," she managed. His tongue outlined the ridge of her ear, sliding slowly along the most sensitive edges.

"Sometimes I can sense emotions. Only strong ones. I can't get inside your mind."

"Emotions." He pulled back to study her face. "What do you feel from me now?"

Cautiously Yarwyn lowered her defenses. She closed her eyes and opened herself up to him, letting him pour inside. The intensity shook her. Love and lust swirled together until there was no room for anything else. The last traces of anger swept away with the rising tide of desire. "I need you," she whispered. Tears streamed down her face as she found his mouth and kissed him the way she'd wanted to all evening.

As if he'd made it his mission to drive out her demons, Seanen took control. His hands worshipped her body, first soft, then demanding, as she arched against him, her body aching for the feel of his touch. His hand stroked down her back until he reached her hips, pulling her more tightly against his swollen cock as he flicked his tongue lightly over her nipple. "Who am I?" he demanded.

"Seanen!" she moaned, as much a plea as a response. The heat of his breath against her neck sent her pulse hammering against his lips.

"What do you want?"

"I want you," she moaned. Her voice broke as he cupped her mound with one huge hand. "I need you."

He slipped a finger inside of her hot, wet flesh, teasing, torturing, promising more as she shuddered around him, already breaking with desire. Pinning her into the pillows, he hovered above her, the tip of his cock resting against her so that she writhed under him, seeking to push up onto him, whimpering in frustration when he simply rose out of her reach.

He brushed his lips over hers, teasing her with his tongue, then taking possession. She fought him now, trying to free her hands. She wanted to touch him everywhere. She rose up against him, brushing her breasts across his chest, her nipples painfully hard.

"Please," she gasped.

"Please what?"

"I want to feel you inside of me."

"What do you feel from me now, Yarwyn?"

It was impossible to tell where he ended and she began. "Everything," she moaned.

"There is only room for one woman in my heart. Can you feel what I feel for you now?"

"Yes." Yarwyn strained against him, urging him to fill the ache within her.

He pushed against her, almost gaining entrance before he withdrew, sliding his hot, rigid shaft up over her swollen lips instead. "Tell me what you feel. Say it."

She couldn't. She wouldn't.

Warm breath caressed her neck, her cheek, her sensitive ear. "Tell me."

"You love me," she gasped, the words tearing from her with a sob.

Her body shuddered to climax as he came down on top of her, driving into her with all the force of unrestrained desire. He released her hands, finding his own necessary to stroke and to hold as he filled her again and again. She crested, and crested again, each wave hitting her harder as he built the need within her, his hands worshipping her everywhere, stroking her breasts and her thighs and her neck.

"Seanen!" she cried, arching mindlessly against him, meeting him stroke for stroke. Her hands raked though his hair, pulling him tightly against her as their lips met again. She felt herself clench around him like a tightly closed fist, shattering her world into so many points of radiant light. He pushed into her again with one long, last shuddering thrust, filling her with a gush of hot, wet seed.

A long, eerie wail broke the still of the chill night air, the mating call of the white arctic wolf. From somewhere far away she heard an answer, only dimly aware that the voice was her own.

* * * * *

She felt so small and vulnerable. Seanen curled around her, trapping their warmth within the shelter of the furs he'd drawn over them, protecting her with his body, wishing he had some way to protect her mind. She stirred beside him, turning in his arms to study his face in the dim light of the stars.

"The more I know of you, the less I understand." He kissed her gently on the forehead. "You are beautiful and talented and held in high esteem by all who have dealings with your Guild. I marvel the fates that brought you into my arms. I would not hold you prisoner, but know that wherever you go, you take my heart."

Yarwyn traced the runes that ran across his chest with the tips of her fingers. "I shall always be your prisoner," she countered. "You hold the key to my heart within yours."

Epilogue

Seanen stood at formal parade rest, eyes forward, feet spread slightly apart, hands clasped behind his back, every ring of his grandfather's blackened mail buffed clean and lying precisely in place. He hated waiting. Always had. Seemed like he'd been standing here for hours. He didn't belong here. He didn't want to be here. Not now. Not for this reason. But one simply did not ignore an invitation from Lady Lochinvar.

A murmur like the buzzing of flies drifted around the crowed anteroom. No one spoke directly to him. That, at least, had not changed. Men glanced toward him, then looked away. Ladies pointed their fans, then slammed them shut. They knew why they had been called here, and they were not happy. He hadn't expected them to be. Not that they would protest. Not publicly. The nobility wouldn't say anything. Nothing at all. They would just look right through him as if he didn't exist, just as they always had.

Seanen wondered, not for the first time, whether anything he had done or could ever do would change a thing. He hadn't cared, not before. Not when he'd been alone. He hadn't ever wanted to fit in with these people. Now he resented their bigotry, if not for himself, then for Yarwyn. She deserved so much more than he would ever be able to give her.

A hush fell over the room as Lady Lochinvar strode in, still tall and proud and straight despite her years. The magic still glittered strongly around her, giving her an aura, as if she stood bathed in a pale light. Her small party of personal aides trailed after her, Tranorva in their lead, looking austere as ever.

Seanen marveled to think that he'd once found Tranorva fascinating. His eyes swept past her now, searching, seeking, coming to rest at last on the smallest member of the great Lady Evalayna's party, the Ranger dressed in fine soft leather and polished Elven mail of a deep emerald green. The ancient bow settled comfortably on her shoulder, its finish polished now to a bright silver gleam, its stones glowing softly, giving it a radiant blue light that mingled with the sheen of her mail to make her look as foreign and exotic as she was.

Yarwyn surveyed the crowded room, her eyes carefully avoiding his, her hands resting easily at her sides. She looked aloof, detached, almost uninterested, her expression a carefully maintained mask that he knew shielded the most passionate of hearts. He half expected her to use her magic to blend into the room, shifting slowly out of sight until she could make her escape.

Would she escape to him, to find her way back into his arms, or was she looking for an escape from him, regretting now the things she had allowed herself to say in moments of danger and passion?

If she left, deserted him now, he would have lost everything. The goals of a lifetime—revenge, retribution, vindication of his family name—these things meant nothing without his woman in his arms and by his side. He felt once again as that young boy had, standing before the woman who would decide his fate.

"Friends and fellow countrymen, it is my privilege to bring ye here this evening to share news of great import with ye. All of ye know of the heroic deeds accomplished in the recent war. Our armies have destroyed the power of the Orc nation, reducing their numbers to scattered tribes and populations surviving in the far reaches of the extreme north. Our peoples can once again travel freely across the tundra. The head of the Orc King stands guard on their pass, a warning to their kind for the future."

A cheer ran through the crowd, bubbling over as if the victory had been their own, and not bought with the lives of the paid mercenaries who had taken the place of their sons and their daughters. Seanen fought the anger that welled up inside him, washing it down with the taste of blood. He had spilled enough of it for all of them. One noble house, at least, had been well represented.

When the noise settled back to a comfortable level, Lady Lochinvar spoke again, her voice commanding silence from the room. "Our armies did not do their work alone. Our Northlanders fought side by side with the Humans, who brought great credit to their race. And while we attacked from the front, another battle took place within the castle."

There was no cheer this time, only a hush that settled over the crowd as they waited expectantly for Lady Lochinvar to continue. She had the gift of a storyteller, Seanen thought as the sound of her voice pulled her audience within the cold stone walls of the Orc King's castle.

"We were aware, when we chose to face the Orc King, that our losses would be high. We were aware that we could not face the Orc armies more than once with the resources and manpower we have available. Toward this end, and at great personal risk, two brave agents undertook to infiltrate the Orc King's castle, setting in motion the seed of our victory. It is my privilege to ask those two people to stand before us tonight, that we might show them our appreciation for a job well done. From the Elven land of Talismar, I give ye Ambassador Yarwyn, of the Talismar Rangers."

Lord Mâkakao himself escorted Yarwyn to Lady Lochinvar's side. A warm round of applause greeted Yarwyn as she came to stand at the Lady's right hand.

When the clamor had settled to an acceptable quiet, she spoke again. "When I asked Talismar for their assistance, they sent me the best that they had. Less than a fortnight gone, I stood before ye here in this room, and I gave that Ranger choice of all that we had to offer. She asked for but one man. To tell the truth of the matter, I could no' have chosen a man better suited to the job. In the years ye have stood by my side, Seanen, thy name has come to be synonymous with loyalty and honor."

Her eyes scanned the crowd, daring anyone to register a challenge. Seanen half expected the Lord of some minor house to remind them all that honor was stripped from a man whose house had fallen into disgrace, but the room held silent.

Lady Lochinvar continued, as if her pause had only been for emphasis. "Once again, ye have offered thy life in my service. I have contemplated a suitable reward for thy valor. When the answer came to me, I realized it was long overdue. It gives me great pleasure to announce the cancellation of all debts against thy house and the restoration of thy rightful title. Lords and Ladies, I present Lord Seanen, House of Lindall."

The room exploded with noise. It was not a cheer, precisely, but more a roar of disbelief. Seanen felt as much as heard the sound, his pulse beating heavily in his temples as he swayed a bit unsteadily on his feet.

This was not what he had expected. An ambassadorship, perhaps even an appointment with military rank, anything that would give him a credible title within the hierarchy of her household, but not this. Such a thing had never been done before. Not in his lifetime. Perhaps not ever.

Lady Lochinvar was speaking again, her voice quieting the crowd. "Know ye all that there is basis for this honor beyond the sacrifice and loyalty Seanen himself has shown our peoples. In the treasury of the Orc King all that was thought lost has been recovered. A great dishonor was done House Lindall these many decades past, and my actions here today canna' hope to right those wrongs. I canna' give thee back the family ye have lost, Seanen, nor thy years of servitude in my household. I can offer little to make amends. House Lindall and all its lands and holdings are hereby returned to thee. A portion of the Orc King's treasury equal to the debt ye have paid shall be restored to thy accounts. In addition, an equal portion shall be settled upon ye as reward for thy part in this mission."

Seanen knew he should speak, should acknowledge the Lady's great generosity, but he could not find his voice. Words could not have made it past the great knot in his throat had he known what to say. He stood mute as a fool, unmoving, as the great Lady dismounted the dais to come to him, her hands extending to take his own frozen ones in her firm, warm grasp.

"Ye have been like a son to me, Seanen. As a boy I remember ye stood by thy account of thy grandfather's honor, refusing to bend even when the other boys used ye poorly for thy defiance. Many in thy place might have become bitter and wasted their lives. I am proud of the man ye have become. I am honored to name ye a member of my household. It is with great personal regret that I dismiss ye from my service to return ye to thine own."

Tears welled up in Seanen's eyes, obscuring his vision and threatening to overflow. He swallowed hard, struggling to find his voice. The words would not come. Instead he sank to one knee, his head bowed, his hands still clasped in the Lady's own. "I owe ye my life, M'Lady, and all that I am," he managed. "My loyalty and my fealty will always be thine."

* * * * *

Yarwyn moved back in the crowd, losing herself in anonymity as the Lords and Ladies surrounded Seanen, offering congratulations and asking already for variances and easements, anxious to cement their place against what had once been a powerful house, and would, from the feel of things, be so once again.

The ladies who had once eyed him with admiration only for his body eyed him now with deference, measuring him for a place at their tables, eager to introduce their daughters to him. The Lords sought to restore age old alliances, eying the boundaries of his holdings with the greed of their kind. All was as it had always been, except now Seanen was also a part of it.

A Lord in his own right. A man of great wealth, and power he would soon learn to wield as he had his battleaxe.

A Lord of a great house would no longer consort with tavern wenches and ladies of the night. A Lord would need a mistress to tend his keep, a woman to bear his children and tend to their education. A Lord would have eyes for a Lady. Perhaps Tranorva herself would look to him now, to form an alliance between their two houses.

The crowd moved and surged like an ocean, pulling them farther and farther apart. It took no magic for her to slip from the room. There was magic enough in the newfound nobility. These were not her people. She would never be one of them. It had been a mistake to allow herself to dream. Love was not meant for one of her kind. Tears stung her eyes as she pulled the door shut behind her.

* * * * *

She knocked back a draft of ale in the hopes that it would dull the pain. It didn't. The tavern's patrons eyed the stranger drinking alone at the bar suspiciously. The thin cloak did little to disguise the arsenal of small arms and the great bow slung over her back, and all appeared to be there for purposes other than ornament. They gave her a wide berth, her presence lending a somber quiet to the evening.

She wouldn't have welcomed their company anyway. There had been a time when a handsome man might have offered her a pint and stirred her interest, but she wasn't interested. Not tonight.

She should find a man. Any man would do. There were several here who might be persuaded, with a minimum of effort and a slight invitation. Unfortunately there was only one man who would ever own her heart, and he would soon forget her, moving on, as she'd always known he would. She wouldn't hold one man while she pretended to make love to another. She had her standards. They weren't very altruistic, but they were standards.

Yarwyn shoved the ale back across the bar half finished. The man she wanted was a Lord now. It was time to move on. Time to return to the life she'd been comfortable in before this assignment. She could learn to be comfortable there again. She was a Ranger, after all. She always had a plan.

Yarwyn sucked in her breath as two huge hands slid down the length of her arms. She'd have killed any other man for such audacity. Instead she forgot to breathe as the hands moved down, finally sliding around her waist.

"Yarwyn, I must speak to you."

As she turned in his arms to face him, all she could think of was that he'd come looking for her. No matter how gently he let her down, she had this. At least he'd come to her to say goodbye. She would not cry.

He moved against her, gathering her into his arms to kiss the tears from her eyes. "I'm sorry," he whispered. "Forgive me, my love."

She swallowed her pride and her heart. "There is nothing to forgive."

"I know this is not what you wanted. I promised you desert and beaches and warmth, not the frozen tundra of Lindall. I can still give you that. Lindall has survived without me for many decades. Surely it cannot demand all of me now. We can work this out. The desert in the winter, the tundra in the summer. Spring and fall in Talismar if you wish. I've never been there. I hear it is very beautiful."

Perhaps it was the waves of emotions rolling off of him—fear and concern and something she'd come to recognize as love. Perhaps it was the ale. Yarwyn slipped off the stool and into his arms, tears streaming down her face. "I love you," was all that she could manage.

She felt his heart slam against his ribs as his arms convulsed around her. "I was afraid I'd lost you. I knew the crowd would scare you away, but I couldn't escape them, and when I did I couldn't find you."

"You found me now."

"Don't ever leave me again."

"Seanen, think what you're saying. You're a Lord of a great house. You need a Lady to stand beside you. You need—"

"I need you. Nothing else matters. If this frightens you, I will give it all away and renounce the title. What use is a grand bed in a great house without the woman I love to lie next to me at night? The houses, the lands—they mean nothing without you. You hold my heart. Wherever you are is my home."

Yarwyn closed her eyes as she sank against him, allowing him to scoop her up into his arms. "The desert in the winter, and the tundra in the summer. I could get used to that."

"And Talismar."

She smiled. "Talismar is beautiful in the spring."

"I've always wanted to see it. I hear the Elves walk in the trees."

"There are paths and bridges. I will show you."

"Yarwyn."

She loved the sound of her name on his tongue, the faint trace of his accent giving it an exotic twist. "Seanen," she whispered, watching his eyes grow as black as the night.

"I want you as I have no other woman. You are all there will ever be for me."

"And you for me."

They made it as far as the orchard in the gardens behind Lord Mâkakao's great house. The grass was still young and fresh with the smell of spring, and the flowers crushed beneath them to give off a fragrance unrivaled by the richest of scented oils. As he sank into her, hard and hot and burning with need, Yarwyn opened herself to him, body and soul, knowing that they fit together as perfectly as the flowers and the bees that came to drink their nectar.

Her body rose up to meet him, slick and wet with desire, aching to be filled as he ached to fill her. She could feel the love and the lust combine within him, building toward the point of no return. Her body responded in kind, meeting him thrust for thrust. She demanded even as she gave, pulling him into her depths, crying out his name as she tightened around him, shaking with need as he brought her to climax over and over again, then shattering as he spilled his seed into her with a hot, fiery gush that left him spent and gasping for breath in her arms.

And if another watched from a window above the gardens, held prisoner as much by his own desires as the restraints they'd fitted him with, they sank into the glory of the night, blissfully unaware.

A Sorcerer's Seduction

Prologue

"Tell me about the gods, Mother."

"Ye know the gods, child."

The tiny hand grasped hers. "Tell me again."

Evalayna laughed, catching the tumble of hair that cascaded over her shoulder as she bent to draw in the dirt. "All right. Once more then ye go to sleep."

Bright green eyes reflected the firelight, so young and innocent. Evalayna kissed her black-haired child on the forehead. "Say it with me, Mel~amin."

The small voice chanted softly beside her as she drew.

Eight diamonds form the star.
One for the Wind, the breath of life.
Two for Water, that lends us sustenance.
Three for The Wolf, Endurance and Faithfulness.
Four for The Bear, Courage and Strength.
Five for the Cat, Swift and Cunning.
Six for the Falcon, Freedom and Vision.
They come together in the center,
Earth, Our Mother.

"The poetry is better in Elven," the mother mused. The child was silent for a moment...a rare thing in a child. Evalayna waited patiently. At last the child spoke.

"We've only named seven, Mother. Sea, Wind, Rain, Wolf, Bear, Cat and Falcon. That's only six points, with Earth in the center to

make seven. But there are eight diamonds. That means there's room for nine gods. What about the other two points on our star?"

The mother's eyes flicked over the child's face. "The other two—the shadow-points—are always with us, though we name them not. They are Chaos and Destruction. We acknowledge them, but we do no' choose to serve them. Doest thou understand the difference?"

The child gnawed pensively on the end of the stick. "Those two, the shadow-points, those are why we're here, aren't they? Chaos and Destruction are stronger than our gods, and we're running away."

"Chaos and Destruction can never win, Mel~amin. We are no' running away. We will wait here in the mountains for thy father, who battles even now against the forces of darkness. The shadow-gods will no' win."

"What if Father doesn't come for us?"

"Father will come. He is a great Warrior, as ye shall one day be, Tranorva. Go to sleep now. Think no more on the gods."

But as she stared into the shadows, Evalayna wondered...They were only two, those shadow-gods, but they were powerful.

They were the authors of doubt.

* * * * *

Sometime in the night he found her, the Fey creature that had been bound to her at her birth. The light touch of a hand on her shoulder roused her. She couldn't ask, couldn't say the words, but he shook his head once, the tumble of blond hair a halo around his head in the darkness.

"We must go," was all Shammall said.

"Go where? I have nowhere to go. I no longer have a home."

"I will take you back to your mother. The Lord of Lochinvar is old. There is no successor to his House. He will accept Tranorva as his own. Tranorva is young. She will learn to call him father."

Evalayna had never been one to cry. She didn't cry now. "I will accept my mother's generosity," she responded wryly, "for the sake of my daughter. Tranorva shall call this man Father. She shall lead his army into battle. She shall be the heir that he requires. But I shall never take to his bed."

Shammall merely inclined his head.

Evalayna packed up her few belongings and bundled them over her shoulder. As Shammall bent to scoop up the sleeping child, she laid her hand on his arm. "How old are ye, Shammall?"

His lavender eyes glowed in the moonlight. "I have seen the moons cycle more than two thousand times, M'Lady."

More than a century and a half. And to the best of her knowledge in all that he had never taken a wife. Never had a family. Never known a place to call home.

"Are your kind immortal, Shammall?"

If he thought it odd that she should ask such questions here and now, he did not ask. "No, M'Lady. We are long lived, but nothing lives forever except Earth Mother herself."

Evalayna sighed. "Ye have always been good to me, Shammall. Ye alone have stood by me unwaveringly. If it were within my power, I would give ye thy freedom now. As it is not, I can only promise ye when I have the power to do so, I shall return what is rightfully thine."

"It is the way of my kind to serve, M'Lady, and it was I who chose you and your house."

"Ye will no' leave me, then? Wish ye no' for freedom?"

Shammall raised one eyebrow quizzically. "What would I do with my freedom, Lady? You are my life."

Evalayna closed her eyes, resting her forehead for a moment against the small bundle Shammall carried. "And when I am gone? What then?"

"I shall serve Tranorva as I have you, M'Lady." His arms tightened protectively around the child. "She is my destiny."

Chapter One

Tranorva took a long swallow from her mug of ale. She surveyed the debauchery around her with growing disgust. The camp had fallen into a sea of chaos and disorder...but what did it matter? There was nothing left to kill. No castles to lay siege to, no enemies to conquer. No more battles to be fought. She would move the men out in the morning, early, too early for most to offer her authority any resistance. The Humans would return to their world. She and her Northlanders would make one last sweep of the plains, routing out the few Orcs who had escaped, and then...

And then nothing. The war was over. For her, there would be no more wars. No more wars, no more battles, no more marching with the men, no more feeling the heft of her broad-bladed axe as it sang through the heart of her enemies. She was destined for another field; she had been since the day she was born. Bile rose in her throat till she thought she might gag. Every woman made sacrifices, but this, this was too much. To be condemned to live amidst the world of politics, for naught else but a twist of fate at her birth...

Mother hadn't even had the nerve to tell Tranorva to her face. Instead Mother had sent Shammall, the pet Mage she favored so much, to Tranorva before they left home, warning her to expect changes. Once the Orc Wars were over, Tranorva's time would begin.

Shammall. How Tranorva despised that damnable Elf. Sometimes she thought Mother kept him around just for his lithe, athletic good looks. Shammall was certainly easy on the eyes, if you liked that type. Beautiful, in a very male sort of way. He had incredible long golden blond hair that never seemed to get tangled or out of place. Tranorva wanted to tie it in knots while he slept just to be spiteful. Shammall was everything Tranorva was not—graceful and sophisticated and polished and a master of politics.

Politics. Well, Tranorva had a few useful talents of her own. She had been born to lead an army to battle. It was what she was good at. What she lived for. Why should that change now? Lady Evalayna was still in the height of her power. There was no reason for her to step down. There was no reason for Mother to saddle Tranorva with such a weight of responsibility—especially one she was totally unsuited for.

Tranorva took another long pull from her mug. Anger always brought heat to her blood. She needed a man. She needed to work off her frustrations in a bout of good, healthy sex. But not just any man would be up to the task. She didn't want a weakling who would cower before her. Most men were too afraid of her to do more than murmur their apologies. She wanted a man who would meet her as her equal, and more. She wanted…an image came to mind. She wanted Seanen Lindall. The man who'd emerged from the shadows today to toss the bloody head of the Orc King into the midst of her men, turning the tide of battle for them.

Funny. She'd never really seen him before. He shouldn't have escaped her notice. He was taller than most and built like a battering ram. He swung those swords of his like they were extensions of his hands. Perhaps—perhaps she had underestimated him.

Seanen had walked among her troops tonight, the conquering hero. Spattered in blood and wearing armor none had seen for decades, he looked perfect—all hard angles and broad expanses of muscle and power. It was the power Tranorva admired the most. She would send for him. She would send an orderly with an invitation to come to her tent. By the gods, if this one proved to be passionless she would turn her attention to women. She wasn't sure she could take another disappointment.

With that thought, Tranorva tossed her empty mug into her satchel and made her way carefully to her pavilion. Her orderly was there, ready to help her strip out of her soiled leather undertunic. She used the washbasin her orderly had provided to clean the worst of the battle grime from her face and arms. The orderly combed out her hair and would have plaited the mass into a thick, heavy braid for the night, but Tranorva ushered him off with a wave of her wrist. "Leave it down for now. I have an errand for ye."

"As you wish, M'Lady."

"Go and find Seanen, of the House of Lindall. Tell him I request his personal report."

The orderly paled, glancing tentatively toward the flap of the tent, but not moving.

"What ails thee? Go!"

"It's just that—M'Lady, I know Lord Lindall is not—available."

Tranorva mused over the words, playing with them like a cat with a rodent. "*Lord* Seanen is unavailable? He's a Lord, now, is he? My, my. And why is he unavailable?"

The orderly trembled visibly, looking anywhere but into her eyes. "Lord Lind—Seanen has retired for the night, M'Lady, to the pavilion of Ambassador Yarwyn, with orders that they are not to be disturbed."

Tranorva felt her mouth knotting into a frown. So. That was the way of things. This had all been arranged from the beginning. Tranorva didn't need to ask how, or by whom. Mother was clever, Tranorva owed her that. With Ambassador Yarwyn's help she'd used the Orc Wars to restore *Lord* Lindall's place in society. It all came down to *politics*. The fact that a thousand Orcs and a few hundred of Tranorva's own men had given their lives to accomplish Mother's political goals was, in the end, of no real consequence. The Orcs needed to die anyway, and soldiers knew well their fate.

Tranorva turned her attention back to the orderly. He might have made a good stand-in for the night had she not known he was terrified of her. He was young, and strong, and a fine hand with a sword. Attractive enough when he didn't know she was watching him. Fear, however, was hardly an inspiring emotion to elicit in a lover.

Tranorva waved her hand in dismissal. "Off with you. I suggest you retire early. We move out at first light."

* * * * *

Élandine hadn't been invited to the reception for the returning heroes — that came as no surprise. He hadn't expected any acknowledgment of his role in the Orc king's defeat. There were no accolades here for a job well done, not in his line of work. When the mission was over, his latest persona would simply fade away…all part of the job.

Something was different this time, though. Too many of those involved in this last little war considered him a villain, and might have still, even had they known all the inner workings of House Lochinvar. And so he was still held prisoner, bound and locked in a tiny stone room high in the great Lord Mâkakao's west tower. Soon, he promised himself, Lady Evalayna would have need of his special services again. She would find him, the prisoner would "escape," and he would be on his way.

Somewhere else, someone else, whoever, whatever, she needed him to be.

Élandine stared out the tiny slit of a window. The air was still fresh with the smell of spring. The bright colors of freedom taunted him. He would have pulled back, turned away from this reminder of his failure, but a flash of movement caught his eye. The Elven Ranger, Yarwyn, appeared, breaking the trance of the scene, slipping quickly through the maze of the gardens. She was almost out of range. Still, he could feel her sorrow, and he envied her even that emotion. For a moment, just a moment, he'd become her, long enough to *feel*…Long enough to know what he'd missed in his life.

He knew he'd never be the same man again.

Yarwyn disappeared through the servants' gate. Élandine felt the void in his mind where she'd been like a hollow ache of longing. He steeled himself against such thoughts. There was no place in his life for that kind of weakness. Still, he couldn't help but wonder if this was all there was ever to be. Shouldn't there be something more, even for one such as him?

Yarwyn's mate Seanen interrupted Élandine's thoughts. The tall Northlander all but ran through the orchard, following Yarwyn's trail. Soon they were back together, their energies combined until Élandine could not tell one from another. The strength of their lusts shook him with a force that nearly wrenched his soul from him. He knew what they were feeling now, understood it ever since he'd become Yarwyn's twin for those few moments. He had never thought himself capable of feeling such overwhelming emotions.

He'd been a fool to think he could steal Yarwyn's form, even temporarily, in order to capture what he needed. He hadn't wanted to steal her identity, not permanently. He'd only wanted to know, to possess her powers long enough to understand. For those few stolen moments he'd seen what she saw, felt what she felt, known what it was to want, to need, to love, until the love itself consumed you, and you became so much more than what you were.

The couple slipped away from him, leaving him alone again. He was only a thief, an interloper, a voyeur at a window. Élandine's nostrils flared as he sank to the cold stone floor. Emotions made a man weak. He would think on this no more.

* * * * *

The guards threw open the massive bound oak doors with a clang that had Élandine scrambling to his feet. Lady Evalayna Lochinvar strode into the room, temper simmering in her eyes.

The guards hastened to scramble out of her way. She dismissed them with a wave of her hand. In her wake they stood staring blankly into space, unblinking, unmoving. Élandine wasn't even sure they remembered to breathe.

"Thou hast been in my service a very long time, Élandine."

Her voice held no warmth. Anger tinged Élandine's reasoning. Yarwyn. She was behind this. Élandine tried to swallow the sick feeling in the pit of his stomach. Lady Evalayna had always trusted him implicitly. "I would not have hurt Seanen."

"Nay?"

Élandine allowed his anger to show. A lesser mortal might have feared him, but not Lady Evalayna. She knew him too well. She knew what he was, and what he was capable of, but they'd always treated each other as equals. "Yarwyn tried to kill me. What was I supposed to do?"

"According to Lady Lindall, ye had *intentions* toward Lord Seanen. Had I been there, I might have killed ye myself."

He rolled his eyes. "*That*? She would hold *that* against me? I was but maintaining my disguise," he growled. "You know me better than that. Seanen is hardly my type. Had I been seeking a lover I would have looked elsewhere—and for a female! But Élandine must do as the Dark Elves do. The Elves of Élandra have their own ways. Had I truly faced an Élandra Priestess and done otherwise I would have begged for my own death to come swiftly." His jaw clenched. "How was I to know Yarwyn had been sent on such a mission as this unschooled in the ways of the Élandra Priestesses?"

Lady Evalayna arched one heavy black brow. "And what part of thy disguise was it that had ye in Lord Seanen's arms, impersonating the Lady herself?"

He looked away, red heat staining his face. Embarrassment—yet another emotion that had previously eluded him. How could he make Lady Evalayna understand what he himself barely understood? Élandine turned back to the window, swallowing hard. "I—that was wrong. That was—I know not how to explain. When Yarwyn thought she had killed me, she came closer than she will ever know. With the last of my strength I cast the spell that preserved what life I clung to. Those two, they cared nothing for the broken being they left on the floor."

Finally he turned back to face her. "You know that my magic often lends me the gifts of those around me. Yarwyn—she feels other people's emotions. Her gift opened my eyes. I lay on the floor at their feet, bloody and broken, and I mattered nothing to them. I was dying, and I was but an inconvenience to them. They had each other. That was all that mattered..."

Pity tainted her voice. "So ye would have taken what ye could not find within thyself."

The red stain on his cheeks deepened. He didn't want her pity. "It was a foolish thing, done without proper thought. I meant only for them to take me prisoner, that I might maintain my disguise. I didn't expect to—to *feel* so much. I have never had another's identity overwhelm me before."

Lady Evalayna sighed deeply. "What am I to do with ye, Élandine? Or shall I call ye Shammall?"

Élandine cursed himself for a fool. He needed Evalayna's trust. What's more he cared what this woman thought of him. The last of his pride crumbled. He slowly dropped to one knee before her. "Call me whatever you wish, M'Lady. I care not. I care only that I have failed in my mission, and that I have broken your trust. I beg your forgiveness."

Her hand touched his shoulder. "Ye have been as a son to me these last few decades, Élandine. That bond cannot be broken by one foolish action. Still I fear ye have won no loyalty for thy service from Lord Lindall and his Lady, nor from my youngest daughter and her new husband. Perhaps it would be well if neither couple were to discover that Élandine and Shammall are one and the same."

Élandine felt the first stirrings of hope in his breast. Forgiveness would not be without personal expense, but Lady Evalayna would not reveal his true identity. That must mean she still had need of him. Thank the gods. He raised his head, meeting her eyes at last. He held out his bound hands to her. "I live but to serve you, M'Lady…"

She might simply have used the tiny ceremonial dagger she carried in her belt. Instead, in a show of power designed, perhaps, to remind him of just who *she* was, Lady Lochinvar passed her hands over his wrists. A shimmering of white fire surged from her fingertips, and his bonds disappeared as if they had never been. In a moment he had shifted, slipping into Shammall, the form of the Elven Mage that he knew she preferred above all others. Lady Evalayna bent to kiss him gently on the forehead, her touch itself a blessing. He felt strength and healing radiate through his battered body. He breathed in deeply, shaking back his long blond mane, reveling in his temporary freedom.

Lady Evalayna stood silent a moment, looking beyond him and that small stone room. "There is always a price, is there not, Shammall?"

She looked older, somehow, and pained. He had not noticed the lines of strain about her eyes before. He'd been too concerned with his own affairs. "Aye, M'Lady," he managed, suddenly afraid for both of them.

Evalayna moved to stare at the rising moons, just visible through his slit of a window. Élandine scrambled back to his feet, moving to stand as close to her side as he dared. "What troubles you, M'Lady, and how can I be of service?"

"'Tis my daughter."

Alarm filled his breast. "Cassadara? Has harm come to Cassadara?"

Evalayna slowly shook her head. "Nay. 'Tis my firstborn. Tranorva, my Warrior-daughter has disappeared from my glass."

Tranorva. Clouds passed before the moons, painting the night sky a dull blood red. Élandine took a deep breath as he regarded Lady Lochinvar. He needed a bath and a change of clothes and a night spent wrapped in a woman's arms enjoying emotions he understood. There was nothing like straight, uncomplicated sex to clear a man's head.

Instead, he would escape now, tonight. Lady Evalayna had given him his freedom, but the price would be higher than he'd thought. Shifting back into the form of the smaller Dark Elf, he bowed low before his benefactress. "I will do everything in my power to restore Tranorva to you, Dear Lady. I will leave at once."

"My prayers go with ye. May the goddess protect ye."

Élandine had never had a favorite among the seven gods, but he figured he could use whatever blessings were available. He slipped through the open door, past the sentries staring slack-jawed into space, and ran down the stairs. He was nearly at the bottom when the commotion began. "What is the meaning of this!" Lady Evalayna proclaimed in her most outraged voice. "Ye have allowed the prisoner to escape!"

Élandine could picture the astonishment on the guards' faces when they woke up to an empty room. "M'Lady, he was here when we opened the door! Surely you saw him, sitting right over there!"

"I see no one but two incompetent fools."

Élandine laughed to himself as he slipped away into the darkness. There were those who feared the night, but it would always be the friend of one such as him. And now he knew the secret of the servants' gate in the orchard…

Chapter Two

She was up with the dawn, dragging liquor-fogged heads to the water to personally revive her unit commanders. Within half an hour she had the men on their feet and the ox carts loaded. None of the men were in any shape for breakfast at the moment. Tranorva chewed contentedly on a hunk of dried venison as she marched beside her men. By noon the troops would be ready for their first repast of the day. By nightfall they would have covered thirty kilometers. She would set up her base camp at the edge of the tundra. Tomorrow the units would begin scouting the vast, empty plains for signs of any Orcs who might have survived last week's battle. She could put off returning to Lochinvar for many days, possibly even weeks, before she was satisfied that the entire region was safe...Let tomorrow bring what it might. For the moment, at least, she was securely in charge of her world.

She could hear his footsteps getting closer. It was the dream again. Tranorva knew it was a dream, but she didn't try to wake up. Oh no. Waking up was the last thing she wanted. She'd had this dream before, each time more real than the last. Tonight, she promised herself as the steps came closer. Tonight would be the night she saw his face.

She was in chains. Shackled hand and foot, spread naked across a cold stone altar, she should have been terrified. The man coming toward her wore hard-soled boots, she could tell from the sound of his footsteps, and he slapped a leather whip against his leg in rhythm to his footfalls. She should have been terrified, she reminded herself. Or angry. Or almost anything but excited.

Why the thought of being held captive should make her body burn with such heat she did not understand. Perhaps it was the man. He stopped close enough to trail the ends of the whip's lashes across her body, touching, teasing, stroking her with the leather until she wanted to scream with pent up sexual frustration. If only she could see his face. But this time he moved behind her head, draping a swath of soft leather over her eyes and knotting it securely.

The next stroke of the whip was firmer, across her thigh, but still not hard enough to leave any marks. A gush of wetness flooded her sheath, bidding him welcome to whatever he wanted from her. "Please," she whimpered.

"Please what?"

She'd never heard him speak before. His voice was low and deep, as smooth as fine aged brandy. A shiver of anticipation passed through her. "I want to feel ye inside me."

The trails of the lashes tickled the fur on her aching mound. He used the whip on her again, harder than before. She bucked off the altar to meet his punishment, aching to feel him inside her. The tip of his cock grazed her mound, just inches away. His voice was a little harsher now, hoarse with his own need. "I want you to beg."

She would. She would do anything to end this sweet torture. "Please," she sobbed, writhing against the restraints. "Please…"

A whimper broke from her lips as he brushed the tip of his erection over her. She bucked against him, trying to capture that cock within her aching sheath, but he pulled back, only to tease her again with the whip. This time it was the leather-wrapped handle, sliding slowly along her thigh, forcing her waiting lips apart, then stroking slowly over her drenched entrance. He massaged her clit with the whip's handle, bringing her closer and closer to shattering, then backing away.

The entire universe focused down to those few square inches of her body demanding fulfillment. A wail of desire broke from her lips. "Now!" she screamed. "I want ye now!"

"But this isn't about you, is it, my sweet?" His tongue replaced the whip as his hands spread her open for easier access. He blew softly on her tender, needy flesh, watching her convulse before him. "You're used to giving orders. I don't obey your orders here. You'll take what I offer you, when I offer it."

"Yes. Anything. Just touch me. Please…"

She shattered as his demanding tongue swiped over the surface of her throbbing clit, then shattered again as he sucked the juices from her, thrusting his tongue deep inside. She thought she had nothing more to offer, until he slid his thick, hot shaft into her wet sheath. Fast. She wanted fast.

He gave her slow. Standing between her widespread legs, he moved in and out of her in long, measured strokes, burying his massive cock until she thought she might split. She strained against him, using her strength to pull him in farther, fighting to hold him within her, clamping down on him to prevent his escape.

He liked that. She could tell he liked that. She squeezed harder, demanding more, assaulting his cock with rigid spasms of hard toned muscles that tried to pull him back whenever he tried to escape. Soon he was moving to her rhythm, faster now, faster, his hands braced on her hips, pulling her harder as he slammed into her hot, wet, sheath. Their bodies slapped together with the sound of flesh on flesh, sucking away with each stroke. Tranorva lost count of how many times she came as he stroked into her again and again.

It was he who was her prisoner now, desperate for his final release, and she ached to give it to him. Words became impossible. A voice that must have been hers cried out in loud moans. He answered her cries of desire. *More, more!* her body demanded. She pulled at him with all her might, sucking the final shattering from him until they both shattered with the intensity of the thing they had built.

An animalistic roar broke from her lips, and he joined her, spilling his seed with a gush of searing wet heat that scorched her raw skin. She convulsed around him, trapping him where he was until she had milked him of his full provision. Then, even then, she would not release him. With a moan of exhaustion he collapsed across her body, his head resting between her breasts.

Tranorva woke with a languorous stretch from the dream that was more than a dream. She was alone, in her pavilion, and her lover had drifted back to the land of dreams where he lived. She smiled contentedly as sleep overcame her again. It was just a dream, but he was waiting for her. Somewhere out there he was waiting for her.

* * * * *

Élandine shook his head, staring at the field of tall grass before him. He checked his position again with the sextant. He had the location right. This was the last place Lady Evalayna had seen Tranorva and her men. The scry glass couldn't be tampered with. Yet there were no signs of a skirmish here. No bodies, no blood, none of the refuse of war.

No army passed by unnoticed. Nothing larger than the occasional leopard had crossed this section of tundra for weeks.

Élandine pressed his fingers to his temples, then wiped them slowly across his eyes. The landscape before him faded. Voices bombarded him. The earth trembled beneath his feet. Holding his hands over his eyes, he sank slowly to the ground...

His vision cleared, as if that army had been nothing more than a distant memory.

Nothing. The vision slipped away as if it had never been.

Whatever had happened here, either it was long ago, or some magic far greater than his had wiped the slate clean.

He had no choice. He'd go back to the beginning and start again.

* * * * *

Still nothing.

Élandine stared up at the massive, ugly fortification that marked the line between the territory of Men and that of the Orcs. He'd searched for two days now, traveling fast, covering ground, yet careful to overlook no evidence. It was impossible to move an army without any trace, yet it had been done. He was back to the Orc King's castle now without any further sign of an army to be found.

As he approached the castle, cautious lest the remaining Orcs on the tundra might have moved back in, Élandine suddenly understood why he'd found no trace of the army out in the field. The army was right here, right where they'd been when he'd been returned to House Yarishet along with Lady Lochinvar's party after the war. He could feel the presence of the men even before he heard the armor clinking and the tread of mail-clad feet on the parapets of the castle.

They were here? The entire army? This made no sense. Élandine stood staring at the Orc King's castle, perplexed and vexed. He'd spent days out searching the tundra, and Tranorva had never left her original base camp, except to move a hundred meters to occupy the castle itself?

Righteous anger treaded heavily on Élandine's common sense. He could understand Tranorva's reluctance to follow in her mother's path. This deception, however, this breach of the military discipline the famed Tranorva was known for, had sent him on a four-day mission to scour the tundra for her, and she wasn't even lost. She could have at least defied her mother openly, rather than allowing Lady Evalayna to worry needlessly.

Well, Evalayna wasn't here to give Tranorva the serious dressing down she deserved. Élandine was. He squared his shoulders. A slight shift in mental attitude, a stretching here, broadening there, and he was a Northlander. Not just any Northlander, either. He was Seanen, Lord Lindall. He entered the castle as easily as he had so many months before, striding through the front gates unchallenged.

The place smelled of fear.

Men stood at the ready everywhere, their faces grim. Tensions ran high. No one seemed in the least surprised to see him. More importantly, he saw no officers. Well familiar with the layout of the castle, Élandine headed for the top floor, where he knew the Orc King had held court, such as it was.

Not a bad guess. He found them in the conference room, pouring over maps, heads bowed in anxious discussion. He surveyed the room. No long ebony tresses spilled down the backs of any of those in view. No husky voice commanded these perusals of whatever maps they searched. More importantly he could not feel her presence. Tranorva had too strong an aura not to be evident if she was anywhere about.

These were men he had known for decades. Captains and Commanders all, their voices containing their strain. He had not stomped into the conference room. Seanen might be a Lord now, but he was first and foremost a thief—too damn good a thief to go barging in on anything he didn't fully understand. Élandine rethought his guise. Whatever was going on here, Seanen would be expected to participate, perhaps take charge. That wasn't the role Élandine had in mind.

Another shift, another wrenching of bone and muscle into the slightly shorter, slightly less bulky form of Shammall. These men knew Shammall, or at least they thought they did. More importantly they knew Shammall was bound by oath of fealty to the Lady Lochinvar. This form carried her authority with it, without the responsibility of solving any mysteries…at least not today.

Commander Garreth was the first to notice Shammall's presence. Garrett snapped his head up, looking, for once, actually pleased to see the pale High Elf.

"By the seven! Tell us you have heard something."

That was a little unsettling. Not at all the welcome Shammall was used to. "Lady Lochinvar has sent me to locate Lady Tranorva, as she has not had communiqué from her. I take it the Lady Tranorva is not here?"

"General Tranorva just disappeared two days after the battle. We had established a base camp here." Garreth pinpointed the spot on the map that looked dangerously close to where Lady Lochinvar had sent Élandine in the first place. The place where no Army or its traces had been found. "We were to send out scouting parties from this point in radiuses to clear up any remaining Orc threat. The day after the battle went as planned, though we encountered no Orcs. We moved our base of operations and established the camp. The second morning, General Tranorva did not report to the Commanders Meeting. We spent the day and well into the night searching for her. The third morning we fell back to our current position. My scouts have found no trace of the General."

An army had moved twice through ground Élandine had sworn untrodden in decades. Shammall ran long, slim fingers over his aching ears as he seated himself at the table. "Start at the beginning and tell me everything." It was going to be a long, long day...

* * * * *

If Garreth was to be believed, an entire army had bivouacked on this spot, and yet there was nothing. Élandine could find not a trace of their scent, not a blade of tundra grass even bent to indicate their passage. Not even a waxed paper wrapper from a ration left lying crumpled beside the spring. Fear closed down around Élandine's heart.

He served Evalayna while she ruled, but Tranorva was his destiny. He had known this since her birth over three decades ago. His life was as inextricably bound to hers as hers was to House Lochinvar. As he had served her mother, he would serve her, and later her daughter. Such was the fate of his kind. It was not a fate he minded, truth be known. Tranorva was headstrong and driven, but she was also beautiful. She had decades yet to grow into her role. Or so he had thought until Lady Evalayna had announced her plan to step down from her place as Matriarch of House Lochinvar early this spring.

If Lady Evalayna did not pass her succession on to Tranorva, there would be no more daughters for him to serve. Lady Cassadara had her own house now, that of her husband. Lochinvar needed Tranorva. He needed Tranorva.

There were other houses, he reminded himself. Other great ladies. Yet this one had been his since the day of her birth. The fear that stole into his heart was more than just the knowledge that her disappearance marked yet another in a list of his failures. No matter how much Tranorva hated him, and he knew she did, she was his. Had he been Human…

But he was not. He was *Fey*, and she could never be his. Not that way. What he felt for her was no more than the love of a protector for the woman he served. Their futures had been intertwined by the fates. He needed to serve her, he repeated stubbornly to himself. Nothing more.

Did he need her enough to risk…

Chapter Three

Élandine drew carefully with the tip of his finger in the fragile soil of the tundra. Every line must be precise. Every word must be perfect. Every thought must be controlled. He chanted softly as he drew, burying the thought of failure in one of the far recesses of his mind.

Eight diamonds form the star.
Give me breath, Wind, even in the void.
Give me sustenance, Rain, when all has been stripped from me.
Guide my heart, Wolf, that I may endure.
Guide my sword, Bear, that I might not waver.
Guide my feet, Cat, that I may not falter.
Guide my Vision, Falcon, that I may see truth.
Guide my soul, Mother, that I may face what lies ahead.
Come forth, ye spirits of Chaos and Destruction, and bow to my will.
Take me to your plane and back again.

Wind rushed around him, cold and angry, ripping at his cloak. Rain pelted him like angry lashes from a cat-o-nine-tails. He heard their voices, Wolf, Bear, Cat, and Falcon, screech out their warnings. Earth opened at his feet with a groan that shook the very foundations of her soul. Then as quickly as it had begun, the noises stopped. Earth sealed over his head. He was trapped in a bubble, a void, a place where nothing existed. Not time nor space nor breath nor life.

"You do not belong here, Élandine." The voice was deep and strong, rumbling as if it came from the bowels of Earth herself.

Sweat drenched Élandine's skin, already damp from the storm. By the gods he was hot. The air was so thin he could barely breathe.

Did one talk to a god? Or gods? Well, it—or they—had spoken to him. Seemed rude not to answer. "I come only seeking a vision."

"What vision?"

Élandine fought to keep his voice steady and calm. "There is a Northlander. The woman called Tranorva, of the House of Lochinvar. I am sent to find her, yet what I have seen cannot be. It is as if the ground has swallowed her up."

The dark mists swirled around him, shades of black on black. "Do you know what you ask?"

Élandine swallowed hard, willing his voice not to shake. "I know."

"There will be a price."

Élandine bowed his head, struggling for breath. "There is always a price."

"Ye may be *Fey*, but ye are yet mortal, Élandine. The price may be too high. Is the Human worth our price?" Another voice, softer, perhaps feminine, though only slightly less frightening.

Human? They considered Tranorva a Human? Perhaps to the gods they were all Human. "Tranorva's life is the price of my honor. I will pay your price."

"Very well." A third voice. This one hollow and echoing. If the first had been Earth, and the second Rain, this one sounded like Wind. Perhaps. Perhaps not. "Tranorva's fate shall be your own. You will live as she lives. You will die as she dies."

Did that mean...No. He was *Fey*. His life was the span of the trees, with an ebb and flow like the oceans. He was almost immortal. He was nearly a century-and-a-half older than

Tranorva herself. That could not be what they meant. They. Whoever the voices belonged to. The room was beginning to spin as the sweat drenched his body. Air. He couldn't get enough air to fill his lungs.

"Do ye accept our terms, Élandine?"

To be truly mortal. To feel what they felt. To see as they saw. To have an end in sight. To know he would age, and in the blink of an eye he would be gone.

To love…

"Think what this means. Ye shall be bound to this Human, from this day forward, Élandine. Her fate is your fate. Her years are your years. From this day forward, your destinies are as one."

He was already bound to her…Élandine bowed his head forward. "As is your will, so it shall be."

Wind swept through the room, filling his lungs. Rain pelted his skin, cooling the awful fire. Wolf and Bear and Cat and Falcon screeched, their voices following Wind as they called him back to the world. The stars reappeared above him. The cool Earth of the tundra appeared beneath his knees. Stars graced the sky. Blackness overcame him as he tumbled into the soft tundra grass. The moons lent their pale shivering glow to the form below, smiling as Élandine drifted off into a deep sleep.

* * * * *

His footsteps echoed across the cold stone floor. He did nothing to muffle them. He knew she could hear him, and the thought sent his blood pumping until he grew hard just thinking of the feast that awaited him.

She was in chains. The great and powerful Tranorva awaited him, shackled hand and foot, spread naked across a cold stone altar. Any other woman would have been terrified. The fact that she was not, that she moaned for him with just the sound of his approach, made him ache for release. He slapped the hard-shanked leather whip against his right leg in rhythm to his footfalls.

It was wrong of him to take part in this ritual. He had no business being here. He needed to rescue her, to return her to Lochinvar. That was his mission. If he followed through on his disguise she might never forgive him. Yet he was being watched. This body he had borrowed had certain duties and obligations. If he did not behave as the Dark Priestesses commanded his life would be forfeit.

And there was more. Tranorva wanted him. He could feel it. His body trembled at the thought of her. He'd never truly understood what it was to be Human before, nor why the gods saw all the races as one. The change in him was complete. He was no virgin, yet he'd never felt like this before. The passion that change had wrought in him threatened to overwhelm more than a century of strict discipline. He wanted her. He ached for her as he'd never ached for a woman before.

She lay there before him, naked and lovely, her skin pale as the moonlight, her hair dark as midnight. Why he should find the look of her helpless so stirring he did not understand. He knew that, despite his anticipation, he could never take her if she denied him. But watchers or no, she would not. He felt the answering need shake her as he trailed the whip gently across those exquisite breasts. The altar was shaped like a birthing table, so that her legs were chained spread wide apart. He walked up the V of the table, stopping inches from her midnight mound.

Tranorva moaned as he slapped her thighs with the whip, harder this time, though still soft enough not to leave permanent marks. Reason began to soak through his befuddled brain. Tranorva was not fighting her bonds. She was trying to reach him. The woman who was always in control wanted him to control her. He slipped his fingers into her wet, waiting sheath. Her body shook with the force of a small explosion. The force of her lust nearly overwhelmed him.

"Please," she whimpered.

"Please what?"

"I want to feel ye inside me."

His throat was dry, almost too dry to manage the words. "I want you to beg."

"Please," she sobbed, writhing against the restraints. "Please…"

* * * * *

Where was a whore when you needed one, damn it?

The vision had left him hard and aching with need. Ridiculous. Utterly ridiculous. Tranorva. Waiting on an altar for him, wanting him to overpower her. Ridiculous. He needed to take some time off. He needed to take a trip to the nearest town and find himself a whore. Maybe two. After a vision like that, he could use two. He wasn't the type to visit their dens, but a man could make an exception, especially after a night like this.

Perhaps there were camp followers in the lower halls of the castle. Where there was an army, there were always camp followers. Yes. That was it. He'd head back to the Orc King's Castle. He'd find that Dwarven wench who had eyed him with such evident approval. He'd….

Unfortunately things he had not paid attention to in the vision began to fall into place. The cold stone floors. The Dark Priestesses. The damp smell of the walls. *Élahandara*. Bastion of the Élandra Priestesses under the mountain, Élahandara was a catacomb of maze-like tunnels that stretched for miles beneath the solid stone of the mountains. Back at the Orc King's castles the other acolytes had spoken of the impending arrival of their High Priestess.

Only a High Priestess could command the magic necessary to wipe the traces of an entire army from the face of the tundra. Only Géndalaine herself could have stolen Tranorva from under the noses of her guards and a thousand devoted troops in the dead of night without a sound.

The whores would have to wait. There was only one way to find out whether Tranorva truly waited for him. He would go to Élahandara. His journey might yet find another meaning to the cryptic message sealed in the gods' promise to him. For in truth he no longer feared death as much as he feared the loss of the woman who had found her way into his soul…

* * * * *

Escape. You must escape.

Tranorva woke with a start.

The reality of the stone altar was cold. Stripped naked as she was, she was chilled to the bone. She wasn't one to let adversity get the better of her, but she'd had no choice in this. Whatever spells the Dark Ones had put her under, she'd had no way to fight them. They should have killed her swiftly, ended it there. This was no way for a soldier to die. Naked. Helpless. Strapped to an altar.

She had to escape. But she was so tired…

Footsteps echoed down the long stone corridor. Tranorva whispered a prayer to the gods for strength and courage. "Let me die well, that is all I ask," she assured them.

"You pray, and yet your gods do not answer you."

The voice was deep and powerful and—female. Not the voice of her dream.

"Perhaps you pray to the wrong gods."

She couldn't see the face. Not yet. But she could feel the power. She whispered a short prayer of protection. This one radiated power the way her own mother did.

"What have your gods done for you, Tranorva? Where have they gotten you? Your gods only take from you. Your prayers go unanswered."

"My gods give me my strength. The strength to endure whatever ye intend to do to me. Save thy breath. Kill me now. Swiftly. It is a Warrior's right."

The woman moved closer, into Tranorva's line of sight. Her skin was dark blue- black, the color of deepest midnight. Her hair hung in long waves down her back, shimmering like fine strands of obsidian. Her face—her face was perfect. Small, heart-shaped, lovely. Her eyes, though, were what held Tranorva's attention. Lavender eyes that glowed with intensity. Surely this was not the face in her dreams. Surely...

"Kill you? Why would I kill you, my love? I have gone to so much work to bring you here safely. If I wanted you dead, I would have seen to it on the battlefield. In truth, it was not I who brought you here, but you, yourself."

Tranorva glanced around the rudely carved stone room, trying to keep the disdain noteworthy in her voice. "I? I think not. I remember marching not into thy city of stone, M'Lady. I would sooner have braved the depths of the hells themselves."

"Think you not? Think again. What prayer did you ask when your mother relayed the news that you would be called to serve in her place?"

Tranorva blinked slowly. Prayer? All those months ago...she had prayed, right after Shammall had left her. "I asked to be spared such a fate..."

A note of triumph sang in the Priestess's voice. "And I have been sent as an instrument of the gods to deliver your reprieve."

The answer was temptingly simple. Of course the best lies were the simplest ones. Twist a fact just a little here and the lines between truth and lies began to blur..."I asked only to die in battle," Tranorva countered.

"You asked first to be spared your fate. You know I speak the truth. The gods have sent me as an answer to your prayers. I offer you another choice, Tranorva. Think you that all of my kind were born to their power? No. It is a gift of the gods. Become one with us, and the gods will gift you as well. You will have power greater than you have ever dreamed of. You will have acolytes to serve you. Our young men will worship at your feet, and anywhere else you desire them. You are young, and strong, and you have what we seek. Join us, Tranorva. We are your destiny..."

The Priestess ran her hands over Tranorva's body as she spoke, touching, stroking, stopping here to bring a nipple to peak, caressing a shoulder, brushing back the hair from Tranorva's face. She ended her invitation with a kiss that Tranorva was too stunned to fight. She didn't want—she wasn't—this was wrong! This was against everything she had been taught! She did not worship their gods, would never worship their gods, would...

The woman sat astride her now, her heat only inches from Tranorva's as she leaned over, her breasts dangling against Tranorva's nipples as she deepened the kiss. She was a fine kisser. The Dark One's tongue stroked Tranorva's lips, twisting around her own tongue, teasing her to respond. Tranorva's traitorous body trembled with need. Her sheath was already aching and drenched. This was not the way it was supposed to be. She had to escape. This was not...

The Dark Priestess slid down Tranorva's body, licking and sucking, devoting her attentions first to those traitorous, aching breasts, then lower. This was not the way the dream went! This was not right...

The Dark Priestess spread her open like a feast to be devoured. Tranorva screamed as the first stroke of that tongue against soft, sensitive flesh shattered her world. She would not respond, not to a woman. Not to this woman. This was wrong! She would not be used so. She had to escape. She twisted and fought, succeeding only in throwing herself harder against the probing tongue. She felt herself peaking and screamed out again, whether in rage or ecstasy she no longer knew...

* * * * *

"Tranorva's fate shall be your own. You will live as she lives. You will die as she dies."

Élandine swallowed hard as he stared at the mountain that was not a mountain.

Élahandara.

If his life was as Tranorva's life, would he still be able to shift? Could he be who he needed to be next? Or would he be trapped in the body of the ageless Dark Elf, forever lost to the races he desired most? For he would be killed on sight in most cities were he to appear as a Dark Elf...

Perhaps the cryptic message meant only that his fate was irrevocably entwined with Tranorva's. Be that as it may. It had always been so. Whatever his fate, whatever awaited him within the dark recesses of Élahandara, it mattered not. He had no future without Tranorva. She was his. She was the one he had been waiting for all his life. He had known that from the first time he held her.

He'd thought it duty, devotion, fealty that bound him to her, and it was all those things, for the child and her protector. But she was no more a child, and he could never go back to the innocent he had been before Yarwyn's touch. The wound she had opened over his heart would never fully heal. She had let in too much of what she was in that single knife thrust. He knew now what he had denied in himself for years. What he had felt for Evalayna's child was nothing to what he felt for the woman. The pity of it was, he was in love with a woman who despised him.

* * * * *

No light found its way into the cold, damp cell. By the gods she was tired. Tranorva huddled under the blanket, repeatedly flexing her muscles. The guard would be here soon. By now she knew the rhythm of the place. The Sun must have just slipped behind the shadows. The inhabitants of Élahandara were beginning to stir.

The cart with its wobbly wheel turned the corner, creaking slowly down the corridor. The footsteps halted often enough as the guard stopped to shove food to some other poor victim locked away in this grim stone fortress. Tranorva tensed as the footsteps drew closer. Two cells away. Another ten footsteps. Another bowl of parched grain shoved through a door. Another ten footsteps.

"Hey."

Tranorva held her breath, lying perfectly still under the blanket. She knew that to the Dark Elves, the cells were moderately well lit.

"Hey. Come get your food."

Thirty seconds. Forty. How long would he wait?

"What the..." Keys rattled against the lock. "Hey! This one's not breathing!"

She had learned to swim underwater almost before she could walk, in the arctic waters of The Northland...Seventy seconds. Eighty.

The door burst open. The guard sprang across the small room, yanking the blanket off of her body. One hundred seconds. Tired as she was, she still could have managed another half minute or more. Tranorva filed the thought away as she sprang from the pallet, ramming the top of her head into the nearest guard's abdomen. That one went down even as the second one lunged at her, his dagger drawn now and ready.

He was small. Much too small to have come after her with nothing more than a wee little knife. Tranorva laughed in triumph as he buried the tiny blade into her arm. Moments later his neck snapped beneath her hands. She held the body before her, an effective shield against the third one who now came charging through the door. The knife was slippery with her own blood. She wiped it on the dead one's tunic. The third one went down, mortally wounded she could tell from the wheeze in his throat, before the whoosh of air at the back of her head warned her too late that she'd underestimated the length of time it would take the first guard to regain his footing.

Damn. She sighed as the guard's weapon impacted with her skull. Next time she would have to make sure the first one stayed down...

* * * * *

Tranorva stretched carefully, trying to determine the extent of her injuries. Nothing felt broken or out of place. Someone had thought her worth expending the energy to heal her arm of that blasted knife wound. Those could be irritating.

Unfortunately, stretching, or trying to, confirmed her fears. She couldn't move. She'd been brought out of her cell and strapped to the altar again. She concentrated on long, slow, steady breathing. There was no need for panic. True enough, she was immobilized and helpless should anyone try for retribution over the guard's deaths, but if they were going to kill her as punishment they'd have done so already.

She was so tired...she would have let her eyes slip shut once again, but she had to think. She needed a plan. There was a way out of this. As long as you were alive, there was always a way to escape.

Instinct told her the Priestess wanted her alive. At least for now. As long as that one thought there was some hope that Tranorva might embrace the Dark gods, she was safe. Except for their torture—or whatever the Dark Priestess's seduction might be called. In truth Tranorva might have been swayed with the strength of their attitude toward sexual pleasures alone, had she not her mother's words still firmly branded in her mind.

"Chaos and Destruction must never win."

As a child she had known that her father would give his life to protect his family from the forces of Chaos and Destruction. Her childhood had ended the night Shammall came to take them to Grandmother's. Father would come for them here, on the mountain. If they left how would he know where to find them? They were to wait for him at the camp. Alone, Mother would have waited there for him forever. If she was willing to leave with Shammall, that could mean only one thing.

Tranorva had screamed out her rage in the night.

Father was dead.

Three decades later, little had dimmed the rage in her heart. As a woman she had faces to go with the gods. Destruction, that was the face of the Orcs. They looted and pillaged and destroyed everything in their paths, leaving nothing of value behind, doing nothing with what they had taken, except the captives. The captives they set to break, slowly, painfully, for no other reason than that they could.

These people, the Dark Elves, they were the ones with a plan. They were Chaos. They would seek to strip her of everything that she valued—her courage, her devotion to duty, her loyalty to her own kind, even her status as a Warrior— slowly, systematically, until they reduced her to clay, to mold to their shape. But she had still one defense against them. She still had her rage.

She had been young, but not so young as to have forgotten. The Dark Elves had attacked in the night, Orcs with them to do their bidding. Father and the other warriors had been roused from their sleep even as the first sentries spread the alarm with their death screams. She still heard their cries in her sleep. Then Mother came and Father had kissed her before he slit the back of the tent with his sword. He had vanished from her world as the hides fell soundlessly back in place in the wake of their passing.

Tranorva flinched despite herself as the shadow on the wall told her the Dark Priestess was here, though without the usual heavy tread of her feet she liked to use to make her presence anticipated. A cunningly evil smile lit the face that might otherwise have been beautiful. The eyes remained focused and shrewd, assessing their victim thoughtfully. Tranorva sensed that today's torture would be of a different sort. Today the Dark One would start on her mind.

How long could she hold out against such power? She was so tired...if she was going to escape she'd have to do it soon. They were wearing her down.

"Your father was a victim of war, child." The voice was soft and reasonable—and laced with sympathetic understanding. "You are a Warrior. Surely you understand. How many have you slain in battle? How many life's bloods have you let fall to the ground? Think you not that those who died at your blade had mothers, wives, children who might miss them? Such is the lot of a Warrior, to leave these broken lives behind."

Tranorva worked carefully to seal off her mind as her mother had taught her. She had not known these Priestesses had the power to read her thoughts. Or perhaps she had not such a gift. This was where Tranorva herself would have started. Shared sorrow. Establish a common ground. "Those that I killed, I killed in battle. I came no' in the night like a thief to take the lives of innocent women and children."

"You came and you slaughtered. You had your orders, and you followed them. You were your mother's right arm, aimed wherever she pointed you. There must have been times when you wondered. Why would she send an army against a few hundred men trying to scrape an existence out of the wilderness? There were women and children amongst the Élandra farms she sent you to loot and destroy. What was their crime? That they were different from you? They were peaceful farmers! There were women and children with the tundra Rangers she sent you to execute. You followed orders. Surely their deaths have been on your conscience. What would you say to those children who watched their fathers die that day had you the chance?"

Tranorva felt her breath hit an uneven note. The Élandra farms had been nothing but aggressive attempts to occupy Northland territories. The Outlawed Rangers, however, had been a hard thing for her and her men. The Rangers' families had fought by their sides..."We fought as we had to fight. Those who died took up arms against us. They had the chance to lay down their weapons. Their victims had no' that chance."

"And so you slaughtered the children, because you had to. Can you not see that we are the same? I follow orders as you must. You lay the blame for other's decisions at my feet. What choice does a soldier ever have? We follow orders. It has always been so."

"I am not a machine. I am a Warrior. I follow orders that are fair and just. I have not willingly laid the edge of my blade on the throats of innocent unarmed civilians. This has never been the way of my people."

"What if I told you your precious father yet lives? That he serves by choice within these very walls? Let me show you our ways. You will come to understand us, even as I understand you. You can do now what you could not as a child. I will give him to you as your initiation gift."

Tranorva yanked against her restraints with all the power of a maddened Northland Warrior. "Ye lie! Thy gods are the authors of all lies! My father died in battle three decades past! Ye blaspheme his name to mention it here in this foul place!"

The Dark One's face broke into an icy smile as Tranorva fought against her restraints. "Roahr VinDall yet lives. Roahr VinDall serves by my side. Your people hid his existence from you that he might not be an embarrassment to them. Would you not do all within your power to protect him? Turn my invitation down and I will kill him while you watch."

The band on Tranorva's right wrist snapped as she wrenched against it. Her momentum carried her half off the table. Blind rage had her hand around the Dark One's throat, spanning it as her thumb bit into the soft, fleshy skin over the jugular. The High Priestess screamed, a high, shrill wail of protest as Tranorva yanked her closer, her rage more than a match for the strength this one possessed.

Tranorva had no weapon, but it mattered not. Escape was within her grasp, one way or the other. She closed her teeth over that fragile windpipe, using her free arm to keep the hands from casting their magic. Only the metallic ping of the door opening behind her warned her that someone had heard the Dark One's cry. Footsteps raced across the room. A Male shouted for help.

Tranorva bit down harder, grinding her teeth into the fragile skin, hoping to accomplish her goal before reinforcements arrived. She felt the first taste of blood pour onto her tongue even as the impact hit the back of her head. She laughed in triumph as the blackness took over…

Chapter Four

Géndalaine, High Priestess of Élahandara, cursed herself roundly for a fool. Tranorva would never be broken. The woman was dangerous. Rage spilled like the blood from the wound on her throat. Arrogance. That was all it was. Arrogance on her part to think that she could win that one over. But it would have been such a victory. It would have broken the morale of the Northland troops to see the Warrior mistress at the head of the Élandra army.

She should have known better. She should have ordered Tranorva's death immediately. By the gods she would remedy that mistake today. Now. Within the hour. Just as soon as —

Géndalaine stopped in mid-stride as she flung open the door to her apartment. The room was not empty. A young male lay on her bed, naked, looking startled and half wild, as if he'd been asleep when she flung open the door. And from his deliciously tousled look, perhaps he had. Géndalaine licked her lips in anticipation. "Who are you, and what are you doing in my quarters?" she demanded, centering her rage on the unfortunate male.

"I — I am a gift, Mistress. From your sword-sister, Nafésti of Talandar."

Géndalaine crossed the room slowly, taking her time in studying this gift. Nafésti had incredibly good taste. He was young. No more than sixty, she'd guess. He sat now half-sprawled on the bed, his legs to one side, his weight supported on one arm, his face still fuzzy with sleep and wild with the sudden fear.

He would be tall. Taller than most of the males — only a few inches shorter than she herself. He was fine-boned, but still solid, in that delicately male sort of way. Beautiful, really. Géndalaine stared down at him a minute before she backhanded him hard enough to knock him flat on the bed. He lay where she'd dropped him, though she could see he wanted to run. Good boy. "I should kill you. Your impudence alone is worth the price of your life."

A smile stole slowly across his face. "But you won't, Mistress."

"Why won't I?"

"Because you're curious. You want to know what Nafésti saw in me that made her think I might be a suitable gift for you."

Géndalaine shrieked as she jumped on the ancient carved wooden bed, landing neatly astride his waist as she swung both fists at that pretty-boy face. His hands closed over her fists, his grip surprisingly strong. She pitted her strength against him, determined to beat the smile from his face. Instead of defending himself, he pulled her fist to his mouth, laying his lips across the inside of her wrist where the pulse beat against the dusky ebony of her skin.

Géndalaine felt her breath catch in her wounded throat. Her vision began to blur as his lips moved slowly up her arm, stopping to lick the delicate point at the inside of her elbow. The sensation of his tongue against her skin made her shudder with rage which was fast turning to an all-encompassing lust.

She made no protest when he rolled with her, her hands still locked in his. Now she lay flat on her back on the bed, his lithe young body positioned over her, his eyes dancing now with laughter. Damn it, laughter was not the emotion she wanted to elicit in a male. She wanted fear. She wanted...

His erection surged against her belly, a white-hot heat burning against her skin. His teeth grazed over her shoulder, then gentled as his tongue moved to trace the injury to her neck, slowly, deliberately licking the blood from her wound. He traced the line where the blood had run down her chest. Slowly, very slowly, their hands still locked, he moved the thin silk out of his way, using only his lips and his teeth to undress her.

She was ready to melt in his hands by the time his lips made their first assault on her aching breast. She heard his sharp intake of breath as he stared down at her. Then slowly, deliberately, he ran his tongue across her nipple, his smile deepening as her body shook with desire and her breasts jutted out to meet him. He lowered his mouth again, suckling like a greedy child, flicking the end of his tongue across the bud of her nipple all the while.

Géndalaine made no effort to stifle the cry that tore from her injured throat. She bucked up against him, grinding her aching mound against his rigid cock. "By the gods," she panted. "Now! I want you now!"

He laughed at her again, the way no one had dared in three centuries. "And I want you to wait. I'm going to make you wait. I want to hear you beg."

"I will kill you, you impudent young fool!"

He merely transferred his attentions to the other breast, licking in an ever-tightening circle around the areola, flicking his tongue across her skin in short little darts designed to pinpoint her concentration on nothing but him. It was working. She was more acutely aware of his body than she had ever been of anyone's save her own. She cried out again as he sucked the nipple into his mouth, giving it at once all the attention she had craved. His cock, hard as an oak shaft between them, ground slowly against her as he began to circle his hips, so close to where she wanted him, so close.

"Please," she whimpered.

"What? I don't think I heard you, Mistress."

She lunged at him with her teeth, ready to bite and tear, but he met her mouth in a kiss that scorched her, leaving her breathless and stunned. He changed the motion of his hips, drawing down, and down again, until the tip of his rigid cock forced a path between her springy curls to the source of her agony. For it was agony now as he moved against her, his cock a burning torch against her aching clit. She arched against him, bringing her legs up and around his waist, attempting to impale herself on him, but he escaped.

"Please," she begged again. "I want you. I want to feel you inside me."

"I want to feel you around me," he whispered, sliding easily into her heat. "By the gods," he murmured against her throat. "You feel perfect. So tight. So hot."

He stroked into her, young and hot and hard, yet still in control. Géndalaine felt the tension of the day slip away. Yes. This one would do. He would do for quite a while. She would wait till later to kill him.

He suckled her breasts again, his touch expert, knowing just how to bring her to the hardest peak. "You are exquisite," he assured her. "So beautiful." He moved to trace the tip of her long, pointed ear between his lips.

Maybe much, much later. The room shimmered with lights like the brightest show of stars in the night as she shattered around him. He stilled within her a moment, letting her absorb the glory, before he shifted, pulling her with him to the edge of the bed. He stood over her now, stroking into her slowly at first, then harder as her body responded to him once again. Her hands were free now, and she used them to explore his body, perfect, hard and well muscled, and covered with a fine sheen of sweat from their efforts together.

"Show me," he instructed as he thrust into her harder, pulling her hips against him now for leverage. "Show me what you like."

She'd never done that before. Done something sexually just because her lover desired it. The thought wouldn't have occurred to her. He was a male. He was there to serve her. He was...enticingly beautiful. And so focused on her. Géndalaine watched his eyes darken to the color of blackest ebony as she traced the circle of her own nipples, raising her fingers to wet them as she tweaked the tips into hard, aching buds. She lifted her breasts, feeling the weight of them, pinching the nipples hard as she shattered around him again.

There was no pause this time. He drove into her harder, faster, the movements frenzied and jerking with need. She ran her fingers up over his chest and higher, pulling his head down until she could stroke the tips of his delicate, perfect ears with her tongue. It was his turn to cry out, screaming her name as he raged within her, spilling his seed in a fiery gush that brought her to her final shattering climax. The room spun around them in a crazy kaleidoscope of colors as he collapsed on top of her, his breath coming in ragged gasps.

"So beautiful," he murmured against her neck.

"So are you," she assured him. And so young and so perfect. Yes indeed. Géndalaine decided she might keep this one around for quite a while before she killed him. A sudden thought occurred to her. An absurd idea, but one she voiced anyway. "Do you have a name?"

"Yes, Mistress. I am honored that you should ask. Élandine. I am called Élandine."

"Élandine," she repeated. "In the old tongue it means 'Beautiful One.' How appropriate."

He managed the strength to move beside her onto the bed, folding his body around hers as he kissed her shoulder at the base of her neck. "You are too kind, Mistress."

She stretched languorously against his warmth, comfortable in their nakedness together. "I may still kill you."

"You have that right, Mistress."

"I should kill you. Your impudence alone is worth the price of your life."

A smile stole across his face. "But you won't, Mistress."

"I won't?"

"Not just now." His fingertips traced the outline of her ear, making her want to purr like a giant cat.

"I will. But not right now."

"No, Mistress. Not now. You should get to know me much better before you kill me."

Géndalaine felt her blood beginning to heat again as he stroked his fingers over her skin. "Much better," she agreed.

"Nafésti was going to kill me herself," he mused, "But somehow she never got around to it. She thought perhaps you might like the privilege."

"I must remember to thank Nafésti, and tell her what marvelous taste she has in males."

* * * * *

Tranorva awoke strapped to the altar again.

She wasn't dead. Surely you couldn't hurt like this if you were dead.

If she wasn't dead, she had to escape.

She felt more than a little disoriented. Tired. She was so tired. Perhaps she would wait just a while longer to escape…

Had she been brought back here before? How long had it been? She couldn't quite remember. She had to escape…

Her head still hurt where she'd been hit from behind, knocked unconscious again. She might have been taken back to her small stone cell. She had vague impressions of a long restless night spent on a hard pallet while her head threatened to explode.

A warm hand stroked gently across her throat, brushing back her wild tumble of hair as the fingertips began probing gently for the beat of her pulse. Tranorva's eyes flew open to stare into those of a Dark Male. He smiled down at her with eyes that looked almost familiar. Eyes that seemed to be trying to tell her something.

Three fingers pressed against the side of her throat. Slowly, deliberately, the fingers spread wide apart. The nails rocked against her, pricking her skin, then pulled away, so as not to leave any mark. The fingertips pressed into her, no longer gentle as they drew down toward her breastbone. Tranorva understood their meaning well enough.

Three slashes across the upper chest. Clan of the Wolf. Tranorva swallowed hard, fighting back the tears that threatened. She'd never been rescued before. Never needed rescuing. It was a humbling experience. The face looking down at her slowly closed its eyes, sending an unmistakable message. Tranorva forced herself to relax as her lids veiled her sight to the narrowest of slits.

"She's still unconscious, Mistress." The voice sounded rich, and deep, and tinged with humor. "So far your methods seem to have been less than effective with this one."

Tranorva forced herself to lie perfectly still. Apparently the Dark One's methods had proven effective enough. She hadn't managed to escape, and the Priestess was still alive. "She is a waste of my time. I should have killed her." The voice sounded a little hoarse, though that might have been wishful thinking. Still, Tranorva smiled to herself. Small victories.

"Why don't you let me give this one a try? Perhaps I can break her." The hand on her skin seemed to be trying to reassure her, though Tranorva thought she might be grasping for any mote of hope.

"Have a care, you impudent young fool, lest I turn my attentions toward you." The Priestess did not sound as displeased with the male as her words implied. Rather the contrary. Tranorva could have sworn she found his impudence flattering.

The male only laughed. "I shall fear you when you tire of me, Mistress, and not before."

"Do what you will with her. I shall enjoy your entertainment."

Their laughter held dark promises jointly understood. Tranorva offered a silent prayer to the seven gods for strength and endurance.

The male stroked his hand gently over her skin. "Open your eyes, my fair beauty. We have so much to offer you. Power beyond your imagination. The best armies in the world at your command. And a dozen such as myself as your personal slaves. What have those who are lost to you offered as compensation for a lifetime of duty?"

Tranorva swallowed hard. Indeed it was difficult to remember with the handsome, exotic creature stroking his hands over her naked breasts. "The duty to family and Clan needs no reward save brotherhood," she managed, proud of the force with which she managed to convey her words.

His fingers dipped between her thighs, stroking up the soft flesh of her inner leg until his palm rested against her heat, grinding rhythmically against her until it became hard to think. "Family. Do you even know what that means? The name of the House you would die for is not even your own."

Anger warred with fear. He knew her too well. He played her body with perfection. "How come ye to know of my family?"

"My mistress has found me ever useful," the male answered cryptically. "I have many talents."

Apparently his talents included those of an experienced lover, for she shattered under his hand, aching for more. She would not. She might be helpless to withstand his physical onslaught, but she would not respond to his treachery. "My House is the House I choose to serve, and my position one I am entitled to by right of my mother's marriage."

Three fingers dipped inside her, demanding her response. "You are the bastard daughter of a disgraced House, and the name that House bears is not even your own, for your mother was but the younger daughter of House Lindall, and now that House is ruled by her sister's son. Were the truth known, you would have no House to return to. You know this, deep in your heart you know I speak the truth."

Ayailla, Evalayna's own mother, was House Lindall? Seanen was her own cousin? Mother had raised him all these years in her own House without one word of the truth? Tranorva fought her restraints, both to escape his touch that continually roused her traitorous body, and to escape the fear his words elicited. Rage surged up within Tranorva's blood. She twisted violently against her wrist cuffs, determined to tear them from their marble mountings. "You lie! Your gods are the authors of lies! You would trick me with half-truths and treachery. I will not dishonor my House nor my Clan!"

He moved away, leaving her body aching with need as he moved to stand at the top of the altar next to her. His fingers stroked her lips, wet with her own juices. Her smell mingled with his. She tore at the restraints mindlessly. "Your Clan is not even your own, for Roahr VinDall was your father, and he was not of the Northlanders. A Second Sister takes the Clan of her husband. Though Roahr VinDall never bothered to grace your mother with his House or his Clan, since he saw no need to formalize their union."

He held her head now, so that she could not bang it into the altar, knocking herself unconscious. "You are a bastard, from a long line of bastards M'Lady. You have no House, no name, and no Clan. No matter how your kind maligns us, we are the ones to offer you truth. Your future is your own to choose. We offer you everything. Position. Power. Wealth. And we offer it honestly. We do not choose to hide behind lies and half-truths. That is not our way. Join us, mistress. We are not evil. Only mal-used by those who fear us for our honesty and our beauty. Come with us, Mistress. Allow us to serve you."

Tranorva cried out in anger and rage as the Dark Priestess moved to join in the assault on her senses. The Dark One only smiled as their eyes met, her eyes already clouded with passion. Tranorva gasped in outrage as the High Priestess ran her hands up the inside of Tranorva's thighs, then over her hips, swirling up to tease her nipples into aching mounds of need. Tranorva wanted to be able to tell the Priestess to keep her hands to herself and mean it, but the aching need threatened to rip her apart.

She'd tasted this one's blood on her tongue. Now her traitorous body responded thus to this woman's touch? Had she ever thought herself immune to such carnal lusts? At least no man she'd ever attempted to couple with had raised such feelings of all-encompassing need. Yet as warm feminine lips closed over her aching breasts Tranorva had to admit that she was far from immune. She should be planning new ways to attempt escape. She should be finding ways to argue against the Male's logic. She should...

Tranorva raised her head as far as she could to watch as the Dark One lowered her mouth over her aching clit. Just as the Priestess's tongue dove into her hot, aching sheath, the Dark Male drove into the Priestess from behind, impaling her as she lapped at Tranorva's throbbing nub. The Priestess shrieked in desire even as a growl shook loose from the young male's lips.

The effect of their combined lusts loosed an answering need that shook Tranorva to the core of her understanding of herself. She was not—she should not—Damn them! They were the enemy. At least the woman was. Tranorva was not sure exactly what the male was about. The Wolf Clan Symbol was no deep secret mystery. Every Clansman bore the matching tattoo. Now that she thought about it, he might have been merely tracing the lines scored into her shoulder. But...

The Dark Priestess licked her rough tongue over Tranorva's clit, demanding response. Tranorva's world shook as she shattered. Her sworn enemy had brought her to climax, and would do it again. The same enemy she'd tried to kill—last night? This morning? Tranorva had lost track of time.

The greedy mouth sucked her juices as she shattered yet again, feeling as if the focus of the universe had narrowed to the burning need centered between her thighs. The Priestess kneaded her fingers into Tranorva's breasts in rhythm to the male's long measured strokes into her own greedy body.

The male. Her benefactor? Her rescuer? Or yet another pawn in the Dark One's game of seduction? He knew too much about her. Lies. All lies. She wanted to believe them lies, but his words held the ring of truth, making too much sense in her ever shifting view of the world of politics.

Tranorva could see the strain in the male's face as he forced himself to maintain control. His hands grasped Tranorva's thighs for leverage as he drove into the Dark One time and again. She was sure there would be bruises from his grip come the morrow. But for now all she felt was her universe shattering as she discovered within herself a need unlike anything she'd ever known before. The Dark Priestess shuddered against Tranorva's waiting clit once, twice, and yet again, and still Tranorva felt herself hurtled toward that final oblivion.

They would be done soon, she could tell. The male's speed increased to a frenzied urgency. The Priestess's tongue drove into Tranorva in an equally frantic pace. Tranorva tested her restraints once again, but the broken manacle had been replaced with a sturdier model. If she could have broken free, would she have tried to escape? Now?

Later. She would deal with escape later. Now she wanted — she needed. Tranorva tried desperately to find something to hold, to touch, some way to urge them on as the final climax built within her, but she was utterly and completely helpless — to protest or to join. The Priestess understood, however, and changed her focus, licking and sucking at her clit until Tranorva shattered with a roar she could not contain.

The Dark Priestess screeched, her body freezing for a moment before she collapsed on top of Tranorva, her hands still gripping Tranorva's breasts as the final shudder shook her. The male, too, added his cry to chorus. He did not, however, collapse on top of the Priestess. Instead, his eyes met Tranorva's as he calmly fastened his hands around the limp, satiated body before him and ended her life. Tranorva watched in perplexed fascination as the Dark One became momentarily aware, and then the understanding in her eyes went dim as she slumped to the floor.

Chapter Five

The Dark Male stood silently before Tranorva, the Priestess forgotten as his fingers brushed over her skin. For a moment Tranorva thought he intended to rape her. Though perhaps it would not be rape. She felt her body respond to his nearness as if all of the other events that had gone on in this room had no meaning.

This was so much like the dream.

He was the enemy.

He had killed for her.

She had to escape.

She was so tired....

His hands trembled against her skin now as he reached for the straps holding her ankles. How odd. Tranorva sensed that his sudden vulnerability had nothing to do with the dead woman at his feet. The broken Priestess was of no consequence to him. He'd already forgotten her.

Well, the Priestess was of consequence to Tranorva. The dead woman meant everything to her. The Dark Male leaned close as he unstrapped her left arm. His hair tumbled down around his face and he shook it over his shoulder, annoyed. Tranorva fisted her hand in his hair and dragged him backwards across the altar with her as she rolled to her feet. Her elbow came down hard against his windpipe as she unfastened the last buckle with her teeth.

She kept her voice low, knowing the guards were listening outside the door. "Tell me one reason why I should not kill ye, little man."

She let the pressure off slightly, but still he chose not to defend himself. He seemed to be concentrating heavily on some point just behind her head. A fine line of sweat beaded his brow as her fingers tightened around his throat. Then he shifted, his image blurring around the edges, until Tranorva wiped a hand over her eyes to restore her sight. When her vision cleared, her mother's pet Mage, Shammall, lay passively under her hand.

"By the seven gods," she whispered. "Impossible."

She stared at the Elf's beautiful, naked body. Her grip went slack. She was so tired...she needed to think. Nothing was as it seemed. Politics and illusions. Mother. Mother had sent Shammall to rescue her.

One man, alone, into a fortress no army could penetrate?

Not a man, no. Not a man at all. No man could command such magic. Nor any Elf, to her knowledge. She had to swallow hard to find her voice. "How did ye manage that?"

He shrugged, his eyes still wary. "It's a gift I was born with, M'Lady."

Tranorva ran her gaze over the body of the stranger she'd known all her life. By the gods he was gorgeous. She'd always resisted picturing him naked, knowing his loyalties lay elsewhere. And indeed, this body was an illusion, created for her benefit.

He was either an Elemental, not a man at all, or he was *Sidhe*—a Changeling or Faerie shape shifter—one of the magical creatures that slipped between this world and the next. In either case neither this nor the Dark Elf he'd entered the room as were his true form. How many other identities had she known him as through the years? How many other secrets had her mother kept from her?

He was also far more powerful and possibly even less trustworthy than she had ever imagined. And yet this ancient creature stood before her as if waiting for her to pass judgment on him. Tranorva removed her hand from his neck.

"Be ye my pet cat, as well? He has been a little too friendly of late."

He flushed as he rolled to his feet. "No, M'Lady. My talents are limited. I can but change my appearance, not what I am. Only your people posses the talent to transform to your totem animal. I envy your family their familiarity with the form of the wolf. I thought this form would at least be more familiar to you, if not exactly welcome."

Tranorva snorted softly. "Ye just killed for me, Mage. Why should ye worry that I might find any of thy forms unpleasant?"

He stared at the cold stone floor. "I am not unaware of your feelings toward me, M'Lady."

Tranorva shook her head. She must have had her brain addled by that blow to the back of her skull. She could have sworn that the Mage not only cared what she thought of him, but that, at the very moment, her opinion mattered more than anything else in the universe. Well, she hadn't even been aware that the ever stoic Mage *had* feelings, let alone that her opinion of him had any bearing on his life. She stifled a sigh. It didn't matter the race. Males made absolutely no sense.

"Mage, it is true there be no love between us. I am no' certain just why the Dark Priestess took such interest in me, but if I had no' eventually agreed to join her she would have killed me. I owe ye my life. 'Tis not a debt that will easily be repaid."

Shammall kept his eyes cast on the floor. "Please forgive my harsh words about your lineage earlier, M'Lady. The Dark One could read my thoughts. I meant only to disguise my true feelings from her."

By the gods, he was blushing! The man—or whatever he was—was embarrassed. Tranorva slowly paced the room, gathering up the High Priestess's clothing. Though Shammall stood eyes downcast, he was watching her. He was trying not to stare at her body, but whenever she moved, his eyes still followed her.

Tranorva took her time digesting this new information as she dressed in the dead woman's garb. The corpse itself was naked, except for a necklace—several gold and platinum keys on a fine Mithral chain. Tranorva removed the necklace from the corpse and placed it over her own neck, still watching Shammall watching her. There was power in this. Circling closer, Tranorva raised her fingertips to trace over Shammall's golden skin. "If the words ye spoke were the truth, then ye have given me the greatest gift of my life, Mage. Ye have given me my freedom. If I return to House Lochinvar now, I come of my own free will, not as a slave bound by my birth. I am doubly in your debt."

He swallowed hard, looking anywhere but at her. "I spoke only the truth, M'Lady. To do otherwise would have meant death to us both. Géndalaine was very powerful. I had not the strength to kill her except at the moment when she was most vulnerable."

"Look at me," Tranorva commanded. "And tell me the truth." His eyes met hers, dark with desire. "I am a jealous mistress. I would not share your loyalties with any other. Are ye bound to my mother, or House Lochinvar?"

"I am my own, M'Lady, bound to no one accept by my own choosing."

"Then choose, Shammall. My Lady Mother or myself. Ye cannot serve us both."

His eyes never wavered. "I made that choice thirty years ago, M'Lady. As I have served Lady Ayailla and Lady Evalayna, so I shall now serve you. I am yours to command."

Great. Now she had her own pet Mage. The ache in her head must have addled her. Hysterical laughter threatened to overwhelm her.

Perhaps she was simply too tired…

She leaned forward to whisper in the Mage's ear. "Doest thou trust me?"

If possible, he turned even paler. "With my life, M'Lady."

His deep voice contrasted nicely with his small, sculptured pretty-boy Elven looks. Tranorva found herself picturing him as a Northland Warrior. No, that would not work, for the first image that came to her mind belonged to Seanen, who was now her *cousin*. Tranorva sighed as her fantasies ended. Another hopeful possibility that would never come to fruition.

* * * * *

"Guards!"

Élandine froze, his clothing gripped tightly in his hands. She meant to kill him. To have him killed. Once the guards saw Géndalaine's broken body his life would be over. There was no place here to run. He thought of shifting. A Troll perhaps. That might give him the power...

Doest thou trust me?

With my life, M'Lady.

His trust seemed to be a short-lived thing. Élandine swallowed hard as the doors burst open. Five guards rushed in, the Priestess Maelyn close on their heals.

"Halt!" Tranorva raised her hand palm out. "Ye will show me proper respect! I have defeated Priestess Géndalaine in combat. Behold her remains. By thy own laws I claim what was hers. Know me! I am Tranorva, High Priestess of Élahandara! Put down thy weapons and kneel at my feet!"

Could this be the same woman who had trembled with fatigue moments before? Élandine marveled at her strength of will. Her voice echoed with power, filling the chamber with her presence. The fear in the room was a tangible thing. The guards dropped to their knees, their swords offered up across their arms.

The Priestess alone remained standing at the back of the room.

Tranorva turned her attention first to him. "Attend me!"

"M'Lady." He dropped to one knee before her, still clutching his clothes before him.

"What is thy name?"

"Élandine, M'Lady."

"What belonged to Géndalaine is now mine."

By the gods, she was brilliant. Or out of her mind. "Aye, M'La—Mistress."

"There are no other witnesses to what happened here today. How long do ye think ye would live if I sent ye into these halls alone?"

She said this before witnesses, who would surely repeat all that they heard? "I am grateful for your protection, Mistress." *If you don't get me killed.* 'Twas a pity she couldn't read minds...

"That is as it should be. See that ye remember thy place." Dismissing him, she turned to face the still standing Priestess. "Who are ye, and how dare ye defy my divine right to thy fealty?"

The Priestess approached, circling warily, her knuckles grown white as she grasped her staff of office. "I am Maelyn, First Priestess of Élahandara, and it is my right to succeed Géndalaine as High Priestess. You are not Élandra! You have not the right to wear the sacred keys! You have not the right to our throne. Why should I lay down my staff before you, when you are nothing to me? For all I know, Géndalaine died of her own excess. She was old, and the strain of your discipline may have been too much for her. I name you Charlatan, and claim the high seat for my own!"

Tranorva threw back her head with a roar of laughter. "Ye? Ye would challenge me, little woman? Ye would challenge a Northland Warrior?" She stood before the First Priestess unarmed, raising her hands in beckoning. "Come to me, sister. Let us test thy strength against mine. I needed no weapon to drop Géndalaine at my feet. Rest assured that a dozen Priestesses of lesser houses stand ready to take thy place, and all will swear fealty to me for a tenth of thy price. I accept thy challenge!"

Maelyn raised her twisted rune staff and brought it down hard against the stone floor. *Remember our lessons!* Élandine ached to scream. Lightning arched through the room, bouncing off floor and ceiling as it converged on Tranorva's head. Élandine barely dared to breathe as the energy cracked through the air. Tranorva shimmered for an instant, surrounded in flames, before her laughter echoed against the walls once again.

"Know ye not that I am the daughter of a great Shaman? I am not ignorant of thy arts!"

Tranorva raised one hand, palm out, and the lingering fire coalesced on the tips of her fingers, spinning there as if in slow motion. Capturing the lightning in her fist, she drew back her arm as if to hurl a discus.

Maelyn screamed in outrage as she charged, brandishing her staff as a weapon. Tranorva opened her fist as she completed the arc, sending the lightning ball hurtling back against Maelyn's attack. The First Priestess staggered as her own blow hit her, dropping to one knee from the impact.

Tranorva pressed her advantage, moving in to rip the staff from the stunned Priestess's grasp. Her left-hand crushed the First Priestess's throat as her right brought the staff crashing to bear as a cudgel. She halted her blow inches from the quivering Priestess's head. "Think no' that I will no' kill ye. Swear to me now and live. Stand in my way again and thy life is forfeit. I will no' tolerate any less than thy full obeisance."

Maelyn's rigid body went slack in Tranorva's grasp. A strangled gasp broke from her throat.

"What? I could not make out thy words."

Maelyn raised her arms, palm up, as Tranorva allowed her enough freedom to speak. "I swear."

Tranorva loosed her grip on Maelyn's fragile windpipe. "Swear by thy gods."

Maelyn ran her fingers over her bruised throat, waves of enmity shining from her eyes. "By all that is holy, by the Lords of Chaos and Destruction, I pledge my fealty to Lady Tranorva, High Priestess of Élahandara."

Tranorva let her eyes settle on the five cowering male guards. "Should I hear my Priestess's name dishonored in any way, thy lives will be forfeit."

All five guards bowed their heads in agreement as they backed closer to the door.

Tranorva placed the staff of office back into the hands of her Priestess. "I accept thy oath, Lady Maelyn, and name ye the First of my Council. Thy first duty is to inform thy sisters of my new office."

Maelyn made an obvious effort not to gape at Tranorva. "You are most gracious, M'Lady. I shall be honored to accept First Chair at your table."

Tranorva gestured to the guards who knelt before her. "Go! Spread the news to thy mistresses on the eight points of the Star. I have defeated Géndalaine in combat and claimed right of succession." She turned back to Maelyn. "Have Géndalaine laid out and prepared for her rights. I will receive the oaths of fealty from each of thy Sister Priestesses at the ceremony for her passage as the sun sets tomorrow."

Tranorva gestured again to the guards. "Away with thee."

As a unit the guards turned to flee her presence. Maelyn trailed in their wake, not far behind. Tranorva closed her eyes, looking suddenly older, and tired. And...Human. Élandine repressed the urge to gather her into his arms and comfort her. Instead he teased her as he pulled on his clothes. "You are a fine actress, M'Lady. You should have taken up touring with a traveling minstrel show."

She sighed, pulling herself back together with a visible effort. "Take me to Géndalaine's quarters, please, Élandine. I must sleep. If no one kills me while I die that little death, tomorrow will be a busy day."

A new respect overwhelmed him. "No one will bother you while you sleep, M'Lady. I swear it."

She leaned on him as they made their way down the long, cold stone corridors. Élandine marveled again at the strength of Tranorva's will that kept her on her feet. He bolted the door to Géndalaine's room behind them. Somehow he doubted Tranorva would even notice the splendid opulence of the chamber. She collapsed half off the ancient carved bed, her face buried in a pile of silk brocade pillows, asleep before she managed to crawl under the coverlets. He hated to disturb her enough to move her, though she seemed to take no notice as he arranged her more comfortably and pulled the bed curtains shut to seal in her warmth. But as he moved to stand guard, her hand captured his.

"I am so cold," she whispered. "Do no' leave me."

His hands trembled as he lifted the covers, but she was fast asleep as he wrapped his warmth around her. Her deep, even breathing assured him that at last he was safe. "I can never leave you, M'Lady," he whispered. "I love you."

Chapter Six

Magic.

She knew it was magic. She'd escaped. There was no reason for her to be back here, strapped to the stone altar again. It had to be magic. The Élandra Priestesses commanded talents far greater than she had ever suspected. To have captured her and held her immobilized right under the eyes of her entire army bespoke of a magic as powerful as her mother's.

Perhaps as powerful as Ayailla herself.

Now they had taken her again in her sleep, and she was once again laid out on that same stone altar. Shammall had promised to guard her while she slept. He had given her his word…where was he?

She shook her head angrily. She didn't need Shammall. She didn't need anyone. She had escaped once, and by the gods she would do it again! Tranorva fought the restraints this time, even as she heard the booted feet approaching down the long echoing corridor.

The dream? This was the dream again?

She froze in place, listening to the footsteps. They hammered in time to the beat of her heart. The footsteps came closer. The man paused at her feet, and her heart seemed to stop. She raised her head far enough to look down. At last, at last the man had a face. Or many faces. A thrill of anticipation ran through her. Shammall had not deserted her. He was here. He shifted now from the Mage she had known all her life to the Dark Priestess, then finally to the smaller Élandra Male known as Élandine.

She knew the rudiments of the ancient language of the Elves. *Élan* meant beautiful. Before the Elven races split, the women of the ebony skin had been highly prized. The Élandra. The beautiful folk. He was Élandine.

Beautiful one.

The name hardly did justice to the form he had taken. He was more than beautiful. His slim, athletic body might have been a sculptor's work of art. Hair black as midnight spilled over his shoulders in long, shimmering waves. Tranorva swallowed hard as he moved toward her.

His hands caressed her, sliding slowly up her body, his lips pausing to pay homage to her most sensitive spots. His fingers lingered for a moment behind her knees, then moved up again, up the inside of her thighs, brushing over the place where her need was already beginning to puddle between her thighs.

"So beautiful." His voice was little more than a whisper, deep and husky, the flavor of liquid sex.

"I am no' beautiful." Even in a dream she could not help but argue. "My sister is beautiful. She is smaller and younger and far more graceful than I could ever be. I am but a Warrior." She knew what she looked like. Too big and too strong and covered with scars. Her hair was plain and straight and black as the night. Her shoulders were wider than many a man's. "Know ye not that men fear me?"

"Their loss, M'Lady." His lips lingered on the curve of her hip. "You are built like a goddess. My goddess. Allow me to worship you properly."

Somehow he lay beside her now, stretched out with his heat so near hers. She could not have objected if she'd wanted to. Not with his lips moving across her shoulder toward the curve of her aching breasts. If only she could move…

She could move. She could never move in the dream.

His lips brushed the tip of her aching breast, and she rolled toward him, encouraging, but he would not be hurried. His fingers moved up, their pace achingly slow, to cup that hot weight of flesh that begged for his touch.

She needed more. She ached to touch him. Her hands were no longer bound. She lifted her fingers to rake through his tangled curls. He shifted, rolling her to her back amongst the rich brocade pillows, suspended above her on forearms rife with muscle as he let his hair cascade down over her. She gathered handfuls of the silken mass, stroking her breasts with his tresses.

He laughed as she moved against him, demanding his touch. "So much fire. So much passion. Patience, my love."

"I do no' want to be patient!"

"M'Lady," his voice whispered in hoarse, husky surprise.

The same voice, but not the same. Tranorva opened her eyes as the feel of his breath against her skin faded. No longer the dream. She wanted to scream in frustration.

Beautiful one.

He lay next to her, propped up now on one elbow, his eyes glowing violet in the soft light that seemed to seep from the walls.

Her fingers were tangled in his hair, and it was as soft as she had imagined. She closed her eyes again, willing the pain away. Why? Why was she always alone?

"You were dreaming, M'Lady."

Well, she could see that. Why did the dream have to be so much more satisfying than any real man?

"It is said that my people have a gift for interpreting dreams."

His lips were so close to her that she could feel the heat of his breath on her cheek. She opened her eyes again, hardly daring to believe she understood what he was offering. His skin shone like onyx in the pale light of the room. Beautiful one indeed. His eyes were hypnotic. "I was dreaming of ye."

He was silent for a moment too long. She should have known better. She would have pulled back, withdrawn her hand, but strong fingers caught her, turning her wrist palm up toward his lips. The first stroke of his tongue over the base of her thumb made her breath catch in her throat. "Do not tease me, M'Lady. That could be very, very dangerous."

A power radiated in his voice that she had not heard before. Tranorva made no move to withdraw her hand from his grasp. "Are ye no' afraid of me?" she whispered, allowing a small glimmer of hope to slip through her defenses.

He laughed, though the sound conveyed more lust than humor. "Afraid? Of you? You are a mere mortal."

Tranorva shivered at the power in his voice. "Men are always afraid of me."

Slowly, holding her mesmerized with his gaze, he bent to capture her mouth, touching gently with soft, warm lips, then claiming all that she was and would be with a wanton lust that shook her to the very core of her being. "You forget, M'Lady, I am not a man."

Tension crackled in the air like its own life force. Her body trembled beneath his touch. Her voice sounded suddenly timid and strained, even to her own ears. "I—I would see ye, Mage. In thy own true form."

Violet eyes stared at her silently for a few blank, desolate moments. She was sure she had asked too much. He would disappear, no more than a memory escaped from her arms. He would...

"For three generations I have served this house. No one has ever asked this of me."

He had not said no, and she was not one to concede the point. And there was more he needed to know. "I would see thy true form, Mage. Not the illusion. I would know the face of the man who takes my maidenhead."

His eyes closed for a moment. He would run. Surely he would run now. He placed her hand against his chest, so that she could feel the beating of his heart. Strong. Steady. Excited. "You do me great honor, M'Lady."

The air around him shimmered with power. The skin under her hands glowed with an unnatural warmth. The shift came slowly this time, almost reluctantly. She tried to brace herself for whatever might come. He could look like a Troll, if he would only take her unwanted gift...

The hair became nearly white, and the dark skin melted to pale, glowing with the power she'd felt in him previously, but so much more intense. And the face..."By the seven gods," she breathed. "Ye will never let anyone else observe this form."

The eyes turned suddenly vulnerable. The aura of power dimmed slightly. "Shall I shift back, M'Lady? Does this form displease you so?"

"Displease me?" How could he think such a thing? "Ye have the face of a god! Ye could not function beside me in this form! Women would throw themselves at thy feet! We would be tripping over the bodies, worse than the carnage of battle!"

The pale golden skin flushed with embarrassment. "You mock me."

Tranorva ran her fingers over the shimmering golden silk of his cheek. "I speak but the truth."

"You are daft, M'Lady. Among my people I am considered quite plain."

"Plain." She blinked slowly as she studied his shimmering skin, so pale against her own sun-weathered hide. "Have ye a name, plain one?"

He looked away again. "No, M'Lady. Nothing that could be spoken in your tongue. Call me whatever you wish."

Her fingers outlined the soft bloom of his lips. "Then I shall name ye Élandine always, my beautiful one. I shall be quite satisfied with thy simple beauty. Any more might overwhelm my senses."

The lips parted to nip gently at the tips of her fingers. Her breath caught in her throat at the power that radiated from eyes that shimmered with lust. They changed color, from violet to blue now, then green, then darkest silver, like the ocean in winter. "I am honored to be your first, M'Lady. I am pleased that you waited for me."

She closed her eyes, trying to hide the pain, but she knew she could not hide the truth that flamed in her cheeks. "'Twas no' by choice. I have a—a gift. Men fear me."

"Look at me, M'Lady."

Warily she opened her eyes.

He seemed taller, now, larger, as he stretched at her side amid the scattered pillows. "I do not fear you."

"But…"

His hands framed her face as his lips caught the taste of her argument, silencing her with a kiss that threatened to wipe all thought from her mind. His tongue asked for entrance, and she allowed it, unsure, but willing to learn. He lay on his side, now, his hand in her hair, supporting her head as his mouth plundered hers.

His right hand wandered lower, lighting a fire wherever it touched, lifting, stroking, exploring. "I want you to sing for me, Wolf-woman," he whispered against her lips. His fingers paused to admire the smooth, soft flesh of thighs before they moved on to brush over her damp curls. She moaned against his mouth as he kissed her again, deeper this time, demanding more than she had known she had to give.

His fingers caressed, gently at first, then dipped inside, pausing as he felt the barrier there. Her heart forgot to beat. One finger slipped inside her, then two, as he made room for what was to come. His fingers taught her the rhythm of their bodies, as the heel of his hand ground against her. She moved in rhythm to the harsh panting of their breath.

"Sing for me." His lips kissed lower, across her jaw and down, over her shoulder to the curve of her aching breasts. She cried out as his tongue teased her nipples into twin mounds of need. She needed to feel. She needed to touch. Her hand sought him out, searching restlessly through the layers of fine flowing silk for the source of her pleasure. He groaned against her as she located her prize.

Hot. Hot satin slicked over hard sword-steel. Molten metal within, still malleable from the forge. He jumped at her touch, and a few drops of liquid heat burst from the tip of his cock, dampening her fingers as she explored.

There was power in this. His body convulsed as she wrapped her hand around him, drawing her fist down his length. "I want thee," she breathed. "I want to feel thy sword within my sheath."

"Patience, my greedy lover. Not yet."

Patience? She surged against his fingers, riding the crest of the wave. What more could he want of her? What more...

"Sing for me, lover."

She cried out as he pushed her past her endurance, rocketing against his knowing fingers as they stroked her to climax. Still it was not what he wanted, but it was all that she knew how to give. She rode him harder, cresting again as her hand fisted around his cock.

With a cry of need he rose to his knees over her, kicking free of the last of his shimmering silks. He captured her hands in his, pausing to stare down at her for a long, unhurried moment. "So beautiful," he murmured. "So young, and so beautiful."

She thought to tell him she had passed her thirty-fourth year, but then all capacity for thought left as he drove his cock into her, ripping her barrier asunder with a wave of searing pain. She cried out again, though there was no lust in her voice this time.

Still. The room was perfectly still. The only sound was the steady rhythm of their long, harsh breaths. She could feel the beat of his pulse as his burning flesh melted her from within. Slowly she opened her eyes.

He looked like one of the gods, translucent and shining, his hair a pale golden halo around his head. He held fast, poised there above her, his gray-green eyes fastened upon her, waiting.

Relief flooded her senses as the pain subsided. "I thank thee," she whispered. "I—"

His lips over hers sealed off words that were inadequate in any case. And then he began to move his cock within her. Silk over hot, molten fire. He moved slowly at first, then faster as she caught fire with him, raising her hips to meet his hot, heavy thrusts. Something built within her. Something more, something new, something uncontrollable. She crested and shattered like breaking bottles of mead, over and over again, but still it was not enough. "Sing for me," he pleaded, driving into her with the frantic force of his final desperation.

The scream built within her until it threatened to rip her apart. She shattered, spiraling over the edge, clawing her way toward some oblivion that threatened her grasp on her shifting world. The scream that was not a scream spilled forth, the sound a deafening roar.

Her arms that were no longer arms clawed at her mate, threatening to tear him asunder. He met her with a force equal to her own, punishing her as he stroked within her, ramming his massive body against her time and again. She stood now, looking down in a weird fascination at the brown shaggy fur that coated her forearms, as he plunged into her from behind, his teeth grasping the loose skin at the back of her neck.

Delicate furniture snapped like twigs as he rolled with her, supporting her weight with his paws. She roared again as the final climax came, an earth-sundering call that challenged the gods themselves to witness their joining. A roar unlike anything she'd ever heard before split the air as his molten seed spilled within her. She could feel his cock quiver helplessly within her, still grasping her tightly in his mighty paws. *At last, at last*, her mind seemed to scream, though her voice crooned another song of mating to the world.

They collapsed heavily together, shaking the floor as their massive forms rolled into a pile of tangled fur and claws. Strong limbs still cradled her. A cold nose nuzzled her cheek. Tranorva opened her heavy-lidded eyes to peer into the soft brown gaze of the massive grizzly who held her. She was surprised to find she understood when he licked her muzzle affectionately. "I love you," his eyes seemed to say.

She smiled her grizzly bear smile and laid her head upon his massive chest, her ear close to the sound of his steadily beating heart. "And I love ye," she murmured in return. And if the words sounded like the snuffling cough of a rooting bear, she worried not that he understood.

He cradled her there in his arms, safe and protected. For the first time since she'd awoken in these ancient stone halls, she was warm.

Chapter Seven

Tranorva sniffed cautiously. She didn't smell like a bear. She wriggled her muscles slightly, still feigning sleep. She didn't feel like a bear. What she felt was stiff, and sore, and mildly abused, like a woman well-loved.

Well, that bear thing was a little over the top. She wasn't sure how he'd done that, but they'd probably broken most of the furniture in the pretty little room. Such things should be left for outside. And some warning would be nice.

A hand stroked her breast, still possessive even in sleep. The noise came again, that little mouse of a noise that had pulled her back to this world. A slight scratching at the door. Tranorva forced her eyes open, anxiously surveying the room. By the gods, it was bad. As bad as she'd feared. And the man laying tangled in the covers beside her was not only naked, but pale. As she slipped from the bed, she drew the brocade coverlets up, hiding his sleeping form.

The air in the room chilled her naked body instantly. She dashed for the bolt on the door then flung herself back into bed, no longer concerned with letting the Mage sleep. His arms found her instantly and his heat wrapped around her. Still the door hadn't opened. The mouse scratched again. "Come in!" Tranorva ordered.

A mouse it was. A tiny creature, no more than half-grown, with skin the color of darkest raw honey. She was neither Dark Elf nor Wood Elf, nor any discernible point of the Star, but some exotic mixture of races. Tranorva stared at the mouse in fascination as she scurried into the room.

"Good morning, Mistress." The child's eyes never met hers. Her attention shifted instead to the shambles of the room as she ordered things to rights.

"Who, and what, are ye, little mouse?"

The mouse tittered softly. "Dahlai. My name is Dahlai, Mistress. And I am your bondswoman. Are you ready for your bath?"

Bondswoman. Such a thing was unheard of in the Northlands. What did one do with such a creature? "Food. I could use some food. As could my...companion."

At that announcement the covers began to stir, and Tranorva caught her breath, fearful of what the young girl might see. There was no containing the awakening Mage, however. The mouse called Dahlai stared as the covers seemed to rise of their own volition.

A deep, resonate voice came from the sheets. "Have you tired of me already, Mistress, that you would suffocate me under this pile of ill-used carpetry?"

Tranorva glanced down, wondering whether to try to explain away the Mage's pale appearance, or simply to order the little mouse to keep silent. Instead she forced herself to snap her own gaping jaw shut.

Élandine wriggled out from under the tumbled pillows and coverlets to sit up against the head of the bed, his beautiful ebony face a mask of hooded desire. "I know exactly how to break your fast, Mistress."

By the gods. He pulled her back until his sinfully beautiful body was cuddled against her, fully erect. She felt her body responding to the heat that spilled from him, forgetting the many aches and pains of the morning. "Ye may go," Tranorva ordered, waving the bondswoman away. Dahlai scuttled out the door, her eyes still fastened in wonder on the beautiful Dark Male.

Hot kisses trailed over Tranorva's spine as his fingers reached around her to splay over her breasts, pulling her tighter against the searing heat of his cock.

"Élandine," Tranorva began, once the door was shut. "I—"

His lips vibrated against the back of her neck as he spoke. "Did no one ever tell you you talk too much, woman?"

"No. No one would dare." She tried to sound annoyed, but the sharp intake of her breath as he stroked the length of her neck ruined the moment. "I would know—"

Curling around her, he quieted her lips with a kiss that threatened to addle her brains past endurance. "You were saying?"

"Ummm…" Even his breath against her cheek as he spoke felt sensuous.

"No singing this morning, my pet," he warned as he slipped his cock inside her. "There are too many too close." She rocked back against him as he rose to his knees, as attuned to his body as he was to hers.

Her fingers knotted in the soft linen sheets. "It feels so good to have ye inside me."

"Ummm," he offered by way of an answer as he stroked his fingers over her pulsing lips. He lifted her hips, granting him deeper access as he moved slowly within her.

"So many wasted years," she sighed. It was the wrong time to ask, but she had to know. "Why did ye wait so long?"

He bent to nip at her shoulder, tugging playfully as she squirmed harder against him. "A man does not take this gift from a child. I waited for you to tell me you were ready."

"I was ready a decade ago. I thought—I thought ye belonged to another. I would no' share ye with anyone. Not even my mother."

One fine ebony eyebrow arched in surprise. "Lady Evalayna? I would have been honored—but no. There was never that between us."

"Then who—" the question drifted away, forgotten, as he ground his palm against her.

"Me. Only me for you. For as long as we have together."

"Yes," she promised. Whether that was a day or a year or a lifetime. "Yes!" she screamed as he rose into her, waves crashing against a weathered shoreline. "Yes!"

And when they came together, the force of the tide and the beach, she knew that no outside influence could mar the day.

* * * * *

"May the gods grant me patience."

"Unlikely, Mistress."

The amusement in his voice only served to further annoy her. "I should kill ye. Thy impudence is worth the price of thy life."

Fine ebony shoulders rose in a delicate shrug. "You have that right."

Tranorva felt her tension ease as he stroked the curve of her shoulder with the soft, sensitive tips of his fingers.

"But you won't, will you, Mistress."

There was something fascinatingly erotic about being touched so in public. Still, she had an image to maintain. Tranorva resisted the urge to let her head fall back onto his chest. "Why will I not?"

Élandine nipped lightly against her neck. "You should get to know me much better before you kill me."

The headache eased as her blood began to heat under his touch. His lips vibrated against her skin as he whispered into her ear. *"Why should anything change with your leadership, M'Lady? These petty quarrels have existed for decades within this court. It is not your place to solve all their problems in the space of one day."*

Relief flooded through her. The lines in her forehead softened from her fearsome scowl. She flicked her fingers at the male who stood behind her, waving him away as she rose to tower over the women before her.

"Silence!"

Her voice echoed through the sudden quiet of the huge stone room. "Ye deafen me with this incessant babble!" She pointed to the loudest of the contenders, praying that she might remember their names correctly. "Maelyn, this dispute with thy sister is pointless. Why should the disposition of one mere male come between the bonds of thy birth? Share him between ye or slice him in half, I care not, but keep the matter away from my court!"

"Parsiony. She is the sister of Lanaie, and they are cousins to Maelyn and Analeas."

She frowned at the male who made a show of admiring her, while inwardly she thanked the gods for his savvy. "Parsiony, have a care lest Lanaie should also prove thy better at swordplay, for I shall certainly rid myself of one of ye and give thy House back to thy cousins to divide amongst themselves."

"Matias, Jeserat, Nellióne and Wayonka."

The feel of his hands kneading the tension from between her shoulder blades might have been worth the price of this trial alone, even without the added benefit of his tongue tickling her earlobe. "As for the rest of ye, Matias, Jeserat, Nellióne and Wayonka, none of these problems began with the rise of the moons, and none will be solved with their setting."

She waved her hand at the nearest guard. Thankfully it was not necessary that she remember that one's name. "Give me thy sword."

The guard blinked in surprise. "Yes, M'Lady."

Tranorva offered the sword hilt first to Élandine. "The lot of ye bicker like children. Ye have become weak. Ye have forgotten the disciplines ye were raised with. I wager this worthless male can defeat any one of ye. The woman who hands me his sword may have second seat at my table beside Maelyn."

Élandine simply stared at the sword laying in his hands as Nellióne drew her sword and began her advance. "I have no training with this weapon, Mistress. Perhaps you would hold it for me."

A hiss of displeasure escaped Tranorva's lips. "Ye canna' fight unarmed."

Élandine shrugged, not bothering to mention that she had done the same thing a scant twelve hours before. "'Tis against the laws of our people for a male to wield a weapon, Mistress. Yet the challenge is issued and I accept."

Tranorva's heart rose in her throat. He would maintain the guise at the expense of his own life? What had she done?

"I accept your challenge." Nellióne apparently saw no moral dilemma in killing a defenseless male. The agile Dark Priestess leaped to the small platform where Tranorva's dais stood. She did not approach Élandine with the arrogance Tranorva had seen in her before, however. Her runed staff extended, she began to circle warily.

There was something here. Some essence of Élandra society Tranorva had missed. Males were expendable chattel. Males were not even allowed, it would seem, the use of a weapon.

So why did Nellióne act as if she were about to do battle with the prize swordsman of all Élahandara?

Élandine crouched low, his weight on the balls of his feet. Tranorva held her breath. The Mage could not use his magic here. Not and maintain his disguise. And he was shorter and less powerfully built than the females of his race.

But they weren't of his race. Would this body retain the strength of the Faerie creature she'd held in her arms last night?

Nellióne struck her staff on the floor and aimed a small ball of fire at the male, conserving her energies perhaps, or testing the waters. Élandine did not reflect the fireball back at Nellióne, as Shammall had taught Tranorva to do. Instead he simply tucked and rolled, coming up behind the larger female as she whirled to face him again.

Too slow. Élandine had already regained his footing. Nellióne found the heel of his hand with her sternum. Nellióne was no unskilled acolyte however. With an amazing display of agility, she rolled backwards out of the blow, kicking out with her heels as she walked over her hands to a pace behind where she had stood.

One kick slipped inside Élandine's guard to rake him across the chest with sharp pointed nails. He looked down at the tears in his fine colorful silks with the first trace of anger Tranorva had ever seen on his handsome face. So, Élandine was as much of a peacock as the strutting Shammall had ever been. She smothered her laughter. She would have to see that she kept the tailor in attendance.

Élandine lashed out with a hard kicking lunge that brought both feet in contact with Nellióne's rib cage before she'd fully recovered her balance. She went down in a tumble unremarkable for its grace, and he landed atop her. Shrieking, she tangled her hands in his hair, twisting with all her strength.

Tranorva spoke softly, but everyone in the room heard the threat in her voice. "Have a care lest ye mar the beauty of my pet. I do not wish him disfigured."

Her warning seemed to calm Nellióne's anger. The pair untangled themselves and began to circle again.

Élandine struck first this time, feigning left first, then striking up with his right hand, catching her behind the left shoulder to toss her over his hip. Nellióne latched her legs around him even as she went down, so that they rolled together, a mass of limbs poking out as they tumbled across the floor. Élandine landed on top, Nellióne's hair fisted in his hand as he buried his knee in her back, pulling her face away from the floor.

"Well done," Tranorva offered as she began to clap. The rest of the room quickly joined her. "An excellent show, Priestess. I admire thy restraint. Take thy place at my table, and let the entertainment begin."

Nellióne gathered her dignity around her, smoothing most of the traces of rage from her face as she bowed before Tranorva. Still, Nellióne's eyes remained cold, and she kept her gaze focused on Élandine. "I am honored, Mistress. Your pet is unusually well skilled in the fine arts of KimJing. Indeed a prized possession."

So. Élandine had attracted yet another bit of unwanted attention through her ignorance of Élandra customs. She would have to keep an eye on Nellióne. Tranorva looked away, clearly dismissing Nellióne. She clapped her hands and the doors at the end of the hall flew open. A dozen young men, outfitted in the colorful silks Élandine so admired, sauntered in.

The music began, and the dancers set their silks to swirling about the room. "Well fought," Tranorva praised as Élandine returned to her side.

"Thank you, Mistress."

"I may still kill ye." She said it loud enough for those closest to hear.

"Géndalaine was going to kill me herself," he mused, "As was Nafésti. But somehow she never quite got around to it."

Chapter Eight

The extravagant feast sat on long tables about the room, trenchers filled to overflowing, the food left mostly untouched. Such food was meant to be savored, its lure a lust of its own. It could not compete with the other delicacies in the room.

Tranorva swirled the amber liquid within her delicate crystal glass in time to the music. Slow. Seductive. Intoxicating. The dancers filtered by her dais, one at a time, performing for her alone. Pieces of colorful silk began to litter the floor like some opulent carpeting. A handsome youth of no more, she was learning, than sixty, dressed in flaming red silks, danced before her now, his ebony skin glowing with the soft sheen of the heat in the room.

The dancer raised his eyes to meet hers, peering out from under thick, curling lashes, half bold, half coy. He ran one slim, dark finger over the length of his thick, rigid cock as he smiled at her.

Perhaps it wasn't the room that had grown warm. Perhaps the heat came from her.

By the gods. She had finally found a man who actually desired to mate with her. Now that she was no longer seeking a man who would lust for her, she suddenly had not one, but a dozen. She was beginning to feel a little dizzy.

This world was so unlike her own. Not that the Northlanders did not value sex. But at home sex was usually reserved for the marriage bed or a lovers' tryst.

Here it practically danced into your lap.

The Dark Male twisted sensuously around the central column that supported the roof, sliding slowly down to the floor, all the while keeping his eyes focused on hers. As he spun his open silk tunic slipped down his shoulders to join the others at her feet. The dancer's hard cock jutted against the thin fabric that did little to cover him anyway. The loose flowing pants needed but a slight tug at the waist to release their cord, and they too floated to the growing pile.

These Dark Elves were slight in their build, slim and graceful, but there was nothing else small about them. Tranorva swallowed hard as this one stood before her naked. His dark hair tumbled about his face as he bowed before her. As the music ended he fell at her feet, the swirling silks settling around him like the drifting fall of frost-brightened leaves.

Élandine stood behind her, his hands on her, stroking, caressing. His fingers moved over her breasts, lifting, molding, brushing gently across the tips until the nipples stood out in tense relief against the sheer fabric of her gown. The music started up again and another young male took the last one's place.

Tranorva leaned her head back against Élandine's chest. He bent to kiss her immediately. *"The males vie for your attention, M'Lady. They come here in hopes of the honor of being chosen as your mate."*

Tranorva stared at the dancer who displayed himself before her now, his silk garb so sheer that she could have seen every scar on his body, had there been even one. His cock was long and thick and very erect. She hadn't known cocks came in so many sizes and shapes and textures. This one was the color of dark burgundy wine, and curved up slightly at the tip, as if planning to tickle her...He ran his hands over himself as if pleasuring a lover.

Élandine's hands on her body moved in time to the music, arousing her senses to the point of almost painful awareness. She found herself arching her breasts against his hands. "Let us leave the merry-makers to their own devices," she suggested, her words meant only for his ears.

"That would be rude, Mistress." He indicated the Counsel of Eight spread around the room. *"You are expected to join your sisters in revelry."*

Sisters in...Tranorva tried not to stare. While her attention had been focused on the beautiful young men at her feet, the Priestesses had made their own choices for the evening. Maelyn had appropriated three of the young men, and her second, Nellióne was surrounded by four. The logistics of the situation alone fascinated Tranorva. She thought she had known all there was to know about sex, despite her limited personal experience.

She had never imagined anything like this. The dancer of the flaming red silks lay beneath Nellióne, her body impaled on his cock, while a second male knelt between her knees. Apparently the other two were there to bathe the Second Chair Priestess with their tongues, for each was washing a circle closer and closer to the tips of her breasts. Already her nipples stood out like arrows pointing the way to her desire. She writhed in pleasure against the tongues that caressed her, her thin keening moan joining the others about the room.

Not all the Priestess had coupled with the young men, Tranorva corrected herself. Jeserat and Wayonka were either fighting like cats, or they pleasured each other in ways that would give credit to gymnasts. Wayonka's feet were latched around Jeserat's neck, while Jeserat arched hard against Wayonka's mouth, her own legs spread over Jeserat's shoulders.

Tranorva's senses screamed for release. The air felt oppressively hot.

"You must pick a dancer, M'Lady. None may climax before you have chosen a mate."

Tranorva blinked slowly as she glanced around the room again. They expected her to...in front of...with...oh no. She couldn't. Not with one of these...She closed her eyes for a moment. "I have chosen my mate."

Relief warred with uncertainty in his eyes. Tranorva wanted to laugh. He was a creature of politics. "Dance for me, Élandine." She hoped her voice didn't sound too desperate.

"Mistress, I—" his eyes met hers, and the startled look faded to one of bemused sensuality. "For you, Mistress. Only for you."

Tranorva smiled back in relief. "Never fear. I will no' share thee. I am a jealous mistress."

A flick of her fingers dismissed the current dancer. He moved to join Jeserat and Wayonka. Tranorva's fascination with the acrobatics of that pair might have pulled her attention to the three of them, but the room went quiet.

Élandine moved to stand before her, stiff as a marionette, arms at his sides, head down, his hair half obscuring his face. As if some message had been transmitted between him and the musicians at the end of the hall, the music changed its gentle beat to a short tempered drum from some exotic jungle.

His body loosening, Élandine began to sway gently to the rhythm, almost as if against his will. The drums hit a stronger beat. He jerked as if someone had pulled him by a string. He flung back his head, his eyes suddenly focused on her.

With a spinning kick that brought his right foot to the tips of his outstretched arm, he rose to his toes, folding in upon himself until he stood balanced on one foot, stretched out like a bird in flight. The music seemed to pause as he hovered there, then take off wildly again as he executed an intricate kick.

As he landed cat-like on the balls of his feet, his hands skimmed over the contours of his chest, his violet eyes searching out hers, teasing her with a glint of primeval hunger. The silk clung to his damp skin for a moment, translucent in the flickering light, leaving little to the imagination. The ageless Elf looked both dangerous and predatory at the moment.

He spun slowly, knees bent, hands tracing symbols in the air that only he could read. His body was poetry, flowing and strong, painting a picture of a lover so in tune with his mate that his every movement was designed for her pleasure. He held her at arms length while he stroked, then pulled her close, worshiping her body with his hands, his kiss, his eyes.

Every gaze in the room followed his dance, yet always his eyes conveyed the message that he danced for her alone. She could not blame the women for looking. She had not taken the time to fully appreciate this body, so like his own, yet so different. He was smaller, yet still lean and powerful, all exquisite lines of hard packed muscle and perfectly trained athlete.

His dance conveyed its sensuality in his perfect control and execution of every movement. Each reach of his arm and twist of his body seemed to promise what more he could do with those muscles. His hair spread out in his wake, always a movement behind, whipping around his shoulders like a predator stalking its prey.

How could he twist the movements of the KimJing into something so sensual? Each curve of his arm felt as if he drew her to his side. Each arched, raised thrust of his leg seemed to skim over her body. He was grace and strength and athletic prowess and lust all rolled into one.

His sapphire blue silks, new just this morning to replace those Maelyn had damaged, seemed suddenly much too sheer as they fluttered around him, exposing more than they hid. Tranorva realized jealously that she did not wish others to see how beautiful he was. She wanted him all to herself. When at last the music fell silent he knelt at her feet, hands outstretched to her, palms up, in a voiceless offering of sheer masculine beauty. She fought the urge to bundle him in the discarded silks, shielding her prize from greedy eyes.

The room paused to draw a collective breath. Tranorva reached out a trembling hand to touch what was surely a piece of leftover magic from her dreams. Élandine raised his eyes to meet hers with a slow, seductive smile. Tranorva slid into his welcoming arms as if at last she'd come home.

As their lips met her jealousy faded away, until the watchers merely added heat to her already sizzling brain. They were of no more import than the fallen silks that padded the floor. "Ye have no' disrobed," she managed, as she slid her hands over the sapphire silk. Her voice sounding thick to her ears.

"Perhaps you would prefer to do that job yourself."

She would. Though she found now she had no need of hurry. The thin, sheer fabric glided down his arms, bright blue silks mixing with the colors of late fall at her feet. Her fingers lingered in their wake, sliding easily over his smooth, oiled skin. She stood close enough to feel his hot, thick cock dance against her as her touch repaid his. She ran her hands over his chest, then lower, pausing at his waist.

She knew what he expected. Could feel his body's anticipation as her fingers moved toward the tie at his waist. Yet there were other ways to torment a man. She had examples surrounding her. She let her hands slide lower, over the curve of his hips, and she folded herself to her knees. Slowly, deliberately, knowing he was watching every move, she used her teeth to pull the cord that would release her prize from its wrapping. His hands gripped her shoulders. She felt him stiffen beneath her fingers, his jutting cock bobbing against the underside of her chin.

By the gods he was exquisite. *Beautiful One* indeed. His skin shone with the radiance of a black onyx stone. The head of his cock glistened in front of her as she rocked back, dark and purple and wanting. Its bobbing head held her gaze in fascination. Almost of its own volition, her tongue reached out to touch.

He tasted like a rich wine marinate, his scent deep and heady. He cried out as she nipped ever so gently, jerking against her uncontrollably. A murmur of approval circled the room. In some dim recess of her mind she knew that the room was no longer quiet. The musicians began to play a low, sensuous beat, and the lovers around the room began to pick up their pace, feeling the heat as she did.

She massaged the underside of his cock with her tongue, marveling at the way his hands tightened on her shoulders. She had not realized there would be so much power in playing the seductress.

"I must—Mistress, you cannot..."

"I can do whatever I want," she reminded him. "Ye are mine."

"Yours," he whispered. And despite the strength that allowed him to fight unarmed against the First Priestess, his knees gave out as she took him in her mouth again, and he collapsed into her arms.

Which was, after all, right where she wanted him to be.

* * * * *

"Do you mean to remain here, M'Lady?"

Tranorva snuggled deeper into his warmth. "Will I lose ye if I stay?"

His arms tightened around her. "No, M'Lady. You lose a fastening off of your shirt. You lose your favorite earring. You cannot lose me."

She turned her head, burying it against the skin of his arm, breathing in the heady perfume that was his scent. No oils of anointing had ever done as much to entice her. "I have a plan," she admitted as she adjusted herself in his arms. He always seemed ready to hold her. This morning just the warmth of his body was enough to content her.

He nuzzled his face into her hair. "Does it involve a stone altar?"

Anticipation filled her as she remembered the dream. "That was not part of my plan, but it could be."

"Would you trust me enough to share your plans with me?"

Tranorva laughed against his chest. "Trust ye? I trust ye with my life."

She felt his heart stutter, then right itself. "Do you?" His lips grazed over her ear. "Am I more than just a sex object to you then?"

Tranorva opened her eyes and forsook his warmth enough to prop herself up on one elbow and gaze down upon him. She saw something there she had not seen before. He looked so serious. "Do ye not know?"

His eyes drifted to some point beyond her shoulder. "I know what you tell me."

Tranorva freed an arm to reach out and stroke his face, turning his head just a little. "I love ye."

He reacted as if she'd struck him. "No. No. Humans, mortals, they do not fall in love with my kind. We live but to serve. We do not become emotionally involved. We—"

"Élandine. Shammall. Whatever name ye go by, 'tis all the same to me. I love ye. I have for years. It angered me that ye took no notice of me as a woman, when I was no longer a child. Angered me because I wanted ye to notice me. Wanted ye to treat me as something more than my mother's daughter, and thy charge of the moment. Wanted ye to love me."

He turned his head into her hand, closing his eyes as he kissed her palm. "I have loved you for years, M'Lady. Loved you and needed you and feared for my soul because I knew it was wrong."

Tranorva bent her head to kiss his closed eyes. "There is no right and wrong in matters of the heart."

Worried eyes sought her out. "I am *Fey*. Such things are forbidden among the *Sidhe*!"

"Why?"

"I will not age, M'Lady, not as you understand time. My lifetime is measured in centuries, not years. We feel not the call of mortals to mate, lest we lose our hearts and our souls a dozen times in the course of a lifespan."

"Would ye leave this world complete without knowing the feelings we share? If my plan does not work and the Dark Ones take our lives on the morrow, are ye less of a man because ye have loved?"

The tension in his eyes shimmered and began to ease. "No, M'Lady. I could never be less for having shared your love."

"And if the fates do not intervene, and thy life should stretch on for centuries, ye will live to love again. But I will always have been thy first."

He kissed her, then, pulling her tightly into his arms once more. "Whatever my fate, I shall be richer for having carried you in my heart. If I die tomorrow, know that I would not have ever lived had I not found you."

"Let tomorrow take care of itself. Let us concentrate on today."

* * * * *

Philosophically, letting tomorrow take care of itself had sounded like a fine plan. Now that tomorrow was here, however, he found the plan somewhat amiss. Especially since the hour of his death appeared to be imminent.

The day had started off well enough. Tranorva had looked quite lovely, decked out in her own polished mail, her sword strapped to her side, as she convened the council. No one had voiced an objection to her plan to place Maelyn as regent during the times she must serve at House Lochinvar. He should have known things were going too well. He'd let down his guard. He'd been too attuned to the brilliance of his lover to notice when Maelyn slipped behind him in the reception, until he felt the edge of her dagger pressed against his throat.

Chattel in a battle between leaders. What an ignominious way to end an enchanted lifetime.

He could feel the fury vibrating through the First Priestess's body. "I have seen the way you look at this one, Tranorva. You will not sacrifice his life to maintain your power. Hand over the sacred keys."

Tranorva removed the chain from about her neck, holding it just out of Maelyn's reach. The First Priestess shifted her hold, reaching for the symbol she could not quite grasp. It was all he needed. Élandine twisted as he threw himself into her blade, tossing the Priestess over his hip. The world shimmered in a haze of pain as he went down, but he had time to see his beloved disappear, and to know that the blood was not all his own as the enraged grizzly shredded the Priestess before him until her broken body was no more than a lifeless toy.

He chanted softly through bloodied lips as the fog rolled into the room, too tired to stem the flow of blood, unable to lift a hand to the wound. Charms and spells left his mind as the cold muzzle sniffed anxiously at his throat. Tears stained the huge brown eyes. "Forgive me," he managed as he drifted away. "I love you."

Epilogue

The enraged scream of a giant grizzly bear disturbed their peaceful slumber. Mother Earth held up her hand for silence as Sister Wind and Brother Rain led the dash for the pool. Soon they were gathered together, nine in all, around the smooth, dull surface of the water. Mother waved her hand over the surface.

The cry came again, the keening wail of a woman this time. The picture in the water wavered and focused, until they could see the vast reaches of the frozen tundra, stretching empty and barren for leagues on end.

A Northland Warrior screamed each of their names in turn as she stumbled and fell, alone in the snow, the wind whipping her hair over her face. She might have kept her balance, but she refused to drop her burden. They looked closer, then pulled back a little, stunned looks on their faces. The burden she carried was a broken body, clasped in her arms, as the tears froze on her face.

"No," whispered Wind. "It was not to be thus."

"His time is not yet," agreed Rain.

"It is the way of things that not all fulfill their destiny," argued Cat.

Bear turned away, ripping up great chunks of Earth to unsettle the air. "I will not see my child so destroyed."

Destruction curled his lip in a sneer. "He made his choice. Let her live with it."

The keening rose again, and the air in the room shimmered, the dust from Bear's paws catching the flickering light.

"Ye gave me thy word!"

Lightning shimmered around the room in angry waves.

"We have not broken our word." Mother's voice carried a warning the Human would not heed.

"No harm. No harm was to come to my children."

"He is not one of yours."

"Can ye not see the life is gone out of my child? Can ye not hear her heart break? Enough! I have sacrificed enough! My daughter must no' pay for my sins!"

"We did not make this choice. We cannot undo what he has done by his own hand."

Wolf shook his shaggy head sadly. "This has not to do with you, Evalayna. Some things neither thee no we can control."

"No!" *The wail of her grief combined with the keening from the water to shatter the ears of those listening.*

"Cease!" *Falcon's voice rose above all. "There may be a way. If ye can find the courage within thyself."*

"Anything." *The woman pulled herself together, regaining some of her characteristic composure.* "I will do anything. I would trade my life for theirs."

Chaos turned on her now. "Would you face your past?"

Mother Earth raised her hand and the room once again fell silent. "Take his body to the source of his life, with all those you hold dear about you, and make your pledge to his king. He may grant you the gift you desire."

"I do no' understand!" Evalayna spun to face them, reaching for something she could hold and touch, but the plain shimmered around her, and heat faded to cold. She gasped as the wind took the breath from her lungs. Her vision blurred then cleared again, until the scene before her came into focus.

Tranorva marched out of the snow, her head down, her stride firm and determined, the body of the Mage clutched to her chest. He looked small and frail in death. He would not have liked that.

Tranorva swayed as she held out the pale, lifeless thing.

Alone out here exposed to the elements they would both die as well. "We will need help," Evalayna answered the wordless plea. "First we must get in out of the storm." Tranorva turned her gaze blankly on the landscape, as if unsure where they were.

Evalayna pressed her fingers to her temples and issued the summons. *Take his body to the source of his life, with all those you hold dear about you, and make your pledge to his king.*

Those she held dear would find them.

But how could they travel to the source of his life? She knew nothing of *Tier na nÓg*, save the stories of myth and legend. And should they manage to find the magical isle of the Faerie folk, would the King of the *Fey* grant such a request? Could he?

She would deal with this all tomorrow. For tonight she must keep her daughter alive. She raised her hands and cast a dome about them to shut out the wind. But it could not seal out the chill in her heart.

"Would you face your past?"

Would she? Could she?

The mournful roar of a giant grizzly echoed across the plains, its direction lost in the wind.

A Warrior's Pride

Prologue

They were gathered together, nine in all, around the smooth, dull surface of the water. Mother Earth waved her hand over the surface. The picture in the water wavered and focused until they could see the vast reaches of the frozen tundra, stretching empty and barren for leagues on end.

The keening rose again and the air in the room shimmered in the flickering light. "Ye gave me thy word! I have sacrificed enough! My daughter must no' pay for my sins!"

"We did not make this choice. We cannot undo what he has done by his own hand."

The wail of her grief combined with the keening from the water to shatter the ears of those listening. Mother raised her hand and the room once again fell silent. "Take his body to the source of his life, with all those you hold dear about you, and make your pledge to his king. He may grant you the gift you desire."

"I do no' understand!"

The mournful roar of a giant grizzly echoed across the plains, its direction lost in the wind.

* * * * *

The ancient grizzly raised his head to taste the message on the wind as the breeze shifted. A once familiar scent caught his attention, bringing him to his feet with a mighty roar.

Mate.

He spun to face the wind and sniffed again.

No.

Human.

Human female.

Familiar.

He let out his grief with another cry that threatened to shake loose the snow along the ridge and bring an avalanche tumbling down the mountainside.

There it was again.

Human. Female. Mate.

He drew in gasping mouthfuls of cold arctic air, searing his lungs as he breathed deeply of her scent.

Human female.

Familiar.

He shook his head, pawing the air in angry denial.

Yet there had been a time, long ago…

Pain. So much pain.

He would not remember. He would not.

Yet the scent came to him again. The scent of her would not allow him to forget. Mate. His mate was here. He raised his voice to the night air and repeated his mournful cry.

No. No, it was not possible.

The memories came flooding back. He had been…He was…He had been gone too long this time. He was losing his mind. Losing his last vestiges of humanity. Of course he remembered. How could he forget? He forced himself to take on Human thought processes, though his body shook with the effort.

The scent came again, but with a great effort of will he forced himself to think past it. She was dead. She had died with the birth of their child.

Yet the scent could not lie. There it was again. *Human female. Alive.*

The Mage had brought him the news, the Mage…

Rend. Destroy. Rip limb from limb.

No. Think like a man. Must think like a man. Must…

Kill. Kill the lying tongued one. Take. Take what is mine. Reclaim…

"*Mine!*" he shrieked in a voice that was neither quite Human nor all grizzly.

Reclaim what is mine. An end to the loneliness. An end to the vast wanderings and the long winter nights.

"*Mine!*"

Standing on his hind legs he pawed the sky, shaking his shaggy head as he roared his challenge to the air, unsure no longer. He dropped to the ground, forty stone of enraged grizzly bear shaking the earth as his screams split the night, charging toward the smell, toward the promise, toward the lies.

Chapter One

"'Tis a fool's errand."

"Aye, M'Lady."

"And if I forbid thee to go?"

Tyrell stopped packing long enough to turn and raise one long, slim, arched eyebrow at the old woman. "Forbid, M'Lady?"

Ayailla thumped her heavy staff down hard upon the ancient stone floor. "Forbid. Yes, forbid. Do ye think I will no'? Ye are my apprentice. Ye are bound to me, goddamn it. Ye cannot just go traipsing off wherever ye wish just because my fool of a daughter Summons ye!"

Tyrell laid the crisp linen tunic neatly on the side table before he turned to face the old woman. Slowly he drew himself up to his full six-foot-eleven inch height, stepping just close enough to her that she had to tilt her head to look up at him. Her eyes twitched with anger, although she did not step back.

He spoke distinctly, controlling his anger the way she had taught him. "I am apprenticed to thee, dear Grandmother, because I requested it be so, and because ye accepted me into thy training. I did this, in part, although ye are a crotchety old woman, because ye are the equal to my temper and stubbornness. Remember that I came to thee voluntarily. I now formally request leave that I might be allowed to attend my Lady Mother, who has need of me."

He held up a hand before Ayailla could speak. "Take heed of thy own advice and think before ye speak, Grandmother. I love ye, and I would no' have ye say something in anger and fear that ye will later regret. No matter what thy decision, I will go. I must answer my mother's Summoning. Ye of all people should understand that. I ask no' for thy permission to attend my Lady Mother. I ask instead for permission to return to thy household once my mother's need has been met."

Ayailla bit her lip, and if he hadn't known her better he might have thought she was fighting off tears. "Of course you can come back, you idiot."

She opened up her arms and he moved into her embrace, bending his head to lay his cheek atop her jumble of thick silver curls. "Thy accent is slipping, Grandmother. Do no' let the servants hear ye. The will think it most odd to hear you speak like a peasant."

"So what?" she sniffled. "I pay them well enough. Better wages than they'll bring home anywhere else, for less hours."

Tyrell rolled his eyes, sensing the danger of their tempers clashing had passed. "I will miss ye, Grandmother."

She sniffed heavily. "No you won't."

Warning bells went off in his head at the sudden change in her voice and temperament. "What possesses ye to say that, Grandmother?"

Tyrell watched Ayailla pull her ruffled dignity back around herself like a cloak. "Very simple, my child. I am going with thee."

He could have reminded her of her age. Just yesterday she had complained that at near one hundred she should not have to do things as strenuous as climbing the stairs to her third floor bedroom. He did not. He did not voice any of the opinions that came to mind at all. Instead Tyrell threw back his head and laughed. "Good."

She eyed him suspiciously. "Thou art no' going to argue with me?"

Tyrell shrugged. "Ye are Ayailla. Ye are as tough and strong as ye were when I first came to know ye. If ye wish to trek across the tundra with me, by the gods, ye will. If Mother is truly in need of assistance, she'd find no better Shaman to fight at her side than thee. If this is but some wild power play on Mother's part, she'd find no more capable adversary."

Ayailla smiled benevolently at him. "Ye have learned my lessons well, my heart."

"Do no' take anything ye do no' wish to carry," was all he said. "If ye can set out across the tundra, ye can shoulder thy own pack."

* * * * *

Cassadara jumped to her feet, flinging Lord Mâkakao's arm off of her as she rose, and, in the process, pulling half the bedclothes along with her.

"Married less than three cycles of the moons and already she steals the bedcovers." Mâk sighed deeply as he rolled out of bed. "What is it, *Mel~amin*? What ails thee?"

"Mother. Mother needs me. I must go."

"*Mel~amin*, it is but slightly past moonrise. You were dreaming. No messenger has entered our bedchamber. Come back to bed with me."

Cassadara turned to rest her gaze on his moonlit nakedness. "Truly I should prefer to rest in thy arms, my love, but I must go. I have been Summoned."

"Summoned?" He was already stretching his long, lean form, bronzed muscles rippling across a broad-shouldered frame that was large for a Human, nearly of proportion to the Northlanders' physiques. "I know not what Summoned means, *Mel~amin*, except I shall get no more sleep this night, and no good reason to stay awake, either. Does the occasion call for formal dress or full armor?"

She kept her voice low, hiding her eyes so that he could not see her tears. "'Tis I who have been Summoned. Go back to bed."

He crossed the chamber in two long strides to wrap his arms around her. "We are one, *Mel~amin*. There is no I. There is only we. Do not shut me out. Tell me of what you are afeared. I will not leave you to face this alone."

Cassadara turned to face him within the circle of his arms, no longer attempting to hide the tears that overflowed her heavy black lashes. "I know not. A Summoning is a powerful spell, like a message sent with the mind, commanding me to my mother's side. I know naught, except she is afraid. My mother fears nothing. I sense some great evil is upon us."

Mâk kissed her once on each eyelid before throwing open the doors of the wardrobe. "Light armor for traveling, then. I will send for Balthain and have him ready a company."

"No. This is a family matter."

He paused, his hands on the laces of his light leather leggings. "I will not be left behind while you run out across the tundra like some madwoman. Am I not family?"

Cassadara ran her hands over the muscles that bunched along the back of his shoulders. She understood, by now, somewhat of his odd compunction to protect her. She found his attitude sweetly endearing, yet dangerous. She swallowed a sigh of frustration. "I only meant ye need no' call the men. Mother has called her own company. We will find the others en route, or they will find us. Leave Balthain to guard thy house of the many beds, lest others see thy absence as a weakness in thy fortifications."

The muscles under her fingers sagged in relief. "I feared you would try to leave me behind. 'Twould drive me to distraction to watch you head out alone."

Cassadara kissed him on each shoulder, marveling still at the way his skin shivered at her touch. "I fear I am too selfish to leave ye behind, love. In truth ye are a fine Warrior. I would stand beside no other in a fight. I trust ye to guard my back."

Mâk turned to kiss her swiftly before he yanked on his tunic. "Then let us slip away without announcement. I will leave brief written instructions for Balthain. We can scavenge what we need from the kitchens without anyone being the wiser. 'Tis best we were away before dawn. Balthain is loyal, and would feel almost as I do at the thought of being left behind."

Cassadara laughed as she ran her fingers over his leather leggings, tracing the heat of his shaft. "Perhaps no' quite as ye do. Write thy note while I raid the kitchens. I will meet ye at our place in the gardens."

"You give me your word you will not seek to slip out without me?"

Cassadara kissed him again, this time taking her time, her tongue sliding between his lips to tease his with promises of things to come. "Wolves mate for life, my love, and we fight as a pack."

Mâkakao lost himself in her arms, burying his fears in her kiss as he tried to pretend he believed her. It would have been easier had she given her word. He closed his eyes and breathed in the smell of her—warm, sexy, exotic. His body was already hardened with desire. He kissed her again, his tongue demanding now as he sucked her bottom lip into his mouth. His hands were rough as he pulled her against his aching erection, demanding her body's response.

Her answer was a low feral growl that rose to a whine as he lowered his head to attack her straining nipples, twisting the small blackened rings with his tongue as she moaned in desire. "I have been Summoned. I must—"

"We will run as wolves across the tundra. Surely we will outdistance the others. That gives us time. At least a little extra time. This won't take long." Not with her leg already hitched around his waist and her hands pulling his head more firmly against her taut, distended nipple.

"Quickly, then." Her fingers fumbled with the lacing at his waist. "Why did ye waste thy time with these foolish knots if ye meant to distract me so?"

Mâk laughed as he nipped at her ear, taking advantage of the distance she'd placed between them to glide his palm over her tightly muscled abdomen and down, until he could tangle his fingers in the dark, damp curls that seemed to cry out for his touch. Her breath caught when he outlined her labia with his gentle caress, and she lurched against the heel of his hand, moaning as he slid one exploring finger into her.

Her body responded to his touch like the note of a perfectly tuned guitar strummed lightly by an expert, and he smiled, finding the chord much to his liking. Had there truly been a time when he had feared her? His pulse quickened at the memory, for he knew well what she was capable of, what she could become. Truly the legends were not all just stories designed to frighten a child. He'd seen the wild light in her eyes, felt her teeth close over the pulse of his life's blood at his throat and yet still, she'd known his touch, she'd trusted herself to him.

"Mine," he whispered against her ear as he slid into her, grasping her hips to fill her more completely. She was ready for him. Tight, hard muscles rippled around him, squeezing, pulling, grasping his straining cock and greedily sucking him in. "You're mine. My mate. My love. My wife."

"Mine," she countered. "My love, my mate, my husband." She strove to meet him thrust for thrust, trusting him to support her weight as she wrapped her other leg around his waist now, too, her hands tangled in his hair as she sucked his lower lip between her teeth, nipping playfully.

Her sheath gripped him like a fist, hard and demanding and leaving him with little room for coherent thought. With a hint of the strength that had won her respect, Mâkakao wrapped his arms around her, one across her shoulders, one supporting her hips as he lifted her free of the wall. He stepped back three paces to drop onto the huge four-poster bed, rolling with her there until he held her pinned under him, her legs still locked around his waist.

His feet found the floor. With a growl he claimed her, stroking into her hard and fast, lifting her legs until her heels rested on his shoulders. Their eyes locked, she raised her fingers to her lips, licking her fingertips before she brushed them over her blackened nipple rings.

He groaned as he grasped her buttocks, changing his pace, slowing to torture her with long, slow, hard thrusts that matched the rhythm of her fingers on her breasts, methodically pinching and twisting the fine black rings.

She came with a stifled cry, her muscles pulling greedily at him as she convulsed around him, her moans of pleasure his reward.

"Mine," he breathed, thrusting into her hard and fast again, pushing her back toward her peak.

"Thine," she agreed as she slipped her legs behind his shoulders, pulling him even deeper into her. "Sing for me." Her fingers found his nipples, massaging the small hard knots of desire, while her eyes danced with laughter. Her words came in fragmented gasps, timed to their now frantic thrusting. "Take me—with ye—wolf-mate."

Their voices intermingled as they broke together, the ancient call of mating wolves, high and fierce and possessive in the still of the pre-dawn light. If there was a hint of desperation in that call, they cared not to voice their fears.

* * * * *

Mâkakao woke up alone, with only a heavy down comforter for company. He sighed as he rolled swiftly to his feet. He was not one to fall asleep after sex. Not like that anyway. Not when there was a job to be done. He suspected some devilment in her final, lingering kiss. He jerked his breeches and tunic back on and donned his light traveling mail. Strapping on his scimitars and shouldering his pack securely, he slipped out the window, scaling the rough stone wall with the ease of nearly three decades of practice.

Anger warred with humor as he considered his wife's deception. He'd been a fool to think he could outmaneuver her. She'd lulled him with her talk of wolves, and packs hunting together. But she would not get away. She had marked him. She was on him like a morning mist, permeating his pores. He could follow her scent anywhere. She knew that. Knew he would follow. She'd meant only to put some distance between them, to protect him.

She loved him, but she had yet to learn to trust him.

He raised his nose to the wind and howled, the mournful call of the lone wolf.

* * * * *

Yarwyn came awake abruptly, searching the bed with her hand. The place beside her was still warm, though empty. Rogue that he was, Seanen had managed to slip from the bed without awakening her. She could see his silhouette in the moonlight filtering through the window, all long lines of hard, lean muscle as he stared out into the night. "What is it, my love?"

"I wanted it." His voice was low, barely audible. "The desert in the winter, and the tundra in the summer. Talismar in the spring, where the Elves walk in the trees."

She could feel his regret, a tangible thing in the air between them. Her voice took on a note of desperation. "You will love Talismar. There are paths and bridges in the trees. I will show you."

"You know me too well, my love. I must go."

She rose to stand beside him, close enough to touch, yet knowing he'd never been farther away. "Go where? When? Why?"

He shook his head, his dark locks disturbed by the action until they resembled a lion's mane. "I—I know not. I have been Summoned. Lady Evalayna has need of me."

Anger furrowed Yarwyn's brow. "So that's it? Evalayna calls and you must go? In the middle of the night? Is this going to happen often?"

At that Seanen turned to her, grasping her shoulders in powerful hands that could well have lifted her over his head. Instead he merely caressed her lightly. "No, my love. I have not been called back. Not like that. No courier has tracked me down and brought me a message in the night. I felt the command, inside me. A Summoning is a powerful spell, and one few Shaman would dare to attempt. I have heard of its use only once before, long before my birth. I felt—urgency. Evalayna needs me. I felt something else, too, that I hardly dare to put into words."

Yarwyn laid her hand against his face, absorbing it all. For a Rogue and a thief, she reflected, he was remarkably honest. He put up no defenses to block her out. She, too, could feel it now. Could almost see into Evalayna's mind. "Fear." She whispered the word in awe. She dropped her hand and spun away toward the wardrobe. "I will be ready to move out in ten minutes. We will need supplies. The vendors will not yet be open. Try the kitchens. The cooks never sleep in a place like this. I'll meet you there."

"Yarwyn, I—"

She didn't bother to turn back to face him. "We will not have this argument."

He laughed softly. "Whatever you feel from me, I know better than to say it. I meant only to tell you I love you."

At that she did turn to him, slipping into the arms he offered, a small sob muffling itself against his chest. "And I love you. More than I ever thought I would love anyone. If you tried to slip away without me, you would break my heart."

He snorted softly against her hair. "And when you caught up with me you would break more than that. I will not try to escape you, my love. But do not blame me if I feel the need to protect you. I was raised that way. I cannot help but feel some small amount of guilt at the thought of leading you into danger. And before you remind me, I do know you are as well equipped to handle danger as I, but that does not change the way I feel."

"Nor does it change the way I feel," Yarwyn whispered against his chest. His body shivered in response when she flicked her tongue over his nipple. She felt the brief argument within him as duty warred with desire, felt the compromise he reached with himself as his body responded to her while his mind considered. She slid her still-naked body hard against his stiffening shaft, helping him decide. "We will travel light, covering the distance swiftly," she whispered, her voice blowing little puffs of warm air over the nipple she had dampened. "No time will be wasted."

His hands slid slowly down her back to cup her hips, caressing as they moved, playing with her, teasing in their slowness. "Lady Evalayna knows well why we were here," he reasoned. "She can spare me these few minutes."

Chapter Two

Evalayna shivered next to the fire, cold beyond its meager ability to chase the chill from her bones. She was too old for this. She was...

"He does no' grow cold, even in death."

Evalayna forgot the chill that had overcome her once she'd expended the energy to issue the Summoning. "When ye were but a child, I spun tales beside the fire for ye, and ye did listen. In this way I taught ye of our people, as was the way of old. Will ye listen to me now, Daughter?"

Tranorva might not have heard her for all the good her words did.

Evalayna rose to her feet and hammered her staff into the ground. "Tranorva! Hear and obey me!"

Grief-stricken eyes focused on her at last. "I am thine to command, as always, my Lady Mother."

"Child, can ye no' see I am trying to help ye? Ye and the Mage? He is no' dead, Tranorva. No' in the way those of our race depart this earth. Behold." Evalayna raised her staff and cast a simple spell upon the empty shell in Tranorva's arms. The small darkling immediately rose to his feet to stand at attention before her.

Tranorva scrambled to her feet. "Élandine?" she whispered in disbelief. She waved her hand in front of his eyes, but he took no notice. She touched his face gently, then spun to face her mother, angry tears smudging her dark lashes. "What foul magic is this? He stands, he breaths, yet he is still dead to me."

"Shammall is Fey, my heart. He is no' like us. His kind live for centuries, mayhap even tens of centuries. 'Tis his spirit that has fled this plane. His body will no' decay the way ours would, yet he is neither dead nor alive. The gods have given him—have given us—a reprieve, to restore the spirit to the body. We have no' much time, and the conditions set by the gods will no' be easily met."

"But it can be done?"

Evalayna lowered her head. "I know not, Child. But I will try. We will try. I would do anything within my power to ease this hurt within ye. My only prayer is that I have no' doubled thy burden with false hope."

Tranorva slowly pulled herself together, her eyes regaining the gleam that had struck fear in her enemies across the lands. "I will no' fail. We will no' fail. Know this, my Lady Mother. I shall rule House Lochinvar and the Northlands with this man at my side, or no' at all. Élandine holds my heart, and when his light is fully extinguished, mine shall be as well."

Evalayna bowed her head. "There was a time when I knew a love such as thine."

From far across the tundra, the call of a great grizzly reached their ears, an eerie echo in the early light of dawn.

* * * * *

Élandine turned his head into her hand, closing his eyes as he kissed her palm. "I have loved you for years, M'Lady. Loved you and needed you and feared for my soul because I knew it was wrong."

Tranorva bent her head to kiss his closed eyes. "There is no right and wrong in matters of the heart."

Worried eyes sought her out. "I am Fey. Such things are forbidden among the Sidhe!"

"Would ye leave this world without knowing the feelings we share? If the Dark Ones take our lives in the morning, are ye less of a man because ye have loved?"

He kissed her, then, pulling her tightly into his arms once more. "Whatever my fate, I shall be richer for having carried you in my heart.

If I die tomorrow, know that I would never have lived had I not found you."

Shaken by the dream, Tranorva threw off her cloak to pace beside the fire, fear and anger radiating off of her in restless waves. She paused from time to time to stare at the thing standing beside her mother as if it were some strange new enemy with which she was about to have to do battle.

"What are we waiting for?" she demanded for perhaps the twentieth time.

"Take his body to the source of his life, with all those you hold dear about you, and make your pledge to his king. He may grant you the gift you desire," Evalayna repeated again. "I have Summoned those I hold most dear. We must wait for them here. There is naught else I can do until the others arrive." Evalayna sighed. "I am old. I am tired. The Summoning has taken much of my strength. If ye canna' sleep, will ye no' cease this haunting, that I at least might rest?"

"Ye are no' old, Mother. Ye have bundled thy cloak about thee and leaned so long on thy staff, pretending it to be a walking stick, that ye have begun to believe thy own illusions. Ye are but sixteen years my senior, and ye are as fit as ye were when ye did first train Cass in the art of the staff. I fear no Warrior in battle as I wouldst fear to face the wrath of thy magic. Abuse me no' with reminders of thy age."

Evalayna rolled her cloak into a pillow and curled closer to the fire. "I was old by the time I was twenty, Daughter. Mind thy tongue and get some rest."

"How can I rest with that—that thing standing there, haunting me with the face I have come to love, mocking me with the eyes of death?"

Evalayna raised her head slightly to look over her shoulder at the animation she had raised. She flicked her fingertips at it. "Go to sleep." It promptly shut its eyes and bowed its head.

Tranorva's harsh sob pulled Evalayna even farther from the rest she craved. Evalayna sat up, abandoning all notions of sleep entirely. "What is it, Daughter? What troubles ye?"

Tranorva further stunned her by sinking to her knees, folding her head into her mother's lap as she had when she was but a girl. "It is no use. 'Tis a fool's errand, Mother. The Faerie King will no' grant us this boon."

"Ye know this for a fact?"

"It came to me in a dream, Élandine's words. Love such as ours is forbidden among the *Sidhe*. I have made him an outcast amongst his own people. His king will no' ever return him to me."

Evalayna thought to comfort her child, but she knew with a mother's instinct Tranorva would not accept her platitudes. "Ye must go and gather much wood, then."

Tranorva looked up, her face wet with tears. "Wood?"

"Aye. As soon as thy sister and Seanen arrive, we shall commence with the funeral pyre. We canna' take the chance that some beast of the tundra might happen upon his cairn and uncover the body."

"A pyre? Ye mean to burn him? But—but Mother, ye said he is no' dead!"

"Aye, no' in the normal sense that a Human might be dead, but he is dead enough, dead to this world, and if, as ye say, it is hopeless, then we must dispose of the body. We canna' have *that* following us about for the next eighty years, now can we? It is helpless as a newborn, and it canna' take care of itself."

Tranorva blanched. "Surely the gods would no' offer us this boon if it could no' be."

Evalayna shrugged. "Yet ye say it is hopeless. Perhaps the gods knew not of his disgrace."

"They are the gods!" Tranorva argued. "They know all!"

"Then will ye trust in them?" Evalayna asked, her voice softer this time. "Or shall we give up now?"

Tranorva's eyes searched hers. "I—I would trust in something, anything, rather than admit there is no hope. Yet I fear the hope as much as the loss, for hope is a two-edged sword."

Evalayna took her daughter's hands and raised them clasped between her own. "The Fey have few rules, Daughter, save they shall no' take a Human life without reason. Shammall himself told me this long ago. If there be a prohibition against the Fey mating with Humans, I suspect it is one that has been broken before, and will be again, for hearts go most oft' where they are directed not to. Mayhap the King of Faerie would be the one to ask a variance for this transgression, as well."

Tranorva nodded slowly. "Ye are wise, Mother. If I must I will give him up, rather than see his life forfeit."

"Let us pray that will no' be necessary." Evalayna glanced at the lifeless form that guarded her, trying to remember his face animated, his wisdom pouring forth when she had needed him most. He had waited over a century to fall in love, and then he had chosen a woman with a will to match his own. Somehow, she doubted the Mage would ever agree to such a plan.

* * * * *

Evalayna came awake to the feel of his hands smoothing over her pregnant belly, caressing, worshipping, making her feel less fat and awkward and more beautiful than she had in the last several weeks. He buried his nose against her neck and sniffed deeply. His teeth closed over the sensitive spot at the base of her neck, sending shivers down her spine. "Mine."

Evalayna laughed as she rolled in his arms. She closed her teeth over the edge of his jaw, very close to the dimple in his chin that she liked to admire. "Mine." *She nipped gently on his lower lips, loving the way his body responded to her, his thick cock instantly anxious to bury itself within her warmth.* "Mine. Ye are mine, Roahr VinDall, now and forever."

"Yours," he agreed, running his hands over her rounded tummy. "Yours and yours alone, now and forever." His hands cupped her enlarged breasts, lifting their weight away from her chest, running his thumbs across the sensitive nipples ever so gently. "Take me, my greedy lover."

Evalayna might have laughed at the audacity of his suggestion, had not her body responded with so much heat and longing to his simple caress. He helped her, his broad, strong hands steadying her as she moved to straddle him, feeling awkward and ponderous. She bit her lip in disappointment. "I'm no' sure this will work."

He raised his knees up behind her, supporting her back. "We can make it work, if it pleases you, my lover."

Her doubts disappeared as she slid down over him, encasing his hot, thick length with her needy sheath. She paused a moment, enjoying the feel of him there within her, relaxing around him as her body adjusted once more to the size of him. Her breath drew in sharply as his knowing fingers swept once again over the taut tips of her breasts, and she shuddered around him. "I have missed this. I have missed ye so much."

"I have missed you. I am sorry to have had to leave you alone so long this late in your term. Let me make it up to you now."

"Yes," was the best she could manage as she braced herself against his arms, his hands locked now on her hips, guiding her as she began the dance, steadying her, demanding, and yet still allowing her to set their pace.

Once again his control amazed her as she rode the heavy, pulsing heat of him, moving slowly, driving herself insane with the slow pace of their mating, the feel of him within her both comfortably familiar and still brand new again. She clenched hard around him on each upward stroke, as if to keep him from escaping, building the speed and the tempo as she found her rhythm, learning how this new body responded.

She lay back against his raised knees, her hair hanging down over his legs as she linked her fingers with his, delighting in the feel of his cock filling her so completely. She felt the light sheen of sweat over his skin and knew what this control was costing him. Good. She wanted to make him sweat. Wanted to make him remember every thrust in the weeks to come.

He brought their hands, still linked, back to caress her heavy breasts again, and it was her control, not his, that snapped. She lurched up to her knees, only to drop down hard on the hot thick length of him as the first fingers of greed wrapped around her, raising herself up to slide down onto him time and again.

His hips moved in rhythm to hers, seeking her heat with as much greedy lust as her own, yet still controlled, still letting her set the pace. She wanted to snap that control. She wanted all of him. She wanted...the first orgasm hit her low and hard, spreading slowly up her belly until the flush set her nipples on fire under his touch and she leaned back again, crying out his name.

Not content to leave her there, he set the pace, faster now, driving her further up the peak, rising into her again and again until the spasms of orgasm shook her like a small tree in a high wind, and she knew not how to contain the pleasure. Then all control left them both, and the hands that held her turned her within strong arms, a man no more, cradling her within the powerful embrace of the giant grizzly, his magic strong enough to take her with him as they changed together.

They rolled together, his soft, dense coat pillowing her, protecting her, as the force of their need shook them, demanding all the passion those huge bodies were capable of. "Yes, yes!" *Evalayna screamed, in a language only her mate understood. She gripped him hard with her bear muscles, demanding, taking, her orgasm shattering around him again and again. He roared out his need and his love as he lost all control, exploding into her with a full load of hot, thick seed that washed over her like a balm. She tightened around him convulsively, milking him of all he had to give.*

Finally, long after the last shudder had quieted into the mixture of their heavy breathing, she felt him shift beneath her, snuffing anxiously as his muzzle sniffed along hers.

"You are unhurt?"

"I am unhurt," she confirmed with an answering snuffle. "Our cub is healthy. Sleep, my love."

His heat still pulsing within her, he held her wrapped in his warmth, shielding her from the arctic cold with his massive coat. "Mine," he whispered as his eyes slid closed.

"Thine," she agreed, burying her muzzle in his fur. "Thine, forever and always."

She came awake slowly, cold and alone, the fire long since died down to no more than a few glowing embers, dotting the night like cats' eyes in the dark. "Thine," she repeated, tears staining her cheeks. "Thine, forever and always."

Somewhere in the vastness of the tundra the call of a giant grizzly echoed her words.

* * * * *

The night was no longer calm. A fierce storm had rolled in, blanketing the tundra with several inches of new snow while they slept. Tranorva stood at the outside edge of the small invisible dome that acted as their tent, her eyes searching the darkness. Something or someone was out there.

Shivers colder than the arctic air ran up her spine as the ancient grizzly called out again. He'd stayed close ever since she'd run from the carnage at Élahandara. She knew it. She could feel him out there, watching them, waiting. He was getting closer, circling, moving in.

Yet she didn't fear the great bear. She knew, somehow, that he was there to protect her. She knew the timber of his voice, could judge his moods by his calls. At times she felt the urge to answer him, to call him into the camp, to come face to face with this piece of her past. Yet if she recognized his voice, surely he would have known hers, for it had been her cry of grief and despair that had brought him to watch over her. If he wanted to see her, he knew where to find her. She would not go looking for him. Not after all these years.

Something beyond the dome caught her attention again. She'd neither consciously heard nor seen anything out beyond their perimeter, but she knew with her Warrior's instinct that they were not alone.

The wind had kicked up again, swirling the snow about like a sandstorm. She was well accustomed to the rigors of the tundra, trained since birth to survive in these lands. Yet without the dome, without the small fire her mother had conjured practically out of nothing, Tranorva would have been blinded by now in this storm, lost, reduced to tunneling into the core of some snowdrift to hibernate with her burden, her body's warmth their only hope of survival.

Whoever or whatever she sensed, it was no Warrior. A Warrior would have approached the fire, dragged himself the last few hundred yards to safety, fought to live another day, that he might die honorably, in battle.

Whoever was out there now would surely die, feeling warmer at last, as the blood had less body to heat, until that final sleep overcame them. No more pain. No more grief. No more...

Perhaps that fate would have been better.

Tranorva stirred herself from her own bleak thoughts, substituting action for introspection, as was her way. "We are no' alone," she warned her mother as Evalayna stirred beside the fire.

Evalayna's expression turned sad. "I know. I have heard him. I have felt his pain."

"There is another. Smaller. Closer. This one needs our help." Tranorva reached out to touch the dome. It gave way as though it did not exist, yet sealed again as soon as she withdrew her hand. Encouraged, she stepped through the edge of the dome, headed unerringly toward the tiny bit of movement she'd felt more than seen in the swirling storm. The storm nearly knocked her over, but she kept her focus. She could feel the presence, almost smell it. She concentrated on her senses, using instinct when reason failed. She could smell nothing, yet she knew it was there.

The storm closed around her until she could see nothing, could find nothing, was as useless to anyone out here as she was to herself. Defeated, she turned back toward the camp.

She spun directly into the path of the largest grizzly she'd ever seen.

He stood on his hind legs, pawing the air, and roared once at her.

To her credit, she didn't scream. That would have been much too Human a reaction. Instinct once again ruled. He wasn't threatening her. He was trying to tell her something.

Tranorva sniffed, extending her nose just slightly to taste the air. Her upper lip twitched, showing a hint of her teeth. Somehow she knew he would not harm her. She backed away from him cautiously.

She almost stumbled over the silk wrapped bundle that lay nearly lost in the snow. So small. So fragile. So ill-equipped to survive out here. She scooped up the little mouse and shouldered past the giant grizzly, ignoring his bulk as she plowed back through the snow toward the relative warmth and safety of the dome.

The grizzly rose on his hind legs again, offering a snuffle and another roar as he backed away. She'd wonder later what he was doing here, how she recognized him with such certainty, why she didn't feel threatened by him...and what he meant by his snuffled messages.

For now there was the little mouse, half-frozen and nearly unconscious in her arms. This was something she could deal with.

"What have ye found?" Evalayna demanded, holding her arms out to receive the burden.

"Her name is Dahlai. In Élahandara she served as my bondswoman. She must have followed us here. Perhaps she was expelled upon my leaving. The bear found her for me."

Evalayna flinched as if she'd been struck. "Ye have seen the bear?"

Tranorva glanced over her shoulder and beckoned. The giant grizzly hesitated, then pushed through the barrier as if the dome didn't exist, as if he, too, had been Summoned within its confines, only to lumber to his feet and split the night air with his roar.

There was pain there, and fear, and need. Tranorva felt them all. But mostly she felt annoyed. "Sit down," she admonished. "Surely all that racket is unnecessary. Whatever the two of ye have to settle, there is no reason to frighten the girl. Behave thyself, Father."

Chapter Three

Evalayna nearly dropped the small bundle as she stumbled to her feet. "No," she whispered, her voice hoarse with denial. "No. Ye canna' be here. Ye are dead. I know ye are dead. I am dreaming again."

Tranorva snatched the pile of wet silk from her mother, endeavoring to set the childling on her feet as she pulled the ruined bedspread away from her skin, wishing she had somewhere to put it to dry. "Hold this!" she hissed at Élandine's animated form, blanching in distaste as he did precisely as she ordered.

"Wonderful," she observed. "My lover is reduced to a drying rack for wet bedclothes."

The grizzly sat on his splayed haunches well back from the fire, his liquid brown eyes fixed on Evalayna. Tranorva could have sworn there were tears in his eyes. His voice broke in soft snuffling sounds, almost as if he were speaking. She found if she listened with her heart instead of her mind she could understand him.

"My heart. My mate. You call me now?"

By the gods, she did not want to think of her mother, the feared Shaman Lady Evalayna Lochinvar, as some bear's mate, nor some man's lover! Especially not now, with her own lover's arms draped in a ridiculous tattered silk coverlet, steam rising off of its wet folds.

"All lost. All gone. So many days. So many years. So alone."

Tranorva flushed hotly, feeling suddenly like a voyeur, eavesdropping on something very personal. She turned away, both to care for the child and to allow the lost lovers some small degree of privacy.

Evalayna shut her eyes tightly, but when she opened them again, he was still there. "I thought I was losing my mind, imagining I heard thy voice in every call that echoed across the tundra." She crossed slowly to the ancient grizzly, trying to see beyond the gray in his fur, beyond the dull, matted coat, to find the man she had once loved. Behind her the little honey-brown bondswoman who was neither Elf nor Élandra shrieked in terror. Evalayna heard her daughter's voice, uncharacteristically soothing, calming the girl, and then all else was gone. Her world narrowed to the shaggy coat, the lean build, the deep musk that was all grizzly, newly awakened from his winter's den.

'Twas not the first winter he'd spent buried in the earth.

Her hand trembled as she touched her fingers to the talisman she wore about her neck. "Roahr...I hardly dare to believe my eyes. How can this be?"

He did not reach out to her as she approached. If anything he shrank farther back into himself, making no move to touch her, either for harm or for comfort. Evalayna lifted a hand slowly to his muzzle, grayed now with advancing years, to wipe the dampness from the fur around those deep pools of suffering. "Roahr."

"Lost. Years lost. So alone."

"I'm here now, my heart. Ye need not be alone any more. Come back to me."

"Lost..."

"I have missed ye as I would miss the air itself, Roahr."

He snuffed her once with his broad damp nose, breathing in the scent of her hair. *"To be small. To be naked. To be afraid. I cannot. I do not remember the way."*

Evalayna wrapped her arms around the shaggy head, stroking through his grizzled fur, trying to reach him with touch where her words failed. "I need ye, Roahr. Our daughter needs ye. Our way is perilous. Do no' leave me to make my way alone once again. Come back to me."

A heart-wrenching cry of grief split the night air as he lumbered to his feet. *"Too late! Too late..."*

The barrier of the dome might as well not have existed as he spun off into the night. He disappeared into the swirling snow in seconds, invisible as the night, but she could still hear his voice split the arctic air. *"Mine! Forever and always. Mine!"*

* * * * *

"I hate winter," Yarwyn snarled.

"I know, my love." It seemed a bad time to remind her that spring was almost spent, and this uncharacteristic snow squall would soon pass.

"I hate cold."

Seanen tried to suppress the laughter that pulled at the corners of his eyes. "Let me warm you, my heart."

"I hate tromping through snow."

It was useless. Seanen knew she could feel the laughter bubbling up inside him as he watched his tiny Elf attempt to match his stride through the drifts. She was far too stubborn to simply travel in his wake, allowing him to break trail. He let the laughter loose as he scooped her up into his arms and settled her onto his shoulder.

"Put me down you big ox. I can run on my own two feet."

"I rather like the feel of you there, your lovely curves so close to my teeth." As if to prove his words he bit gently into the curve of her hip as he doubled his speed. "Would that you had the gift of your mother's people. You surely share their affinity for long naps in the hot sun."

"My mother had no gift but to make bottles of mead disappear," Yarwyn reminded him crossly.

"Oh?" He ran his fingers over the curve of one long pointed ear, feeling her purr despite herself. "Are these not a gift from your mother, then?"

"I got nothing from my mother. She was Human, a tavern whore, little more than a slave. I remember nothing of her except that she told me my talents were too precious to waste, and the Priestesses would pay well for me."

"Your father was Elven, then."

"I know not. I suppose he must have been, since I bear someone's likeness, and I was born in Talismar."

"The Priestesses who taught you how to harness your power, did they not teach you the gifts of your race?"

"They did not consider me one of their race. Half-Elves are the bastards of the world, homeless wanderers, destined to roam the earth looking for Barbarians to tote them about."

"Well, this Barbarian may be the bastard son of a bastard house, but he would prefer to travel on four feet rather than two across this expanse of wasteland. Especially since winter has decided to renew her grip on the tundra. Would that you had learned this art from your Priestess benefactresses. 'Twould seem a useful skill for a Ranger to possess."

"Put me down. Now."

The change in her tone brought him instantly to a halt, her edgy wariness putting him on guard. He set her upright, his fingers spanning her small waist. "What is it, my heart?"

"Seanen, explain this slowly for me, that I might understand. You can shape shift into a wolf, as your Shamen do?"

He blinked in confusion. "All my people are capable of this. We live as men, but we hunt as wolves. Wolf Clan fights as a pack."

"How? How do you do this?"

He fastened his gaze on the depths of her violet eyes, concentrating, letting go, letting himself flow until he was one with the Earth Mother and her sons.

Yarwyn watched, absorbing all she could as the eyes that held her gaze turned black as the night. One moment he was a man, standing before her, seven foot tall and broader of shoulder than the average doorway. The next he was a wolf, ragged and rangy and ready to run for miles across the tundra, his black coat tipped with silver like a mask around his muzzle.

"Too quick," she gasped, barely managing to contain her awe. "Does it take too much out of you? Can you do it again for me?"

Black eyes blinked up at her, and he was a man. She stood next to him in the snow, open to him, all her barriers down. "Don't think. Feel. I need to know what it feels like—the joy, the pain, the wonder of it."

She felt first his love for her, which still overwhelmed her, and then something stranger—his understanding of the gods and his place in the divine universe—and then the slight pain as bone melded to another shape, and the swift changes in his senses as he tasted the wind.

The gods. Of course. His people were so close to their god. This thing that he felt inside, it went beyond love. It touched on unity of the spirit. She had never learned such a thing from the Sisterhood. She had known, of course, known that the Sisters shared a faith that led them to train the Rangers to protect their lands. But she had never been schooled herself. Had never believed in anything beyond the grasp of her own two hands. Was she capable of such understanding? Such an elemental response to the gods, so personal, so intimate?

"Again," Yarwyn whispered.

The man leaned in to claim her mouth, his breath hot against her lips, his tongue gentle as he tasted her, his teeth sharp as they nipped at her.

She felt what he felt, let it flow through her veins, let it touch her heart and her soul, until she looked into the depths of his midnight eyes, her muzzle a few scant inches from his.

She hissed, a screech of protest falling from her mouth. "*A cat! By the gods I did not wish to be a cat!*"

His wolf eyes laughed at her as his tongue lolled out of his mouth. "*You cannot be aught but what you are, my mate. And you are a cat. Such is the lot of the folk of Talismar.*"

"*Well I do not like it.*" She sprang forward, clearing a damp patch in the snow by several feet. "*I hate wet. I hate snow. I hate cold.*"

"*Yes, my love.*"

"*Don't seek to placate me, you — you — mangy — dog.*"

Dark eyes laughed at her as he loped at her side. "*Never, my love. I must say, you make a gorgeous leopard. Very sleek and sexy.*"

Yarwyn shook her head in disgust. "*You would mate with anything, you lech.*"

"*No, my love. I would only mate with you. As that is not possible just now, I shall race you from here to House Yarishet. We shall be safe from the storm there. Even Evalayna herself cannot move about much in this weather. Once we reach the splendor of Mâkakao's great house, I shall tumble with you amidst piles of brocade pillows and satin damask before we take up our journey again.*"

Yarwyn smiled a feral cat smile. "*I like the way you think, my love.*"

"*You like the idea of being warm by the fire nestled in silks.*"

"*I like the idea of your naked man-skin beneath my hands, and your body mine to command.*"

"You make a fine cat," Seanen laughed again. He nipped lightly at her muzzle as they streaked through the night, unlikely companions at best, too attuned to each other to take notice of the far off roar of the ancient grizzly.

* * * * *

The storm was getting worse. Even with her excellent night vision it was almost impossible to see more than a few feet in any direction. Cassadara stopped just below the crest of the hill, her sharp lupine senses alerting her to the small party that lay in wait over the ridge. Four, by the smell of things. Four nasty, filthy Orcs who would have done much better at trapping her had they taken a few minutes to scrub themselves with the snow before they headed out to hunt.

Cassadara surveyed the terrain before deciding on a strategy. The edge of this hill sloped down to the right, funneling into a natural valley that would leave her at the low point, where she would be vulnerable to attack from above and behind as she moved in on her prey.

To the left the way was steep and rocky, but she'd wager it was passable — for a wolf. She could skirt the end of the hill and come in behind the Orcs, finishing them off before they even realized she had discovered their ruse. She licked her lips in eager anticipation. She had been born to fight. Adrenaline sharpened her senses and lent new strength to her tired legs. She scrambled up the side of the hill, moving in for the kill.

* * * * *

Tyrell pitched his voice deeper, his words carrying clearly through the steadily falling snow. "Who are ye, and what are ye doing out here alone?"

"He would be thy brother-in-law," Ayailla commented dryly. "And ye need no' think to intimidate Lord Mâkakao by bellowing at him in our tongue. He speaks more languages than ye are aware of."

Mâkakao bowed deeply as he moved in to shake himself off by the fire. "Lady Ayailla. Sir Tyrell. Well met."

"Yarishet? Ye are here alone? Where is thy Lady Wife?" Tyrell's voice turned harsh as he attempted to scan the blanket of drifting snow that surrounded the small camp.

"Your sister travels as the wolf, and has outdistanced me in this storm," Mâkakao explained reluctantly.

Ayailla offered a most unladylike snort. "She ran off and left ye."

A flush lit Mâkakao's face. "Aye, M'Lady. I fear my young wife thinks to protect me from time to time, whether I have need of her protection or not."

"How much of a start has she on thee?"

"Not more than an hour, at best, M'Lady, though her speed surely outdistances mine. The storm would not have impeded her progress as badly as it did mine."

Tyrell shook his head. "No wife of mine would be running off alone across the tundra to leave me to follow at her heels."

Ayailla raised an eyebrow, waiting to see how Mâkakao would react to Tyrell's challenge. Men were unpredictable things, needed much guidance, but she sometimes found it amusing to watch them viè for a superiority they would never rightfully claim.

Mâkakao simply threw back his head and laughed. "The voice of a single man knows no humility, Brother. Cling to your illusions whilst you can."

It was Ayailla's turn to laugh now. "Spoken as a true husband. Come. Join us at the fire, Lord Mâkakao. Once the storm passes we will travel together, as a pack. For tonight we shall feast. Tyrell's fine skill as a Shaman has caught us a rabbit."

Mâkakao dropped his pack near the fire, ignoring the irony of Ayailla's words. "Rabbit makes a great stew, with a bit of greens to flavor it."

Tyrell's eyes lit up with reluctant interest. "Ye can cook?"

"Aye."

"Perhaps ye could teach me a thing or two, Brother. The Lady Ayailla has no such skills to pass on to me."

"Is it my fault this century cannot conjure a microwave?" Ayailla demanded, taking personal affront to Tyrell's comment.

Mâkakao's hands stilled in his pack. "Mike-row-way?"

"Microwa—never mind," Ayailla conceded with a sigh. There was no way to translate words whose concepts simply did not exist. "An ancient device used to cook foods quickly with beams of energy."

Tyrell raised one eyebrow and shrugged slightly. Mâkakao found something interesting in his pack that required his attention.

"'Tis no secret I never learned to cook," Ayailla added defensively. "'Twas a different world, a different time. The skills a woman needed were based on technology, no' sheer survival."

Mâkakao raised an eyebrow in surprise. "Technology? I have heard stories from the past, but in my culture these stories are from the ancient past…I would have thought such artifice much older than the span of your years, M'Lady."

Ayailla nodded in agreement. "Aye, 'tis true. I am from an older time. I was Summoned, as ye were, but with a much more powerful spell. 'Tis a long story, for another night. Suffice it to say that I owe all that I am, my life, my loves, my daughters, to the Fey creature Shammall. It is for him, as well as my daughter, that I trek across this tundra. And, perhaps, for myself. I am old. I thought to make no more great journeys again in this lifetime. It comforts me to know I am no' too old yet to repay this debt."

Ayailla seemed to snap back from her musings, her fierce matron's scowl pulling the wrinkles back into her face. "Enough talk of the past. Two men, and I still canna' get a decent meal. Are ye going to cook that rabbit, or worry it to death with thy voices?"

"Tis already dead." Tyrell stood up to drop the skinned rabbit parts in Mâkakao's small pot of boiling herbs. After brushing his hands clean with snow, he turned to plant a kiss of affection on his grandmother's forehead. "I love ye, old woman, no matter how odd ye are."

Ayailla laughed at that, returning his hug as they settled in to watch the pot bubble over the fire.

* * * * *

Evalayna raised her head to sniff the night air, though she needed no such aide to follow him. Roahr had made no attempt to conceal his tracks. 'Twas not arrogance. He would not have thought of it. He had no natural enemies, other than his own kind.

She sniffed to catch the flavor of the night, the feel of the air rushing in, overwhelming her super-sensitive olfactory nerves. She sniffed to remember.

It had been long since she'd tasted the night.

Too long.

It had been longer still since she'd caught the scent of him on her tongue and savored it as a relished spice...

Grief for the long years lost threatened to overwhelm her, but she forced it aside. No time for that. No time for anything but the mission at hand.

The mission. She should be focused on the mission. On her daughter. What in the name of the seven hells was she doing out here in this blizzard chasing a dream? What was she thinking, running off into the night after...

After him.

After the man she'd loved more years than she could count.

After Roahr VinDall.

"Too late! Too late..." He stopped at the top of the snow-covered slope to roar out his grief. *Lost.*

He'd lost her again.

Away. Must get away. Too old.

He was too old. Defeated, he ran, now, forsaking his territory. Another, younger, stronger, would take his place. He was done with the battle. He could not be what he had been in his youth.

She'd touched him. She'd touched him with her hands, and her heart.

"Stay with me."

She'd touched him with her words.

Did she not understand? Did she not know of the months, the years of the vast alone?

Grief gave way to anger. *Rend. Destroy. Eliminate the betrayer. Kill the lying tongued one. Reclaim what is mine…*

But he could not make that claim. She was lost to him as never before. For she had chosen her path.

She had chosen the man who stood at her back. He looked different, but the smell was the same. There could be no doubt.

How could she ask him to stay, when the betrayer stood at her side?

He ran, lumbering out of sight in the snow shrouded night, his voice growing dimmer as his long stride outdistanced her shorter legs. She was old, and unaccustomed to such strenuous exertion. She would never catch up with him this way. She stopped at the top of the slope to pull his scent back to her on the night air. She could not catch up with him in this storm running across unfamiliar territory. She had to use her wits. The gods had armed her well enough.

She dropped her shaggy butt down into the snow and lifted her head back in song, rending the night with her melody. *"Thine. Thine, forever and always. Come to me my heart."*

There was a long silence — so long that she began to think he would not answer. When his voice reached her again, it was a wordless call of grief and pain.

"Forever and always," she repeated.

"Too late. Too many years. Too much pain."

He hadn't moved again. There'd been enough time in between to tell her that both answers had come from the same place. *"Forever and always."*

"*You ask too much.*"

"*What is a year in the drop of forever?*"

"*A year? A decade times three.*"

"*Thine. Forever and always.*"

His wordless, haunting cry split the night again, but still he had not moved. She was catching up to him, she could tell. His scent was growing stronger. His huge paw prints in the snow might have been a map to follow him by. She rounded the end of a small ridge, and there he was.

She moved forward cautiously, extending her nose to him, letting him get his fill of her scent. "*Mine,*" she whispered against his muzzle. "*Forever and always.*"

"*Yours,*" he acknowledged, laying his muzzle against hers with a snuffled sob. "*Yours, forever and always.*"

Chapter Four

"Halt!"

Seanen snapped to attention, pulling his military dignity around him like a cloak. "What is the purpose of this outrage? Is the hospitality of House Yarishet so short lived, then? Wouldst thou deny the Talismarian Ambassador entrance? The double moons have no' lit the night twice since thy house did offer me the keys to thy gates, and already House Lindall is defamed by thy discourtesy?"

Yarwyn thought to tell Seanen she would tolerate the breach of protocol, considering the hour, but his uncharacteristic use of the formal language of his rank dissuaded her.

The guard, though tall for his race, still had to tilt his head to look up at Seanen, and might, therefore, be excused his fear. "Forgive me, M'Lord Lindall, Ambassador Yarwyn, but the House is under full security, and I did not recognize you upon your approach. Please, allow the Lieutenant to escort you to Captain Balthain.

"Captain Balthain? Are we to be interrogated, then, rather than given audience before Lord and Lady Yarishet as honored — and trusted — guests?"

The Sentry shook his head, emanating undue worry, though Yarwyn began to suspect it was not the sheer size of the Warrior at his gate that had intimidated the man. She felt more. A stronger, deeper fear than that of the moment. "Be not offended, My Lord. I can only grant you audience to one who is here, and the senior officer within these walls is Captain Balthain. Lord Yarishet and his lady have disappeared and I am posted to guard the gate. I know not else."

Yarwyn laid her hand over Seanen's arm, squeezing gently with the tips of her fingers. She pitched her voice low, trusting the guard did not speak Thieves' Cant. "*He speaks the truth, my love. There is no deception in him, nor animosity. Allow the man his duty. He cannot tell you what he does not know.*"

Seanen did not openly acknowledge her information, but the tension in him relaxed perceptibly, though a new wariness took its place. "Fear not, young Sentry. I shall report to Captain Balthain that ye have managed thy task admirably."

Yarwyn hid her desire to giggle behind a cough, holding her hand over her mouth a moment longer than was necessary. Admirably indeed. Seanen could cut to the quick with his sarcasm. "*He is but a boy,*" she cautioned. "*Try not to frighten him too badly.*"

Seanen merely nodded his head as he turned to follow the Lieutenant down the long stone corridor. "*I was fighting for my life in the streets of Lochinvar before I was half his age. These Humans grow up too slowly, if at all.*"

"*Had either of us grown up within the walls of a house of privilege, we too might have known such innocence.*"

"*Innocence? The pair of you? I have my doubts.*" The voice was soft, and deep in timber, laced with the subtle cynicism inherent to the spirit of the Thieves' Cant.

One moment Seanen was beside her, as relaxed as he ever was outside the bedroom, and the next he simply vanished. Yarwyn stepped back into the shadows, instantly on the defensive. She had seen no one. She had felt no one. The Lieutenant moved on down the hallway, unconcerned, as if he'd seen and heard nothing. Which was as it should be.

"*Identify yourself,*" Seanen's voice hissed.

"*You know me well, Lord Lindall. You taught me to dance.*"

Yarwyn blinked slowly, trying to picture Seanen as a dance instructor. Trying harder to read and feel real the meaning behind the spoken words.

"*Rat?*"

"Aye, M'Lord."

"What in the name of the gods are ye doing here?"

The deep voice offered a rumbling laugh. *"A Mercenary goes where he is paid to go, my friend."*

Both men ceased their disappearing act and moved to clasp arms, attracting the Lieutenant's attention so that he halted and turned to face them. "Captain Balthain. My apologies, Sir. I did not hear you. Lord Lindall and Ambassador Yarwyn are here to see you, Sir."

Balthain himself was a member of Seanen's Guild? And he was head of Mâkakao's security, just as Seanen was Lady Lochinvar's head of security. Interesting. Another piece of the puzzle of the Rogue's Guild fell into place. Perhaps their reputation as thieves was no more accurate than the reputation the Ranger's Guild managed to cloak themselves in...

"I can see that. I will escort them from here, Lieutenant. You may return to your post."

"Aye, Sir."

Balthain led them to an office in the second story of the guard tower overlooking the front gates. *"Mâkakao and Cassadara disappeared before the dawn yesterday just before the storm hit,"* he began abruptly, his words still masked in Thieves Cant. *"I found but a cryptic note saying the Lady had been summoned and I was to maintain security in his absence. I can tell you nothing else except that he left in light armor and well armed, with perhaps a two to three day supply of food from the kitchens. We do not know how the message reached the Lady. The guards reported no page at the gates. The head of the Bards Guild has no report of any note being delivered. I have received no word or token from any member of our Guild traveling through."*

Balthain drummed his fingers lightly on the desk. *"There is word from the north that the Dark ones are showing their faces in daylight well past the gates of Talandar. That ruined city is said to be on the mend, though no open attacks have as yet been reported. Yet I fear Lord Mâkakao travels straight into the path of danger. At the very least he travels directly into the heart of the storm."*

Seanen and Yarwyn exchanged glances. "'Twas about the same time, then. Early in the morning, well before dawn yesterday, I received the same Summoning. Your security has not been breached. There was no written or carried message. Word came to me as a voice in my dreams, compelling enough to wake me from a deep sleep. I believe that word to have been sent by my patron, Lady Evalayna Lochinvar. I go to her now, and Yarwyn with me. We would seek a few hours rest here before we move on."

"You would do well to wait out the storm here. There is nothing to be gained by attempting to travel in such weather. The apartment you used last is empty. I shall provide you with an escort."

"We can find our way. We shall be on our way at first light, weather permitting. Forgive me if we do not say our formal good-byes in the morning. The fewer who know we travel here the better…and you are well to maintain your defenses. If Talandar is indeed on the mend, our Guild must be alerted. Spread the word as quickly as you can."

"It shall be done. Well met, my friend. Good journey to you. May we meet again under better circumstances."

"Well met indeed."

Yarwyn blinked, looking around what appeared now to be an empty room. Only Seanen's hand on her arm guiding her steadily out the door betrayed his presence, so that she could focus on him once again. She could have sworn his image had less substance than his own shadow.

When she would have spoken, to ask him how he accomplished this, he turned enough to grin down at her, his eyes wolfishly hungry, and she forgot what it was she had wanted to know. His apartment seemed suddenly miles away, instead of merely at the other end of the great house. Tomorrow seemed even farther away.

* * * * *

A lone wolf's cry split the night air, the only warning they had. Mâkakao surged to his feet, his scimitars singing as they cleared their sheathes, whirling to face the unseen enemy. He knew that voice. 'Twas his mate's call. Fear pumped through his veins as he answered, his voice singing out clear and true through the night, a beacon to guide her to safety.

The attackers moved in swiftly, appearing out of nowhere, dark shadows twisting across the frozen ground.

Tyrell, too, leaped to his feet, staff at the ready, but it was Ayailla who saved them. She looked up from her stew without spilling a drop to flick her fingers at the night. A wall of fire more than four feet high suddenly surrounded the camp, pushing back both the night and the storm.

Orc voices raise in hideous shrieks as those caught within the flames perished instantly. Unfortunately only those caught in the flames were affected. At least six attackers had made it inside the circle of fire, and more awaited just beyond the perimeter of the camp.

The ones outside could wait. Mâkakao set his blades to the ones within as Ayailla calmly wiped her chin and reached for her staff, sending a globe of light to hover over the camp, allowing them to see the forces massed on the far side of the dying flames.

Many. Too many. Mâkakao made the assessment even as the Orc whose head he'd just severed rolled to the ground. Tyrell's current attacker stepped back into the gore, losing his footing as his bare toes tangled in his dead comrade's hair.

Ayailla lifted her staff to point it like a mother pointing her finger at a naughty child, and three of the attackers outside the circle ran screaming into the night, the smell of burning fur trailing in their wake.

The lone wolf's cry came again. Ayailla shifted the focus of her staff, quelling the flames in her fire ring long enough for Cassadara to leap safely through. Mâkakao moved to fight at her side as she shifted, raising an eyebrow at the long bloody gash that ran the length of her left arm, but offering no words of reproof.

Ayailla renewed her wall, and the three Shaman turned their attention to blasting those on the other side into oblivion, while Mâkakao finished off the two who remained intent on impaling themselves on the blades of his scimitars. Once they were down, he turned to Ayailla, indicating with a brush of his blades where he wanted the funnel to point. She obliged him instantly, peeling the flames back until they formed a chute, as for ushering farm animals toward their sacrifice at a butcher's altar.

It was bloody, gruesome work, for the Orcs had not the intelligence to see that for all their comrades who lay dead, the only blood they had yet drawn was the gash on Cassadara's arm and a few small tears in Mâk's favorite traveling tunic. It took the best part of an hour to kill them all, and for all the carnage, Mâk had nothing to show but an angry heart and a fouled campsite. When there was nothing left to kill, he turned to wipe his blades, but could find no unadulterated ground.

It was Tyrell's voice that broke the deadly calm of the after-battle silence as he moved to examine Cassadara's wound. "I see ye did not fair so well alone, Sister."

Mâkakao fought to contain a smile at his brother-in-law's gentle reproof. Cassadara's gaze met Mâk's as she answered her brother. "I made a foolish mistake, Brother. I underestimated both the strength and intelligence of my enemy. I thought to out-trick the tricksters. I was lucky to get away with my life. Had ye not been here—all of ye—'twould have been a much shorter night for me."

"Wolves fight as a pack," Ayailla observed, her tone a less gentle reproof.

Cassadara shook off her brother's ministering hands as she moved to Mâkakao's side. "'Twas a foolish misjudgment. Forgive me, my husband, for forgetting the ways of my people."

Mâkakao stepped outside the charred circle to clean his blades in undefiled snow. "You cannot protect me, *Mel~amin*, if you are not at my side."

Cassadara winced as her brother found her arm again. "Nor can ye protect me by sheltering me within thy great house."

Mâk drew in a long breath as he sheathed his scimitars. "Agreed. We fight together, as a team."

"As a pack," Ayailla corrected. "And as a pack let us move out. This place smells of death. Storm or no storm, I will no' rest here longer." She ran the tip of her finger lightly along the long gash Tyrell had just cleaned. "I am sorry, Granddaughter. I am too late. Ye shall have a scar to remind ye of this night's misadventures."

"No matter. 'Twill no' be the first." Cassadara held out her hands toward him, and her eyes met his across the wreckage that had been their camp. "'Tis only the scars of the heart that do not fade with time. Join with me, my mate."

Mâkakao met her halfway, the battle rage cooling as quickly as the blood that congealed all around them. He took her hands, and laid his cheek against hers, breathing in her scent as the magic consumed him, and then once again they were wolves, and the night was their home.

* * * * *

Even for wolves, traveling in such a storm was not easy. They took turns breaking trail, plowing through snow that was nearly chest high now, leaping through drifts and scrambling over unseen obstacles that lay buried beneath the smooth white surface.

They made but a few miles before Tyrell brought the party to a halt in the lee of a sheer cliff that towered out of sight into the night. "Let us camp here and continue on in the morning, when the drifts have crusted over again."

He said nothing about Ayailla's age, or the way her breath came harder than theirs, although they had carefully kept her from taking the lead. Instead he turned his attention to the night around them. "I would have something more than just a conjured campfire this night, Grandmother. Mayhap ye might teach me a few of thy tricks?"

Ayailla donned her Human form once again. "'Tis no trick. Picture the thing that ye want. Then make it so."

Tyrell closed his eyes, frowning heavily. "It's no' working."

Ayailla shook her head. "Ye work too hard at the magic, my heart. The spell is no' important, or at least it is no more important than ye make it to be. I teach ye the spells because ye expect them. Ye believe in them. 'Tis what thee believes in thy heart that makes the magic work. Ye receive what ye expect to receive."

"I do no' understand."

Ayailla waved her hand at the clearing beneath the shelter of the cliff. "What do ye want? Do ye wish tents?" She waved her hand and three tents appeared, each of tight woven white canvas, their sides lit from within by small glowing fires. "Or would ye prefer something more substantial?" She waved her hand once again, and the tents turned into small cabins, with thin trails of smoke issuing from their chimneys.

Cass blinked in surprise. "How did ye do that, Grandmother?"

Ayailla shook her head. "I was no' born in this time. I was no' taught the magic as ye were. Perhaps it is easier for me because I have no' the constraints of thy knowledge. I simply picture what I want and it appears. But the elements must be at hand. Ye canna' make a log cabin out of the air. Ye must have wood about, that the elements are to be formed from. For a tent there must be vegetable matter, that the magic might spin the cloth, or the thing ye make will be insubstantial, no more than an illusion. I canna' create food to feed an army with no more than a puff of the wind...Do ye understand at all, Granddaughter?"

"Some," Cass admitted. "I was a poor pupil when the Mage sought to teach us our spells. I mastered the combat spells early, but gave too little heed to the everyday necessities of life. I am only now learning many lessons I should have learned years ago."

If Mâkakao understood that she meant more then The Book of Ways, he kept the thought to himself, his face still dark and brooding as he took her arm to accompany her to their cabin.

"Figuring out what ye need to learn is half the battle," Ayailla offered as she turned toward her cabin. "We move out in the morning, with the dawn. Try to get some sleep."

Ayailla's eyes met Mâk's, and Cassadara could have sworn the old woman was grinning wolfishly at her husband.

Impossible.

Mâk was surely not grinning as he led her toward their cabin. His grip tight on her arm, as if afraid she might once again try to escape. Cass turned to face him as the door shut behind them, ready to meet his arguments with apologies, but he had other ideas.

Her mouth had but barely opened when his clamped over hers, his tongue rough and demanding, his hands yanking her against the hard muscled length of his body. His anger lent him a strength that matched her own, and she felt, for the first time, some small fear of this Human.

"I have paid the price we agreed upon," he hissed. "I have earned my freedom. I am no longer your slave. I am your husband, and as such I have certain rights."

"Yes," she agreed, her body flaming as his hips pressed hard against her.

Quickly, efficiently, he stripped her of her armor. One hand claimed her breast while the other held her pinned close against the heat of his pulsing cock. "I may not be born to your clan, but I am well trained as a Warrior. A Warrior does not sit at home while his mate puts her life in danger."

Her eyes closed as his teeth fastened on her neck in the traditional grip of a pack leader demanding acquiescence. She was shocked to feel her body respond so completely to his dominance. A shiver of anticipation washed over her. "Wolves fight as a pack," she repeated, her voice sounding breathy to her own ears.

"And I will be an equal member of your pack, or no member at all. If you cannot trust me to fight at your back, I will not share your bed. I am not just a toy for your amusement."

"No," she agreed as he tugged on the small blackened rings that adorned her nipples. "Ye are no toy to me. Ye are my husband, my pack mate, my soul mate."

He buried his face in her hair, so she could not see the pain she felt in his voice. "When I heard you call out tonight, the fear that raced through my heart was nearly my undoing."

"When I rounded the ridge, when I faced the trap I had allowed my pride to lead me into, I felt nothing but remorse, for I feared I would lose my life without ever having the chance to apologize for having wronged ye so."

Mâkakao scooped her up into his arms, surprising her once again with his show of strength, and carried her to the bed Grandmother had so thoughtfully provided. She watched in fascination as his own armor followed hers to the floor. The soft undertunic followed, exposing hard, vein-roped muscles that rippled with every movement. He pinned her arms, holding her helpless beneath him. "I do not want your apologies, at least not for nearly getting yourself killed. I want only your promise. I want your trust, as an equal."

"I trust ye, Mâk, as I have trusted no other."

She made no move to break his grip on her hands as he slid slowly into her, their gazes locked as she tightened around him, pulling him in, asking for all he had to give, and more. He held her captive, as much with his eyes as with his strength, punishing her slowly for the torture he had been through. She let him set the pace for once, quivering in anticipation of each stroke as he pumped his thick shaft into her, submitting as long as she could before the agony of his pace drove her over the edge.

"Mâk!" she called, demanding, begging, writhing against him in wanton need. "Claim me," she pleaded. "I am thine. Take me. Now."

A smile settled on his lips as he thrust into her, harder now, and faster, their flesh making a sucking sound with each stroke, her breathing harsh in the night air. She heard her own voice crying out in little moans of pleasure. Mâkakao twisted the small rings in her nipples with his tongue, claiming her fully, pushing past some barrier she had not known she harbored in her mind. She felt herself surrender, giving control over to him completely.

"Sing for me, Wolf-Woman."

And she did, as she broke again, the ground giving way as she plummeted over the cliff, falling helplessly into the dark void, but he was there, his voice rising with hers to guide her through the night.

Chapter Five

Evalayna stood face to face with the ancient grizzly who blocked the path before her with his enormous bulk. A sea of conflicting emotions battled within her. Anger that he had let her think him dead these many years. Pain for all she had lost in those years away from him. Fear for all she stood to lose did she bring him back. Doubt that said he was too long gone from her to still hold her in his heart. Concern that the man she had known no longer existed. Need — the need to touch, to heal, to claim what was hers. But above all, there was hope. She laid her muzzle against his, allowing her eyes to close in pleasure as he hesitantly returned her caress.

The first stroke of his cheek against hers was soft, tentative, fur on fur so close she could peer straight into the depths of his wet green eye and see into the vast reaches of his soul. Later, later she would speak to him with words, tell him of the long nights by the fire at their camp, ask the inevitable questions. For now she wanted nothing more than to touch, to hold, to nurture, until she found the man hidden within those endless depths.

If the man was no more, what then? If he rambled off into the night, his shaggy fur shrouding him like a barrier she could not penetrate, if she lost him again, would there be anything left of her that was Human? Or would she be nothing more than the thing her mother had wished her to become? Would she be the great matriarch once again, her soul forever lost in the vast white snow of the tundra?

Evalayna closed her eyes and followed her heart, as she had once before, so long ago. She nuzzled her cheek along the length of his still powerful neck, until her chin rested across the hump of his broad shoulders. He laid his head over her neck, his broken, snuffling cry both a demand and a surrender.

He turned suddenly, lumbering away down the path he'd been on when she found him, but he looked back over his shoulder to make sure she followed. She did, nearly running to keep him in sight as the storm sought to blind her.

The den was fresh and clean and at the same time well lived in, the dirt floor comfortably compacted and free of annoying litter and rocks, as if he'd raked the dirt with his claws, cleaning it for her. An absurd notion. He could not have known she would follow him here. How could he. She hadn't known herself.

Perhaps he cleaned the den for himself. As a man, he had never been one who was wont to wallow in his own filth. She wondered briefly if he used the same den year after year, something true bears rarely ever did, and then she forgot to wonder as he pulled her down into his arms with a short, piercing cry, his broad chest and thick fur cradling her head as she snuggled back against him.

His head slipped over her shoulder from behind and he laid his muzzle alongside hers, his warmth contrasting sharply with the cold that had cut through her bones for days, now.

She felt another warmth from him, down low and tight against his belly, still sheathed but already trembling with need when he brushed against her. He shifted his body slightly so she might not notice, as if his desire embarrassed him. Her heart raced as she felt the heat of him trapped between them, just as she remembered him, long, thick, hard, and quivering with need as she pressed back against his body, refusing to allow him to hide his desire. Her body's answering surge of lust surprised her with its force.

"*I want ye*," she breathed against his shaggy muzzle. It was no more than the truth. Whatever she had thought, however this had started, she no longer cared. A flood of desire dampened the fur at her opening.

His long, thick cock rose out of its hood to jump against her, as if it had a mind of its own, even while his voice protested. "*Here? Now? Like this?*"

She felt the question he did not ask, the silent plea for acceptance, for understanding of what he had become. "*It has been so long. Too long. Wherever ye are is where my heart lives,*" she countered. She rocked her hips, stretching her legs out behind her until she could rub her yearning slit down the hard, burning length of him. "*I have waited long enough. Years. Decades of wanting. Take me. Here. Now.*"

He ground his cock against her, letting her feel the hot pulsing need he could barely control, yet still he hesitated. "*You. Only you.*"

His voice was the voice of the bear, but was there a man's lust behind his snuffled words? She reached out to him with her heart, trusting him with her secret. "*There has been no other for me. How could there be, after what we shared? I feared I had grown too old, too—too respectable—to feel like this again. Make me feel alive again, Roahr. Make me remember how it was between us.*"

She pressed back against him, letting him feel the rising heat of her passion, drenching him with her need. His cock seemed to grow even harder, as if its enormous length were about to split the long, smooth sheath that held its root bound against his lower belly. She felt the weight of his lightly furred balls rubbing against her, contracting with desire as they brushed against her damp welcoming, then pressed against her once again.

"*Take me!*" she demanded. "*I want to feel ye within me once again. I need…*"

His control snapped. No matter how ready she was, she could never have been prepared for the fury with which his enormous cock plunged into her, his body shaking with need as he buried himself fully. She wanted to hold him there, to savor the feeling, but his teeth closed hard in the fur at the base of her neck, above the hump of her shoulders, rendering her helpless as he drove his hard length into her with a passion that assaulted her senses.

Rolling her beneath him he pinned her down to the dirt floor with his enormous weight, his quivering haunches moving so furiously as he pumped into her that she wondered if her body could contain him. She met him thrust for thrust, arching her pelvis hard against him, her muscles clenching around him desperately as she felt her climax build, then burst with release. Still he continued his assault, driving her farther and farther toward the limit of her endurance, demanding more when she shattered around him yet again.

The pleasure built until it was a nearly inescapable pain, a need so strong she felt she might break from the strength of it. "*Now!*" she screamed at the night. "*Now!*"

She felt the almost imperceptible change in him, felt his balls tighten as he surged into her again, harder and deeper with every stroke, the quivering need in him making his breath harsh against her neck, his heartbeat wild where his chest crushed against her shoulders. "*Now!*" she breathed again, her need as strong as his own. "*Now!*"

He broke.

With a roar that threatened to bring the small earthen den down around them he erupted into her, still thrusting against her as she tightened around him like a vise, shrieking out her pleasure in a cry as fierce as his own. The sweet stream of his seed washed over her, soothing her battered flesh as he grew still within her. His teeth released her as he laid his muzzle along hers, his heartbeat echoing through her like a bass drum in the sudden silence, his breath coming in long, drawn gasps.

Her heart beat in rhythm to his. His spent cock still pulsed within her as the aftershocks of their lovemaking coursed through her. Like a memory revisited, she held him, cherishing the sensations as they slowly subsided.

His weight crushed her in place, leaving her unable to move more than was necessary to draw in a labored breath, but she would not have moved had she been able. How could she have lived without this? How could she have endured these last decades with nothing more than his memory? If he left her now, if the man he had been was indeed too far gone to be brought back, how could she ever go on as if life had purpose and meaning without him?

"*Mine,*" she sobbed against his grizzled beard. "*Mine. Forever and always.*"

His forearms tightened around her as he rolled them to their sides. She pressed tighter against him to keep from breaking their bond. His body wrapped around her, sheltering and protecting even as his breathing became steadier. "Yours," he whispered gently against her ear. "*Yours and yours alone, M'Lady. Never have I been anything else.*"

* * * * *

Yarwyn raced on ahead, Seanen close at her heels as they made for his apartment. He was tall, and long of leg, incredibly agile for a big man, but no match for her Elven speed. She was through the door and starting to undress before he caught up with her. Her hands stilled as she felt him enter the room.

"Seanen?"

"I could be some thief, stealing in to take possession of you as my prize."

Despite herself she shivered at the suggestion. "You must teach me this trick of fading into the walls…"

He stepped from the shadows, advancing on her like a predator. "Do not stop now. Undress for me."

She searched his eyes, feeling suddenly small and vulnerable. "I — I am unpracticed in the art of seduction, I fear."

Seanen laughed softly. "Your every move seduces me." He helped her lift her fine mesh shirt free of her close-cropped silver hair. "'Tis your very lack of artifice that seduces me most."

Yarwyn peeled out of her undertunic, anxious to feel his hands on her skin. Only when she was naked did she realize that he had not yet begun to undress. "Where is my thief, come to steal my virtue?"

Seanen laughed at that. "Sometimes a thief uses a more direct approach to take what he wants." He drew her into his arms, his mouth slowly descending upon her neck, his hands skimming over her body, her breasts smashed against the cold steel of his mail shirt. "You should run, little one. Your virtue is not safe with me."

Yarwyn ran her hands over his thickly muscled forearms. "I cannot run. 'Tis too late. You hold my heart hostage."

His mouth nibbled its way up her neck in a series of small kisses, working its way closer and closer to her ear. She shivered in anticipation, already wet and wanting. One large hand clasped her buttocks, pulling her tightly against him, so that she could feel the hard length of his thick shaft through his leggings. His voice whispered hot against her ear, sending electrical shock waves of desire skimming down the length of her body. "Then I claim you as my prize, my captive heart, to do with as I will."

"Yes," she agreed as his tongue traced the outline of her ear. "Anything. My body is yours to command."

He released her abruptly. "Undress me."

She smiled her cat smile as she reached to help him shrug out of his chainmail shirt. Slowly, deliberately, she skimmed her hands up his sides, then down the length of his muscular arms as she pulled the undertunic over his head. Loosening the ties on his leggings she managed to brush her fingers across his bulging erection several times as she struggled with the knot. Finally she lowered her head to set to work on the knot with her teeth.

By the time she had it undone he was trembling beneath her fingers, his hands fisted in her hair. But when she would have taken him into her mouth, he moved away, lifting her easily until her mouth met his own, claiming, possessing once again. He supported her easily with one hand under the curve of her hips as he carried her to the ancient four-poster bed.

"My captive must follow my rules," he whispered. He laid her gently out on the bed, taking the time to settle her head carefully in the pillows, arranging pillows under her hips, leaving her knees spread wide, so that he had full view of her swollen labia, puffed with desire for him.

"What do you want me to do?"

"Nothing."

"Nothing?"

"You must simply take whatever I give you. Keep your hands to yourself." And then he proceeded to make that nothing nearly impossible, as he worked his way up from her ankles with slow, tantalizing kisses.

She felt the flood of moisture drench her channel before he even reached the top of her inner thighs, and she wanted desperately to pull him against her, tangling his long, heavy hair in her fingers, but instead she arched off the pillows, offering her mons up to him as a sacrifice. He laughed, but continued to kiss his way up her thighs.

Inspiration claimed her. If she could not touch him...she reached down to spread herself open before him, making sure he had a clear view as she circled her swollen clit with her finger, moaning wordlessly as the need to climax shook through her.

"You cheat."

"Do not." Her voice came in thick, hard pants. "You said I could not touch you."

His tongue nudged her fingers aside, circling, then lapping over her throbbing clit. Yarwyn surrendered her position to him, only to move her fingers to tweak her jutting nipples. She heard him groan as he looked up to see her stroke and pinch the aching tips. "Cheater," his whispered again, though there was laughter in his voice.

"Thief," she countered. She came almost instantly as he slipped two fingers deep into her, thrusting gently in time to his expert sucking. She shook beneath him like a willow in high winds as the power of it tore through her, sure she would shatter and break like some delicate vase.

Seanen only slipped his hands beneath her hips to raise her up so that he could thrust his tongue deep within her, stroking her inner walls as he pushed her to the limits of her endurance, withdrawing only long enough to lave her aching clit once again. She screamed out his name as she shattered around him again, forgetting the rules as she reached for him, her hands stroking his ears, pushing him down harder against her as she shook beneath his touch.

"Seanen!" she cried again. "I cannot—I—"

"Is there something you want, my love?"

"You. Inside me. Now!"

He moved to oblige, kneeling between her thighs, lifting supple legs until her heels rested nearly against her own shoulders as he slid slowly between her swollen lips and into her tight, drenched sheath. She cried out again with his first long, slow thrust, straining to hold him deep within her, moaning with desire as he withdrew, only to thrust in again, stroking into her with an infuriating control that threatened to shatter her mind as well as her body.

"Tell me," he demanded. "Tell me what you want."

"Anything. Everything."

"More."

"Yes, more!"

He shifted again, sitting back on his knees as he hooked her legs over his elbows, granting him even deeper penetration. She started to reach for him, then decided instead to torture him as he did her, using his own rules. Lifting one breast to make sure he had a perfect view, she licked her fingers, then deliberately outlined the nipple, watching his eyes darken as she slowly massaged the aching bud of desire.

She watched his control snap as she pinched the tip, then rolled it between damp fingers. He slammed into her harder, slow forgotten as her body responded to him, meeting him thrust for thrust, clenching around him tightly with each stroke. She came again as he increased his pace to a furious pounding, driving her backwards into the pillows as he lost all control, screaming her name as he came within her. She shattered again as the hot gush of his seed washed over her, her muscles spasming around him as she milked him of all that he had to give.

"You never play by the rules," he laughed as he collapsed over her.

Yarwyn wrapped her legs around his waist, holding them tied together as he grew smaller within her, his hot length still pulsing with the aftershocks of their collision. "I never was good with rules," she admitted, still struggling to catch her breath. "We can try again, if you like. Perhaps I'll get it right next time."

"Give me a few minutes to recover," Seanen managed, his head curled against her chest, his arms still wrapped around her possessively.

Yarwyn stroked her fingers through his tangled hair. "Will you not tire of me, M'Lord, now that you have the entire Clan of the Wolf to choose from?"

"Did I not tell you?" he answered, his voice already heavy with sleep. "Wolves mate for life."

* * * * *

Roahr tightened his paws around her possessively as he felt her body shift within his arms. But as he came more fully awake he understood what was happening.

Her magic was fading.

The dream was ending once again.

He wanted to wake her up, to warn her before she slipped away completely, but he merely held her, knowing it would be no use. She was what she was. This form was only magic for her. She could not live like this. Not as he could.

He wanted to open his muzzle and scream out his pain to the world as his heart shattered within him once again. He would not lose her again. He could not. Without her he was nothing. Less than nothing. The man he had been was as lost as his people, yet the bear was no true bear. They knew the difference and shunned him, as well they should. He was an impostor, masquerading, welcome nowhere. He would never be accepted as one of their kind.

Yet to be a man, to think as a man, to feel as a man...to hurt again. To risk again. His arms tightened around the small, frail being who held his heart. To love again...

There were others to think about as well. The woman at the camp had called him Father, and he knew not so much as her name. Logic said she must be Tranorva, his firstborn, for he sensed within her no fear of the thing he had become. He remembered her as a child still in his heart, so small and so fragile. Yet Evalayna had been sure she would grow to be a Warrior, as he was himself.

As he had been, so long ago.

How had she known him? His firstborn would be named to his clan as her inheritance. Was there more than years of established tradition behind that custom? Could she truly be one of his own? Tyrell had clearly inherited his mother's magic, as well as her heritage, being able to assume her clan totem form almost from birth. The wild-child had spent more time as a wolf than as a boy. What would the little hellion have grown into?

Did he yet live?

What of the one Evalayna had carried when—no, not when he'd lost her. When the poser had separated them. For surely the lying tongued weasel had done this apurpose.

Evalayna moved within his arms, burrowing more tightly against his thick fur. He sniffed at her hair, remembering the scent of her, the feel of her in his man-arms so long ago. He'd seen her expression when he'd followed the Warrior-woman back to the dome. He'd felt her fear when the understanding hit her. Seen too the sorrow in her eyes when she moved to touch him…it was the pity he'd run from, as much as anything.

Yet she'd come after him. She'd followed him here, knowing. Surely, if she could accept him as a bear, she could accept him as a man.

No. It was too late. He had spent too many years here, alone, hiding from what he had been, what he had lost. Yet he sensed this was yet another lie he told himself. The feel of her body in his arms was too familiar, too comforting. The desire he felt for her was too strong. Perhaps the change was no longer his choice. Perhaps the change had begun the day her scent had first reached him on the night air. Perhaps his future was as inevitably locked within hers as was his heart.

Chapter Six

The storm had spent its fury during the night. As the early morning light began to chase the shadows back down the wall Evalayna awoke to the feel of arms around her, cradling her, protecting her.

Her magic had faded. She was once again a child of the Northlands. The arms that held her tightened as she came awake.

They were a man's arms.

Roahr had come back to her.

Smothering a sigh of relief, she snuggled closer, content just to be near the man once again.

"I have been so alone without you."

"And I." She turned slowly in his arms to face him, feeling him tense, prepared for her rejection. She tried to steel herself, to contain whatever she felt. Whatever he looked like now, she would not send him back to where he had been with one careless word. She looked up to meet his eyes, searching the deep green depths for the man she had known. She saw uncertainty there, and a need for acceptance.

Whatever she had tried to prepare herself for, this was not it. He was but a man. Older, perhaps leaner, but the naked skin beneath her hands was soft and clean, and the hands that touched her were the hands of a man. There were subtle changes — small lines framing his eyes, silver streaking his long unruly beard. There were much less subtle changes. His beautiful red hair hung in a twisted mass that reached nearly to his waist. It too was streaked heavily with silver. But beneath it all was the face of the man she remembered.

She smiled as she slipped her arms around his shoulders and up, until she could coax his head close enough to taste his lips in the strange custom of his people. They were soft, and warm, and gentle against hers, his touch asking a lifetime of questions. She kissed him again, asking him to feel, and not think. But he needed the words. She teased him with a gentle nip on his sensuously curved lower lip. "I missed ye as the tundra misses the spring. I love ye, Roahr."

He searched the depths of her eyes with that intense stare of his. "How can you say that, after all this time? After what I have allowed myself to become?"

She ran her fingertips over what he had become. The smooth, pale skin. The narrow waist above lean hips. The hard-muscled chest. The broad, powerful shoulders. "Never have I ceased to love ye. Forever and always, remember?" She closed her eyes as his mouth dipped towards hers, his lips gentle as they explored, the tentative touch of a butterfly's wing brushing over her skin, so soft and so poignantly sweet.

As the kiss ended he stood up abruptly, offering her his hand to help her to her feet. "Come. Let me show you something."

Evalayna moved a little more stiffly, the night's activities and the dirt floor having taken their toll. Laughter sparkled in those deep green eyes as he swept her into his arms. "Put me down!" she insisted. "We are no' children any more. Have a care for thy back."

Roahr merely laughed again as he moved deeper into the back of the den.

No. It was no true den. She hadn't taken enough time to study the place last night. He'd dug in the earth and shaped the front, but the back narrowed to a passage into the rock that made up the Earth Mother herself. "Have ye become as the dwarves, then, burrowing into the mountains?" Her arms tightened about his neck as the passage descended steeply. Not bad footing for a bear, but not a place a lesser man would have walked along so blithely, let alone a man carrying a woman who was no longer young, nor small.

"No, my love. This is a gift from the Mother herself. Behold." As he spoke, the passage widened out, and he came to a halt, setting Evalayna back on her feet before him.

It was a room. A large room hidden in the depths of the Mother. It should have been dark, so deep underground, but the walls were studded with luminescent crystals that gave the place a soft flickering glow. The light reflected off the water, shimmering through its surface to reflect about the small cavern. The surface of the water broke toward the far side with small effervescent bubbles, and waves of moist heat rose through the air.

This was why the den had felt warm. This and the fact that the man himself had always been a virtual furnace. Evalayna smiled as she turned to face her beloved once again. "Tis beautiful. I thank ye for bringing me here."

"Come bathe in the water with me."

"What? Would ye parboil me like some sea creature about to be served up for dinner?"

He laughed again, the sound of his voice becoming stronger and less hesitant. "Trust me. I would take no risk with your safety. Come in the water with me."

His hands moved to the sash that bound her robe of office, and for the first time Evalayna hesitated. She placed her hands over his, stilling his fingers. "I—I am no longer young, Roahr. Things are no' so different under the spell of the magic. The bear is the same. But the woman...she has changed."

He lifted her fingers to touch them to his lips. "'Tis not the magic I fell in love with. How sad it would be if I had indeed aged alone. The same time that has given us these changes in our bodies has given us, perhaps, more wisdom in our hearts. Fear not, though your shyness becomes you. Do you remember the first time you undressed for me, when you came to my pavilion before the siege of Talandar?"

Evalayna blushed, feeling as nervous as she had all those years ago. "I was sure ye would mock me for my foolishness."

"You were so beautiful, and so afraid. You took my breath away. You still do."

Evalayna closed her eyes, letting the robe fall back off of her shoulders as he pushed it aside. His hands, so large and powerful, skimmed over her, as gentle as he had been touching their babies. They outlined her hips, then gently lifted her breasts, the thumbs brushing lightly over the hard buds of her waiting nipples.

"So beautiful. The years have been good to you."

She wanted to tell him he was daft, but as his hands drifted up to frame her face she felt beautiful again. "The years have no' changed ye," she whispered in return. "No' in the ways that matter. Though I fear untangling this hair may take hours."

He laughed again as he kissed her. "You may spend as many hours as you like playing with my hair, or any other part of me you wish, my love. I am yours, to torture as you see fit."

She relaxed in his arms as he carried her down into the water. The lake was warm, yes, but not too hot. She pictured him bathing here through the years, long years as both a man and a bear, and knew things had never been as bad as she feared. He had never truly lost touch with his Human side.

Bears did not seek heat in the winter.

Her thoughts turned fuzzy as he turned her to face him once again, the water high around their waists. "You are so beautiful, my love. Never a day has gone by that I have not thought of you."

She reached out to trace her fingers over his cheek. "I married again, Roahr, after I thought ye gone, but only for the inheritance I could give to our daughters. It was understood between us that I was to be his in name only. He was an old man, dying heirless, and I thought only to give the children a future."

He leaned in to brush his lips over hers. "Once I might have been angry, but with age comes an understanding of the way of things. There is naught to be gained in punishing either of us now for decisions we made decades ago. You did what you had to do. You survived. The children are well?"

A shiver of anticipation ran through her as his hands caressed her shoulders. "The children are well." The rest could wait till later.

Roahr paused, his fingers lifting her breasts. "When I had been gone too long, when I was not sure I could remember what it is to be a man, I would think about touching you like this, remembering your breasts, heavy in my hands, sometimes filled with milk to suckle our children. I kept you alive in my heart. Always you have been my anchor, my focus when the world of man seemed to slip from my grasp."

Evalayna looked down, a hint of a tear blurring her vision. "I fear they are no' as ye remember. A woman's most prized possessions go first with age."

He only smiled. "I remember them hot and hungry for my touch. Has that changed?"

Evalayna watched in fascination as his thumbs grazed her nipples, surprised to see the skin tighten quickly at his touch, so that the points stood out hard and ready under his fingers. "Perhaps some things have no' changed so much as I feared…"

Roahr backed up a few more feet in the water, toward what she had taken as a small rock outcropping. As he sat, she realized it was a sort of a naturally formed bench, worn smooth through the ages by the bubbling water. He pulled her astride his lap as he sat, so that her breasts floated on the surface of the water. "I remember other things. Those little noises you would make when I touched you so."

As touching her so involved the gentle grazing of his teeth over the hard buds of her nipples, her head fell back into the water, and a small moan rewarded him for his work. His hands slipped down to her waist, letting the water support her upper body as he sucked at her nipples like they were some exotic drink he'd missed for too long.

She wondered briefly what he would think when he realized his hands no longer spanned her waist, but lost the thought as they slipped around to caress her hips and then pull her forward on his thighs. She pulled herself up to run her hands over his chest, then down along his sides, until she slowly brought her fingers in to brush over his hot, slick length.

His eyes closed and his tongue went still as she stroked slowly up the length of his erection. "I have missed this," she whispered. "The feel of thy skin. The heat of thy cock in my hands. The power of politics canna' begin to compare with the power a woman feels when she knows that, for this moment, she owns a man's soul."

"For this moment, and any other," he assured her. "How I have missed the feel of your touch."

"I want to feel ye within me."

The serious look disappeared as he grinned at her. "I am yours to command, sweet Lady." Yet he moved slowly, drawing her up against him so that he entered her inch by inch.

Slow was good. The way his hands caressed her ass was good. The feel of his lips on her breasts, his tongue lapping at her nipples, was better than good. Evalayna tangled her fingers in his hair, clasping his head tightly against her as he began to move within her. Slow was good. And faster was even better.

"Sing for me, Wolf-Woman. It has been too long since I heard your voice."

He wanted Lady Evalayna of House Lochinvar to sing? Impossible. Yet as he worked her body like a musician playing a harp, she lost track of Lady Evalayna, moving in rhythm to his touch. The years slipped away until propriety and station made no difference. All that was important was the feel of his thick, hot shaft pulsing within her, stirring her blood to a fevered pitch, while he licked and caressed and worshipped her body.

She came the first time like a soft warm glow building within her, heating the water a few more degrees. "Sing for me," he pleaded, not content to stop there. She shuddered with anticipation as his hand slid lower, his finger circled her other opening. She came again, harder, as he pushed into her more fiercely, driving her back onto his waiting finger. She bucked against him, moaning out in surprise and pleasure. His teeth tightened over her hard, needy nipples, first one and then the other, and then his mouth moved as his free hand tangled in her hair, pulling her closer as he tasted her temples, her nose, and the soft skin of her eyelids.

"Sing for me, Eva," he whispered as his tongue outlined her ear.

She was breathing so hard, yet she could not catch her breath. Momentarily frightened, she tensed as his finger moved within her. She wanted to tell him it was too much, she was too old, she could not endure—and then the room went dark, the world narrowing to the feel of his cock thrusting into her, his balls contracting against her. The clear note of a wolf's mating call sang through the huge, echoing cavern. She knew not whether the stars she saw were her love for him shining through as she broke at last, flooding over him with her release, or whether she was, indeed, losing consciousness from the strain her body had grown unused to.

His own song echoed with hers, the triumphant roar of the mighty grizzly, as he surged up within her, marking his territory with the wash of his seed, pulling her tightly against him as he thrust into her one last time, reluctant to let go of the long missed sensations.

Slowly the glowing lights of the cavern came back into view. She had not passed out. She was not too old. She was young again, young and tight as she held his still throbbing cock locked within her.

"I love you, Eva."

The sound of his voice, still shaken from what they had shared, made her feel younger and stronger, still. "And I love ye, Roahr. Forever and always."

"Forever and always. No matter what the day shall bring."

Evalayna laid her forehead against his shoulder, searching her memory for a spell that would generate some form of tangible clothing…for surely a man did not go to meet his daughter and her betrothed dressed in no more than the finery supplied by the gods. Even if the intended groom was a member of the walking undead at the moment.

* * * * *

"Yarwyn?"

Yarwyn licked her lips as she eyed the massive posts at the corners of the oak bed.

She pushed on his chest with both hands, but she might as well have been pushing against a wall. "You are awake too soon. Lay back down."

Seanen flexed his right arm experimentally, watching the silk scarf tighten around his thick wrist, as if to assure himself he could escape if he wished to. Yarwyn trailed the ends of the scarf she held over his chest, then slid it under his arm, tugging the fabric gently across bulging muscles and roped veins, down the path to his left wrist. Their eyes met as she looped the ends through the fold, effectively noosing his hand.

"The storm is fading. We should be on the move."

Worry clouded her eyes. "The sun is not yet up. Surely we can afford just a little more time to ourselves."

She had gone to a great deal of work to arrange this, gathering an assortment of brightly dyed scarves from some resource within the castle he knew naught of, and setting dozens of candles around the room. A hint of cinnamon reached his nose.

He would not disappoint her. Seanen forced himself to relax, one muscle at a time, laying back into the pile of assorted brocade pillows. "'Twould seem the decision is not mine to make."

Yarwyn's grin promised him he would not regret his acquiescence. She knotted the ends of the scarf securely around the bedpost, stretching his arm out until he lay quite flat against the damask sheets.

Seanen raised his head as far as his restraints would allow, watching her tie his ankles to the lower posts in a similar fashion. His breath hissed in sharply with each knot, and his cock sprang to attention like a soldier facing review on the field.

There was no sound in the room save the steady whoosh of their breathing. Yarwyn lit the candles one by one from the lamp on the dressing table. As the heady smoke of the spiced candles filled the apartment, she stepped up onto the raised bed, standing above her captive, staring down into his eyes.

He still had no clue what she was about, she could tell. She had his attention, but all she could see was lust. Slowly, methodically, she ran through the litany she had memorized. Black. She would be black this time. Black as the night. Stealthy as the leopard stalking its prey. Bones twisted and stretched as the fur sprang from her skin, and still she held his gaze.

She growled softly as he twisted within his restraints, warning him that she was in control. She could tell he was afraid of her now, the lust overshadowed by fear of the thing she had become. He could fight her, probably break those bonds, but would he? Yarwyn narrowed her cat eyes, staring down at her victim, willing him to trust her. She dipped her head and very slowly ran her rasp-like tongue up the length of his sternum.

"Yarwyn?" he whispered. He shivered under the feel of her tongue, lust once again surfacing in his eyes. "This is not right. It is not permitted…"

She silenced his protests with a swipe of her tongue over his nipple. He bucked off the bed so hard she feared for the fabric of her scarves. "Yarwyn, we cannot—"

His nipples tasted hard and sweet, like little candies ornamenting the tables at one of those infernal receptions she was always expected to attend. A jolt of lust tore through her, surprising her. This was supposed to be for him. She hadn't expected to feel—He smothered a cry as she sucked harder, savoring the taste of him. She rubbed her great furred head across the breadth of his chest, then down, watching his cock jump with desire, hearing his protests die as she touched the tip of her tongue to its head.

She ran her barbed tongue slowly up the underneath side of his rigid cock, watching the veins swell until they looked as if they might burst.

"Yarwyn..."

It was no more a protest, but more a plea for mercy. Tasting experimentally, she teased his balls with her tongue before she sucked them into her mouth. She could feel his body shaking with the strength of his desire. Her own lust would surely drive her mad at this rate. She'd never expected to feel so much. She lapped his balls against the roof of her mouth, watching his member surge helplessly as she savored the moments, gauging how far she could push him before her efforts would snap his control.

"By the seven gods, you will be the death of me..."

Yarwyn chuckled, though the sound came out more like a low growl. She released him, only to swipe her rough tongue over the inner surfaces of his thighs, licking him from knee to balls and all around his cock and back down the other side again without once touching his raging erection.

When she was sure he could stand no more without spilling his seed , she crouched down between his spread legs, so that he had to strain to see even the top of her head. Slowly, methodically, she rubbed her fur against his legs, touching him with as much of her body as she could, savoring the sensations of her cat's fur against his skin for as long as her desire would allow before she permitted the woman to rule again.

There were rules. In a clan filled with shape shifters, one had to have rules. A man did not mate with an animal. True enough, he could shift, even now, but one did not, simply did not, *ever* mate outside of one's own species. Two shifters might mate, but only if they were of the same form.

Yet Yarwyn had grown up without rules, an outcast both because of her birth and her upbringing. She knew rules only as things to bend to her will. His traitorous body obeyed only the force of her lust. He had never felt anything like the sensations of her huge barbed tongue abrading his skin. He shook with the effort of controlling himself. He could not allow this. He must not. Yet he had not the strength of will to attempt to snap the frail silk scarves.

He feared he might spill his seed as she ran her tongue over the sensitive tip of his penis, nearly shattering him with the strange sensations. "Yarwyn," he breathed, no longer knowing whether he asked for mercy or completion.

He was a fool not to have seen this coming. Of course she would want this. It was not her fault he could not shift with her. Wolves mated for life. She knew that. He had told her he loved her, yet he had not thought to find a way for them to join as his people would. He had not spoken of his regret for their inability to tie as wolves, yet she must have felt it too, this thing that was missing between them. This was as close as she could come to the pair-bonding he had not offered her.

Now she would take all that her newfound magic had to offer.

He closed his eyes. He would deny her nothing. He had not the strength. Whatever she wanted of him, she would have it. At least this time. He would try to explain to her later why such things should not be. For now he was her prisoner. For now there were no rules.

Still he nearly sobbed in relief as he felt her hands—Human hands—move up his legs, her fingers raking through the thick growth of hair shielding his skin. He shuddered as she stroked his balls again, lifting them as if testing their weight. Her eyes met his, still feral, as she rose to sink down over his hungry cock.

He surged up into her, straining against the silk bonds as she clenched around him, fighting to possess and capture her even as she rode him, taking all he had to give and demanding more. She cried out, her muscles gripping him with a fierce strength, determined to lock him within her. He rocked his hips as high as the restraints would allow, lifting her small body easily as he thrust into her, driving her over the edge again and yet again.

Her nipples stood out in harsh relief, jutting like two flames of desire needing his touch, but he had no way to reach them. Regaining her perch on her knees, she rocked forward, thrusting the greedy peaks hard against his chest, raking them across his own small hot buds. He bobbed his head, trying to reach her, feeling like a child playing party games. Her hips jerked hard against his as he finally captured one nipple, sucking it deep into his mouth so that she could not easily escape, teasing its tip with hard thrusting swipes of his tongue.

Yarwyn cried out, shuddering hard against him as she squirmed, whether to escape or attempt to get closer he was no longer sure. She rose up on her knees, the cool air of the room hitting his cock in a cold wave of shock before she drove back down again, her control shattering as the waves of release washed over her. His own control snapped. He thrust into her with short, hard jabs while he grazed her rigid nipple with his teeth then sucked it hard again.

Seanen sucked desperately for air, still reluctant to let lose of his captured prize. The room went dark again, though the candles were but half burned. The sound of the blood rushing in his head made a noise like waves crashing on the shoreline. He wondered briefly if he might pass out. Then Yarwyn's fingertips found his nipples, pinching, twisting, demanding. He screamed out a roar of both pleasure and pain, blending with her cry until the two were one song, one note, one long wave of ecstasy they rode out together.

When at last their breathing calmed and the room grew brighter, this time with the glow of the rising sun, Yarwyn raised her head enough to meet his eyes. "Perhaps when we meet up with Evalayna the Mage might lend us his magic that we might truly join as wolves. I would honor the traditions of your people in this."

"I love you, Yarwyn. To tie with you as my life mate is a tradition I would be honored to share." He smiled up at her with a sly grin. "Perhaps the Mage might allow me to join with you as a cat. I would know you in all the ways that there are."

Yarwyn ran her tongue over his nipple, as if daring him to respond, though he expected more might be too much for either of them. "I think I would like that."

He forced his voice to sound relaxed as she untied the silk sash from about his wrist. "There are other traditions my people share with yours."

She cocked an eye at him, at least willing to listen.

"In the one I am thinking of, we stand before a Priestess, agreeing to join our lives as well as our bodies, for as long as we both shall live."

Her hands paused on the knot. "What?"

He tried to make his voice project a confidence he did not feel. "Marry me, Yarwyn. I am already bound to you in every way that there is. Marry me."

Her eyes opened wide as she stared at him, the silence stretching on too long.

He was a fool. She'd already lived twice his lifetime. Seen more of the world than he could dream of. He was but a plaything to her. She hesitated now, trying to find a way to tell him gently, to save face. She was an ambassador. Diplomacy was her line of work. "You don't have to answer me right away. I don't mean to rush you into anything. I understand how—"

"Yes!"

He laughed as she dove in to kiss him, pouncing on him like a playful kitten. "Yes?"

"Yes! I love you, Seanen. If you'll have me I'm yours."

"When?"

"Now! Today! This morning."

He laughed again, snapping the bond that held his wrist with the sharp sound of ripping silk. "Not that quickly. I want you to have a real wedding. The kind you dreamed of as a girl. We will stand up before your Priestesses. There will be feasting and dancing far into the night. All of Talismar will know you are the Lady Yarwyn Lindall."

She grew quiet, her hands falling still in his hair. "Seanen, I have no family to give me such a wedding."

"We will ask Lady Evalayna to present you, as you were a member of her household when we met. I have family to spare. I will loan you a few. We can invite all of your Guild sisters to attend. They dare not refuse an invitation from the High Houses of the Northlands."

Yarwyn cuddled her head against his chest. "I love you Seanen," she repeated again. "You don't have to do this for me."

"Finally I have something more to offer you than a hollow title and a name you dare not mention in public. I want to do this for you. For us. I would not have it any other way. I love you, my beautiful Elf. More than life itself."

Chapter Seven

The noise brought Cassadara awake instantly. It was a loud, undignified screech. There could be no other word for it. She rolled to her feet as she reached for her staff. Nor could there be any doubt as to the owner of the voice. The screech had issued from the esteemed Lady Evalayna Lochinvar.

Cassadara emerged from her tent in time to see Tranorva take a protective step backwards in defense of her charges.

"Mother! What in the name of the gods are ye doing here?"

Ayailla raised one eyebrow, surveying Evalayna and her Warrior with something akin to temper in her eyes. "I might ask the same of ye, Daughter. Ye took long enough deciding to wander back. Half the day has gone by while we sat in wait for ye. We abandon our lives and our livelihoods to trek halfway across the tundra at thy Summoning and when we arrived, we find naught but a cold fire and a shivering child awaiting us. Could ye not at least have taken the time to conjure up a few tents? Where in the name of the gods have ye been? More to the point, where did ye dredge up the remains that trail at thy heel?"

Evalayna's hasty attempt at affronted dignity crumbled in the face of her mother's raised eyebrow. Her voice hadn't quite regained its normal low, dignified tones of power. It was more fury that took control of her tone now. "Where indeed?" She waved her hand at the Warrior who stood at her side. "I suppose ye know nothing of this? Ye would claim innocence of the lie that kept us apart these last decades? Tell me ye did no' order Shammall to carry out this deception!"

Tyrell moved to his grandmother's side, ready to defend her, just as Seanen silently moved to stand behind Evalayna, Yarwyn at his side, her hands resting on her ancient bow. But it was the huge man who had followed Evalayna into the circle of tents surrounding the fire pit who moved now to stand between the battling women. Cassadara drew in her breath sharply as the ancient, tattered Warrior who could be none other than the legendary Roahr VinDall himself held up his hands, palm out, to silence the opponents.

"M'Ladies. Please. Do not allow this evil creature's deceptions to come between you and cause division within your clan. Let us leave the explanations to the perpetrator of this crime." His voice was as deep as the earth itself, and rumbling with power. Though he spoke in her own native tongue, his odd, clipped accent made the phrases sound strangely foreign. Cassadara shivered as she felt both the cold malice and raw power in the Warrior's words. Despite his ridiculous garb—she could swear Mother had loaned him one of her own robes to wear beneath his tarnished mail shirt—he would not be one to be easily reckoned with. "Let the lying tongued vermin speak for himself 'fore I feed his carcass to the scavengers of the tundra."

At that Tranorva stepped forward, her axe at the ready, her weight on the balls of her feet, slightly spread. "Whatever lies have been told and retold through the years, blame no' the messenger. Ye shall no' touch what is mine, Father."

Oh, no. Not Tranorva too. By the gods this was bad. Cassadara raised her staff to issue a command of quiet, but Mâkakao's hand on her shoulder steadied her.

"Diplomacy might work better, my love."

Mâk smiled down at her as if he could read her thoughts. Cassadara bit her tongue and allowed the tip of her staff to rest once more beside her, though still at the ready. She could have sworn he was laughing as she forced her fingers to relax their grip. By the gods, this trusting thing was not easy.

Mâkakao stepped into the circle of angry Barbarians, feeling small for the first time in his life. Only Ayailla herself did not outsize him, though she was but a few inches his junior.

Fortunately, he was not in the habit of relying on his size to intimidate his opponents on the diplomatic field.

"Ladies. Lord VinDall. Please. Let us discuss our current situation calmly, as befits our rank and station." He might have quit there, given them a chance at rebuttal, but he cared not to listen to their protests. Instead he continued, allowing his voice to win them over to his side. "Let us begin first with the proper introductions." He turned his attention fully on the legend himself, Roahr VinDall. No matter how odd the man looked, Mâkakao was quite sure that if Roahr lost his temper, it would take the combined powers of all the Shamen present to keep the man from ripping Shammall limb from limb.

"I am Mâkakao, Lord of House Yarishet, and husband to your beautiful youngest daughter, Lady Cassadara, formerly of House Lochinvar." Cass inclined her head slightly, eyeing the old bear with an assessing gaze. Mâkakao reached out his hand to clasp the huge Warrior's in his own, but allowed Roahr no time to speak. "I am honored to find myself in the presence of such a renowned Warrior as yourself, M'Lord."

Mâk turned to face the other members of the pack, for he felt them as such, now, though he was not sure just what kill they were circling. "Lady Evalayna you obviously have become reacquainted with. I know you will remember well her Lady Mother, Ayailla of House McTofflinn, formerly of House Lindall, which is, incidentally, no longer in disgrace."

Ayailla, for once, merely inclined her head, keeping her caustic tongue well within her mouth. Mâkakao said a silent prayer of thanks to the gods as he quickly moved on. "Your son, Tyrell, Apprentice to House McTofflinn, now apparently First Shaman of House Lochinvar, as your reappearance creates political changes that shall be felt across the entire realm of the Wolf Clans. You met your daughter, the Warrior Tranorva, last evening, I understand. Tranorva, by a strange twist of fate, is now both High Priestess of Élahandara and now moves from First Apparent to House Lochinvar to her rightful position as head of your own House VinDall."

Mâk spoke too quickly to do much more than mesmerize and confuse as he twisted the intricacies of family loyalties to his advantage. "At Lady Evalayna's side stands the Ambassador from Talismar, Lady Yarwyn, and her betrothed, Seanen, Sister-Son to the Lady Evalayna. As Seanen's mother, the Lady Travanya, had adopted the Lady Ayailla's second house, House McTofflinn, and as the Lady Travanya died without giving birth to a daughter, Lord Seanen is now heir to both House Lindall and House McTofflinn."

Leaving that one to settle as Seanen and Evalayna exchanged quick questioning glances, Mâkakao turned to face the last player in the grand game of family politics. "And last but not least the bondswoman Dalai stands before your daughter Tranorva's betrothed, the Mage known as Shammall, or Élandine. Now personally, since I bear the estimable Mage no particular good will, myself, I would not mind if you were to end his miserable life."

Here Mâkakao paused for dramatic effect as the crowd stared at him in consternation and utter confusion. "Unfortunately, Lord VinDall, you shall have to wait your turn to kill the deceitful Mage. For you see, he is already dead."

The Warrior woman who was his daughter hissed something at the dead thing and it moved back into her shadow. Her hands on her axe, she stood before it, shielding its body from him, death in her eyes. Her upper lip curled back in a snarl Roahr knew only too well.

The orator—his son-in-law?—Lord Mâkakao—had managed, in those not so few words, to remind Roahr of exactly why it was that he had never been welcome within Lady Ayailla's family. The politics made his head swim. He would not play her game, pitting one faction against another. Roahr raised his head slowly to meet his daughter's eyes as he stepped toward her, his hands well clear of his weapons.

"I have never been a creature of politics, Daughter. I have always followed my heart. Yet my heart leads me two ways now. I would have my revenge for an old wound, the one that has separated my family these many years, until we are no more than courteous strangers. Yet what is revenge but a dry and tasteless meal if it cost me my family once again?"

"I will not let ye have him, Father."

She would not make this any easier for him. Roahr sighed. "What is he to you?"

Defiance shone in her eyes, and worry. He knew she was assessing him as an enemy, judging his weaknesses, preparing to defend her territory. "Mâkakao has spoken no more than the truth."

Roahr softened his tone, trying for something that sounded friendly, perhaps even understanding. "I would hear the words from your lips, Daughter, see the truth in your eyes."

Tranorva squared her shoulders self-consciously, standing eye to eye with him, so close now that he could read the strain in her cheeks as she swallowed once, hard. "Whatever he was to ye, Father, to me he has been a teacher, a friend, and a lover. Élandine owns my heart, and I would defend him with my life, as he did me. He fell in battle at my side, and only the strength of his Fey will has preserved his body. We travel now to ask the King of the Faerie to restore his spirit, that I might once again hold his love in my heart."

Roahr let his focus drift from her intense gaze to study the thing that stood behind her. "I fear my reappearance has already done you a great disservice, Daughter. You are my first-born, and by all rights heir to all that I own, which is precisely nothing. There is no House VinDall, nor any other House left standing within the circle that was once the Clan of The Bear. Those of us who are left wander the lands, singing a song of heartache for what is lost. I know what it is to lose everyone you love. I cannot take from you the one thing you have left. Nor can I kill what is already dead. Yet a great crime has been committed against our family, and the guilty must be punished."

Some of the tension eased from Tranorva's shoulders. "Géndalaine of Élahandara told a fantastic tale of holding thee and thy brethren hostage in her dungeons. Is that why ye did not return to us?"

"Géndalaine..." He swallowed hard, remembering those long years. "I should have fought to the death, as becomes a Warrior, but 'twas not to be so. I was captured in the last great battle of the Dark Elf Wars, even as Talandar fell. 'Twas in the dungeons of Élahandara that Shammall found me some years later and helped me to escape. He told me then of your supposed deaths. I wandered for a time as a bear, until I heard that others of our people yet lived within Géndalaine's dungeons. I thought to free our people, or die at their side. Instead I joined them again for a time. But that was long ago. I have lived ever since near that mountain, exacting my revenge on those who stray too far from the fortress."

Roahr lifted his eyes to survey the crowd gathered about. He read distrust in Tyrell's eyes, and a cool distance from Cassadara. "Géndalaine told me that you yet lived, but I thought her words a lie, meant to further my torture. Still, I could have come in search of you these many years gone by. I could have made sure of the truth of the Mage's words. I do not expect you to forgive my cowardice. I see now what I have lost. Tyrell, I regret that I was not there to see my son grow into a man, and Cassadara, you cannot know what it means to have missed seeing you open your eyes for the first time, or running for cover the first time your power unleashed itself. I will understand if you have no need for me now. But know that I love you, and you were never far from my heart."

Ayailla stepped forward to break the uneasy silence. "I never liked ye, Roahr. Never did. Ye were a fine Warrior, but I never thought ye were good enough for my daughter. No social position. Just an aimless, wandering man from a tribe of gypsies. But ye were my daughter's husband, and the father of my grandchildren. I know not why the Mage would have reported thy death were it not so. But know that I was no' part of this deception, if deception it was. Let us no' judge him till he can speak for himself."

Roahr glanced over at the animated corpse. "It would seem a bit late for that. He's dead."

Tyrell tried vainly to smother a laugh. "We go to recover the spirit of the Mage. That is the mission that has drawn us together."

Roahr studied the lines of worry in his daughter's face. "I will not seek personal retribution against the Mage. Yet if he was responsible for destroying my family, he must be punished. When the Mage is himself, he must answer for his crimes."

Tranorva nodded slowly. "Élandine must have a chance to clear his name of this suspicion. He will answer before the Clan Elders. Will this satisfy thee?"

Roahr nodded. "I will accept the Clan's judgment in both his guilt and his punishment. I will do no harm to your betrothed, Daughter. By the seven, this I swear."

Tranorva's hands slowly lifted clear of her weapons. She raised them toward him, palms up. "I know 'tis no' light thing for thee to give up thy revenge. I am in thy debt, Father."

Hands trembling, he reached out to capture her fingers, bringing them to his lips. She was shaking as he pulled her into his arms. "I love you, Daughter. I have never ceased to love you."

Ayailla broke the uneasy silence. "Perhaps we should get on about it, then? 'Tis a long time for an old woman to stand about in the snow."

Roahr grinned as he released Tranorva. "Where do we go?"

It was Evalayna who answered. "Mother Earth spoke to me in answer to my pleading. *'Take his body to the source of his life, with all those you hold dear about you, and make your pledge to his king. He may grant you the gift you desire.'* When I sent out my Summoning I dared no' hope for such wondrous results. The gods have restored my family to me. All those I hold dear are indeed gathered around me. We travel once again as a pack. We go in search of the King of Faerie."

"Faerie." Roahr looked thoughtfully about the gathering once again. "I don't suppose any of you know where to *find* this Faerie King."

No one answered. He closed his eyes, wishing for a moment that he might go back to being a bear once again. "Do any of you know anything at all of Faerie?"

"I do."

All eyes turned to fasten themselves on the source of the timid words.

Roahr dropped to one knee before the strange little creature, his voice carefully pitched so as not to frighten the child. "What do you know, child? Have you been to *Tier na nÓg*?"

Dahlai wrapped herself more tightly in the faded silk coverlet, looking clearly annoyed. "I am not a child. I am just small."

Roahr attempted a smile—something at which he found he was dreadfully out of practice. He'd never considered himself very good at dealing with people, especially women. His very size tended to frighten them to insensibility. He tried his best now to offer up a placating tone. "Forgive me, M'Lady. How do you know of Faerie?"

"Being small does not make me slow of wit. I am no more a Lady than I am a child. I know of *Tier na nÓg* because my mother was born there."

Roahr rubbed a hand through his grizzled beard. It was Tranorva who came to his rescue. She made no attempt to be gentle with the little imp. "Where is this isle, Dahlai, and how do we get there?"

Dahlai's entire attitude changed at once. "I know not precisely, Mistress, only that my mother said it was a beautiful place, lush and green and surrounded by water, and that the sun rose always to shine on her village. They lived by day on co-coa-nuts and danced on the beaches by night. She said it was a wondrous place, filled with magic and laughter, and that the weather is always warm like summer."

Roahr quickly regained his feet. "South, then."

Mâkakao fingered his chin as if searching through a long missing beard. "Must be near the equator if the weather is always warm."

Seanen nodded his head in agreement. "We can travel by foot for three days or so to City of Port where the ocean meets the desert. From there we can book passage south."

"South to where?" Cassadara argued. "If none of ye, as well traveled as many of ye are, know of this place, then what assurance have we that the mariners will?"

It was Mâkakao who answered her. "You are a Shaman. People expect you to know the casting of spells. We too expect the mariners to know the finding of this place."

Ayailla pointed her staff at the tents. They disappeared as if they had never been, leaving a scattering of personal belongings in their cleared circles. "We will know better once we make our way to Port City. The day is wasting."

Roahr grinned at her, winking mischievously. "It worries me, Mother, when we think alike."

Chapter Eight

They made an odd pack. Six wolves, a panther, two bears, and a small childlike sprite who clung to the she-bear's back, accompanied by one animated corpse. Evalayna decided they might have inspired some brave bard, had he not feared for his reputation.

They traveled fast, running side by side in the open, too large a pack to brook interference from the few stray bands of wandering Orcs who occasionally dotted the hillsides. Yarwyn took point, with the Warriors, Tranorva, Roahr, Seanen, and Mâkakao behind her, and the Shamen, Ayailla, Evalayna, Tyrell, and Cassadara each taking a flanking position off their respective Warrior.

By common consensus they chose to travel in a nearly straight line to Port City, with one night's stop at Lord Mâkakao's great house along the way for clean garb and a night's rest in a real bed. The route by necessity funneled them through the pass of St. Gregory, rather than skirting the mountains by traveling the more circuitous route through the plains formerly guarded by the Orc King's Castle, now held by their allies under Garreth's command.

Evalayna's concentration rested on Mâkakao's kitchens, where there would be serving girls with hot water to bathe in and hot mead to drink by the fire. Tranorva's claim to the Élahandara throne and the size of their party made the pass of St. Gregory seem relatively safe, though it brought them very near the front gates of Talandar itself.

She had never seen Talandar, nor its sister city of Élahandara, the two guardians to the northern expanses of the barren wilderness that was the arctic. She had been big with child when the Dark Priestess declared war on the Bear Clan, too far along to follow Roahr into battle, unable to fight at his side as his Shaman or his wife.

She could have delayed the pregnancy, of course, had they had any warning that the world as they knew it was about to cease to exist…

"*'Twould have made little difference.*"

Evalayna looked up into Roahr's eyes as he lumbered along at her side. "*What?*"

"*You were blaming yourself. You were thinking that you should have been there beside me on the battlefield.*"

"*I was thinking no such thing.*"

"*You snuffle when you brood. You were thinking that somehow your presence would have changed the time that we lost.*"

"*By the gods, Roahr, I should have been there. A Shaman fights at her Warrior's side. A Shaman—*"

"*Dies beside her mate? Though I could be wrong. You might have lived to see the dungeons of Élahandara with me, but our youngest daughter would have been born a slave, and you would not have had these years to watch Tranorva grow to be the fine Warrior she has become, nor to see Tyrell grow into his promise as a Shaman. A mother's duty outweighs a Shaman's call to battle. I regret what we lost, but never would I blame you, and had I to do it again, knowing the outcome, I would still have been waiting for you in these mountains, my heart.*"

Evalayna laid her head against his shoulder for a moment as they ran. "*I do no' snuffle.*"

"*I beg your pardon. Snuffle is a bear term. I guess you woofle.*"

"*I do no'.*"

"*Of course not, my love.*"

"*And though I know ye to be right, I still regret the lost years.*"

"*As do I, my heart. But we shall make new memories to gradually replace the lost ones. And we shall have many years yet to watch the cubs grow and blossom.*"

"I would like to test my powers against the forces of Talandar some day, that they might feel the wrath of my vengeance."

"That day may be sooner than you think."

Evalayna followed the line of his muzzle as Yarwyn dug in her cat claws, sliding on the icy pass as she attempted to bring the party to a quick halt. *"There are only three. We can take them."* She shifted quickly, setting both hands before her on her gnarled old walking stick.

Roahr indicated the slopes above the pass with a flick of his chin as he shifted, his hands already reaching for his ancient blades.

"Ogres!" Evalayna hissed, loud enough for those around her to pick up her warning.

The Shamen drew back, taking up their stances as befitted their stations. Yarwyn held the bow Nemesis at the ready. The deep blue Iolite gems set in the risers caught fire in the sunlight, an unearthly glow blazing forth as she notched her first arrow, her aim steady on the High Priestess who blocked their way.

It was Tranorva who took the lead, striding forward to meet the Priestess, her face a mask of outraged dignity. "Know me! I am Tranorva, High Priestess of Élahandara! Put down thy weapons and kneel at my feet!"

Cold laughter rang out across the crystal ice walls of the pass. "Know me, poseur! I am Nafésti, High Priestess of Talandar! Put down thy weapons and beg for mercy, that I may kill you swiftly!"

Tranorva reached beneath her tunic to draw forth the symbol of office she wore about her neck. "Ye will show me proper respect! I have defeated High Priestess Géndalaine in combat. I have defeated First Chair Maelyn to defend my throne. By thy own laws I claim thy fealty. Step aside and let me and my party pass!"

Roahr knew even as he watched his daughter's display that it was only a show, designed but to buy them time as the pack members took a tighter formation behind her, and the Shamen picked their targets and silently formed a strategy.

As for himself, Roahr's own strategy was simple. Kill everything in his path and keep himself at all times between the enemy and his Shaman.

Nafésti raised her staff and struck it into the frozen ground with a loud echoing ring. "As there are no witnesses to this so-called defeat you claim over Géndalaine, I contest thy claim, Human, and I challenge you for the throne of Élahandara. I shall take back what is mine!"

Inexplicably, the Dark Priestess seemed to be indicating the not-quite dead Mage who had taken up his accustomed place two paces behind and to the right of Tranorva.

Tranorva's laugh boomed out across the tundra. "Ye think to impress me with insults? Ye are not the first to face me, Sister, and ye shall not be the last. I accept thy challenge! Ye shall not live to see the sun rise again. I shall have not only Géndalaine's trophy but all thy worldly possessions as well. Thy harem shall be mine to command as I drink thy blood!"

They were to fight over possession of a dead man? Roahr shook his head in confusion. The world was indeed a strange place.

Tranorva turned to speak quickly over her shoulder to the party standing ready behind her. "Ye will not enter into this fight. Roahr, I ask ye to act as my first. 'Twill be thy duty to see that none from our party interfere in any way with the challenge. Do ye accept?"

Roahr nodded once, sending his unruly red curls spiraling into the wind. He understood only too well. He was to stand by and watch his daughter get killed, without once raising his hand.

"Believe in me," she whispered as she strode forward. The breeze brought her words to him like a twisted song echoing across the frozen tundra.

Nafésti was not High Priestess without reason. She dispensed with the formalities of the challenge to strike first and strike hard, bringing her staff once again to quick impact with the earth. Blue lightning shot out across the ice, wrapping itself around Tranorva's ankles and bringing her quickly to the ground.

Tranorva should have pulled back, writhing in agony, but instead she dove into the attack, her momentum carrying her free of the snaking energy almost as soon as it touched her. She came up hard and fast, the top of her head her weapon as she toppled Nafésti to roll with her in a tangle of limbs that left Roahr no clear view of who was winning. Moments later both women were back on their feet, cautiously circling as they looked for some sign of weakness or tiring in their opponent.

Forgetting the artifice of her lost staff, Nafésti raised her hands, fingers pointed out, and shot jagged beams of fire hissing through the air at Tranorva. Tranorva merely laughed, raising her hands, palms out, to deflect the energy back at the user. "Ye underestimate thy opponent, Nafésti! I am no mere *Human!* Know ye not that I am Tranorva, daughter of Evalayna, High Shaman of House Lochinvar? Granddaughter to Ayailla, the most powerful Shaman who has ever walked this Earth? Think thee that I would fall for such an apprentice's trick?"

She was trying to anger her enemy with insults, goading the Dark Priestess into making a mistake she could take advantage of. Roahr nodded his approval at his eldest as their eyes met across the frozen pass.

"So ye are skilled in the arts of self-defense," Nafésti sneered. "A High Priestess must not only serve our gods, but must also defend our peoples. You would lead us to butchery by the thousands, all in the name of revenge. You are a traitor among traitors, and ye shall never rule over the Élandra!"

Tranorva tucked and rolled, coming up behind the tall Priestess's back, grabbing her arm and pulling it up towards her shoulders until the bones began to twist. "The only butchery I intend this day is of ye, Nafésti. Surrender and swear to me thy oath of fealty and I may let ye live out of the goodness of my heart."

The Dark Priestess laughed as she lifted her feet off the ground, though the pain must have been incredible as her shoulder dislocated from her own weight. Roahr flinched as the pop of bones separating echoed through the stillness of the pass.

Nafésti's shriek was not a cry of pain, however. Lightning issued from her staff as she spun to face Tranorva, and madness shone in her eyes. At the sound of her command the Ogres who had previously looked on with no apparent concern now swarmed, leaping down the icy cliffs with reckless abandon as they charged. Tranorva loosed her hold on Nafésti's arm to unsheathe her war axe, dodging most of the damage from Nafésti's lightning bolts, though a dark singe marred the finish of her fine mail shirt.

Roahr screamed out his own war cry as the Ogres descended, heading first for the Dark· Priestess herself, but he needn't have bothered. Tranorva's blade swept past the space where the fine dark head had once attached to the neck, quelling the evil laughter that echoed through the pass one last time before the Dark One dropped to her knees, reluctant to die even without her head.

Then he was too busy to pay further notice to anything but the Ogres who found it necessary to end their lives on his blade.

There were, he estimated, twenty or more of the dark foul beasts, lumbering toward them at an incredible speed for their bulk. He had not time to assess their fighting style. The first one went down from a blast from Evalayna's staff before his blades had a chance to close over its neck, but the second one had time to look him in the eye as it died, its pike dropped neatly to the ground along with the arm that had held it.

They were big. They were strong. They were fast. But they were no match for the Wolf pack they faced that day. The carnage stained the snow red with blood until the ice became slick with it, yet still they came, the battle lust too strong to heed the senselessness of their deaths. Piles of singed and headless bodies began to make the pass difficult to negotiate as the wolf pack worked their way down the mountain, fighting now with their backs toward Yarishet as they descended, no longer individuals, but one cohesive killing machine, leaving a trail of bodies in their wake.

And still the Ogres càme, more than thirty by now, their numbers as staggering as the quantities of their blood left dripping down the icy slopes. Roahr looked up once from his own butchery to see Lord Mâkakao raise a horn to his lips, sending three long shrill blasts ripping through the frosted air. Roahr gave no further thought to the horn until he found his flank supported by a large Warrior who wore Mâkakao's green livery. On either side men appeared, though none so large as that first, and the Ogres at last began to hesitate in their attack, the sheer numbers of the defender's ranks apparently reaching their diminutive brains when the score of their own deaths could not.

Roahr's swords were beginning to feel heavy and his arms were aching as the last of the Ogres turned to flee, only to fall in their tracks as Yarwyn and her deadly Nemesis chased them down. For the first time since the battle had begun Roahr had time to appreciate Yarwyn's marksmanship as her arrows landed precisely at the base of the creatures' skulls, dropping them instantly. The Shamen also pursued the fleeing monsters, sheathing them in coats of fire, so that their burning bodies left a foul stench in the air as they fell next to their companions.

Wiping his blades in the snow, Roahr turned to survey the pack. The blood that dripped from Tranorva's arm might have been in part her own. Mâkàkao sported a gash across his cheek that was being ministered to by Ayailla, while Cass looked on as if absorbing some lesson in the finer arts of healing. Yarwyn rested heavily against Seanen's arm, looking both older and more frail than he remembered. Even the dead one was dripping with blood, his blade sheathed once again. Tyrell walked quietly among the Humans, healing small wounds and speaking words of encouragement as the Warriors cleaned their weapons and assessed the damages.

Evalayna appeared at Roahr's side, grim and bloody, but otherwise looking no worse for the day's battle. He draped his arm around her shoulder, heedless of the gore that covered them both as he pulled her close. "I believe your count topped mine. You fought well, M'Lady. I am honored to fight beside you again."

"We fought as a pack," she observed. Then her pride faded as she sagged against him wearily. "Never did I think to see such cohesiveness within this family again."

"You raised them well."

Evalayna looked up into his eyes and smiled, a smile that reached beyond the blood and the stench of battle to touch his heart. "They are Warriors all, my heart. Ye bred them true."

* * * * *

The hospitality of Lord Mâkakao's House Yarishet offered amenities Roahr had not known for many a year. Bathed and groomed by anxious servants who were horrified when he suggested they simply sheer his hopelessly tangled hair, he endured their ministrations with less grace than those of the tailor and armorer, both of whom seemed to take great delight in clothing him more suitably in the latest of fashions. Nearly two hours after their arrival at Mâkakao's great house Roahr finally escaped the women from the bath house, only to be captured by other servants and led into the dining hall, where their party had reassembled to feast on delicacies that could not be produced over an open pit campfire.

Ayailla held out her hands to him as he entered the room, her smile worrying him more than the Ogres' attack. "Ye look most handsome, my son. The diligence of the serving wenches astounds me. I never would have thought that hair salvageable."

"They near ripped it from my head," Roahr complained. "'Twould have been easier to simply shave the lot and start over."

Ayailla laughed, and, though he had no understanding of her humor, he realized that he had finally found a place in her heart as she reached up to kiss his cheek. "Keep him, Daughter. He is useful in a fight and not too unpleasant to the eye. But never allow him to dress himself or make any decisions about his grooming."

Evalayna laughed in agreement as she moved into his arms, "Aye, my love, 'twould have indeed been a great loss had the wenches heeded thy wishes."

Roahr closed his eyes at her touch, savoring the feel of her fingers running through the hair the servants had struggled over so relentlessly. "Perhaps 'twas all worth the aggravation if it pleases you, my heart."

"Everything about ye pleases me," she assured him as she offered him a bite of roasted pheasant from her fingers. "Everything."

Roahr felt a blush stain his cheeks as her fingers roamed elsewhere beneath the laden table, promising the night would not end any less passionately than the day had begun.

* * * * *

"Shhh."

Evalayna tried unsuccessfully to smother her giggles. "Thy children will be scandalized if we are caught."

"'Tis good for them. They are so proper, much like their mother. And we will not get caught unless you give us away."

The gate to the gardens swung open silently, its hinges well oiled. Roahr slipped through the shadows as easily as he might have strode down a path in broad daylight. Once clear of the house walls, he set her back on her feet and tucked her arm though his, steering her safely past mud puddles and potholes in the dirt track that led to the common places beyond the great house. Evalayna looked askance at the seedy tavern doors. "Are ye sure 'tis safe?"

"Let yourself live a little, Evalayna. When was the last time you downed a pint in a tavern?"

She laughed as he pulled her into the dimly lit room, his broad shoulders assuring them a place at the old wooden counter. The barkeep eyed the huge Warrior with caution. "What'll ya have, Mate?"

"Draw a pint for my friend," a man's voice suggested softly from the shadows at the corner of the bar. "And a glass of white wine for the Lady."

Roahr shifted slightly, his fingers brushing her arm as they moved to rest over the hilt of his sword. The figure shifted slightly, letting himself be seen in the flickering light of the tavern's smoky oil lanterns.

"Seanen," Evalayna whispered in chagrin.

Yarwyn laughed softly from his elbow. "I thought we were the only ones to flee the hospitality of our fine hosts."

Roahr's laughter made the lantern wicks tremble. "'Tis against my nature to clothe myself in so much civility. 'Twas beginning to choke me more tightly than this damnable tunic. I've no use for silk. Hot in the summer and cold in the winter. Give me linen any day, or better yet the fur the gods cloaked me with."

"What? Doubt you the quality of my tailor's goods?" Mâkakao challenged, reaching automatically for the pint the barkeep slid to him. Cassadara joined her mate at the bar, though her gaze lingered on the spot where Roahr's hand caressed Evalayna's shoulder almost unconsciously. "Would you not have a whole wardrobe of fine tailored silk tunics and smart foppish hats so you might prance about at the fine courts throughout the land?"

Seanen's laughter mingled with Roahr's answering growl. "We are of a build, M'Lord. I will find you a linen tunic before we move out in the morning, though it might be a bit well broken in. At least 'twill not rub your neck raw."

Evalayna relaxed against Roahr's side, sipping her wine as Yarwyn smiled at her from under Seanen's shoulder, losing track of the conversation. Roahr was no longer an outsider, feeling his way back to humanity. Today they had fought together. Tonight they drank together. With the sunrise they would travel together. And no one would ask why Roahr was there, or if he belonged. They would accept him, and in a way she had never been, he would be part of the pack.

*****

They were up again with the dawn, slipping away as silently as they could, yet they had not gone far when another bear joined the pack. Evalayna watched as the two huge male grizzlies sniffed each other cautiously, though no further introduction was made. Evidently several of the party knew the newcomer and were neither surprised nor offended by his presence.

It was not until nightfall, when they camped in another of her mother's circles of tents—Evalayna promised herself that she would learn that spell—that the new party-member revealed himself. She remembered the man. He had joined them on the field yesterday, the first to reach them after Mâkakao sounded his horn, and he had been with Mâkakao on the ill-fated mission to meet with her daughter back in the early part of the year. That seemed like a lifetime ago now, rather than mere weeks.

"Captain Balthain, if I remember correctly?"

Balthain bowed low over her hand. "Aye, M'Lady. I am honored you remembered me."

Or chagrined, she thought, though she said it not aloud. There was something about him—a half-overheard whisper, a way he had of disappearing when she was sure he had been near—that reminded her of Seanen's Guild mates. Evalayna smiled at him, testing her theory. "Since I have no token to pay ye with, I assume ye have joined us purely for the adventure?"

"Token, M'Lady?" he answered with a hint of amusement in his eye. "I know not what you mean. I am here because Lord Mâkakao is here. I am but a Mercenary, like all of my kind, traveling where I'm paid to travel."

Evalayna laughed to herself. "Indeed. Well met, then, young man." Mercenary. Well, that was as good a term for the Guild with no name as any other.

Chapter Nine

"What troubles ye, *Mel~amin*?"

Roahr pulled absently at the neck of the dress cloak Mâkakao's tailor had supplied him with. The garment was fashionable, but much like his tunics, hardly designed for comfort. "I was never one for large cities."

Or fancy clothes.

Evalayna surveyed the City of Port from their position on the last hill above the hard-packed earthen walls. It was hardly worthy of the name. More a squalid hovel of buildings gathered against the water, the wall more to keep in its riff-raff than to keep anything out. "'Tis only for one night."

"Let us hope so."

She was more of a mind to get him into a room away from the crowds on the waterfront than to worry over what he might mean by his cryptic response.

"Follow me," Seanen ordered, taking up point once again. "'Tis not much of a town, but I know where to find the worst she has to offer."

Yarwyn's growl of disapproval met with quiet, easy laughter as they trudged down the sandy hillside, hampered now by their Human forms.

* * * * *

Cassadara watched them together, sometimes so familiar, sometimes like strangers, trying to gauge the man who had given her life. She was reluctant to trust this stranger, yet the effect he had on her mother was so astounding as to shake the foundations of Cass's world. Roahr said something meant only for Evalayna's ears, and moments later Mother was laughing again.

Surely this could not be the same woman who had brought fear to entire armies with no more than her presence alone. This could not be the woman who had held her daughter to the same high standards her own mother Ayailla had exacted from her, reminding Cass always that she was both a Lady and a Shaman.

Not the same woman who was laughing just now because, unless Cassadara was vastly mistaken, the man's sly fingers had reached around when he thought no one was looking to goose Evalayna's butt.

Cass slipped her arm around Mâk, leaning her head on his shoulder.

"Tired, *Mel~amin*?"

"Tired, footsore, and confused," she agreed. "Naught is as I knew it to be. My grandmother treks across continents. My mother laughs like a young girl. I begin to feel the old woman of the crowd."

Mâkakao laughed softly against her ear. "Once I get you to myself within the walls of our room, I will massage your tired feet and give you things to think about that will not cause you such confusion."

Cassadara brightened at the thought. "Mayhap ye might convince me I am no' yet an old woman?"

His teeth nipped lightly on her ear. "Mayhap," he teased. "All things are possible, *Mel~amin*, to she who believes."

"I believe in thee," she answered. "The rest let us leave until tomorrow to sort out."

* * * * *

"Did ye not enjoy the dancers, my love?"

"The dancers were passable."

Passable indeed. Any one of the scantily clad offerings could have been had for the price of a single gold coin, with change left on the plate. Even the whores in this poor excuse for a town were mediocre at best.

Evalayna ran her fingers through Roahr's long flame red hair, trying not to laugh. "Ye seemed in a hurry to leave the tables. Was the food not to thy liking?"

His voice came in a deep rumble as he took the stairs to their apartment two at a time. "There is only one thing I am hungry for."

"And what might that be?"

"The dancing girl who stole my heart years ago."

Evalayna sighed, remembering the first time she had danced for him. "I fear she is lost with the years, my love. I have no' danced in three decades or more."

Roahr shut the door behind them with one hand and dropped the bar in place as he let her feet find the floor. "Find her for me, my love. Dance for me once again."

The length of his body was hard and lean, the muscles standing out in firm definition under her hands. She was soft, soft with the years that came from sitting behind a desk, writing papers and reading documents and negotiating for more. More power. More money. More of all of the things that had brought her no pleasure. "I—"

"Shhh." He leaned in to kiss her, slowly touching soft, warm lips to hers in the gentlest of caresses. "You will always be that long ago girl to me. Dance for me, Eva."

With trembling hands she pulled the pins from her hair, letting it fall about her as it had so long ago, a cloak that reached down past her hips, silver now in the moonlight. The faint rhythm of the drummers below reached up through the night, like the beat a dimly remembered song. Evalayna closed her eyes and searched for the girl she had been, swaying softly as the music came stronger in her head, raising her arms now to move with the rhythm. She bent with the music and swayed to its beat, shy at first then bolder, her hands skimming over her breasts as the flames caught her, the hunger in his eyes as he watched a reflection of her own.

The soft shimmering silk robe floated to the floor as she released its clasp, leaving her body naked as she turned and twisted before him, clothed now only in the long cascade of her hair. With a shake of her head and a twist of her shoulders as she turned the silver curtain fell away, leaving her softly rounded curves fully exposed. Her nipples, grown larger from the nursing of their children, puckered up harder now as his breath drew in sharply. Perhaps the moonlight flattered her, for she felt once again that slim young beauty who had shamelessly wooed the fiercest Warrior to treat with her mother, determined to have him for her own.

She watched Roahr's eyes darken with passion as his gaze followed her every move, held spellbound by the beat of the drums as the tempo increased, his body vibrating with every twist and turn. The drums built to a crescendo as she spun into his arms, trusting him to catch her as she arched back, her breasts lifted moonward as he crushed her against the length of his body.

"You are as lovely as you were the first time I saw you. You still take my breath away. If ever I needed proof of the Divine Mother's blessings, I knew I had found it the day my eyes first rested on you."

She could feel the thick length of his cock, swollen and wanting, as he brushed slowly against her, teasing her body with the feel of his still clothed skin abrading her soft, smooth nakedness. He grasped the two round mounds of her buttocks firmly and lifted her against his raging heat as his teeth closed over her nipple. "Roahr..."

His voice was hoarse and husky with need as his words slipped over the damp tip of her nipple, sending shivers of desire washing over her. "I love the sound of my name on your lips. Say it again for me, Love."

"Roahr..."

"Tell me you want me still, my love. Tell me the years do not matter."

She raked her fingers through the thick masses of his hair, pulling his mouth more firmly against her breast. "Surely it was only yesterday that I first saw ye, a giant among the Warriors, the only man to compete for my hand that I ever would have allowed to claim me. I want ye now as I did then, Roahr, in my bed, in my house, and in my heart."

"Then take me," he offered. "I am yours."

If the fancy cloak lost its clasp as she divested him of it, the sturdy linen tunic Seanen had delivered as promised faired better, slipping off easily under her demanding fingers. The leggings followed the tunic to the floor, hobbling the man as she had not prompted him to remove his heavy leather boots, but she cared not as her hands stroked over the prize she had sought. Roahr managed somehow to kick free of the boots and the leggings, scooping her up into his arms once again as he carried her toward the inn's ancient bed.

Evalayna pulled her knees up self-consciously as he laid her there to stare down at her in the moonlight, but his fingers stroked over her, spreading her so that he might look his fill at the small tangle of curls that covered her aching desire.

"When I despaired of ever escaping the dungeons of Élahandara, I would call up an image of you waiting for me like this, so real I could almost touch you." He dropped slowly to his knees beside the bed, lifting her hips until his breath stirred her curls. Moisture drenched her sheath, her need for him strong enough to make her hands less than gentle as she pulled at him, her fingers finding his ears to stroke over them, first trying to urge him upward, then pulling him closer.

She cried out at the first touch of this tongue between her sensitive folds, her body shaking beneath his touch. His clever fingers spread her fully before him, so that he dined on her like a feast set before a Lord. "Roahr!" she pleaded, without being able to name what she would have. His tongue drove into her, plundering her depths, his laughter vibrating over her exposed skin as he sucked up her juices.

The feel of his tongue darting far into her reaches and his breath blowing over her clit was more than she could withstand. She cried out his name again as she shattered, the pleasure washing over her in waves that her left gasping for air. Her fingers knotted in his hair as she pulled at him, demanding more, wanting, needing, too lost in her ecstasy to voice more than a wordless cry as he pushed her mercilessly toward her limits.

"Roahr," she demanded, riding out the waves. "Roahr!"

His mouth, damp with her own juices, pressed hard against her nipple as he found her at last, stroking at last into her waiting sheath, burying his thick, hard cock into her fully, the pleasure so sharp it was almost a pain. She raised her hips up to meet him, welcoming his length and his fullness, her muscles tightening to hold him within her as she broke around him again.

Relentless, he thrust against her, his breathing coming as hard as her own, the drums below echoing through the room once more in rhythm to their fierce mating.

"Sing for me, Wolf-Mother," his hoarse voice challenged against her ear. "I want to hear your song once again."

The howl broke from her lips even as his hips made their final mad thrust, breaking against her as she tightened around him, tying with him as surely as any wolf mating ever could have claimed her. Her voice cried out to the city, proclaiming him mate to all who could read her scent on the wind.

Through the shutterless window scattered voices returned her call, and Roahr laughed as he tumbled beside her, still holding her locked in his arms. "We are not alone, my love."

Evalayna smiled against his cheek. "Wolves rule the night."

* * * * *

Leadership was not a responsibility Roahr accepted nor a mantle he put on, Evalayna decided. It was in his blood, as ingrained in the man as his need to breathe. She watched with wondering eyes as Seanen, Mâkakao, and Balthain conferred briefly with Roahr, the younger men accepting his leadership as easily as he offered it. Roahr would be good for Seanen, she reflected. Fortunately the fool her sister had married had died before he had a chance to make too much of an impression on the child. The man was grown now, long past a child's need for hero-worship, yet still he looked to Roahr with respect, offering his opinions freely but accepting Roahr's decisions gracefully.

"Why must we wait while the men seek a ship?" Cassadara demanded. "We could question the ships' pursers more efficiently if we all had a hand in the task."

"'Tis no' safe," Tyrell chided. "Can ye no' see that, Sister? How many women do ye see about on the docks? There is a reason."

"Yesterday a dozen Ogres died at my hand and today I must be guarded like chattel? I am no fool of a Human tavern wench. I can take care of myself."

Evalayna sighed as her gaze flicked over her daughters, then back to the crowds below on the docks. There was much her youngest had to learn. Fortunately Lord Mâkakao seemed to have infinite patience with her. "'Tis no' our world, Daughter. Those below have an agenda that does no' include us. Tranorva alone might be safe striding about these docks. Her axe and her stance both mark her as a Warrior, and the criminals and thugs might respect that. In a city like this gentlewomen would do well to stay out of sight or travel with bodyguards. Only the whores walk amongst the riffraff unguarded."

"I have less freedom than the whores," Cassadara complained. "I should do well to dress as one of them and wander the streets. Mayhap I might learn something useful."

Evalayna shook her head. "Ye are too tall and too comely to walk these docks unnoticed. Someone would try to snag ye for service in a brothel in some foreign land, and ye would undoubtedly kill that man and his companions, and all those who came to his rescue. While the wharves would benefit from thy cleansing, we would no longer be odd strangers about in an unfamiliar land. We would be marked."

"I should have been a man," Cassadara muttered grimly.

"I suspect Lord Mâkakao would hesitate to agree," Evalayna argued.

The soft laughter that rippled across their small gathering did little to ease the tensions.

"The men do not seem to be accomplishing much," Tranorva noted grimly. "I should have known no task the gods set before me would be so simple. Take him to the place of his birth. That sounds easy enough. I thought I had steeled my mind against failure. I thought I had prepared myself to accept any terms the Faerie King might ask. My life for that of the man I love. 'Tis no' too hard a bargain. For what is my life worth as it is. But this. To have come so far, survived so many perils, and yet find our goal insurmountable, this is worse than any torture the Faerie King might ever have called down upon me. The men have been combing the docks for over an hour now, and still nothing. This waiting shall be the death of me."

The men gathered again, their faces grim as they looked up at the party above, then disbursed after another few minutes of quick consultation. Balthain sprinted up the stairs toward the porch from which Tyrell guarded the women, looking hot and discouraged as he approached.

"M'Ladies. Tyrell. The news is not good. We have tried to be discreet in our questions, yet already the docks grow quiet around us as we approach. Anyone who knows of that which we seek will not talk to us. It is as if there is a prohibition against even speaking of the island. Perhaps it is some sailors' superstition that clouds the land. Yet it is a place, like any other. A people live there. They must have some commerce with the outside world. It is as if there is some code about it which we know not how to break. I fear we may be here for days, perhaps even weeks."

"We have not weeks!" Tranorva exploded. "I feel it. He drifts farther from me by the day, by the hour even. His skin grows cooler to the touch. If it takes weeks to find passage, we will have no need of it by the time it is secured. I will no' lose him! Not now. No' after all we have come through."

"Mistress? Please do not cry, M'Lady."

Tranorva looked down at the distressed face of the small creature who reached for her hand. "I am no' crying. I am only angry. Forgive me, Dahlai. I did no' mean to frighten ye with my outburst. It is just that I waited so long to find love, and now I feel it slipping away. I must take the body of Élandine home to the Faerie King, or he will truly die. I have not much time left."

Dahlai leaned far out over the banister, seemingly directing her attention to the ships rather than to the men. "I can help, but they are too far away. I must touch them."

Evalayna frowned at the diminutive sprite. "What do you mean, child?"

The Faerie-spawn stamped her foot angrily, her mood as volatile as the weather. "I am not a child! Why do all of you insist on calling me child? I am nearly forty!"

Evalayna smiled at the small temper tantrum. "Because ye look like a child, dear heart, and were ye in Faerie ye would still be considered a child. Shammall told me once that he was no' considered a man and allowed to leave his father's house until he reached his fiftieth year. We seek no' to offend thee. Among my people, the cubs are precious, and we strive to protect and nurture them. Please forgive me. I shall endeavor to remember thy age. Now tell me, why do ye wish to touch the ships?"

Apparently mollified, Dahlai looked back out over the water. "The *Sidhe* are everywhere, Mother told me. She said I would know them if we brushed in passing. I would be able to feel them speak to me. 'Tis so. I felt the light within the one you call Élandine from the first. I felt his presence as if he had changed before me, as my mother would when we were alone. If

I touch the ships, I believe I can find one that has been to *Tier na nÓg*."

A small muscle twitched around the corner of Tranorva's eye. "'Tis no safe for a woman to wander these docks alone."

"I will take her," Balthain offered.

"We will all go," Ayailla announced firmly. "I too am tired of waiting, hiding here as if we are no more than ornaments. We are Clan of the Wolf. Let those who watch know us and fear us. Lead on, Child."

And because it was the old woman who spoke, the child-sprite grinned widely this time, rather than taking offense. She held out her arms to Balthain, who scooped her up to set her upon his wide shoulders as the Shamen swarmed toward the dock. The Warriors saw them coming and said naught, but moved to their sides, hands resting upon the hilts of their weapons. Dahlai whispered something to Balthain and he strode down the longest pier, stopping when she told him to move closer to one ship or another.

Spirits began to sag again as she rejected all the ships they passed, turning away from most before she even laid hands upon them. They neared the end of the pier before her small voice hissed out a sharp word of command.

"Put me down."

Murmurs of approval spread through the party. The ship was bright with fresh paint and outfitted with new sails, and the crew that watched them approach wore crisply pressed matching uniforms, almost like a military crew. "A racing yacht," Balthain observed in a subdued voice.

But it was not the yacht that drew Dahlai's attention. It was to an older, less elaborate ship, partially hidden behind the large yacht and looking far from seaworthy that she ventured.

The Captain stood at the top of the gang plank, his arms crossed over his chest, frowning eyes and dark presence enough to intimidate lesser men, yet Dahlai walked calmly up the plank to him, as if she had done so every day of her life. At the top of the plank she reached out to lay her small hand over his arm, and the small child-like creature they had known disappeared. In her place stood a tall, slender beauty, her dark honey-colored skin shining with a light that glowed from within, her long ebony hair floating past her knees as the breeze lifted it gently.

The Captain stared mesmerized at the beauty before him, forgetting to blink.

"You have been to *Tier na nÓg*."

The Captain merely nodded.

"I want to go home," the Fey creature explained, her hand still laid over his arm. "Will you please take me home?"

"Aye," he managed, pausing to clear his throat. "Aye. That I will, M'Lady."

* * * * *

The ship rolled gently on the waves, the City of Port but a distant memory. Roahr moved to stand beside her, his arm warm and comforting as he pulled her against his side. Evalayna laid her head against his shoulder, watching the setting sun painting a picture of great beauty across the distant horizon.

"What troubles you, my love? You have accomplished your mission. On the morrow we shall land at the Faerie King's docks. The rest is in the hands of the gods."

"I feel guilty, Roahr, to be so blessed, so fulfilled, when our daughter is in such pain."

Roahr dipped his head to brush warm lips over her mouth. "I had thought to end my days alone on my mountain, drifting off to sleep one winter never to awaken again. You have given me back all that I thought I had lost, my heart, and more. You have given me a family, and a reason to live. Together we are stronger than ever we were alone. Tranorva has our strength to draw upon now, as well as her own. Perhaps this was the real mission the gods charged you with. Whatever happens, whatever the judgment of the Faerie King, Tranorva knows we will stand beside her. We are a family. We face the future together."

"Together," Evalayna agreed. "I like the sound of that."

And as the sun drifted below the water, the last of her fires outlined the lovers standing at the ships rail, two lost souls who had found each other again at last.

Epilogue

Tranorva stood far forward on the upper deck, looking out over the water toward the spot where the island must appear that would decide her fate. She spoke to the night air, averting her eyes from the shadowed man who stood always beside her. "I know Mother says ye are gone in spirit, and this thing is but an empty shell, yet I fear ye are instead trapped within, aware of all around ye and unable to tell me what ye would have me do."

She reached out blindly to find his hands, pulling his arms around her in the darkness where no one could see her foolishness. "I miss ye so. Always ye have been here for me, guiding me, protecting me from myself. I do not understand why ye chose as ye did, to sacrifice thyself rather than trust in my strength, but perhaps I do not need to understand. I wish I was sure ye would desire to attempt this thing, to bring thy spirit back to the body it has deserted. If I have chosen wrong, and ye want not the gift of the Faerie King should he decide to grant it, my spirit shall surely fly away with yours."

Tears that she would never have shed in the daylight tipped her lashes. "I need ye, Élandine. I need ye now more than ever. My heart dies a thousand deaths a day without ye." The ship lurched slightly as it skipped over a wave, and for one brief moment the arms wrapped around her tightened, holding her steady as her footing shifted on the tilting deck.

It was only the reflexive movement of the thing that he had become, straining to right itself. Wasn't it? Perhaps she had even imagined the gesture. Perhaps...

"I love ye," Tranorva whispered, holding him tightly there in the darkness. "Forever and always, my heart."

An excerpt from
The Song of The Bear: The Northlanders II

Prologue

He had the strangest feeling that he was floating, watching himself from a long way off. Surely that thing, that shell, couldn't really be him. His present form was so much lighter, so much less tied to the earth.

He would have drifted away, but for the woman.

Her name came unbidden to his lips.

Tranorva.

He knew her, knew her in ways he could not precisely remember, knew the feel of her skin under his hand, the warmth of her breath on his ear, knew the sound of her voice calling to him.

She stood far forward on the ship's upper deck, looking out across the moonlit ocean toward the land he had once called home. She looked right at him, as if somehow she sensed his presence lingering near, although he knew by now that no one alive could actually see him.

Her words haunted him, stole a piece of his soul and bound it to her.

"I know Mother says ye are gone in spirit, and this thing is but an empty shell, yet I fear ye are instead trapped within, aware of all around ye and unable to tell me what ye would have me do."

'Twas not so far from the truth.

She reached back, pulling the corpse-like thing's arms about her, tears drenching her thick, dark lashes, making her eyes glisten like wet emeralds in the moonlight. "I miss ye so. Always ye have been here for me, guiding me, protecting me from myself. I do not understand why ye chose as ye did, to sacrifice thyself rather than trust in my strength, but perhaps I do not need to understand. I wish I was sure ye would *desire to attempt this thing, to bring thy spirit back to the body it has deserted. If I have chosen wrong, and ye want not the gift of the King should he decide to grant it, my spirit shall surely fly away with yours."*

Sacrifice...It was so hard to remember life in his mortal body. What had he done to cause this one so much pain? The only thing that felt real was the taste of her skin on his lips as he tried to comfort her. But she could not see him, could not feel his touch.

"I need ye, Élandine. I need ye now more than ever. My heart dies a thousand deaths a day without ye."

Élandine. He had been Élandine.

He had loved her.

That love was the one thing that could not die.

He slid slowly back into the thing that had once been his body, trying it on for size. An uncomfortable fit. Body and soul were not truly united, and it was all he could do to make her feel his presence.

"I love ye," Tranorva whispered, holding him tightly there in the darkness. "Forever and always, my heart."

And because she willed it, he began to remember...

About the author:

Shelby knew from an early age that she wanted to write. Growing up with Tolkien's **Lord of The Rings** and TV's "**Star Trek,**" Fantasy Literature seemed the natural choice. The only problem--her favorite genre didn't have a place for Romance! Shelby pursued a degree in Communications, graduating from Shepherd College in 1981. Since then she worked as a Radio On-Air personality until she and her husband started their own business. When Shelby found Ellora's Cave, she finally felt her writing had found a home!

Ellora's Cave has provided Shelby with yet one more valid reason for avoiding 'housework' of the common type. Residing in West Virginia with Bill, her husband of 21 years, Shelby enjoys building computers and online role-playing games. When she's not on-line, Shelby can be found in the garage tinkering with her motorcycle--or anywhere but the kitchen!

Shelby Morgen welcomes mail from readers. You can write to them c/o Ellora's Cave Publishing at P.O. Box 787, Hudson, Ohio 44236-0787.

Also By Shelby Morgen

- **Redemption**
- **All I Want For Christmas**
- **Plain Brown Wrapper**
- **The Marker**
- **Too Hot To Handle (*Way of the Wolf* series)**

Song of the Bear series

- **A Mercenary's Prize**
- **A Prisoner's Desire**
- **A Sentinal's Secret**

Why an electronic book?

We live in the Information Age—an exciting time in the history of human civilization in which technology rules supreme and continues to progress in leaps and bounds every minute of every hour of every day. For a multitude of reasons, more and more avid literary fans are opting to purchase e-books instead of paperbacks. The question to those not yet initiated to the world of electronic reading is simply: *why?*

1. *Price.* An electronic title at Ellora's Cave Publishing runs anywhere from 40-75% less than the cover price of the <u>exact same title</u> in paperback format. Why? Cold mathematics. It is less expensive to publish an e-book than it is to publish a paperback, so the savings are passed along to the consumer.
2. *Space.* Running out of room to house your paperback books? That is one worry you will never have with electronic novels. For a low one-time cost, you can purchase a handheld computer designed specifically for e-reading purposes. Many e-readers are larger than the average handheld, giving you plenty of screen room. Better yet, hundreds of titles can be stored within your new library—a single microchip. (Please note that Ellora's Cave does not endorse any specific brands. You can check our website at *www.ellorascave.com* for customer recommendations we make available to new consumers.)
3. *Mobility.* Because your new library now consists of only a microchip, your entire cache of books can be taken with you wherever you go.
4. *Personal preferences are accounted for.* Are the words you are currently reading too small? Too large? Too…**ANNOYING**? Paperback books cannot be modified according to personal preferences, but e-books can.

5. *Innovation.* The *way* you read a book is not the only advancement the Information Age has gifted the literary community with. There is also the factor of *what* you can read. Ellora's Cave Publishing will be introducing a new line of interactive titles that are available in e-book format only.

6. *Instant gratification.* Is it the middle of the night and all the bookstores are closed? Are you tired of waiting days—sometimes weeks—for online and offline bookstores to ship the novels you bought? Ellora's Cave Publishing sells instantaneous downloads 24 hours a day, 7 days a week, 365 days a year. Our e-book delivery system is 100% automated, meaning your order is filled as soon as you pay for it.

Those are a few of the top reasons why electronic novels are displacing paperbacks for many an avid reader. As always, Ellora's Cave Publishing welcomes your questions and comments. We invite you to email us at service@ellorascave.com or write to us directly at: P.O. Box 787, Hudson, Ohio 44236-0787.

Printed in the United States
27035LVS00001B/17